Heretic

Accipiter War # 4

Patrick Seaman &
Blake Seaman

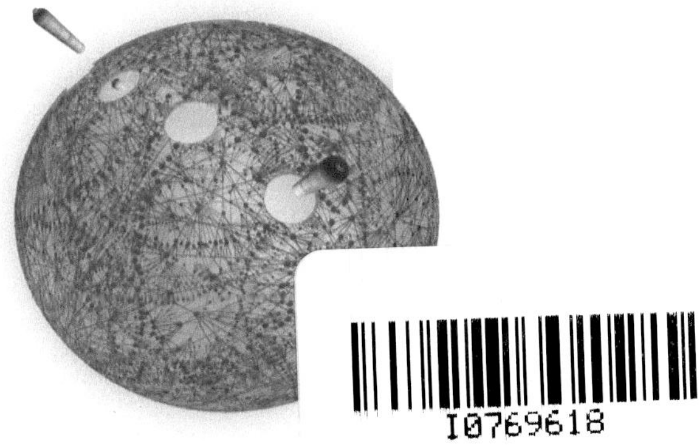

MILSTAR BOOKS • FORT WORTH, TEXAS, USA

HERETIC

by Patrick Seaman & Blake Seaman

1ˢᵗ Paperback Edition: ISBN 979-8-9878511-0-4

Cover Art by Ron Miller

MilStar Books
MILSTARBOOKS.COM
ACCIPITERWAR.COM

Printed in the United States of America

1ˢᵗ Edition, December 2023
First Hardback Printing: December 2023
First Paperback Printing: December 2023
First eBook Edition: December 2023

This work is dedicated to the men
and women who selflessly defend
freedom and civilization every day.

- Patrick and Blake Seaman

BERTIE

● ● ● ● ● ● ● ● ● ● ● ● ● ● ● ● ●

Ascendance
Resurrection Chamber
Accipiter Capital System

Alberta "Bertie" Sinitskaya slowly drifted toward the outer edges of sleep. Eyes still closed, she inhaled sharply, her lungs filling with strangely floral-scented air that reminded her of something between ginger and honeysuckle. She felt… strong. The constant aches and pains of hard work in low-g were gone, but sleeping like this in null-g was both delicious and… wrong. She could feel her long hair drifting loose and caressing her naked breasts.

Wait, what?

She blinked her eyes open and winced as her pupils shrank from the light. She shook herself awake and curled up, pulling her knees to her chest. As soon as she moved, she suddenly felt a multitude of tendrils release and pull away from her body.

She shivered and tried to shrink away from the vine-like tendrils as they disappeared into… a wall of flowers. Her throat was dry as she tried to gasp aloud. She forced herself to swallow as she looked around the large… room. Nothing made sense.

I was… I was on Mace… we were fighting the Accipiters…. and…. and I think I died. Why is my hair so long?

She looked at her arms and hands… and her body. It was….

My tattoos… they're gone, and… my skin! It's like I'm….

She looked closer at her hands and arms. The scar on her left index finger, there since she'd busted her hand working on her first Harley….

Gone. She swallowed and looked down… the small C-Section scar was gone, and… The sudden realization stunned her.

I look… young!

"What the hell…." She sliced off her sentence abruptly in shock. Her voice was a high contralto, like from when she was a teenager or… before she'd smoked enough that her voice had dropped. Her eyes widened as the realization began to sink in. She was no longer the same person.

Shit…. This can't be good.

Looking desperately around the room, she saw that it was cavernous… a cavernous arboretum like some kind of weird botanical garden full of plants that she didn't recognize. She was no botanist, but she was confident that few, if any, had originated on Earth.

She sensed motion to her left and saw… a tendril moving toward her, pushing… folded clothes? The tendril slowed and stopped, holding the clothes within her easy reach.

She snatched them away from the tendril, and it slunk back into the garden wall. Pulling them open, she saw that they were a kind of silken pajamas… no… a jumpsuit… with booties. Hesitating for only a moment, she flexed a practiced null-g movement and pulled the jumpsuit on. There were no fasteners or zippers. The edges sealed themselves seamlessly, but with a bit of experimentation, she found they pulled back apart again with minor effort.

Bertie took a deep breath and looked around, trying to discern an exit or any kind of pattern to the place.

Where is the light coming from?

A single phosphorescent tendril, no thicker than a finger and woven with strands of ochre, extended from the stone wall like an arm. It clasped a green and red flat rectangular object between two digits of its appendage: one half glowed hot green, and the other pulsed with soft blue light. She could feel her heart pounding in her chest as she mustered the courage to reach for it. She swallowed and slowly and cautiously extended her hand toward it until she felt the object's coolness in her fingertips. The tendril released the thing and, as before, slunk back into the wall, disappearing from sight.

She pulled it closer and saw that it had a flat surface that reminded her a little of a tablet computer.

Suddenly, a rock-crushing rumble filled the air. Bertie recoiled in surprise, twisting sharply in the air as the flowered wall split apart behind her. The rumbling crescendoed to a warm set of dulcet tones. Tones that came from a resplendent ten-foot-tall Accipiter, who glided through the new doorway with an effortless grace. It stopped directly in front of her, its gaze piercing and commanding.

Her eyes widened, and her heart pounded in her chest as she desperately tried to swim backward in the zero-g away from the enormous creature.

The flat surface on the tablet changed, and text in English began to scroll across it as an odd-sounding voice repeated the words aloud.

GOOD MORNING, ALBERTA. I AM HAPPY TO SEE YOU WELL. WOULD YOU JOIN ME FOR BREAKFAST?

Bertie stared at the enormous bird analogue alien. She'd seen pictures of the alien captured in the Keeper raid but never… in person, and certainly not close enough to smell its enormous… perfumed… body. It had six limbs: two large, clawed legs, two smaller, wickedly jeweled clawed 'arms,' and another, much smaller pair of arms with 'hands' ending in articulated, but still dangerous looking 'fingers.' One of those hands held a duplicate of the tablet Bertie now clutched in her own hands. It wore an intricately inlaid breastplate. However, what captivated her most was the creature's enormous head. Its large beak was covered with flowing glyphs that glowed and faded in and out of vision. Its huge sapphire-colored eyes, though, froze her heart. They were riveted on her as it approached, cold, like a frozen ocean.

She stopped trying to fruitlessly swim away from it. She set her jaw and straightened, trying to make herself as large as possible as she faced the alien. Her heart threatened to burst from her chest as her eyes narrowed, and she forced herself to calm down.

Stiffening her spine, Alberta clenched her jaw firmly and declared in a voice laced with steel, "I am Captain Alberta Kincaid Sinitskaya, service number zero zero five two eight four nine one seven. I will not answer your questions, make false confessions, or denounce my government. I…"

A deep rock-crushing rumble cut her off, followed by sounds she wasn't entirely certain she could hear. The tablet she was holding vibrated slightly as new text scrolled across it.

WE DO NOT NEED YOU TO ANSWER ANY QUESTIONS. YOU ARE, AS YOU SAID, ALBERTA SINITSKAYA. A CAPTAIN IN YOUR MILITARY. YOU WERE BORN ON YOUR HOME PLANET IN A PLACE THAT WAS CALLED BOYD LAKE IN

WHAT USED TO BE YOUR STATE OF MAINE. YOU RODE AND WORKED ON TWO-WHEELED MOTORIZED VEHICLES WITH YOUR FATHER. YOU GRADUATED FROM YOUR COUNTRY'S NAVAL ACADEMY AND LATER SERVED ON TWO OF THEIR UNDERWATER WARSHIPS. YOU MARRIED DOCTOR DIMITRI SINITSKAYA, AN ENGINEER, AND HAD TWO CHILDREN WITH HIM. A SON, RONALD, AND A DAUGHTER ANNA. RONALD WAS NAMED AFTER A DECEASED FORMER LEADER OF YOUR COUNTRY. ANNA WAS NAMED AFTER YOUR MATERNAL GRANDMOTHER. MOST RECENTLY, YOU WERE IN COMMAND OF A BASE IN ORBIT AROUND A PLANET YOUR PEOPLE CALLED ARI'NELL. WHEN THE FLEET SENT THERE BY MY PEOPLE ARRIVED, YOU FOUGHT THEM USING A WEAPON YOU WERE TESTING. YOU DIED. WE RECOVERED YOUR REMAINS AT THE SCENE AND EXTRACTED EVERYTHING YOU KNOW FROM YOUR BRAIN BEFORE WE DECIDED TO RESURRECT YOU.

Bertie couldn't help it. Her eyes widened at the realization. *They know where New Texas is!* Her pale skin flushed crimson as pure rage exploded within her. She screamed as she tried to attack the alien with her bare hands, "What have you done!"

She struggled to reach the creature in the weightlessness to no avail before regaining control of herself and stopping. She managed to spin, orient herself again, and stretch herself back to her full height. She sneered, chest heaving. *Maybe it didn't find out enough. Don't give it anything.* "Do you have a name? Monster? What about my crew? The station?" Her heart fluttered… *Dimitri….*

More rumbling followed, and a singsong-like melody warbled from the creature itself. The tablet spoke,

THE CLOSEST HUMAN APPROXIMATION IS XURAENS. I HAVE BEEN APPOINTED AS COUNCIL ADJUDICATOR. I AM… LEADER.

"Leader of what?" she spat.

More rumbling, followed by short hoots.

THE LEADER.

Bertie blinked. "You mean, leader of all your people or just the ones wherever it is that we are? Where the hell are we, anyway?"

This time, the tones were more extended, more upswept.

LEADER OF ALL CLANS. EVERYWHERE. YOU ARE AT THE ASCENSION. WHAT YOU WOULD CALL OUR CAPITAL SYSTEM

So, it is not just some local interrogator like I assumed... "Why would the leader of all Accipiters, for the entire galaxy, be my interrogator? You said, Adjudicator. Are you here to judge and execute me? If so, go ahead and kill me. Whatever it is you're up to, I won't cooperate."

THERE WERE NO INTACT BODIES AMID THE WRECKAGE OF YOUR VESSEL. MOST WERE NOT SALVAGEABLE. ONLY THREE OF THOSE INCLUDED INTACT HEADS. WE DETERMINED THAT YOU WERE THE LEADER. INFORMATION FROM THE OTHERS WAS REDUNDANT. AS FOR THE FATE OF THE STATION YOU COMMANDED, WE DO NOT KNOW. THE SECOND GROUP OF VESSELS WE SENT DID NOT RETURN. THE THIRD FOUND ONLY DESTRUCTION. WE BELIEVE THAT YOUR PLAN TO DETONATE YOUR POWER DEVICE WAS SUCCESSFUL. AS FOR THE FATE OF THE HUMANS THERE AND OF YOUR HUSBAND, WE DO NOT KNOW.

The creature paused, then continued.

I AM UNCERTAIN REGARDING HOW TO INTERPRET YOUR BODILY OR FACIAL MOVEMENTS AND EXPRESSIONS; HOWEVER, THE NEXT LOGICAL QUESTION THAT YOU

WOULD HAVE WOULD BE ABOUT THE FATE
OF YOUR HIDDEN BASE AND THE FATE OF
YOUR CHILDREN. I DO NOT KNOW THE
ANSWER TO THOSE QUESTIONS. HOWEVER,
WE LEARNED OF ITS LOCATION FROM YOUR
MEMORIES. THE VESSELS WE SENT THERE
DID NOT RETURN. INTERESTINGLY, WE ARE
UNABLE TO…. SEND MORE TO INVESTIGATE.
THE … DOOR … TO THAT PLACE NO LONGER
FUNCTIONS. IT IS MOST CURIOUS AND
TROUBLING.

Bertie scowled, not believing him, but she noticed how its command of English was improving quickly. "My heart bleeds."

The Accipiter stared at her for long moments, and Bertie wondered if her expression confused it.

The Accipiter seemed to almost grumble, and then more multi-tonal sounds followed.

YOUR REBEL FACTION OF HUMANS IS
INTERESTING TO ME. MUCH TIME HAS PASSED
FOR THE PEOPLE OF YOUR HOMEWORLD.
THEY WOULD NO LONGER UNDERSTAND
YOU. THEY HAVE BEEN ELEVATED TO THEIR
POTENTIAL. YOU ARE A RELIC OF THEIR
PRIMITIVE PAST. YOUR PEOPLE BLINDLY
LASH OUT WITH TECHNOLOGY THEY BARELY
GRASP. AND YET, YOU WERE ABLE TO, AS
YOU WOULD SAY, REVERSE ENGINEER NOT
ONLY STARSHIP TECHNOLOGY BUT ALSO
LEARN TO CONSTRUCT WEAPONS WHOSE
ANCIENT DESIGNS YOU EXTRACTED FROM
WRECKAGE YOUR PEOPLE DISCOVERED
ON YOUR PLANET'S OCEAN FLOOR. AND
YET, YOU ATTACK WORLDS YOU CANNOT
COMPREHEND. YOU, FOR EXAMPLE. YOU
LEFT YOUR MILITARY AND JOINED A SECRET
MILITARY. YOU WERE GIVEN COMMAND OF
A HIDDEN BASE ON YOUR MOON. YOU WERE

IN COMMAND OF THE VESSEL-BUILDING PROGRAM THERE. WHEN MY PEOPLE ARRIVED, YOU YOURSELF PERSONALLY DESTROYED THE BASE AND FLED, LEAVING BEHIND YOUR WORLD.

Nothing in Bertie's physiological response reacted to the pronouncement from the Accipiter. She *knew* it was false, but she also *remembered* the memories. Something *prevented* her from saying something differently. She shook her head, "So? There was nothing we could do. You brought over fifty thousand ships and kinetically bombarded every major city and military base. We had *one* ship, and it wasn't even armed!" She screamed, "You *monsters murdered our world!*"

YOUR BRAVERY AND LOYALTY ARE UNDERSTANDABLE. YOU SEE MY PEOPLE AS DESTROYERS; HOWEVER, NOTHING COULD BE FURTHER FROM THE TRUTH.

Bertie crossed her arms and tried to look as stern as possible. "You pulled my memories. You know everything I know. Why am I here? Why didn't you leave me dead, or did you resurrect me just to annoy me with your lies?"

YOU WERE CHOSEN TO BE RESURRECTED BECAUSE I WANTED TO KNOW MORE ABOUT YOU THAN YOUR KNOWLEDGE. I WISH TO, AS YOU WOULD SAY, KNOW MY ENEMY. YOU DO NOT KNOW HOW BEAUTIFUL YOU ARE.

Bertie blinked, "What?"

WE LOVE YOUR RACE. WE HAVE PRESERVED AND VENERATED IT.

Bertie snorted derisively, "Bullshit. Humanity is not a butterfly collection for you to hang on your goddamned wall! What's wrong? You didn't take the opportunity to get to know any of my people before you slaughtered and enslaved them, so now, since we bloodied your nose, you decided to play catch up? Maybe you underestimated us?"

BY UNDERSTANDING YOU, I HOPE TO PREVENT FURTHER NEEDLESS HORROR AND DESTRUCTION.

Her laughter came out as a menacing cackle, her eyes blazing with disdain. "That's what I thought. You were surprised when your butterflies stung you. You're not used to your decisions coming back to haunt you." She shook her head and spat at him. "Maybe you should have thought of trying to talk to us first instead of nuking the fucking planet!"

YOUR WORLD WAS FULL OF WAR THROUGHOUT ITS HISTORY. YOU EVEN, AS YOU SAY, NUKED EACH OTHER.

She rolled her eyes, "That was generations ago, and it prevented millions of deaths and STOPPED a war that the other side started!"

A BLINK OF AN EYE. YOUR PEOPLE WOULD HAVE SPREAD ACROSS THE GALAXY LIKE A PLAGUE. BRINGING YOUR WARS AND YOUR DESTRUCTION WITH YOU, JUST LIKE THE VA'SO VROKGONGON JADAKLOT.

Bertie's chest heaved as she shouted, "We were no threat to you or anyone else! It never occurred to you to just show up one day with a fleet and tell us that, hey, settle your petty differences. You are not alone. Get your act together, or you will remain bottled up forever on your little world."

YOU WOULD HAVE DESTROYED IT AND YOURSELVES. WE COULD NOT STAND BY AND LET THAT HAPPEN.

She shook her head vigorously. "You can't know that! You had no right! You destroyed everything that we were!"

YOU ARE ANGRY AND, NO DOUBT, DESPITE YOUR OBVIOUS STRENGTH OF SPIRIT, FRIGHTENED TO FIND YOURSELF HERE IN THE VERY CAPITAL OF YOUR ENEMY. I

INVITE YOU TO TAKE THE OPPORTUNITY TO LEARN EVERYTHING YOU CAN ABOUT US. WHO KNOWS, PERHAPS ONE DAY YOU WILL EITHER ESCAPE OR BE REUNITED WITH YOUR CHILDREN, HUSBAND, AND FRIENDS. IN THE MEANTIME, I DID INVITE YOU TO A MEAL. YOU MUST BE FAMISHED. YOUR NEW BODY HAS NEVER EATEN BEFORE. I DO CAUTION YOU TO EAT SLOWLY AND GIVE YOUR BODY TIME TO ADJUST. ALSO, YOUR NEW TASTE RECEPTORS WILL NO DOUBT BE SURPRISED. NO FOOD THAT WE OFFER YOU WILL BE HARMFUL. I WOULD PROVIDE YOU WITH FAMILIAR THINGS FROM YOUR WORLD. HOWEVER, THE ARK CONTAINING OUR RECORDS OF SUCH WAS STOLEN BY YOUR PEOPLE. I AM AFRAID THAT YOU WILL HAVE TO EXPERIMENT WITH WHAT WE HAVE TO OFFER YOU TO FIND THINGS TO YOUR TASTE.

Tears had formed in her eyes, but without gravity to make them fall, they simply welled up on her eyes, distorting her vision. She bit back, "I am obviously at your mercy."

AN INTERESTING CONCEPT.

Ari'Nell

● ● ● ● ● ● ● ● ● ● ● ● ● ● ● ●

*Ari'Shevn Star System
near planet Ari'Nell
NTN Revenge*

Commander Jermaine Cutter stood watch in NTN Revenge's CIC. He was tall, at just over six feet, with broad shoulders and a lean, muscular build. It was a testament to nearly three decades of dedicated Jujitsu practice. His skin held a deep shade of brown, and his black hair was closely cropped to his scalp. Dark and intense, his eyes seemed to contain a world of experience and pain. A pain stemming from a lost world and the struggle of not entirely fitting into either the old or the new. He stood rigid and straight, the embodiment of discipline and command. His voice, warm, deep, and resonant, carried an unmistakable authority, demanding respect and obedience from those around him. With quiet strength, he exuded a deep sense of purpose and determination, his aura palpably radiating from him.

Though raised in an environment of wealth and privilege, he never truly felt he belonged. At eighteen, he secured an appointment to the United States Naval Academy, forging a storied Navy career over two decades, culminating in his command of SSN-795, the Hyman G. Rickover.

Even before the Apocalypse, something set him apart from other officers. An innate clarity of vision and an inner fire that elevated his performance beyond his personal demons. On Earth, he'd been a rising star. After Awakening Day, that luminosity had ensured that he was one of only four people competing for command of mankind's inaugural starship. Phil Underwood and Gene Morton had been lucky enough to be in command when the last technical hurdles were overcome, "winning" the competition, with Charles Cross and Jermaine as the Blue and Gold crew alternate commanders.

Of course, he wasn't alone in bearing his ghosts and demons. That was virtually a job requirement after the Accipiter invasion of Earth and the subsequent trauma of awakening over sixty years later inside a four-thousand-mile-long hollow McKendree Cylinder.

While Revenge's actual "bridge" was relatively spacious, owing to the large size of the original Builders, its controls included only those necessary for navigation, flight, and related functions. It lacked the facilities required to track the mines and coordinate battlespace activities within the Ari'Shevn star system where Ari'Nell was located. A forty-foot shipping container was outfitted with computers, displays, and additional communications equipment to address this, forming a rudimentary Command Information Center (CIC). The shipping container CIC occupied nearly half of the cargo bay.

Revenge had a crew of just twenty-two men and women. Eight of them were in the CIC, including Executive Officer Alister Gordon, COB Gerald Beltran, Weapons Officer Moreno Guerra, Jermaine himself, and others.

Using the remaining half of the cargo area, Jermaine and the crew of NTN Revenge had spent the last few months ferrying people and supplies back and forth from New Texas to the rapidly growing FAB at Ari'Nell.

Once home to trillions of the now-extinct Builders, Ari'Nell had been utterly obliterated by the Accipiters over three hundred thousand years ago. The planet, now a cratered remnant surrounded by vast rings of shattered orbital megastructure debris, was all that remained of the Builder colony.

The Ari'Nell workforce, now numbering over a thousand men and women, fed the FAB with highly refined alloys and rare elements from the planetary rings to construct thousands of mobile bomb-pumped X-ray laser mines to protect the star system. Plans were in place to begin construction of a shipyard.

Then, three days ago, an Accipiter fleet transited through the Nexus Junction Point and found them.

Commander Alberta 'Bertie' Sinitskaya and NTN Mace, one of the two sub-FTL landing craft stationed at Ari'Nell, went out to confront them and attempt to slow down their advance using a newly constructed experimental weapon copied from ancient Builder files.

She succeeded. Until the weapon finally overloaded, killing everyone onboard. Some Accipiters escaped, and more would doubtless soon follow.

Three Days. It had been three agonizing days since the attack.

Back on Earth, Jermaine had *only* had to worry about the

responsibilities of his command and the crew of his submarine, whose lives depended on him. Now, it was different. Not only did he have to worry about the thousand-plus civilian engineers, scientists, and support staff, but it never left the back of his mind that each and every one of them, as well as his own crew, now represented one of the precious few surviving humans still in existence. Their actions…. And his decisions might well impact or potentially even decide the fate of mankind as a species.

Three Days. It had been three agonizing days since the attack.

Three days of expecting a new Accipiter fleet to arrive and finally crush them, as there had only been one copy of the experimental weapon and not enough time to produce another.

Three days to keep pumping out mines to try and slow the enemy down.

Three days for the single remaining ILC, NTN Kukri, to ferry hundreds of people up from the surface of Ari'Nell.

Three days to stretch Revenge's rings to the limit so they could encompass the ramshackle assemblage of habitat modules with over a thousand men and women crammed into them. Jermaine privately referred to it as a trailer park in space. Revenge couldn't simply ferry batches of people back to New Texas. There wasn't enough time. It was over twenty-six hours of transit time each way, and mankind only had two starships, and the other one was off on its own mission somewhere else.

Decisions.

Teams worked feverishly to rearrange the ugly, bulky, blocky HABs to make them fit within Revenge's rings, which were now stretched to their limit. When he'd first seen the HABs, Jermaine had wondered whether the Builders were the only other creatures in the galaxy with less style and panache than humans.

The micro-ZPM-powered HAB modules offered only basic air processing, life support functions, and a built-in 'food' replicator. However, it only produced inedible pellets, mockingly termed Builder-Chow by some people. These were worse than merely unpalatable; they contained toxic, chiral versions of certain amino acids.

Useless food pellets aside, the HAB units could keep people alive for weeks, although without resupply, food would become a severe problem before long. Still, New Texas was just a day away, so everyone would just have to tough it out for the trip back.

Meanwhile, Dr. Dimitri Sinitskaya, shattered by the death of his wife Bertie and the destruction of Mace and her crew, had entered a manic overdrive, leading the work crews in the FAB to produce as many mines as possible. He was a man on the ragged edge, teetering on the brink of collapse. It wouldn't be remotely enough to actually stop the Accipiters, and would be scant payback for Mace, Bertie, and her crew, but it was something, even if it was only spitting into the face of the Devil. Hopefully, the mines would be enough to slow the Accipiters down, should they arrive before the evacuation was complete. He was determined to ensure that Bertie's legacy would not be forgotten, even if it meant driving himself and the rest of the staff beyond exhaustion.

The civilians had all been evacuated from the surface, and the HABs were finally secured and crammed to the maximum their life support could sustain. Jermaine was on his way back from Revenge's tiny galley after managing to drink half a cup of coffee.

Alister Gordon's voice boomed throughout the vessel,

"GENERAL QUARTERS! ALL HANDS, MAN YOUR BATTLE STATIONS! SET CONDITION ZEBRA THROUGHOUT THE SHIP!"

The Accipiters had returned.

Jermaine dashed into the CIC module, shouting, "Report! How many are they?"

Alister shook his blonde head angrily, his blue eyes flashing contemptuously. "Too damned many, Captain. At least TEN of their big motherships, and God only knows how many of their smaller ones. Maybe half a million."

Jermaine's face hardened. "Hell, Bertie and Mace kicked the snot out of them. Guess they're not fooling around this time. ETA?"

Alister sneered derisively. "They're not even slowing down for the mines. They've got a shell of ships in the van soaking up all the hits. When one goes down, another takes its place. Forty-five minutes tops."

Jermaine paused. "Well, we're not slowing down, either. Proceed as planned. Blow the settlement on the surface and finish the FAB evacuation. Have Dimitri…" he cringed at the thought of how the loss of Bertie was affecting the man, "…have Dimitri go ahead and set the timer on the nuke in the FAB. He wasn't sure if he could get the Zero-point energy module to overload, so it'll be insurance in case it doesn't work. Who knows, maybe we'll get lucky, and the damned thing will blow after all, and we'll catch some of their fleet in the blast."

He added with finality, "We are done here!"

Immediately after securing the last hatch, with everyone evacuated and Kukri safely docked inside the rings, Revenge hastily warped away from Ari'Nell. They urgently avoided any path towards New Texas, quickly plotting a series of swift course changes to nullify any chance of pursuit.

A light-hour out, they stopped, waited, and watched.

The FAB's power supply was an enormous Zero-point energy module designed to meet the voracious power demands of matter-energy conversion and fabrication. Dimitri Sinitskaya had warned that the device seemed to have countless built-in safety measures to prevent what they were trying to do from being possible.

Jermaine paced the deck, waiting for the light to catch up with them. The lights in the CIC dimmed for a fraction of a second, and the gravity… flickered.

Alarms sounded throughout the ship as Jermaine momentarily lost his footing and grabbed a railing. "What happened? Report!"

Revenge's personality answered:

Captain, I apologize. There was not sufficient time for discussion. The effects of the explosion were much more energetic than expected. I had to take us into an emergency warp to avoid damage. I've taken us to a distance of ten light hours out. We will need to wait and see if this is a safe distance from which to observe what has transpired.

Alister exclaimed, "Much stronger than expected? A blast wave hit us at a light-hour out? My God, that's farther than the Sun is to Jupiter!"

The alarms from around the ship began to shut off. Gerald Beltran reported, "Captain, no damage. Just a few minor falls, bumps, and bruises. Nothing serious."

Jermaine steadied himself. "The Enemy? The HABs?"

Captain, the status of the enemy is unknown. The HABs appear to be intact. None have lost pressure.

Jermaine nodded, "All right. Check with the people in them. Make sure they're OK. If we had a bunch of bumps and bruises on board the ship, I could only guess what it was like inside all those tin cans. It looks like we've got several more hours to wait to see what happened at Ari'Nell. Let's use that time to make sure we lock everything down for the trip back to New Texas.

✪ ✪ ✪

10 Hours Later

At Jermain's orders, NTN Kukri's CO, Commander Rafferty Youngman, escorted Dimitri from Kukri over to Revenge. Until the Accipiter attack, Kukri had been stationed at Ari'Nell. It, along with fifty-two of the ninety-eight-foot-long HAB modules, were now crammed inside the confines of Revenge's twenty warp rings, like toys inside a massive hollow Christmas tree ornament stretched taller than a 'modern' aircraft carrier.

Alister Gordon led Rafferty and Dimitri from the airlock through the maze of survivors packed in the cargo area of Revenge to the CIC. Alister exuded a calm and measured demeanor, complemented by deep reserves of inner strength and resolve. Despite being just five foot eight inches tall and only thirty-three years old, he carried himself with an aura of confidence that belied his past experiences. Growing up in the Red Hook neighborhood in Brooklyn, New York, near the docks, Alister had endured ridicule and scorn due to his height, leaving him with a scar on his right cheek from a brutal fight with a much larger boy. He had short blonde hair, watchful blue eyes that missed little and sparkled with intelligence, and a sharp sense of humor lurking just beneath the surface.

In contrast, Rafferty Youngman was a man of about thirty-eight, of above average height and slender build, with dark hair and brown eyes that expressed a mixture of sternness and kindness. He had lost his first wife and two children in the apocalypse. A year later, Roberta Wilson had, somehow, in ways he still didn't understand, steered him away from the path of nihilism he and so many others felt after Awakening Day. They'd married and had twin boys that, while not replacing the family he'd lost, had restored some measure of hope in his heart for a future.

Dr. Dimitri Sinitskaya, holding a Ph.D. in Electrical Engineering, was a forty-something man with a tall and lean build. He typically sported a neatly trimmed beard, which now appeared somewhat unkempt, and his dark hair stood in stark contrast to his striking green eyes. Wearing a grime-covered brown jumpsuit marred with traces of metal and chemicals, his appearance was weary. His face was drawn and pale, and his hands, calloused and stained like his jumpsuit, trembled slightly.

Earlier, during the final moments of the evacuation of the FAB, Kukri's Marines almost had to forcibly remove Dimitri at the eleventh hour. He had been adamant about including certain "essential" supplies in Kukri's already overburdened cargo bay. Upon boarding, he demanded that these containers be secured under armed protection. After that, he wove his way through people and stacked containers and, shambled towards a nearby bulkhead wall, turned his back, and slumped down to the deck before passing out from exhaustion, desolation, despair, and spent rage.

Despite the few hours of fitful sleep aboard Kukri, his eyes were still sunken and hollow from three days of frantic, backbreaking work and grief that coursed through him like a blood-borne poison. He'd lost not only the love of his life and mother to his two teenage children, but he had personally known each and every one of the members of Bertie's crew. All 27 of them. Including… especially… desperately… Bertie.

As Alister, Rafferty, and Dimitri stepped into the crowded confines of the CIC module, Jermaine soberly greeted them. His face tightened as he looked into Dimitri's hollow eyes and said, "Doctor Sinitskaya, we haven't had a chance to talk. Please accept my deepest condolences. As you know, I offered to go in her place. I knew she had a family. I've never met a finer officer. We are all shaken by her loss and for the rest of her crew. None more than you, though, and I just want you to know that if there is anything I can ever do for you or your family, you need only ask."

It took a long moment for Dimitri to react, to process Jermaine's words. Everything felt as though he were viewing the universe in the third person. His own body felt numb and disconnected. Slowly, the words registered, and he swallowed before answering, his voice thin and tenuous. "Thank you, Captain. I heard your offer to her and, well, you know there was no way in Hell she would have accepted. She was…. I was…." His voice cracked as he shook his head. "I was a moth to her flame. I left MIT to be with her… took the job at Bechtel so we could be together. I…."

◇◇

Captain, I apologize for the interruption. However, I have news. It appears that the explosion at Ari'Nell was not only of greater yield than anticipated, but its effects were also rather extraordinary. From this distance, as the light from the detonation caught up with us, I observed the events as they unfolded. Please watch on the monitor. The detonation of the Zero-point energy device not only triggered an explosion, but the energy released was evidently sufficient to initiate a fusion chain reaction within the matter in the surrounding area. If you look at your monitor, you can see that, although there was insufficient matter for actual star formation, a significant portion of the planet of Ari'Nell and its surrounding ring structure were engulfed in a cataclysmic explosion for a few brief moments. What little remains of Ari'Nell is in the process of being ejected from the star system. I predict that the orbits of the other planets have already been, or will soon be, disrupted.

Furthermore, the star at the system's center will be subjected to a powerful shockwave, likely leading to significant coronal mass ejections and other severe events. The Ari'Shevn system is now irrevocably hazardous. As for the Accipiter Fleet, from our relative position, I was unable to directly observe what happened when the blast wave overtook it. However, neither the Accipiter vessels nor anything else could have survived being engulfed by the equivalent of a star going nova.

Not a sound could be heard in the CIC module other than Revenge's narrative, as all eyes were held in rapt attention and awe as they watched the scene unfold on the monitor.

The former ecumenopolis planet of Ari'Nell was the third in the Ari'Shevn star system. It possessed a barely breathable Oxygen-Nitrogen atmosphere, courtesy of the greenish algae-analog that ringed the planet's innumerable water-filled craters. Redder than Mars, only a few wispy cirrus clouds drifted above its ravaged surface. Three hundred thousand years earlier, before the Accipiters attacked it, it had been a lovely earth-analog home to trillions of Builders and a stupendously massive orbital infrastructure that housed most of their population. Aeon's later, when the humans discovered it, the planet was a glassed-over wasteland, and all that remained of the orbital megastructure was a vast set of brilliantly glinting rings composed of highly refined alloys, transuranic elements and quadrillions of *pieces* of the desiccated remains of slaughtered Builders.

Seismic surveys had hinted at subsurface structures that begged future exploration, but there had never been time. A small encampment on the surface had provided some relief for the orbital FAB workers. It was a chance to stretch their legs and escape the confines of their spacesuits and the lived-in, smelly, pressurized HABs and "breathe 'fresh' air."

On the display monitor, Revenge had framed the exotically beautiful planet and its rings with strident red icons marking the advancing Accipiter Fleet on its shoulder. The FAB wasn't distinguishable from the rest of the orbital ring debris at this distance, so it was tagged with a green chevron. Without the markers, the scene would have made a lovely wall poster.

Within a fraction of a second, the green chevron was replaced by a brilliant expanding ball that swelled to engulf much of the planet and rings as they fed the ensuing planetary funeral pyre. Within mere moments, the white-hot ball ballooned even more, blotting out the Accipiter fleet icons and expanding more and more until it finally consumed itself and continued to expand outward as a shell of superheated plasma.

Dimitri's brows rose in surprise and disappointment while Jermaine, Rafferty, and the rest stared in shocked amazement.

Jermaine's jaw tightened as he traded worried glances with Alister.

Alister swore, "My God, no wonder they built so many safeguards into the damned thing. People were nervous about nuclear reactors melting down back on Earth, but this! If this thing blows, it takes your whole fucking solar system with it! It's a goddamned doomsday device!"

Jermaine looked at Dimitri. "Doctor, would you care to explain? What the Hell happened out there?"

Dimitri shook his head slowly. "Priya and I argued about it. We were never really certain just how much energy the device could generate. Its yield varied depending upon what we needed, and we were feeding in complex molecules and high atomic number elements so that it didn't have to do as much matter-to-energy conversion."

Alister asked, "Priya?"

Rafferty nodded, "Dr. Patel. A physics professor from the university. She came out with the last batch of support personnel from Fort Brazos when work started on the weapon."

Dimitri swayed momentarily before he steadied himself, his fatigue catching up with him. He corrected, "Priya is the university department head. She's been studying the ZPM back in Fort Brazos."

Rafferty reached out and put a hand on the man's shoulder. "Doctor, we know you're exhausted, and this is a lot to ask of you right now...."

Dimitri closed his eyes and sighed, "Yes, well. You see, it was all theory until now and not well accepted at that. Ages ago, Richard Feynman and John Wheeler calculated that the Zero-point radiation of the vacuum was so powerful that even a teacup of it would be enough to boil all the oceans of Earth. But we really didn't understand the physical structure of the device or how much of it was extracting the vacuum energy and how much was devoted to handling, storing, routing, and managing all that it extracted. For that matter, we only surmised that the device was using vacuum energy… nothing else we could think of matched."

Jermaine nodded, "And now?"

Dimitri rubbed his ragged beard and swallowed, "Well…. Priya did the numbers. If the portion of it extracting power was, oh, say, fifteen centimeters by, say, thirty-five centimeters and the rest was support structure, and if we assume Feynman and Wheeler were correct, then the maximum total output would be, well…."

Jermaine nodded patiently, "Yes, Doctor?"

"2.225×10^{31} Joules per second. She calculated that the total power output per day would be that of over fifty-eight thousand suns, but what we saw didn't come close to that. Had the full power been released, the results should have been much more…. Energetic."

Alister shook his head, "Doctor, that thing just wrecked a star system!"

Dimitri shrugged, "Perhaps we underestimated its power, or perhaps it isn't possible to release all the energy, or maybe we still don't understand what it is doing at all. Maybe some sort of fratricide took place in its internal structure. There's just no way to know right now. Maybe Priya and the others can figure something out from the data."

Jermaine's expression tightened, and he swallowed hard before replying. "God forgive us if we decide to build more of the things and use them as weapons against the Accipiters. It might be the only thing that would give them pause."

Alister and Rafferty blanched.

Gerald Beltran's jaw dropped, and he stared at him. "Sir… Captain… You can't be serious? Wipe out entire systems, completely destroying all life in them? We'd be…."

Jermaine nodded slowly, "Monsters. Yes, I know. But that's not for us to decide and not our worry right now. Right now, we need to get these civilians back to New Texas. Thankfully, there were no serious injuries that can't wait that long."

Dimitri's breath caught in his throat, his eyes widening as he remembered something crucial. "Oh, Captain, Commander, those containers I had brought onboard from the FAB. I asked that they be kept under guard for a reason. They could be vital to our future."

Everyone turned to look at Dimitri, their faces set with a mixture of annoyance, frustration, and dread.

Jermaine asked carefully, "Doctor, what exactly is inside those containers?"

Dimitri wore a sickly smirk of triumph as he replied in a low voice, "ZPMs. I had the FAB crank them out for us over the last day or so, in-between cycles."

Alister gasped in shock, eyes wide with disbelief. "You destroyed a planet and wrecked an entire star system with just one of those things, and you brought a dozen onboard in boxes, and you didn't think it was important to mention that little detail?"

Dimitri shrugged off Alister's outrage with a weary sigh. He frowned, fighting to keep his eyes open as he explained. "Don't be childish, Lieutenant. They're much smaller than the ZPM used to power the FAB. Maybe only a petawatt of output. Same size as what we used to power the weapon. Besides, you can't set them off like a box of old dynamite by dropping them on the floor. Even a nuke wouldn't set one off. Getting one to explode is damned hard."

Jermaine eyed him suspiciously, his face set in a severe expression. "Doctor...these devices will undoubtedly prove invaluable, now more so than ever without the FAB...but please try to remember that we need to be cautious of...."

Dimitri waved him off dismissively as he swayed unsteadily on his feet. His face contorted with frustration, and his words were tinged with venom when he spoke again. "Yes, Captain, you're right. However, right now, I've lost the love of my life, and I really don't give a damn. There just wasn't time to debate the issue. Right now, though, I need to find a corner to collapse in."

His shoulders slumped, and he swallowed. "And now, Lieutenant, I'd really appreciate it if you would mind helping me find that corner before you have to carry me there...." you have to carry me there...."

Hephaestus

● ● ● ● ● ● ● ● ● ● ● ● ● ● ● ● ●

DownSide: Fort Brazos

Alexander Marcus took Gail's hand and led her to the sanctuary entrance as Richard Wagner's Bridal Chorus played. The church sanctuary was packed to standing room only, not including cameras. Security was, needless to say, heavy and tight.

Gail looked up at Alexander's face, looking for reassurance.

He smiled down at her and mouthed, "You've got this."

She nodded, turned back to look down the aisle, and focused on the dais where John and the former Mayor, and now 'just' Pastor Tom Parker, stood waiting. Hector Alonzo stood by John's side while Gwyneth waited for Gail. Matti played a combination of Flower Girl and Junior Bride's Maid as she carried the Bridal train. When the procession finished, she would stand next to Gwyneth.

When Gail got close enough to see the look in John's eyes, everything was suddenly okay, and the weight on her shoulders fell away. She smiled.

Suddenly, the ground and the building shook, followed by the roar of an explosion as the sanctuary's stained glass Dove of Purity and Creation shattered inward.

Gail ripped her veil aside and had only the briefest of moments to steal a look into John's eyes as they both cried in unison, "No! Not again!"

The next few seconds were a blur for Gail as her security detail rushed to her side. Nate Hopper grabbed her bodily and carried her out a side entrance while she screamed and struggled to be let go. As he got her to her SUV, he attempted to heave her inside, but she managed to twist free.

She shrieked in fury, "Take me to him now, or I will shoot you dead where you stand. That is not a warning. That is a promise, Nate!"

For months, an Accipiter Wardog/Stalker hybrid that was literally on the other side of the world, on the other side of the suntube, had grown larger and larger as it attempted to target the city of Fort Brazos with its kinetic projectiles.

While John and Gail sat in the back of the SUV together, still in their wedding clothes, the phone rang. It was Alexander Marcus.

John answered and put it on speakerphone. "Yes, Alex, what's the word?"

"Show's over, Mr. President. Ramona Henry and NTN Dagger got lots of pictures before they killed the damned thing, but it's done. It's dead. We may have gotten lucky with where the explosion hit. The area where it hit was Barnett Park. We'll need to investigate, but we're crossing our fingers that no one was there at the time."

Gail sank back into John's arms and closed her eyes.

Before ending the call, John nodded tiredly and said, "Thank you, Alex."

He leaned his head against Gail's. "Shall we try again? Back to the church?"

Gail sighed. "Everyone's left by now, and there's glass everywhere."

"Tom's still there, I'm sure. He can make it official."

Gail quipped, "It's already official. We signed the papers. The church service was just the public part of it."

"It's OK, we still have it rented. The Food is still there, too. Might as well eat some cake."

"They actually made you pay for it?" She snickered, "This is, like, an official State wedding. I just declared it so." She grinned crookedly. "Consider it a decree!"

"Okay, let's...."

Abruptly, a new sound grew from outside the vehicle. Before anyone could stop them, John and Gail leaped out to see what was going on, although the effort was rather more difficult for Gail, who cursed and nearly fell on her head, struggling with the dress, before she joined him.

They were not far from the Town Square. The over three-hundred-foot-tall black spire placed there by the Gardeners before Awakening Day was glowing with green St. Elmo's fire.

John shook his head, roaring angrily. "No! God Damn it, No!"

The ground shook as green fire erupted from the tip of the spire and soared straight up through the sky, nine hundred miles to the suntube, where it licked along its path.

The suntube began to dim and darken.

All around them, the weather… stilled.

John's phone rang again. Gail's was still in the SUV.

"Alex, what the hell is happening?"

Alexander Marcus's voice was horse and dry. "Mr. President. I… I regret to inform you that the Accipiters have arrived in… in-system. They're here. Somehow, God knows how they found us. They are attacking."

✪ ✪ ✪

The sky turned red as the motorcade raced to the pre-planned emergency location, the defunct old First State Bank next to the town square, with its large central vault.

Flanked by their combined detail, Gail and John ran hand in hand towards the entrance while Corporal Jose Cruz grabbed Gail's bridal train. John's ten-year-old daughter Matti and her personal Marine Security Guard Roxanna Darling were already in the vault.

As John and Gail entered, Matti rushed into John and Gail's arms, and the three hugged each other.

Gail looked the question to the detail's commanders, Sergeant Roberts and Corporal Hopper. "What do we know?"

A secure network terminal sat in the corner. Jesse Roberts looked up from it. "Other than the initial report of the inbound enemy, nobody has a clue. This is all new."

Abruptly, the lights went out, and a dusty yellow emergency light flickered on.

Gail pulled herself loose and snapped, "Jermal! Clothes from the go-bag. Get me out of this damned dress now!"

Before he could answer, suddenly, the ground shook, and gravity itself nauseatingly fluctuated.

Everyone blinked hard and looked at each other.

Gail's eyes widened. "Give me a coin. Now!"

Jose Cruz dug into a pocket, fished out a challenge coin, and handed it to her.

She stared at it for a moment, then outstretched her hand and dropped it. The coin fell straight down. She nodded to herself. "The world has stopped spinning. We're back on some kind of artificial gravity."

From outside, an enormous boom shook the building. Dust settled slowly from the ceiling. Corporal Gabriel Pérez, from John's detail, glanced at Jessie, who nodded at him before dashing out the bank vault door. Moments later, he ran back inside and pulled himself to a stop, then started to speak, stopped, shook his head, then continued, "Uh… I think you all need to see this."

Outside, everyone looked up and stared at the enormous hologram that had appeared around the obelisk. It was the star system where New Texas was located. The hologram wasn't to scale, but the scene was easily recognizable. What was different was the large, stridently blinking cloud of red icons that appeared to be inching toward New Texas.

The Accipiters had found them.

Matti was still wearing her bridesmaid's dress for the interrupted wedding. It had been altered to fit her somewhat taller-than-normal ten-year-old body, at an even five feet tall. She whispered, "Dad… Are they going to get in… or are they going to just blow us up?"

Gail shook her head. She crouched down next to Matti and said breathlessly, pointing up at the hologram, "Look! We're… moving."

John blinked. He asked incredulously, "This thing can move?"

They watched as the image of their cylindrical home shifted out of its orbit and accelerated, veering away from the incoming Accipiters.

Gail shook her head again. "They must be at least a light-hour out or more. They won't know we've moved."

John wondered, "What are they doing? The Gardeners, I mean? Surely, they don't think that simply dodging the Accipiters will work forever? Where the Hell are we going…"

Without warning, the sky and the hologram went black. There was a sudden…. Lurch. As if they had stepped sideways into a direction that didn't exist. Where they didn't exist. Where nothing existed.

And then, in a transition that no one could ever adequately put into words, the world stepped *back*. The transition was indescribable. One moment, they were in their familiar star system, facing annihilation. The next, they were somewhere else. Somewhere very different.

The hologram reappeared in the darkness, showing a completely new star system that appeared to have *three* stars, although they were dim to almost dark themselves. A new icon appeared that could only be New Texas. Only now, instead of the grey rock they were used to, the image was of a dully gleaming metallic cylinder.

A cylinder that was already moving, heading for one of the stars. The hologram zoomed in, revealing that the star was not a star at all. It was a vast structure with circular openings or portals of some kind.

Another icon appeared, labeled NTN Blood Phoenix.

John gasped, "They made it! But that means…."

Gail finished the sentence, "We just traveled almost 75 light-years in an instant. This place… it must be able to use Nexus Junction Point travel as well as warp or whatever they used to get to the NJP. But what's to stop the Accipiter fleet from following us?"

The hologram shifted, presenting an abridged timeline of their recent escape. It depicted New Texas moving and the Accipiter vessels drawing nearer. Then suddenly, New Texas shimmered out of sight, and a massive shockwave billowed outward. It consumed everything in its path, including all the asteroid belts and the encroaching Accipiter fleet, leaving nothing behind but particles of dust and searing plasma.

Thunder boomed, the ground trembled, and the wind started to move. The hologram blinked off as gravity nauseatingly fluctuated, making everyone dizzy. Green lightning shot out from the Obelisk upwards to the suntube. The suntube slowly brightened to its normal yellow color, bathing the world in warm light.

All across the city, cheers, claps, songs, and car horns blared in nervous, happy refrain. They were alive. The world wasn't over yet.

A booming voice that crackled and resounded from the Obelisk suddenly crushed the raucous noise.

You have returned to the beginning. To the genesis of worlds. In this place, many things will be possible. You have exceeded our expectations where others failed.

The hologram faded, and the breeze stiffened. A stunned silence fell over the world.

John shook his head in understanding. "Hephaestus. The Forge of the Gods. We're at Mount Olympus."

Gail looked up at him, her eyes wide and still full of adrenaline. She nodded slowly, and then the corner of her lips twitched. "Are you sure? We could be at Lemnos, where Zeus cast Hephaestus down from Olympus? That would seem to be more consistent with our luck."

John reached over and pulled Gail and Matti to him. "Let's not push Lady Luck any further, then. You're still in the dress. Let's go find Tom and get married before something else happens."

Gail held John tightly, pressing her face against his chest. She inhaled deeply, letting out a sigh. "Wouldn't it be wonderful to forget all of our responsibilities for just a little while and be ordinary people?"

John let out a soft chuckle as he rocked her back and forth. "Do you remember our first dance?"

Gail smiled softly. "It feels like it was a thousand years ago…."

"I couldn't take my eyes off you," he murmured.

"You weren't so bad yourself," she replied with a sniff. "And now… we have to…."

Matti grimaced and pushed away from them. "TMI, you two."

John chuckled and sighed. "Raincheck, Mrs. Austin?"

Gail's eyes twinkled. "We'll work something out, Mr. Finley."

Matti rolled her eyes and turned to whisper something to Roxanna Darling.

Gail and John stood back, silently gazing at each other for a long moment. Finally, Gail broke it with a shaky exhale. "So, where should we go? The base? Riverbend?"

Then, she and John had the same thought and simultaneously turned to look at the Obelisk.

John nodded. "Right."

Gail began formulating their plan aloud, "It's a place to start. People will be gathering there anyway. We should go and reassure everyone that everything's okay. But first, you—Mr. Finley—are going to follow me into the SUV and help me out of this blasted wedding dress," she smiled wryly, "…so I can change clothes. No time for funny business."

He retorted, "I have nothing remotely *funny* in mind."

Matti groaned.

Just then, John's phone started ringing. He fished it out of his pocket, expecting it to be Alexander Marcus. However, instead, the caller ID read "Gardeners." Only a half dozen people had his number. He cocked his head in suspicion and showed it to Gail.

At first, she scowled. Then she glanced back at the Obelisk and worriedly snapped her gaze back at John, her eyes wide with surprise. "I think you should answer it, John."

He swallowed and nodded slowly. The Gardeners had never engaged in direct personal contact. Martin Williams had discovered that he could, occasionally, type and receive cryptic answers from them on what remained of the Internet, but no one had ever "spoken" to them except via the Obelisk. He accepted the call and put it on speakerphone, holding it out between himself and Gail. "This is John and Gail Austin. Who is this?"

A voice identical to the one used by the Obelisk moments earlier announced:

We will help you further, but not until you discover the traitor. Until then, we will be watching.

The call ended.

John and Gail looked up at each other in shock from the phone that John still held outstretched.

John grimaced, "Let's talk in the car while you change clothes."

Gail nodded curtly, then turned and struggled to get herself and the dress through the car door that Nate Hopper, her protection detail leader, held open for her.

Once inside, Gail struggled to free herself from the gown. In frustration, she angrily shook her head, "I can't believe I let Gwyneth talk me into wearing this damned thing."

John sighed, "Stop struggling and let me help. I will remind you that, whether you choose to admit it or not, you *wanted* to need help to get out of this dress. *My Help*. It was supposed to be under... better circumstances." He undid the fasteners down her back and helped her slide the dress off her shoulders. He held his hands on her shoulders and steadied her. "I promise... I'll make it up to you."

Gail twisted and glared at him for a moment before softening her expression. She swallowed, "We'll make it up to each other. Somehow. Until then...."

John smiled sadly, "Yes, until then, let's get you out of this thing without ripping it to shreds, which I promise you would regret *someday*, and talk about what just happened."

Amid the loud rustling of fabric that followed, John smiled at what Gail had worn underneath.

Gail glanced up, noticed his expression, and blushed fiercely, "Later, Mister!" She opened the go-bag containing her emergency change of clothes and her backup Sig P365 pistol. She hastily stretched and pulled on the jeans and long-sleeved blouse without bothering to remove her extremely non-utilitarian wedding day undergarments. "So," she said, breathing deeply, "they know about our traitor. What do they want us to do, take him out back and shoot the bastard?" As she strapped on her pistol, she scowled, "I'll do that in a hot minute!"

John started to reply, then hesitated. He sat back and wondered aloud, "They said… *discover* the traitor. But we already know who it is?"

Gail hesitated, pausing in place for a moment. "Maybe they don't know that, or maybe they mean co-conspirators? Or worse, something or someone we haven't discovered yet? What do they want us to do, start a witch hunt?" She finished dressing, pulling on a thin leather jacket and running shoes.

John shook his head, "You don't suppose… no, that doesn't make sense."

"What?"

"The prisoners. That engineer Grant, the women, the Keeper, or even the Accipiter. We already know about them."

Gail shook her head, "These Gardeners built an entire world and recreated our city, our bodies, and whatever the Hell this place is, they've taken us to. My God, if it really is what it looked like, it's a God-damned Dyson sphere! I can't believe that the semantics of the word "Discover" is a mistake they could possibly make. No, this must be something new…."

Just then, a thought occurred to John, and he slumped back into the seat, his expression full of dread.

Gail stopped and swallowed, "What."

John whispered, "Ari'Nell. If they hit us here…."

Gail's eyes widened, "Fuck. Even if they didn't… how will they find us? John…. We have to do something. All those people!"

John's phone started ringing again, as did Gail's, though it was buried somewhere underneath the discarded wedding dress.

He glanced at the caller ID and showed it to Gail. It read 'Alexander Marcus, Secretary of War.'

DownSide: First United Methodist Church

Fellowship Hall

Over the vociferous objections of every security detail member, John, and Gail decided there was nothing else they could really do at the moment and that they wanted to return to the Church. The sanctuary itself was strewn with broken shards of stained glass. However, Fellowship Hall, where the post-wedding reception had been scheduled, was on the other end of the church complex and was unaffected by the blast. The guests had all left, of course, but after several hurried calls, Alexander Marcus and Sheriff Hector Alonzo returned. Tom Parker had still been there, surveying the damage to the sanctuary and sweeping up what glass he could.

John, Gail, and Matti were the last to arrive, even though by then, the Presidential emergency evacuation bunker (the bank) had been closer to the Church. Alexander had been halfway back to his office at Riverbend, and Hector had returned home to check on his wife Antonia, who was in labor. Hector made calls, and a third of the police force, as well as more than half of the Sheriff's department, converged on the Church to hastily re-secure it.

John and Gail's security detail heads, Jesse Roberts and Nate Hopper, steadfastly refused to move an inch until word came back that the Church was secured.

Now in their 'street' clothes, John, Gail, and Matti entered the hall, followed by Hector, who had greeted them outside. Antonia was still in early labor and insisted that Hector stand with his friend. She was surrounded by her nine children and extended family and 'would be fine.' Alexander's wife, Alisha, was already back home with their older twin girls, Faith and Hope, and their three-month-old triplets, Grace, Joy, and Love.

John shook hands with Alexander and hugged Hector. "Thank you both for this. I know it is crazy doing this now, with everything going on."

Hector shook his head. "Jefe, with all that's happening, if you don't act now, you may never get the chance."

Alexander smiled in agreement. "You may not believe this, Mr. President, but this wedding has been anticipated by everyone but the two of you for a very, very long time. It is your moral imperative to get across that finish line."

Gail couldn't decide how to respond to Alexander. Striking or shooting her former commanding officer was overkill. Maybe. Finally, she closed her eyes and shook her head as she rushed to his side and wrapped her arms around him in a fierce hug.

Just then, Surgeon General Gwyneth Elliot Duncan rushed into the room, her face flushed and her own red hair askew, exclaiming. "Don't you dare start this without me!"

Tom and Dotti Parker followed shortly behind. Tom smiled amiably and said. "Okay, people. The world may be coming to an end again any minute, so let's get this show on the road."

Gwyneth stood to Gail's left and Hector to John's right as John and Gail faced each other with the wedding cake in the background.

Dotti set up a camera on a tripod and began recording the event.

Tom paused, giving John and Gail a chance to soak in the moment. He began. "Dearly beloved, we are gathered here today under uncertain circumstances. The day started full of hope and joy, only to have that serenity shattered by narrowly avoided catastrophe, and, to be honest. A second near apocalypse which was shortly followed by a pronouncement of hope for a future. No one would blame the two people before us were they to focus on the crisis at hand. And yet, despite the urgency of the situation, these two souls have instead decided to forge ahead and complete what was interrupted and bind themselves together, just as they have bound themselves to their shared responsibility to the rest of humanity."

"In doing so, they demonstrate their faith not only in each other but in a future full of hope for all of us. Therefore, today, we come together not just to witness the union of John and Gail but to celebrate the enduring power of love and hope in the face of adversity."

"Before Awakening Day, they did not know each other. Indeed, on that fateful day, their destinies, as were all of ours, were forever intertwined. I was part of the conspiracy to push them both into roles they did not want. To take a terrible burden that none of us wanted to bear and thrust it upon their shoulders. In carrying that incalculable weight, the very survival of the human race, we forced them into a situation where the only other person who could grasp what each of them was going through… was each other. I won't lie to you. The others and I saw the potential chemistry brewing between them even before then. Of course, they were both too stubborn to see it themselves. Indeed, later, even as they began to realize it, their personal honor forbade them from acting on it. And yet, crisis after crisis pushed them closer and closer."

"Thankfully, they finally came to their senses!"

"Today, as we witness the union of John and Gail, we are reminded of the power of love to bring light into the darkest of times. Their journey to this moment has been fraught with trials that would test the strongest of souls. They have led us, fought for us, and now they stand together, not as leaders alone but as partners and as symbols of our collective resilience and perseverance."

"This ceremony is a testament to the fact that even in the shadow of destruction, in the aftermath of a calamity that shook the very foundation of our existence, love endures. Love thrives amidst chaos, grows in the face of adversity, and brings together not just two people but an entire community."

"John and Gail's vows today are not merely words spoken in the presence of witnesses; they are a beacon of hope, a promise of a shared future, and a testament to the unwavering spirit that defines us as the people of New Texas."

"John and Gail, today you join your lives in the most extraordinary of circumstances, forging a bond that is a testament to the resilience and hope we all share."

He paused and smiled beatifically. "So now, John Hugo Austin, do you take Gail to be your lawfully wedded wife, to live together in the covenant of marriage? Do you promise to love her, comfort her, honor and keep her, in sickness and in health, and forsaking all others, be faithful to her as long as you both shall live?"

John, his gaze lost in Gail's eyes, nodded and firmly answered. "I do."

Tom continued, turning to Gail. "Gail Anson Finley, do you take John to be your lawfully wedded husband, to live together in the covenant of marriage? Do you promise to love him, comfort him, honor and keep him, in sickness and in health, and forsaking all others, be faithful to him as long as you both shall live?"

Gail's eyes glistened as she answered, her voice husky and certain, "I Do."

Tom intoned formally, "John and Gail, please exchange your rings as a symbol of your love and commitment to each other."

Matti Austin struggled to contain her excitement, almost skipping forward as she eagerly extended her hands to present the rings.

John and Gail took the rings from Matti and placed them on each other's fingers, then said in unison, "With this ring, I thee wed."

Tom was perfectly glowing as he pronounced, "Now that John and Gail have given themselves to each other by solemn vows, with the joining of hands and the giving and receiving of rings, I pronounce that they are husband and wife. Those whom love has joined together, let no one put asunder. John, Gail, may your life together be a beacon of hope and a testament to the enduring power of love in the face of all odds."

"Congratulations, you may now seal your vows with a kiss."

John and Gail fell into each other's arms in a passionate kiss that would be broadcast over and over again for months.

Senate

● ● ● ● ● ● ● ● ● ● ● ● ● ● ● ●

Riverbend Mall Senate Chamber
Former Carlson Movie Theatre

Prior to the Apocalypse, with notable exceptions, most shopping malls across the United States had generally fallen on hard times. In the 1980s, there were over 25,000 malls in the United States. By the 2020s, there were less than a thousand. Empty malls became a morose hobby for rubberneckers of a dying epoch of consumerism. Despite this trend, in Fort Brazos, Riverbend Mall had defied the odds and stayed open.

Until the Apocalypse and Awakening Day.

By the time anyone thought to lock down the mall to protect it from looting, they found that it was largely untouched. People had other concerns. Later, when New London was discovered, the remaining stocks of clothing and consumer goods were appropriated and given out to help the over twenty-two thousand men, women, and children with nothing but the clothes on their backs. It didn't take long for the shops to be emptied out, leaving the 1,110,000-square-foot facility mostly empty except for the store fixtures.

Then came the horrific bombing at City Hall.

With the Gardener's gun to their heads and a mission to strike back at the Accipiters already underway, a new seat of government was needed. However, the Fort Brazos survivors were short on everything - resources, manpower, and, most especially, time. Building something new was out of the question. New London offered a vast array of vacant buildings and space, but it also presented a logistical nightmare.

Most of the New Londoners had been evacuated DownSide to Fort Brazos. There was no food supply in New London. Every scrap of food had to be ferried down, or up, depending on your perspective, the six-hour elevator ride, three hundred miles through the 'skin' of New Texas, to the city. Placing the new government headquarters in New London, when well over ninety percent of the population was DownSide, was an idea dismissed as quickly as it was proposed.

At Riverbend, the now empty Macy's store was turned into a makeshift government center, with various offices and a new "Oval Office" on the third floor overlooking the atrium.

The newly elected Senate needed a place to meet, something that, in the coming years, would accommodate a growing number of representatives. The original plan was to use the broad Macy's atrium. But then someone remembered the movie theatre next to the mall. Less than two years before the Apocalypse, as part of the mall's revival and general updating, the theatre had been upgraded to include luxury reclining seats, laser projectors, the latest sound system, in-theatre dining, and a full bar service.

Lamentably, by now, the bar inventory had been thoroughly looted by parties unknown. With no fresh supplies, 'luxury' items like beer and liqueur from Earth were worth their weight in gold on the burgeoning black market.

The largest screening room was requisitioned to become the official Senate Chamber. It already had the facilities for corporate events, so only minor modifications and security measures were required. After the City Hall massacre, no one objected to closing off the rest of the theatre complex for public access. It wasn't as though there was much demand for pre-Apocalypse movies, anyway. Of course, there weren't any post-Apocalypse movies yet, either.

The first official Senate session wasn't even scheduled to begin for another two weeks. However, an emergency session was called after the incredible events of the past few hours, probably the most momentous since even Awakening Day. It would be broadcast live. It took several more hours of frantic work to make the arrangements.

During that time, Livia Milner, one of the new Senators and wife of Vice Admiral Preston Milner, lobbied hard to be the leader in any negotiations with the Gardeners. In truth, she had little choice in the matter. Her mysterious blackmailer had demanded it and even went so far as to outline specific leverage points with the other Senators.

In the weeks leading up to the election, Gloria Vargas had helped Livia assemble a new wardrobe. As one of the New London/Groton survivors, she had arrived in the new world with only the clothes she wore the night of the Accipiter Attack. In her case, somewhat infamously, she wore a black Chanel full-length gown. Gloria had dug deep into her own closet to help, and the rest was assembled via the brisk Fort Brazos barter system and no small amount of gentle arm-twisting.

Gloria had worked miracles, and today, Livia wore a genuine, if a few years out of date, black Giorgio Armani blazer jacket, matching slacks, and, incredibly, an equally dated but serviceable pair of Prada ankle-strap platform sandals. The black fabric contrasted sharply with her bone-pale skin tone and, now, waist-length straight black hair. As intended, the outfit helped her stand out from the other Senators as someone used to power and who carried the sophistication of an "old Earth" leader. It had been a small challenge to tailor the clothes to fit her size four frame, but it had worked out better than she'd hoped. Indeed, with no new clothes or designs coming from outside Fort Brazos anymore, tailoring was a blossoming business. Were it not for the threat of blackmail, she might have actually begun to feel like her old self again for the first time since before Awakening Day, not counting the loss of her daughter and the rest of civilization.

She paid no attention to Senator Gaspard Boyer, one of the so-called "New Arrivals" who had been a Colonel in the French Expeditionary Infantry when the Gardeners abducted his unit and left them outside the Joint Reserve Base (now Fort Underwood) on Awakening Day. Gaspard drew a striking figure. He was lean, muscular, and tall, at six feet two inches, and he eschewed the custom of former military officers who became politicians and wore civilian clothes. He still wore his uniform and the blue beret of his original unit. His short brown hair and deep-set blue eyes gave him a piercing look. Gaspard was a cultured Frenchman with a vision. In his mind, he was the only possible choice for a diplomatic role.

Former Council members Esmerelda Collins, Dale Hubbard, and former County Judge Maria Gonzalez were easier to bring on board. For Senator Collins, promising to support land reform and issues beneficial to the surviving Fort Brazos cattle ranchers was sufficient. Gonzalez and Hubbard were even easier – all it took was a call from Gloria Vargas.

Mira (Yeager) Cross and Alphonse Halkias (former Navy Captain) were easy enough. Mira wanted support for more Wardog and Stalker patrols, and Alphonse wanted support for more resources for Navy families. Darnell Lewis and Caesar Salangsang both wanted more resources for their new settlements.

The former Mercenary and New Texas Ranger leader Ignacio was a tougher sell. In the months after Awakening Day, he and his band of former South American mercenaries had been chartered to recreate the Texas Rangers as the senior law enforcement agency with responsibilities outside Fort Brazos-proper. His men now already had positions of respect and authority. What they lacked was better equipment and visibility. Livia proposed special land grants and hazard pay for the Rangers. Ignacio agreed, but only on the condition of an unspecified favor at a future date. Livia nearly balked at the blank check, but looking into his eyes, she decided she would trust the swarthy Columbian.

That left two remaining Senators. The former Russian Marine Captain Valentin Gorshkov and Sybil Blanchard. Valentin tried to give the impression of being a stoic, but a lot more went on behind his eyes. Livia had met him on several occasions and decided that the former Muscovite was simply angry at the universe and wanted to take out his revenge. God help anyone in his way. She'd probed for some sort of deal. Her blackmailer had not provided any useful ideas. After trading pointed barbs back and forth, the man had laughed, saying it was evident that she knew how the game was played, given who her father had been, but that things were different now and the stakes much higher than she understood. Eventually, his only offer was a not-so-thinly veiled suggestion of his support in exchange for sexual favors. The offer didn't shock her at all. She came from Boston political 'royalty' after all. It was the taunt in his eyes that told her the truth. The man didn't expect or even want what he was asking for. He had bigger ambitions and thought little of her or anyone else along the way.

It was Sybil who mystified her, though. The tiny, very busty trucker's wife was a puzzle to her. The woman had radically evolved since Awakening Day. Gone was the quiet, even timid, mouse of a woman. In her place was something new. Sybil was confident, gregarious, and... *knowing*. She acted as if she'd known everyone around her for ages. It wasn't just a sense of general confidence and social affability. There was something about Sybil that left Livia... unsettled. Livia had dealt with political operators and schmoozers her whole life. Sybil was something.... Else. It was almost impossible to dislike the woman, and that made it even worse.

Still, however, when Livia met with her and asked for her support, Sybil simply stared at her with that penetrating look of hers and simply answered, "Of course, Livia. You're the ideal person for the job. Oh, and by the way, what do you think it says that the Senate has chosen for its official meeting place, a movie theatre? A venue formerly devoted to the lies and fictions of fantasy, high entertainment, and the suspension of disbelief?"

What hurt was what wasn't said. Livia felt that she could almost read the other woman's mind and that what she had really meant to say was, *You're just the sort of lying, devious, duplicitous woman we need to negotiate with aliens who can't be trusted.* Or perhaps it was simply Livia's own guilty conscience.

The encounter had left Livia shaken in a way she'd never felt before.

✪ ✪ ✪

Security was tight both inside and outside the theatre. Every bag had been checked and double-checked. Every crawlspace, plumbing access, adjacent rooms, roof, and nearby parking area were searched, blocked off, or both. Ignacio's Texas Rangers' responsibilities now included Senate security, working alongside the Marine Security protection details. While the Marines wore full combat gear, the Rangers stuck to the service's traditional western-style civilian suits, cowboy hats, and various concealed and not-so-concealed weapons.

Three senators were not physically present. Colonel Caesar Salangsang was on the other side of the world in the New Philippines. Darnell Lewis was hundreds of miles away in Jamestown. Mira Cross was rushing to get to New London in time to greet Captain Charles Cross, her newlywed husband before the Blood Phoenix docked.

Four people were seated on stage. President and Vice President John and Gail Austin, Secretary of War Alexander Marcus, and Dr. Takumi Nakamura.

John scrolled through reports on a tablet while Gail opened the meeting. "Dr. Nakamura, what can you tell us about where New Texas has been moved to? Where are we?"

Dr. Nakamura, an astronomer, former Dean of Science and Technology at Bonham State University, and newly appointed Superintendent of the Eugene Morton Naval Academy, looked grave. He nodded solemnly. His black and grey hair, as with so many other people, had reverted to its former hue, in his case, a lustrous jet-black. He brushed it back with a distracted gesture, shrugged his shoulders slightly inside his ten-year-old black suit, and adjusted the narrow grey tie his wife Mizuki had picked out for him that morning.

He began with his patient, unhurried professor's cadence. "Madam Vice President, Senators. Our analysis indicates that the New Texas McKendree Cylinder, our home, somehow transported itself approximately seventy-four point four light-years to the Ari'Chawig system. That's the same destination to which Captain Cross and the Blood Phoenix were dispatched some fifty-two days ago. Clearly, we did not travel via warp, like the Phoenix did, but rather, we presume that our habitat traveled via a Nexus Junction Point."

He paused and glanced up at the movie screen behind him as three images were displayed side by side. He continued, "The Ari'Chawig system lies deep within a dusty nebula, and it appears to be a trinary star system, composed of a Class L brown dwarf, the star you see on your left, a Class T methane dwarf, the star you see on your right, and most intriguingly, the image in the middle is actually a red dwarf enclosed within an artificial spherical structure, a form of Dyson Sphere, whose purpose and capabilities are unknown."

Gail nodded and said, "Thank you, Dr. Nakamura."

She turned to Alexander. "Secretary Marcus, please give us an update. What's the status of the enemy, the Blood Phoenix, our people at Ari'Nell, the Revenge, and the aliens who brought us here."

Like Dr. Nakamura, Alexander Marcus's short-cropped hair, which had begun to turn silver back on Earth, had now reverted to its former glossy black. His skin, too, which had likewise lost some of its dark sheen, was once again the rich dark shade it had been ten years earlier. Unlike Senator Boyer, Alexander, the ex-Air Force major general who had commanded the Fort Brazos Joint Military Reserve Base, had adapted to wearing civilian suits after he was appointed Secretary of War. He didn't care for pinstripes, but the dark grey suit was the best he'd been able to barter for.

Alexander's barrel chest swelled as he drew a deep breath, frowned, and spoke. "The Gardener hologram appears to have shown that the Accipiter fleet was destroyed. Even if they weren't, we don't believe that there is a way to tell where a vessel that travels via Nexus Junction Point has gone. We were not followed. Our new location appears to be some sort of Gardener base, and given the tone of their message, it appears that we are currently not at risk, at least not from the Accipiters."

"The Blood Phoenix is approaching to dock as we speak. I've spoken to Captain Cross. It seems they were immobilized by the Gardeners as soon as they arrived in the system and have nothing new to tell us. Approaching us and docking are the only maneuvers they have been allowed to do."

"We have no information regarding the disposition of Revenge, her crew, or any of the workers and service people stationed at Ari'Nell. Rest assured, we will do everything in our power to locate them and bring them home."

"As for the Gardeners, here in Fort Brazos, I expect everyone saw their hologram above the obelisk and heard their announcement. So far, all attempts to communicate with them have been met with silence. Anything further, at this point, is guesswork and speculation."

Senator Boyer spoke with his heavy French accent, "So, we 'ave nozing but ze Gardeners' word zat ze enemy was destroyed. 'Ow can zey Gardeners say zat zey know what 'appened after we left? For zat matter, 'ow do we even know if zere was an Accipiter fleet on ze way in ze first place? Everyzing zat light show showed us could 'ave been a lie."

John, Gail, and Alexander all started to speak at once.

Livia beat them to it, standing and facing the other senators as she coolly interjected, "Senator Boyer is correct that we only have the Gardener's *word* for what happened. That's true. But then, we also had only their word that the Accipiters existed at all and that they had conquered Earth and destroyed our civilization there. And yet, when we *went* there, we learned that everything that they had said was indeed true. I don't trust the Gardeners any more than our esteemed President or Vice President famously do themselves, but I don't have to trust them to know that nothing they've told us so far has been disproven by the facts. We even have an Accipiter high priest in custody, and everything *he* has said has been consistent with what the Gardeners have told us. We owe a blood debt to the five percent for what was done to them by those same Gardeners. However, for now, we are here. We need to face reality and engage with the Gardeners if we want to move forward. Even if that means that we must go into the belly of the beast."

She pointed behind her at the image of the Dyson Sphere enclosed star on the movie screen, "If they won't talk to us, then we have to go to them. We are an investment that the Gardeners did not want to lose. We must be careful to approach them from a position of strength. They need us."

Gaspard retorted, "All ze more reason why a diplomatic expedition must be led by a leader with ze most experience dealing with sophisticated and delicate international sensibilities, but who is also a seasoned military professional who will recognize dangers to our community and lobby for ze resources we need to fight zis war."

John Austin sternly interrupted the tit-for-tat, "Senators, I have already spoken to Secretary Marcus. A special committee will be formed to address relations with the Gardeners and evaluate next steps. The Committee will be chaired by Vice President..." he hesitated, "By the Vice President. Dr. Nakamura has already agreed to be the scientific representative on the Committee. The military representative will be General Gideon Markovic, who not only has extensive international diplomatic experience but who we all know was the gallant leader of the ground forces on the mission to Earth. The Senate representative will need to be chosen by the Senate itself. In addition to any potential negotiations with the Gardeners, the Committee will evaluate and recommend priorities for possible future military construction projects that may be proposed by the Gardeners. They talked about *possibilities*.... I expect this might imply the construction of new ships with which to engage the Accipiters. Even if such were handed to us on a silver platter, we don't have enough trained crews to man them. Not yet. Furthermore, any decisions about how to employ them and for deciding the best strategies for engaging the enemy are not to be taken lightly and will demand blood and treasure that are in terrifyingly short supply."

Gaspard smiled, obviously confident in the outcome of the Senate vote, "Of course, Mr. President, and on behalf of ze entire first Senate, may I be ze first Senator to officially congratulate you and Mrs. Austin on your marriage."

Gail smiled a thin, crooked smile, "Thank you, Senator Boyer. President Finley and I accept the Senate's gracious congratulations."

Gaspard blinked in confusion while most of the rest of the Senators laughed and chuckled.

Later, when John and Gail were alone, she looked sideways at him. "We never talked to Alexander about any of that. You're lucky that Nakamura knows how to keep a poker face. And what was that bit about Markovic having *extensive diplomatic experience?* For God's sake, the man was just a colonel in the IDF!"

John chuckled, "Well, Gideon did at least travel to what was once Peru, and he did have extensive, uhm, *exchanges* there."

Gail punched him in the ribs, "The man fired missiles there and set off a nuke and killed God knows how many Accipiters and.... others."

John winced at the pain in his ribs, "Yes, exactly. And he won't take shit from that frog, Gaspard."

Lost

● ● ● ● ● ● ● ● ● ● ● ● ● ● ● ●

Observation Point
Outside the New Texas Hideaway System
NTN Revenge

I soft spring breeze with a hint of honeysuckle wafted across John Austin's 2-acre backyard as birds chirped and tweeted their delight. Ringnterstellar spaceflight and galactic war were new to mankind, but war, and the planning and preparedness that went with it, were certainly not. Soon after voyages to Ari'Nell and beyond began, a number of standard operating procedures were established. Lacking any form of faster-than-light communication, there was no equivalent to even the encrypted satellite communications that 'modern' warships back on Earth had relied on.

What's more, even submarines could rise to periscope depth to check for radio messages during non-combat operations. On the other hand, submariners were used to being out of direct communications for long periods, and towed long wavelength arrays were not always an option.

While it wasn't perfect, and the information wouldn't be as current as desired, a standard practice of stopping twenty-four light-hours outside a system and using the starship's warp shell lensing to image the system to visually check for what danger might have been there a day ago, was the best that they could manage.

So, outside the rubble-strewn system where the New Texas McKendree cylinder was located, SOP was to stop and check things over from a distance. The system itself held no planets that would have ever supported life. It was mostly made up of massive belts of debris—failed planets, dust, and planetoids distantly orbiting a small, low-mass white dwarf.

NTN Revenge stopped well above the nominal plane of the ecliptic and far from the known Nexus Junction Points that functioned as an interconnected web of spacetime weak points that the Accipiters used for effectively instantaneous travel between certain classes of stars in the galaxy. Their ships were only capable of sublight flight and did not use warp technology. They'd never felt a need to use anything other than what the race that had uplifted them had gifted. That the Accipiters ruled the galaxy gave credence to their choices.

The NJP's for a star are not located in a fixed location. They move with the relative motion of the star, the nearby stars, and the overall flexure of the galaxy as a whole. That said, their location relative to the star is largely determined by the collective mass of the star and its planetary system. In general, absent the influence of nearby stars, the larger the star, the closer the NJP(s) are to it. The mass equation results in sufficiently large stars having NJP location(s) actually inside or dangerously close to the star itself. Conversely, the smaller the stellar mass, the further away the NJP's are until they reach an effective vanishing point, requiring too much energy to open. So, for small stars, travel time for sublight ships to the system interior can be significant.

In the case of the system where New Texas was hidden away, the closest NJP was just over a light-hour out, though there were additional NJPs further out-system.

In the crowded shipping container-turned-CIC, Jermaine, Rafferty & Alister stood expectantly, watching the monitor, waiting for the now-familiar sight of New Texas to fill the screen. The four-thousand-mile-long world had been disguised by the Gardeners as just another airless, cratered space rock. As they looked on, however, what they saw instead seemed to mirror the disastrous scene from Ari'Nell in the now wrecked Ari'Shevn system. A fading but massive expanding ball of plasma.

Rafferty recoiled back into the container wall, his face turning ashen, "No… God… No, no, no, no, no!"

Alister's reaction was different. Of Scottish heritage, his complexion was quite pale, so the rage that boiled within him nearly left his face beet red. He turned to Jermaine with fury in his eyes.

Jermaine, in contrast, clenched his jaw and tightened his lips as his face hardened. He turned and looked the other men in the eyes and finally said aloud, "Revenge, we're waiting. Report."

<hr>

Captain. I am so sorry to have kept you waiting. I
was just becoming aware of a significant disturbance near

> *the location of one of the system's Nexus Junction Points.*
> *A wave of gravitational energy was released, and it is still*
> *shaking the system. I am detecting gravity waves that do*
> *not correspond to any phenomenon I am familiar with. The*
> *release of energy seems to have shattered much of the matter*
> *in the system, but a significant amount of it also appears to*
> *have undergone fusion, as we saw happen at Ari'Nell. The*
> *signatures, however, do not correspond to what we saw happen*
> *there. What happened here was different. It was cataclysmic,*
> *and there is no sign of New Texas. Not even debris. I*
> *recommend that I move us further away until I can lens what*
> *transpired here.*

Jermaine rubbed his chin and frowned. "How long ago did this happen?"

> *Approximately thirty-seven hours ago, coinciding with*
> *the final attack on Ari'Nell. It is unlikely to be a coincidence.*
> *I conclude that the Accipiters attacked both systems at*
> *the same time. To learn more, it will take a few minutes to*
> *traverse thirty-six light hours and begin to lens the system.*
> *Longer, to analyze the data. More, if I need to reposition*
> *multiple times.*

✪ ✪ ✪

Twenty-two minutes Later

The men stared in horrified awe as events replayed before them on the monitor. A brilliant flash of light announced the arrival of a massive Accipiter armada in-system. Icons representing Ten enormous motherships were accompanied by a hazy cloud of smaller dots marked with a legend indicating over a million support vessels. Moments later, the gargantuan New Texas habitat began to *move*. It accelerated faster and faster with every passing second but soon began to shimmer before vanishing in a stupendous explosion that rippled across the system. Space itself stretched and compressed into stress bands that generated their own titanic energies. As the time index rapidly advanced, the approaching Accipiter fleet was snuffed out of existence like so many dust mites in a blast furnace.

*It appears that New Texas was not only capable of
warp travel but was also able to travel via Nexus Junction
Point. The mass of such a large object, at over four thousand
miles long, however, far exceeded anything I believed possible
to travel that way.*

*Opening the rift appears to have actually, for lack of a better
metaphor, ripped a hole in spacetime, resulting in the release
of the energies that you witnessed. Anticipating your question;
however, as with any Nexus travel, I cannot determine its
destination or if it even survived the effort.*

Gerald Beltran and SWO Moreno Guerra traded horrified glances. Gerald swallowed hard and said, "¡hostia!"

Alister said in a wrathful voice, "Well, at least they took a bunch of the bastards with them."

Jermaine grimaced and looked at Rafferty, who seemed lost. He reached out and put his hand on the man's shoulder. "I'm sorry, Rafe. Truly. I'm sure they made it and that Roberta, Jordan, and Sean are safe. The Gardeners invested too much in New Texas and in us humans. They'll be okay, and we'll do our damnedest to find them."

He took a deep breath and released Rafferty's shoulder.

Rafferty braced himself and shook his head, forcing himself to consider the present. "We have a lot of people to get to a safe harbor somewhere. And soon."

Jermaine nodded in agreement, "You're right, Rafe. We need to figure out what to do next. First, however, we need to act quickly and secure our supplies of food and medicine. Supplies need to be transferred somewhere where they can be kept under guard and humanely rationed out. If someone were to hoard supplies, it could kill us all. Rationing will need to be transparent with oversight. No one, most especially command staff, is exempt. Also, I want to set up a meeting of all department heads for medical, operations, and maintenance. We've got Kukri, Revenge, and fifty-two HAB modules, over a thousand civilians, and a grand total of a dozen dedicated security personnel. We'll supplement security from Kukri's and Revenge's crews, but we won't have nearly enough to cover every location. After I make the announcement, there may be… unrest. All of these people volunteered, and all of them are, by definition, the best we had, but this news… all of it… is going to hit hard."

He held his gaze with Rafferty for a long moment.

Rafferty slowly nodded, "Yes, Captain. I understand."

Jermaine added, dropping his voice an octave, "We cannot afford to lose a single man or woman. It is possible that we may be the last. The last surviving humans in the universe. Even if we're not, we're going to need the skills and determination of every one of us if we're going to make it through this. Understood?"

Alister and Rafferty both swallowed and answered in unison, "Yes, Captain."

"Also, I want a complete headcount, along with names, specialties, and skills. We need to know what we have to work with as we deal with problems that arise. Rafe, Alister, Beltran, get on it. I need to make an announcement now before word gets out."

✪ ✪ ✪

After they were built by the FAB, one of the modifications made to the HAB modules was a communication system and display screen.

Jermaine paused, closed his eyes for a moment, then stepped over and rested his hand gently on Ensign Molly Crawford's shoulder, who sat at the communications station. She had short blonde hair that was even shorter on the sides, with an almost boyish face. Her father had been a Navy Captain, and she spoke seven languages. Molly had graduated from the Naval Academy, completed the Nuclear Propulsion Officer Candidate Program (NUPOC), and had a degree in electrical engineering. Like most onboard Revenge, Kukri, or, for that matter, the Blood Phoenix, wherever it might have ended up, Molly was overqualified and a volunteer. Her face was grim as she returned Jermaine's gaze.

Jermain smiled softly, "Ensign Crawford... Molly, connect me to everyone. All the HABs, and Kukri. All hands announcement."

Molly nodded firmly, "Aye, Captain. Connecting you now." A moment later, an electronic boatswain's pipe signaled the announcement.

Jermaine stiffened and stood at practiced attention as he looked into the camera mounted on the wall amid the displays, "Attention all hands, and all civilians. I have news. We have arrived outside the system where New Texas was formerly located." He paused. "You heard correctly. Over thirty-six hours ago, it appears that the New Texas habitat escaped the system shortly after an Accipiter fleet arrived. We believe that the attack was simultaneous to the one that hit us at Ari'Nell. In escaping the system, New Texas caused an energy disruption that appears to have destroyed the Accipiter fleet. That was the good news. The bad news is that we do not know where New Texas went. Neither this system nor Ari'Shevn is safe. We will shortly begin working on determining where we should go next."

He swallowed. "Every one of you has worked against insurmountable odds. The devastation at Ari'Nell has left us shaken, and now we face an even greater challenge. I have complete confidence that we will find solutions to the problems that face us. We will devote every available resource to reunite us with New Texas… and all of our friends and loved ones there."

"Meanwhile, remember that every person here represents the brightest and most courageous mankind has to offer. At Ari'Nell, you moved mountains. We will get through this, and we will survive. We will find our friends again. In the meantime, I need your help. All of you. We've devastated the Accipiter's fleets, but you know just as well as I do that they have many, many more. They will be back, and we will be ready for them. Until then, we must work together to conserve our supplies and resources. Until we can find a safe harbor to rest and create new supplies, I'm asking each and every person to pass along any critical medical and food supplies they have. A medical committee will be formed to manage these supplies until they can be replaced. No one, especially the command staff, will be exempt from the rules set down by the committee."

"Hoarding could cost lives."

"Think about the people around you and their families and friends, as well as your own. We are all, quite literally, all in this together. Please remain calm and help each other. Look out for each other. We need each other. Each and every one of us is precious. So, I'm calling upon each of you to bring the same ingenuity, brilliance, dedication, and bravery you showed at Ari'Nell to our current situation. Remember Mace. Remember Berti and her crew. Do it for them. Do it for the people in New Texas who will be looking for us. Most of all, do it for the people next to you."

✪ ✪ ✪

Two Hours Later

The Builders had been larger than humans, but the area used as "crew quarters" was distressingly small. The reason for this is that the Builders slept communally. It was part of their psychology as prey animals. After the discovery of the ILCs, modifications were made to accommodate human use and physiology. The "crew" space was subdivided, with a tiny cabin allotted for the CO and the rest given lockers and hot swap bunk beds in the submariner tradition.

Jermaine sat on his fold-out cot in his cabin, with Rafferty seated at the tiny desk. In the corner of the desk lay a small fire safe. The kind you might buy at a big box retail store to safeguard important papers. Jermaine opened it and lifted its meager contents to find a black envelope at the bottom. He retrieved the thin plastic and held it in his fingers carefully as though its contents might somehow carry some dread pathogen. He pursed his lips and looked up at Rafferty. "I can't believe we're going to have to open this."

Rafferty's expression was morose, and his voice was thin, as though he had no air in his lungs. "We already had one apocalypse. What's one more?"

Jermaine braced himself, "Rafe, we'll get through this. We'll find them. Somehow. I know we will."

Rafferty nodded slowly, but Jermaine knew the man didn't believe him. In the back of his mind, he wasn't entirely sure he believed it himself. "Keep it together, Rafe. I need you. We all need you. Are you ready to witness?"

Rafferty straightened slightly. "Aye, Captain."

Jermain took a breath, broke the seal, and removed a single sheet of paper bearing the seal of the new government in Fort Brazos. It read:

FINAL CONTINGENCY ORDERS:

IN THE EVENT OF THE DESTRUCTION OF NEW TEXAS, THIS AND ANY OTHER SURVIVING VESSELS ARE COMMANDED TO SEEK REFUGE FROM THE ACCIPITER THREAT AND USE ALL AVAILABLE RESOURCES TO PRESERVE HUMANITY. THE CONTINUITY OF THE SPECIES IS YOUR PRIORITY. SHOULD INSUFFICIENT BIOLOGICAL DIVERSITY SURVIVE TO ACCOMPLISH THIS, YOU ARE INSTEAD DIRECTED TO ATTACK AND HARASS ACCIPITER FORCES FOR AS LONG AS POSSIBLE.

SHOULD IT BEFALL YOU THAT YOU MUST STRIKE THE ENEMY IN FINAL DEFIANCE, I PARAPHRASE DYLAN THOMAS:

"DO NOT GO GENTLE INTO THAT GOOD NIGHT,
MANKIND'S END SHOULD BURN AND RAVE AT THE CLOSE
OF DAY; RAGE, RAGE AGAINST THE DYING OF THE LIGHT."

MAKE THEM BLEED FOR IT. GOD BLESS AND GOOD LUCK.

SIGNED,
PRESIDENT JOHN HUGO AUSTIN

Jermaine read it and handed the orders to Rafferty.

Rafferty blinked and shook his head. "Well, that's a hell of a thing. Go hide somewhere and make babies, or go out in a blaze of glory."

Jermaine sighed. "What else would you suggest? Are you surprised? What else could he have possibly said? Can you think of anything different?"

Rafferty hissed, "It's all mute! Where exactly are we supposed to take these people? Ari'Nell was our backup site, and now it's less than dust. You know as well as I do that any decent or even half-decent planet out there will already be under the Accipiter's thumb! That was the goddamned point of New Texas in the first place! Any, and I mean any, habitable planet will already be occupied. After their losses in the last two days, the Accipiters will be in a mad-frenzy looking for us under every rock! Maybe the only thing we can do is use the engineers to build weapons and focus on hitting the Accipiters. Maybe Dimitri can rig up those Zero-point modules to blow up Accipiter planets. Make 'em bleed for it like President Austin said!"

Jermaine shook his head slowly. "We've only got what food we have with us. How long can that last, Rafe? A few weeks at most, even with rationing? We're going to have to find a hole to hide in somewhere where we can at least figure out how to find or make more food. Failing that, we all either starve, or we just decide to warp into one of their ships and blow ourselves up like Gene did. But that only kills *one* of their ships. Besides that, Rafe, think about it. Between Kukri and Revenge, we've got a total crew of fifty-six men and women who are responsible for the lives of over a *thousand* civilians! We owe it to them to at least try to save them. We *might*, and I mean *might*, have enough food to make the trip all the way to Earth, the only place we *know* we would find ships to kamikaze into, assuming we could get through the mines that Charles ran into? Chances are, we'd have to leave almost immediately. Do you really think you could convince those thousand-plus civilians to give up now without even trying to find another way? Without even trying to find a way back to their families?"

He paused, stood, and put his hand on Rafferty's shoulder. "Rafe, I know you're hurting. I also *know* that Roberta, Jordan, and Sean would want you to do everything possible to find your way back to them. They survived, Rafe. I'm convinced of that. You owe it to them to survive, too."

Rafferty ground his teeth and stared back at Jermaine defiantly for a moment. Then his shoulders slumped. He closed his eyes, bowed his head slightly, and nodded.

Jermaine's voice resonated with a sense of urgency laced with determination, "Revenge, take us out another few light days from this location and initiate a comprehensive scan of the nearby star systems. We need a list of viable destinations we can make within a two-week timeframe. Prioritize those sectors that are in the worst parts of town. I'm talking about the Red or Brown Dwarfs. Or high-mass stars that tend to be overlooked due to their challenging environments and bad Nexus Junction Points."

He paused to ensure his orders were clear, "I want you to also focus on star systems that are rich in asteroid belts or have a significant number of rocky bodies. We're in need of raw materials. Asteroids we can easily mine and process into food and other essential supplies. Our survival may hinge on our ability to sustain ourselves, and I'm counting on you to identify where we can best do that. Begin the survey at once and maintain a vigilant eye for any signs of pursuit. Once you've compiled the necessary data, report your findings directly to me. Time is a luxury we do not possess."

Acknowledged, Captain.

"Rafe, I want you to manage a survey of all the HABs. Take Commander Parker and Assign whomever you need, but make sure that every seal and every hatch is good and the environmentals are solid. If a HAB is suspect, we'll have to move those people and anything critical out of that HAB, but supplies don't matter if people don't have air to breathe. Round up Doctor Garcia and take her with you, along with Doctor Araki. I want a report from them on the status and health of… all of our people. We've got a lot of stubborn people, and I don't want some unreported injury to sneak up on us. Someone might have a concussion and get complications or something. Also, I'll have Alister coordinate on rounding up and securing the supplies. We checked everything over for the trip from Ari'Nell, but we were not expecting to need to keep people cooped up for more than a couple of days."

"Yes, Captain. I'll take POs Matlage and Tian from Electrical and Ramchandani, Ruttenberg, and Rutledge from Kukri. I'll spread our four marines out with them as helpers but keep them low-key." He paused, shook his head, and added, stating rather than asking, "Visually inspecting fifty-two HABs is going to take time. The systems in them, especially the seals and hatches, are pretty much foolproof. They've been lived-in non-stop for months now, and we have a self-aware AI monitoring everything. This is really as much for PR as it is for safety."

Jermaine looked at him levelly, "We've got over a thousand people in the midst of an insane war, and all of us are survivors of the Apocalypse, and they were all just cut off from the only real lifeline they had…. We just lost Mace. Like Bertie, many of the crew were friends or were family to some of the civilians with us now. These are all smart people, but we're all only human, Rafe. I'll be making the rounds myself. We can't afford for people to feel any more isolated than they already are. If someone goes off the deep end, they could do a lot more damage than to just themselves."

Reunion

● ● ● ● ● ● ● ● ● ● ● ● ● ● ● ●

TopSide: Main Hangar Bay

The moment Senator Mira Yaegar Cross saw the icon of the NTN Blood Phoenix displayed in the Gardener's hologram above the obelisk, she charged her newly christened security detail to get her to the New London elevator post haste. In truth, they had trouble keeping her from leaving them behind. After the explosion near the church, she had been whisked away from the danger like the other newly elected senators. They'd almost made it to her house when the hologram appeared. Still wearing the dress she'd worn to the wedding, she leaped back into her Range Rover behind the driver's wheel — before Mira remembered she'd reluctantly surrendered her key to Corporal Amos Horowitz. Not bothering to go inside her house to change, depending only on the go-bag in the back of the Range Rover, she'd clambered into the back seat while muttering obscenities she'd learned at a tender age while on safari with her father.

As they drove, Mira's thoughts turned to her new husband, Captain Charles Cross. He had departed on the Blood Phoenix only five days after they had tied the knot, and she clung to the hope that he was still alive and well. She faced a six-hour trip "up" the elevator to New London, but nothing would stop her from being there when Blood Phoenix came back to dock. The unspoken terror in her heart was whether Charles, or indeed any of Blood Phoenix's crew, still lived. The hybrid starship had returned once before with her captain and most of the crew dead.

By the time she got to Fort Underwood, its namesake yet another grim reminder of Blood Phoenix's tragic past, Danielle Richardson's breathless coverage of current events on the radio mentioned that Blood

Phoenix had been heard from and that all the crew were safe. The news lifted the leaden weight from Mira's heart, but she still felt like a schoolgirl as she rode the massive three-hundred-foot square elevator. The half-way point flip wasn't the only reason for her stomach to do somersaults.

After New Texas arrived in-system, it took several hours to rendezvous with Blood Phoenix. The massive cylinder moved at a stately pace compared to the blistering speed it had shown when it had fled from the Accipiter fleet. Some later speculated that it had used up so much energy during the escape that it was now, for lack of a better word, exhausted after its daring dash away from danger.

By the time Mira passed through the security checkpoints, Blood Phoenix was already entering the titanic caution-striped airlock doors at the far end of the cavernous hangar bay.

The starship drive was composed of twenty rings that converged at the top and bottom of a comparatively slender spindle. The rings were about twenty feet wide and more or less torus-shaped, with a flat interior surface. Squat bulbous nodal structures filled perhaps a tenth of the upper and lower space at the rings' interior top and bottom apex. Suspended in the middle by the spindle was the highly modified copy of the former USS Montana, SSN 794, a Virginia class submarine with an ILC hanger attached. A recent addition was large water tanks spaced around the hull, providing a measure of radiation shielding for occasions when the warp bubble was turned off or, worse, overloaded.

The colossal hangar loomed overhead, soaring an additional awe-inspiring twelve hundred feet above the formidable silhouette of the Blood Phoenix. The sheer scale of the hangar was a testament to the gargantuan ships it must have been designed to accommodate, and it dwarfed the vessels within it, making them seem like toys in a giant's playpen.

To one side, shimmering in a resplendent sheath of gold, the Keeper Ship stood nearly eleven hundred feet tall. It commanded attention, its lustrous hull reflecting the artificial lights, casting a warm glow over its surroundings. Despite its elegance, the atmosphere was heavy with vigilance; a protective cordon of armored vehicles and tanks encircled the golden giant, their gun barrels a silent promise of defense against any threat.

Amos guided the Range Rover towards the designated area for visitors. Despite being a relatively large parking area, it was dwarfed by the backdrop of the Keeper Ship and Blood Phoenix.

Meanwhile, the Blood Phoenix completed its graceful journey along the hangar floor, carried by the embedded rail system designed for such leviathans of space. It settled with an air of finality.

Almost immediately, the hangar sprang to life around the newly arrived vessel. A mobile construction elevator trundled across the hangar floor. It came to a standstill, and a gangplank extended next to the modified sail/airlock, and it rose to begin offloading the crew.

The construction elevator hummed with activity as the ship's crew streamed out of the airlock, and it carried them from down the crowded confines of the former submarine to the expansive, airy freedom of the hangar floor. Many of the men and women, weary from their voyage, seemed to leave the elevator with a spring in their step, their fatigue momentarily forgotten in the rush of return. Some sprinted towards awaiting friends and family, their reunions a burst of joyous noise lost in the cavernous space.

After several elevator loads of tired but eager-looking crew and officers exited, some dashing away to meet with the scattering of friends and loved ones who had managed to arrive in time, Mira's heart soared as she saw Charles step out of the airlock and pause as he looked down.

She'd been worried that, at this distance, she might not recognize him. However, their connection was palpable as he looked down from the great height, and his eyes found hers with an unerring instinct. He leaned casually on the safety railing as though drinking in the sight of her, sending a silent message across the space that separated them, saying, *I see you, and only you.*

Despite the hammering in her chest, she swallowed hard and managed to compose herself well enough to not wave hysterically.

As Charles entered the elevator for the descent, Mira's anticipation grew with each floor he passed, bringing him closer to her. The descent seemed to take forever, but finally, the elevator reached the hangar floor, and Charles stepped out. No longer able to contain herself, Mira broke into a run, her earlier composure forgotten, and flung herself into his open arms.

They stood that way for what seemed an eternity. Eventually, she relaxed her grip and looked up into his eyes with a crooked smile.

Charles smiled back and hesitated. There was something mischievous in her eyes. "What? What's happened?"

Mira shrugged, "Well, apparently, a Wardog and a Stalker somehow merged together and grew to the size of a small building and started launching projectiles at Fort Brazos from the other side of the world."

He stared back at her and nodded slowly, "Uhm, okay, that's weird."

"Oh, and President Austin and Vice President Finley got married today."

Charles digested that for a moment, "Okay, I can't say I'm terribly surprised, but somehow, I suspect that's not what you're avoiding telling me."

Mira's cheeks dimpled as she chuckled, "Well, you see, it's like this. "We're going to need a bigger car."

He blinked in confusion for a moment before his eyes widened in understanding. "I see. And just how much is my command growing beyond our respective security details?"

She swallowed. "Well, you see… We're going to need room for three car seats. You're going to be a daddy!" She shook her head in disbelief, "Triplets, my God!"

Charles was very still for a long moment as the news sank in. Then he closed his eyes, hugged her even more tightly, and lifted her off her feet as tears formed in the corners of his eyes as he whispered in her ear, "I love you so much. I couldn't wait to get back to you after this long cruise, and until New Texas showed up, I wasn't really sure if I ever would. God, it's so good to see you!"

✪ ✪ ✪

Vice Admiral Preston Milner and Rear Admiral Andre Johansson stood nearby, waiting as Captain Cross hugged his wife.

Andre cocked his head as they waited and said, "Twenty bucks says she's telling him she's pregnant."

Preston shook his head, "No bet."

Tinker Tailor: The Admiral's a Spy

● ● ● ● ● ● ● ● ● ● ● ● ● ● ●

DownSide: The next day
Fort Underwood Testing Lab

Andre Johansson, Rear Admiral Lower Half, strode into the testing lab with purpose. He was here to inspect the latest test results from the Zero-point energy module that had been snatched from the North Koreans on Morgan Island.

The module was a potential doomsday weapon. When pressed on the issue, Dr. Nakamura had once compared it to the difference between a bubble gum 'pop' and a hydrogen bomb. And this one had been in the hands of Colonel P'aeng Jin-Hwan, a madman who had experimented on it with primitive tools. God alone knew what damage he might have inflicted on the device.

Reassuringly, the initial inspection had shown no signs that he had even managed to scratch the thing with his tampering. Still, Andre wasn't about to take any chances with something that, quoting Dr. Nakamura, "in the wrong hands, a Zero Point Module is more than a power source; it is a weapon of cosmic proportions, with the ability to wipe out entire star systems."

The lab was practically a fortress, surrounded by layers of security, but Andre was puzzled to see that most of the lights were off when he entered. The room should have been buzzing with activity, with university professors and engineers poring over the data. Instead, a haunting silence enveloped the space. The only other person in the room was a navy commander in dress uniform, standing in the shadows in a corner, his back to Andre.

"Commander," Andre called out. "Where is everyone? We have a status report meeting scheduled here."

The commander turned slowly and smiled. He didn't bother to salute.

Andre felt a surge of irritation at the breach of protocol. He opened his mouth to reprimand the man, but his words died in his throat as the commander stepped into the light. He recognized that face. The face of a dead man. Thomas Harding, the traitor who had bombed City Hall and killed many innocent people. The man who had been shot dead by Vice President Gail Finley herself. The man whom Andre had manipulated into that very act of political assassination.

Decades of cold, practiced self-control were the only thing that prevented Andre from gasping in shock as he stared into the specter of his wicked past. Thomas Harding stood before him, an apparition bathed in a menacing aura. His arms were crossed, and he cocked his head as a sly grin stretched across his face. His cold grey eyes sparkled with malice as if daring Andre to confront him.

The surrounding air thickened with tension until Andre felt as if he had been suspended in a void of soundless terror. Every breath came hard for him as Thomas leaned closer, reveling in the moment's power like some demented player in a twisted game.

Andre's throat went dry as he stared at the impossible sight. Thomas Harding was dead, struck down by that bitchy little Air Force Captain turned Vice President.

And yet, here he was, alive and well, mocking Andre with his presence.

Then, suddenly, the moment was shattered by the concussion of doors slamming behind Andre, startling him and making him jump in surprise. He spun around as the lights flickered on. A group of lab-coated men and women loudly burst into the room, talking excitedly amongst themselves.

When he turned back to confront Thomas, the man was gone. Disappeared. Had it been a hallucination? A trick of his mind? He felt a wave of confusion. Dread washed over him as he tried to make sense of what he had seen.

The lead scientist exclaimed, "Admiral Johansson! You're early! We're so glad you're here! We have some fascinating news to share...."

Andre turned back to face the group and smiled a thin reply, the corner of his lip twitching slightly. He'd felt his heart race with excitement for the first time since Awakening Day. Whether or not he was going crazy, this was something *new.*

As the scientists began their presentation on the Zero-point energy module, Andre couldn't help but be distracted by the image of Thomas Harding that had haunted him just moments before. He tried to focus on the data before him, but his mind kept wandering back to that impossible sight.

But then, as the lead scientist started explaining that the module was undamaged, a thought occurred to Andre. What if Thomas Harding wasn't a hallucination at all? What if he was a manifestation of something else entirely?

The idea was absurd, but Andre couldn't shake it. He had seen too many strange things since the cosmic event known as Awakening Day had changed the world. *Could this be some trick by the Gardeners?* After all, they had recreated everyone, including himself. *Who was to say that the dead couldn't be brought back to life in some form or another?*

On the other hand, what if Harding wasn't actually dead? Everyone *knew* that the useful idiot was dead. No one could have survived the wounds given to him by Gail Finley. He'd read the autopsy report.

His heart racing with anticipation, Andre decided to investigate the matter further. He made his excuses to the scientists and rushed out of the lab, his mind consumed with the possibility of the impossible.

✪ ✪ ✪

Oval Office

Riverside Mall

John Austin, Gail, Alexander Marcus, and Colonel Martin Williams finished watching the hidden camera footage on the TV mounted on the Oval Office wall.

Alexander shook his head and swore, "My God, that could have gone so badly! How the hell did you get Harding to cooperate?"

Martin shrugged, "I didn't. That was a lookalike with some makeup and prosthetics. That's why we didn't have him say anything. Also, it meant he could quickly take it off and not be recognized by anyone else after his disappearing act."

Gail closed her eyes and sighed. "I can't believe we agreed to this. We know the bastard is guilty. We should just get rid of him!"

Alexander put his hand on her shoulder. "Madam Vice President, you know we don't have actual physical proof he was involved, and we don't know if anyone else was yet, either."

Martin cleared his throat. "Actually, I do have evidence of *past* guilt, at least."

John cocked his head. "Colonel, you always had a flair. What are you holding back?"

Martin smiled thinly, "Over the last few months, I've been feeding one of the late generation AIs, from before the Accipiters, data that the Gardeners provided to us from the Earth's computers. You'll recall that they not only copied the entire Internet but also hacked into firewalled corporate and government computers and networks from all over the planet. I've had the AI indexing and organizing some of the juicier bits so that we might be able to search for technologies and things that might be useful for us now."

Gail chided, "And of course, the fact that the same data might be used to find out things about the New Arrivals and potential spies among us never crossed your mind."

Martin halfheartedly feigned indignance. "Perish the thought. But since you mentioned it, and after Admiral Johansson's reported guilt was revealed a few days ago, I decided to find out if he'd been naughty *before* Awakening Day."

John nodded, "And?"

Martin shrugged again, "And it wasn't easy. I looked at his bank records first. I did not find any red flags. There were no unusual bank deposits that would typify a spy getting paid. So, I instead was able to locate the GPS records from his car and his wife's car. I used it to compare those with the movements of known foreign operatives based on both friendly government records as well as records from unfriendly ones. It is frankly terrifying how easily the Gardeners seemed to have penetrated every Earth government's computers. Anyway, that's when some interesting patterns started to emerge. Chinese agents visiting dead drops correlated within a few hours to *both* his movements and his wife's, going back thirteen years."

"What's more, half of those dead drop movements correlated with either he or his wife stopping at any of a dozen different stores and pawn shops where gold coins or gold bullion are bought and sold. I then looked at social media records from themselves, their friends, etc. Starting thirteen years ago, the Admiral's wife's wardrobe abruptly changed from discount big box store brands to progressively higher fashion brands. From off the rack to tailored. About ten years ago, the Admiral's wardrobe began a similar transformation. Their physical appearances also changed, including cosmetic surgery for her, for which no credit card or insurance records exist. The Admiral's personnel records include several interesting notations about dramatic improvements in the man's Professional Military Appearance. Whereas in his earlier career, his appearance had been borderline acceptable, his fitness reports began to reflect marked improvements in his uniform, personal grooming, and general deportment."

Gail grumbled, "It's hardly definitive proof."

Martin smiled more broadly this time, "Until a few years ago when there was a pattern change. The Admiral began to have in-person meetings with a Chinese handler. I only found the link because the handler had to file receipts. Then, the AI matched his face to social media photos from someone's birthday party at a restaurant. The birthday pictures captured Andre and his handler in the background. Apparently, Andre and the handler would meet at the restaurant and sit back-to-back in adjacent booths. I have GPS records putting Andre at the same restaurant with the Chinese handler, who filed receipts on the same day and time on six occasions."

Alexander grimaced. "He'd just claim that he liked the restaurant and that the Chinese must have been spying on him."

Gail fumed. "The bastard conspired to kill us, John. You too, Alex. You were hurt bad enough, and John almost died. Others did die. We can't let this go on. Taunting him with the Ghost of Thomas Harding past will shake him up, but sooner or later, he'll catch on to the fact that we're on to him. Probably sooner. You've seen his personnel records. The man is brilliant."

John sighed and sank back into his chair, "How long can we sideline him before he figures out that something is up? How long will the Gardeners let us?"

Alexander looked at the fire in Gail's eyes and shook his head, "I know what you're thinking. I'd just as soon shoot the bastard myself, but while I believe Senator Blanchard is telling the truth, do we really want to set a precedent, even a secret one, of executing someone based solely on the word of one person, regardless of how compelling their testimony is?"

Gail shook her head, "Obviously, we're beyond just Sybil's testimony now. The Colonel's evidence is certainly enough to suspend him from his duties. Besides, we don't want to ignore the lessons from 911. The FBI's mindset was to gather evidence so that a legal case could be made against terrorists. The CIA knew better, but State, the FBI, and the CIA didn't share notes or views. I suppose what worries me most right now is that, for all we know, the bastard may have other irons in the fire. He may have other plans in motion. Other bombs to explode somewhere or other pawns like Harding he's groomed to carry out attacks. What does it say about us if we do nothing now and the worst happens?"

John nodded, "Okay. Colonel, give it a week. See if there is anything you can find out. Is he doing anything now that is suspicious or that could lead us to co-conspirators? We'll meet again then and decide how to deal with the SOB."

Priest

● ● ● ● ● ● ● ● ● ● ● ● ● ● ● ●

DownSide: Fort Brazos
First United Methodist Church

Tom Parker took a deep breath as he sat in the Pastor's office, determined to focus on his work. Like others, since Awakening Day, his grey hair had returned to the soft brown of his youth, and the worry lines that years of being Mayor and running his car dealership had softened. Even his golf game had improved, though he still felt pangs of guild whenever he indulged in the sport. It seemed wrong to spend so many hours doing something that wasn't directly helping solve some problem or other. He'd resigned as Mayor and now devoted himself to the church congregation and the community as a whole. After the latest series of events, he felt guilty about not being there in the middle of the crisis.

The church sanctuary was still a mess from the shattered stained glass windows, but he'd held an impromptu prayer service there anyway, for those missing from Ari'Nell and was now trying to work out details on how the church could help their families. Sitting in this office, though, never ceased to remind him of the man who, by all rights, should still be here. The man who's kind and gentle hand should be the one giving comfort and inspiration to the community. The *real* church pastor, Joseph Gilmore.

Tom still had nightmares about the horrific accident on Awakening Day, just hours after the Apocalypse when he'd been in the driver seat next to Joseph when the herd of frightened dear had collided with their truck and the huge buck had crashed through the windshield, impaling Joseph with its antlers.

As Tom contemplated his guilt and grief over Joseph's death, he looked up at the memorabilia that still lined the office walls and asked himself, *What would you do, Joe? How would you lift these people up and give them hope?*

He was startled out of his reverie by a knock at his open door. He looked up in surprise as Dr. Eva (Sanches) Becker, D.V.M., and her husband, Dr. Jacob Becker, Ph.D., entered.

Eva smiled. She was six and a half months pregnant with triplets. However, these days, *most* women were either pregnant or between pregnancies, most with multiples. It was so common now that the fact of being pregnant, by itself, was the norm and rarely prompted comment anymore. She said, "Mr. Mayor, may we have a word with you?"

Tom stood and walked around his desk to greet them, extending his hand to shake theirs. "It's just Tom now, Eva. Jacob. What can I do for you?"

Jacob towered a full thirteen inches over Eva's five-foot frame. He shook Tom's hand and explained, "Well, you see, we've been studying the remains of the two Accipiter Priests who were killed during the Keeper raid. Us and other faculty members. Anyway, some things simply don't make any sense at all about their physiology."

Tom gestured for Eva and Jacob to sit. "Well, they *are* alien, after all. I suppose I'd be surprised if there weren't things we didn't understand. However, I don't understand why you've come all the way here to talk to *me,* of all people, about it?"

Eva chuckled, "Understatement of the Century… Tom. No offense. Honestly, it's way above our heads, too. Anyway, we were hoping that perhaps the next time you have one of your chats with the surviving Accipiter Priest, you might ask him about it. It's not just scientific curiosity. We're concerned that not understanding what is going on with him might affect our long-term ability to provide for its, I mean, his, health."

Jacob lowered his voice, "We're worried about some of the numbers we are seeing. We fear it might be slowly dying, and we don't know why."

✪ ✪ ✪

TopSide: Accipiter Holding Cell

Tom stood outside the airlock to the holding cell and silently prayed, "Heavenly Father, let my eyes be open that I might see, and my ears be open that I might hear. If my lips do part, let it be your word on my tongue. If this creature be a child of yours, may your Spirit shine forth through him, however far through darkness it must. Help me, I pray. Help me build a bridge of understanding between his people and mine. The blood shed between us seems insurmountable, but we are finite creatures. You are infinite. If there is a way for us to find understanding and peace between us, speak through me. Let me be your instrument of healing and forgiveness, starting with my own fear and hatred for his people and what they have done to mine. I accept your will...."

The Accipiter Priest looked up as Tom entered the vaulted ceiling metal room. The room needed to be tall to accommodate the ten-foot-tall avian-like alien. The Accipiter stood up from its oddly shaped bench, which was the only 'furniture' in the room. It's clawed feed clacked on the hard floor. It rose to its full height and stared down its beak at Tom through its enormous Topaz eyes.

It had been noted that its eye color changed depending on who it was talking to. With President Austin or other 'interrogators,' its eyes were a darker Sapphire. With Tom or Leo Talib, its eyes turned a lighter shade of Topaz. As always, Tom was struck by the Accipiter Priest's magnificent, almost frightening beauty. It was the eyes, though, that captivated him.

A low rumbling erupted from within it as it withdrew its truehands from within its multihued chest feather analogues and began to sign. Glyphs flowed across its beak as it did.

Translated audio played from hidden speakers:

You come to. Long Time. Talk once again. What has happened? Untranslatable. Sensed. Not possible. What. Happened. This place.

Tom hesitated, then walked over and sat cross-legged on the cold metal floor in his usual spot. He waited for the Accipiter to sit back down, intently terrified that someday the enormous creature might grow angry enough and decide to rend Tom's still living body from head to toe and....

The Accipiter slowly sat back down.

Tom answered, "Help me understand. I don't know what you are asking."

We felt. Untranslatable. Moved. Not possible. Only. Untranslatable. Can. Untranslatable.

Tom stared at the creature for long moments before understanding dawned. "Do you mean you felt when we... uhm... moved? When the world moved?"

It was the Accipiter's turn to stare. It took a full minute for it to reply:

Not possible for world to. Untranslatable. Only.
Untranslatable. Can. Untranslatable.

Tom suddenly worried that perhaps he shouldn't be having this conversation. That he might reveal the nature of New Texas. *On the other hand*, he thought, *that cat's well and entirely out of the bag anyway, isn't it*. "This world *can* travel through Nexus Junction Points. This place where we have taken you to is a world ship, not a planet."

Not possible. You have constructed a.
Untranslatable. Ship of your own? How? You are
primitives.

Tom smiled. *He doesn't need to know how we got it*. "Yes, we have our own mothership. It is far larger than any of yours. Your people have grossly underestimated humanity."

Not believing. Matters not. Accipiters number as
many as the stars. Why you come. Untranslatable.
Talk once again. Many days passed. You have
considered our words?

Tom struggled to hide his relief at the change of subject. "What did you plan to do with the frozen people in the Keeper ship? What did your people plan to do with them?"

Did not your people have. Untranslatable. where.
Untranslatable. were displayed? Accipiters.
Untranslatable. biological diversity in all expressions.

"You mean museums? Yes, we found fossils and reconstructed what we believed ancient creatures and our ancestors looked like. We studied them to try and learn from them. We used museums to try and teach people about our world's past. We know that Accipiters venerate biological diversity."

Yes. Venerated. They were to be... venerated.
Shared with other clans.

Tom nodded and sat quietly for a while, thinking. He took a deep breath and continued. "Accipiters watched homo sapiens emerge as the dominant species on Earth, and we know that 'we' haven't changed an awful lot physically in at least half a million years or longer. Oh, I mean, we spread out, and there are lots of superficial differences in skin color, hair, that sort of thing, but underneath, we're still mostly the same creatures as the earliest Homo Sapiens."

"That said, our oldest tales and stories tell of humans behaving in ways very recognizable to anyone in modern times. Who we are and how we interact with each other hasn't really changed all that much. Our capacity for both compassion, love, and savagery seems constant. The tools we use change but transpose our most ancient stories to modern times, and they are the same stories."

"However, mentally, now that's another story. We've had dramatic transformations in our worldview and understanding of the universe, as well as in our spiritual souls. All of that happened through the centuries as a consequence of our maturing as a people."

"My question is, you see, Accipiters didn't go through that. You were uplifted as a more or less bronze age culture into a starfaring one by beings that seemed like gods to you. That had to have had a profound impact on your view of the universe as well as on your spiritual lives."

"How has it changed you? Are you really the same as you were before, or are you different, and if so, in what way?"

The Accipiter considered Tom for several long minutes before answering. Its eyes shifted color to a darker, almost purple shade:

When we were. Untranslatable. We raced the
death. Always we. Moving. World turned slowly.
The deathfire chased us always. Then the.
Untranslatable. came. Gave new purpose. Time to
think.

Tom considered the world the Accipiters came from. The Gardeners had already filled in that part of the story. The Accipiter home world rotated exceptionally slowly. Life on the surface could only survive by fleeing the terminator, where temperatures rose hundreds of degrees Fahrenheit. The Accipiters evolved into a nomadic culture that rarely, if ever, warred amongst themselves. Their world was hostile enough already.

"Your clans, your culture evolved on that hostile world. You depended on each other. I understand that you've kept that part of your nature intact. What I'm wondering is, what else has changed? What is different? I mean, we know that you used the technology you were given to modify your own biology. That has to have made profound changes in your society?"

We were given the knowledge of life. We venerate life now. Instead of fear and flight from the deathfire, now we venerate all life.

"I wonder what those who uplifted you would think of the changes you've made in your own biology. Would they not have made those changes themselves when they found you? You were good enough to fulfill the mission they gave you before. Why change? I mean, the changes were not small. You transfer your consciousnesses to new bodies periodically, and you added a *third gender!* And there are organs in your bodies that we haven't figured out what they are even for. How did your culture survive such enormous changes to your own physical reality?"

The Accipiter's enormous eyes turned a shade darker, and Tom worried that he had pushed too far.

Changes needed. Untranslatable. Stability. Prevent divergence across galaxy. Memory trees. Untranslatable. Preserve. Balance.

Tom nodded, "Okay, if you say so. It's just hard for me to understand how you could not become radically different as a people with all those changes or if you would even know that you had changed at all. Still, you've apparently had a stable society for at least a million years, so it would seem to be working for you."

"That said, if it is okay, I'd like to ask a more personal question. And it is out of concern for your health and well-being. I've been told that the doctors who are trying to keep you healthy are concerned. We don't understand your metabolism and biology all that well, but the doctors and scientists are worried that your health might be in decline. Do you feel okay? Are you well? Is there anything you need?"

Your concern is. Untranslatable. I was. Untranslatable. Renewal. Too long. I will die soon without.

Ice

● ● ● ● ● ● ● ● ● ● ● ● ● ● ●

NTN Revenge: Bridge
Unnamed Star System

While the bridge of the Revenge had originally been designed for the much larger deer-like physiology of the Builders, or their predator Masters, it wasn't designed for very many of them to be there simultaneously. With the Builder's cybernetic enhancements, fewer 'organic' crew had been needed. For the humans, however, Navy doctrine demanded a separate crew person for each primary function. Captain Jermaine Cutter, Commander Rafferty Youngman, and Lt. Alister Gordon stood next to co-pilots Yūki Rikuto Miyashita and Dennis Park, who were in their VR frames, and Navigator Darrel Shirazi and Communications officer Ensign Molly Crawford filled out the bridge stations. Crowded next to Jermaine and Alister were Dimitri Sinitskaya and professors Priya Patel and Patrick O'Connell. Behind them, peeking over their shoulders, stood medical doctors Inés Garcia and Revenge's mission doctor, Lt. Amelia Araki.

Priya had been Bonham State University's physics department dean. As for Patrick, he served as the closest approximation to an astronomer among the Ari'Nell castaways. His specialty lay in the realm of quantum physics and nanotechnology, albeit with a passionate amateur interest in astronomy and a close friendship with Dr. Nakamura.

Everyone wanted to see the planet.

Such as it was and what there was of it. There was no discernable atmosphere around the stark and desolate rock. Only jagged mountain peaks and endless ice fields tinted red from the light of the system's red dwarf star.

Alister's brows contorted disdainfully as he peered through the lone window of the bridge, his disappointment mingling with a sense of foreboding. "Doesn't look like much, does it?" he commented, his voice tinged with a touch of desolation.

Jermaine pursed his lips, a flicker of concern crossing his face. "Well, that was the idea," he responded, shaking his head. Turning his attention to the two individuals in question, he prompted, "Dr. Patel? Dr. O'Connell?"

Priya's dark brown hair cascaded around her shoulders, and her eyes carried the warmth of her parents' Indian heritage. They had hailed from Nashik, but Priya had been born and raised in Houston. She'd previously been an Assistant Professor of Physics at the United States Military Academy. She grimaced at Alister's remark. "I'm afraid I have to concur with Lieutenant Gordon. It certainly doesn't beckon us with warm, open arms, does it?" she lamented. Then, her gaze shifting to Patrick, she urged, "Patrick, enlighten us on the findings you and the Revenge have unearthed regarding our prospective...." Her voice wavered slightly, "...home?"

Priya stood considerably younger than Dr. O'Connell at forty-two, but if her seniority and age disparity bothered him, he didn't show it. Patrick, renowned for his amiable nature and teaching style that attracted post-doctoral students from across the country, maintained an air of affability. He also had a small internet following from his physics lectures and yet another side-hobby of molecular gastronomy. Patrick was sixty-three, with formerly grey hair now turned brown again and a matching close-cropped goatee.

He drew in a deep breath, shrugged, and began in his practiced, genial, and ebullient professorial style. "Well, as Captain Cutter rightly pointed out, this is precisely what we sought. A place so repulsive and inconspicuous that it would never grace the Accipiter's hit list of potential hideouts. And let me tell you, the entire solar system adheres to that principle."

Gesturing with a nod towards the planet, he continued, "The source of that... captivating hue lies with the system's primary star. An M7 V Red Dwarf, notable in particular for its relentless onslaught of frequent and ferocious solar flares. Now, keep in mind this star is a mere third of Earth's sun in terms of mass, and yet its explosive tantrums are nothing short of formidable. Those flares and their radiation, by themselves, are yet another reason for the Accipiters to disregard this system as a potential haven for us. But that's not all."

He paused briefly, allowing his words to sink in before delving further into the specifics. "The planet itself is a desolate and icy expanse, its rocky terrain concealed beneath frozen layers. Any trace of atmosphere it may have once possessed has been mercilessly obliterated by the relentless solar flares, and it has no appreciable magnetic field, leaving it defenseless against the ravages of cosmic and solar radiation, I'm afraid."

Raising his hand for emphasis, he continued, "Its radius measures at approximately ninety-three percent that of Earth, resulting in a slightly smaller scale. Furthermore, gravity is lighter here, amounting to just over eighty-one percent of Earth's standard. While, at least to those with older bones, that might sound lovely, trust me, you want a planet with something close to our familiar gravity."

"Some people suggested we just build out an asteroid, but I assure you we are not ready to try and build a low-g or zero-g colony. Aside from health issues and the smell, everything is harder without gravity. The Ari'Nell workers certainly learned that, the hard way, working on the FAB there. At least, however, we all were able to periodically go down to the surface of Ari'Nell and reset our bodies in a gravity well. Anyone who spent much time actually working in orbit, though, will tell you that the real reason for going down to the planet was," he closed his eyes and wrinkled his nose, "Was so they could get clean. Take a shower. The average human body sheds about a pound of skin cells every year. Multiply that by a thousand workers. Even with many of them devoted to nothing but trying to keep FAB and HABs clean, it wasn't nearly enough. That is why the rotation ground-side was mandatory. There is no good way to clean the inside of a spacesuit without gravity, either. I shudder to think of what living conditions would devolve into in a low or null-g asteroid colony.

"That said, the planet itself is just the beginning."

With a sweep of his hand, he indicated the broader picture of the star system. "The celestial neighborhood we find ourselves in is primarily composed of diminutive planetoids, a multitude of asteroids, and a pair of minor gas giants akin to our very own Neptune."

A wry smile tugged at Alister's lips as he quipped, his voice laced with a touch of sarcasm, "Ah, a true home away from home, then. Just lacking in vibrant nightlife and with beaches that probably suck, I presume?"

Priya's response came in the form of a thin smile, her amusement tempered by the weight of their situation. "Initially, the Revenge will provide a protective magnetic field for the habitation modules," she explained. "Once we have settled in, we can utilize the salvaged Zero Point Modules, courtesy of Dr. Sinitskaya, to construct a new FAB."

Her gaze shifted towards Dimitri, who stared intently at the desolate world beneath them, his anger simmering beneath the surface. With a solemn nod, he acknowledged Priya's words. Time had allowed him to rest, but the searing pain of losing his wife and children still smoldered deep within.

Dimitri shook his head ruefully. "It will be a time-consuming endeavor," he admitted, his voice tinged with determination and resignation. "Revenge can calve off a seed for the FAB core, and the core can Von Neuman itself into a full-size FAB. However, this time, it will take longer since we don't have access to the wealth of heavy and exotic elements that littered the debris rings around Ari'Nell. The time will be somewhat mitigated since we have extra power from the ZPMs, but not a lot. We must carefully prioritize between constructing the protective dome and addressing other pressing needs... such as sustenance, I suppose."

The weight of their situation hung heavily in the air, a reminder of the challenging path that lay before them. They would need to navigate the scarcity of resources, striking a delicate balance between building the necessary structures and ensuring their survival amidst the unforgiving embrace of their new, icy home.

A collective unease settled over the bridge as the topic of food arose. Jermaine turned to Lt. Araki and Dr. Garcia, the only actual physicians among the castaways. Amelia, an Undersea Medical Officer in the Navy hailing from Honolulu, had previously served on the USS Virginia, while her husband, Dr. James Araki, had been a pediatrician at Naval Health Clinic New England. However, he did not survive the events of Awakening Day. Since then, she'd thrown herself into her work, eschewing any semblance of a social life.

In contrast, Inés was a family doctor with a practice at Methodist Hospital in Fort Brazos. She had not been stationed at Ari'Nell. Her presence had been part of a rotation of doctors who traveled back and forth with the Revenge to provide medical checkups and care for the inevitable and primarily minor injuries among the engineers and support staff. Initially slated for a three-day stay, she now found herself marooned with everyone else. She was only supposed to be away from her husband, Carlos, and her two children, Sofia and Mateo, for a grand total of five days. One day each way to the system and three days doing checkups on the engineers and support staff. The despair etched on her face painted a bleak picture.

Amelia nodded solemnly, her expression grave. "Captain, we've made the rounds through all the habitation modules. Alongside addressing minor injuries and general health concerns, we held meetings in each HAB to discuss the food situation. We made it clear that in order for the

FAB to produce food, we would require samples to replicate. We don't have seeds to plant crops, and that's for the future anyway. I'm sure some people have stashed away food. We made it clear that the ONLY food we're going to be able to have once the FAB is going is the food we can copy. If we don't have samples to copy *from,* then there won't be any. Captain, I know some people heard us, but a lot of them are still just shell-shocked by what has happened."

She continued, her tone laced with a tinge of frustration, "Unless we resort to ransacking each and every HAB from top to bottom, which would undoubtedly worsen the already fragile morale, then what we have is what we have. Maybe once the FAB is up and running, we can offer rewards for individuals to come forward with anything they miraculously stumble upon, innocently tucked away. A few more things might trickle in, but anything left by then would be small, probably things like candy or snacks. Luxury items. While the food scarcity is indeed dire, my greater concern lies with the mental well-being of our people. We have already observed individuals skipping rations, and it will undoubtedly take a toll over time."

She gently put her hand on Inés' shoulder, urging her to contribute. "Inés?"

Inés blinked slowly, lost in her own melancholy thoughts. "Yes, well, to be honest," she began softly, her voice tinged with sorrow, "it's worse than after Awakening Day. At least then, we had a whole city where people could, for a brief moment, except for the alien sky and creatures, people could almost delude themselves into believing things were almost normal. But here? Here, the reality is inescapable, and there are a few people we must keep away from airlocks and others who need to be safeguarded from sharp objects."

The bridge fell into a heavy silence, each person grappling with the harsh realities of their new existence. The challenges they faced extended far beyond mere physical survival, encompassing the fragile fabric of their mental resilience in the face of a reality where, even if every single person survived, their lives would never resemble a shadow of their former selves.

Jermaine nodded, "I expected as much. Let me reiterate to everyone here that the individuals we have with us are all we've got. We cannot afford to lose a single person. Not one of them is... dispensable." He addressed Amelia and Inés, "I want you doctors to collaborate with Commander Youngman and devise a plan."

His gaze shifted to Rafferty, "Rafe, do whatever it takes. If we need to rearrange personnel to ensure those most vulnerable receive proper care, then make it happen. Losing even one person is utterly unacceptable.

Should someone decide to inflict harm upon themselves in a manner that endangers or, God forbid, takes others with them, the consequences could be catastrophic. Assign each person a purpose, something to be responsible for. God knows there's no shortage of tasks to be done. Sitting idle without purpose is a recipe for disaster."

Rafferty acknowledged Jermaine's instructions with a knowing nod, his eyes bearing the weight of his own grief. "Understood, Captain. I'll see to it."

Amelia hesitated for a moment before speaking up. "Captain, there's another matter we'll need to address sooner rather than later."

Jermaine turned his attention back to her, his expression expectant. "Yes, Lieutenant?"

Amelia closed her eyes briefly, then shook her head. "Given the potential for radiation exposure, the personnel at Ari'Nell were strictly warned about engaging in sexual relations. As you know, despite that, we still had the occasional… lapse, and those cases were dealt with and shipped back to New Texas on the next return flight. That being said, it's only a matter of time before pregnancies start occurring here, and we have only a limited number of pregnancy supplies and tests available, much less all the things babies need."

An uncomfortable shift rippled through the room, and Jermaine closed his eyes, shaking his head before reopening them to respond. "Noted, Lieutenant. I can only hope that when such occurrences arise, they will serve as joyful events, speaking to a promising future. Meanwhile, shifting gears, what is the status of the Builder food extruders in the HABs? Revenge?"

Captain, the food extruders were not designed to be changed. They're not programable to provide different things. They were intended only to make food pellets for the Builders. What you would consider… pet food. As you know, the chirality in the molecules makes the pellets somewhat toxic to humans. The equipment is, as you would say, hardwired to do only one thing. It is not a matter of altering it… the entire system will have to be replaced, and you have already prioritized creating a new FAB core, which will consume nearly twenty percent of… myself.

Rafferty let out a snort, his amusement tinged with a hint of frustration. "Seems like a cart before the horse situation, or is it the chicken and the egg? Damn, I just hope we don't reach a point where people forget the meaning of those idioms." He shrugged and turned to Amelia. "Amelia, what's the nutritional value of those emergency MREs?"

She wrinkled her nose at the thought of the MREs. "Commander, I've checked and rechecked the food stocks. Between the MREs and everything else, by the time the FAB is up and minimally running, we'll squeeze by. Of course, we'll all be pulling our belts a lot tighter, but we can make it. The problem is our meager selection of items to replicate once we have the ability to do so. We won't be facing scurvy, thanks to the MREs providing some vitamins. I looked it up. They average around twelve to thirteen hundred calories and contain varying amounts of vitamin C. The fruit components or spreads provide C2, and there's also calcium, iron, and other nutrients, along with protein, fat, and an abundance of carbs. Lots and lots of carbs. And lots of sodium too, too much really, but that's a different discussion. However, do you really want to subsist on MREs for the rest of your life?"

She grimaced as she shook her head, "We'll be eating lots of beef stew, cheese spread, peanut butter, crackers, cookies, and the like."

A hint of relief touched Amelia's voice as she continued, "Oh, and thank God, at least some of the MREs have some chocolate. Not the good kind, but at least it's something. We do have other supplies, including canned foods, but by the time the FAB is operational, many of the fresh fruits and vegetables will have spoiled. We're doing our best to freeze whatever we can salvage. I've also got a dozen people looking through everything to see if they can find any uncooked seeds we can save for the future. All in all, though, it's going to be a dreary menu for the foreseeable future."

Priya couldn't help but chuckle at the situation, her amusement breaking the tension in the room. "Patrick, maybe your weird hobby will finally prove useful," she remarked with a playful tone.

All eyes turned to Patrick, who momentarily shrunk back under the sudden attention. He blinked, trying to gather his thoughts. "Oh, right. Yes, well, molecular gastronomy involves using innovative ingredients, tools, and techniques, such as treating things with liquid nitrogen; however, it isn't really designed to create food from raw atomic elements or space rocks, but who knows, I'll of course be happy to do whatever I can to help."

Jermaine looked at Dimitri and worried about the man's state of mind. "Dr. Sinitskaya, once the new FAB is operational, what patterns do we have available to load into it?"

Dimitri's gaze never left the sight of the red-hued icy planet beneath them. He grunted. "Fort Brazos had an entire city and a copy of the pre-Awakening Day internet to start with, plus all the infrastructure there… tools… equipment… instruments… even military resources. We had endless workshops in New London filled with state-of-the-art machinery, machine shops, computers, and more. But here… what we have is what we have."

He paused, the weight of the situation evident in his voice. "The truth, Captain, is that we have more than we might have expected and less than we truly need. When the first FAB was built, someone had the foresight to pull 3D printing designs from the copy of the Internet the Gardeners saved. They pulled designs from commercial sites and even from government files from around Earth. Scary. It is scary how primitive our security must have been to the Gardeners."

"Anyway, so, we have designs for anything from hinges to guns to jet engines to Pokémon figurines. The FAB itself was equipped with scanning capabilities, so our staff had the task of scanning items sent from New Texas, mostly military equipment. Occasionally, they scanned various odds and ends we had around, mostly hand tools and testing equipment." His voice grew strained, "But when it comes to food, the only items we ever thought to scan were Bertie's smuggled coffee, her Cherry Cordials, and the odd airplane mini-bottle of alcohol smuggled among personal gear allowances."

Alister snorted, "Well, maybe there is a God out there after all."

Livia

● ● ● ● ● ● ● ● ● ● ● ● ● ● ● ● ●

DownSide:
Lake Texoma, Freetown Beach

Every time her nemesis, her unseen blackmailer contacted her, it felt like another slice was carved away from her soul. For years, as Preston had grown colder and more distant, Livia's heart slowly shrank in response. She had a face and body that had drawn men and not a few women to her flame from an early age. She'd fallen head over heels for the handsome Naval officer, though, and she'd always turned down subsequent advances with an amused and self-satisfied eye. Eventually, though, her inner satisfaction dwindled as Preston's career ascended to greater and greater heights, in no small part due to her and her family's influence. The higher he rose, the colder he became.

Then, one day, she'd run into an old flame at a conference and decided, *what the hell*, and accepted his invitation to drinks and then to his room… and his bed. Her regret and shame were short-lived when Preston's indifference angered her more than her own self-loathing.

In time, the veil on her behavior to spite Preston grew ever thinner, eventually disappearing altogether. It became an emotional crutch. An endorphin high that became an addiction. The thrill pushed her discretion closer and closer to the edge. Instead of old flames, she began targeting people within Preston's orbit. Other officers. And then there was Karl Johansson. Rear Admiral Lower Half Andre Johansson's studly nineteen-year-old All-American football player son. She was almost twenty years his senior, and robbing the cradle brought a new kind of thrill and excitement she'd never imagined. Teaching and guiding the young man was an entirely new level of fun with which to bury her heart.

And then came the Accipiters. Livia had awakened in one of the tens of thousands of "hotel" rooms in the Gardener-created artificial city the survivors later named "New London." Awakened, that is, in bed next to young Karl. In the chaos that followed, she reunited with Preston, now the senior surviving military commander, alive.

In private, afterward, they'd fought. The loss of their daughter Helena, and of course, the Apocalypse, broke the dam holding back Preston's anger towards Livia. Her actions had been a ticking time bomb within him, and he'd finally had enough. He threw her out, but she convinced him that the appearance of their marriage and relationship was more valuable to him in their new circumstances. He needed her and the appearance of family stability if their new political leaders were to trust him.

The cold war of their marriage morphed into a sullen arrangement of convenience, complete with separate but adjoining penthouse apartments.

And then there was Karl and the convenient diversion her dalliances with him provided. It wasn't enough, but it was *something*.

That is, until the bombing and the recurring nightmares that followed, which had reduced her to a shell of her former self. She'd been there when that madman had exploded his bomb. Dazed and in shock, Livia had found herself disoriented and stumbling amid that murderous scene's gore and acrid horror. She'd witnessed Vice President Gail Finley stand and calmly, dispassionately shoot the madman dead and then take charge of the situation, giving orders and staying in complete command of herself, all while the man that Livia and every other surviving human knew she loved, even if she didn't admit it to herself, lay horribly wounded nearby.

Livia couldn't help but compare herself to Gail's example and see the shallow, empty, vain, and pointless woman Livia had become. Night after night, nightmares and self-loathing had finally broken her.

Preston had found her emaciated and semi-conscious on the floor. She'd lost twenty pounds and weighed just ninety-six. For reasons she still could not bring herself to comprehend, Preston had gently picked her up, carried her to bed, and cared for her. He nursed her back to health, and…. miraculously, they had reconciled.

She confessed *everything*, although Preston already knew or suspected much of it. In turn, he admitted that he'd lost himself in his career, taken her for granted, and lost her in the bargain.

For the first time in a very long, long time, she'd felt… alive. The pain of Helena and the Apocalypse still loomed over her, not to mention the

Accipiters and the Gardeners and, oh, a galactic war. Still, she'd started to feel at peace with herself. She'd grown quite close to Councilwoman Gloria Vargas and others and felt like she was finding her place in this strange new world.

And then the blackmail photos were delivered, reminding her of just how damned her soul truly was.

Her blackmailer never missed a day tormenting her. Pushing her. Driving her to run for Senate. Spying for him. From his choice of words, she knew it was a man.

But then, not long after that Senate meeting, the messages just stopped.

Not hearing from him suddenly became worse than hearing from him. *What if he'd been caught?* Surely, there would be evidence leading back to her, exposing her secrets….

Livia felt her stomach drop as she realized the full implications of what was happening. Sure, she would be humiliated and shamed publicly if her past caught up to her. But what hurt even worse was how much it would hurt Preston. He already knew all about her past, so it wasn't the news that was the worst part. It was the prospect of public exposure.

Not only would her own reputation be ruined, but, to her amazement, the thought of damaging the relationship she'd built with Gloria was excruciatingly painful. Livia had initially dismissed Gloria as a flyover country nobody to be used to Livia's advantage. Instead, the older woman had quickly become what Livia suspected was the closest and most genuine friend Livia had ever had. Livia's disgrace would, by association, taint Gloria's reputation.

Worst of all, though, is how the whole thing would paint Preston as a cuckold and destroy him as well.

It was something…. Something she knew she would not… could not… endure.

The penthouse patio door was open, and the omnipresent soft breeze tickled the open drapes. Only the soft glow of the false night illuminated the room.

So here she was, once again, lying on the floor with a bottle nearby. Not that she'd actually taken more than a sip or two from it. She didn't need to. It was more symbolic than anything else. She wore only her simple department store white slip. Her long black hair was unkempt and loose against her pearlescent skin. Her Beretta 92FS pistol lay on the table nearby.

When she heard the sound of the apartment door opening through the open doorways, she steeled herself. It took a few minutes for Preston to come looking for her. His tie, service jacket, and shoes were off. His shoulders slumped as he saw her, and he sighed and shook his head slowly.

Before he could say anything, Livia spoke, her voice high and tremulous. "I think maybe this time you need to really kick me out for good. Publicly. File for divorce and get ahead of it while you still can."

Preston gently padded to her side, bent down, and effortlessly picked her up. Instead of carrying her to bed, he simply hugged her close to him, swaying slowly back and forth, cradling and rocking her as he'd done with Helena as a child so many times.

He swallowed. "Whatever it is, we'll get through it."

Livia couldn't hold back any longer. She burst into tears and wrapped her arms around him, sobbing. "I'm so sorry. I'm so sorry. It's not your fault… it's all me. Me and my…. Oh God, Preston. It finally caught up with me!"

He carried her to an armchair and sat down with Livia curled up in his arms.

After long minutes, her sobs slowly ebbed. Huskily, she said into Preston's chest, "Just… hate me. Throw me out. Don't let both of us be destroyed."

He waited and said nothing, just holding her until she fell asleep. Then, he stayed there, holding her while his arms grew numb.

When she awoke, she lifted her head to look up at him. She swallowed and said in a small voice. "It's bad. You need to distance yourself from me. Do damage control while you still can."

Preston stared into her bloodshot jade green eyes. "Tell me."

✪ ✪ ✪

Preston poured himself a drink of very recent vintage Fort Brazos gin, and waited while Livia showered and dressed. He sat in 'his' apartment living room in an armchair identical to the one on Livia's side and considered the situation.

When she entered, she was barefoot in jeans and a T-shirt, with her wet hair combed and pulled back into a ponytail. She slowly walked to the side of his chair and knelt beside him.

"Preston…. I'm so sorry. I've packed a bag, and I will leave. I'll… I'll make an announcement. Resign."

He turned and looked at her, studying her face. He asked, "How did the blackmailer get the photos?"

Livia blinked in surprise. "What?"

He repeated, "How did the blackmailer get the photos? You said yourself that you always went to anonymous hotel rooms. It doesn't sound like the blackmailer would have had time to set up a camera in advance. So, how did the blackmailer get the photos?"

Livia continued blinking in surprise. Then she stopped, and her eyes widened in shock and betrayal. Her chest heaved as she exclaimed, "Oh God…. No! No, no, no, no, no… it can't…. he couldn't…. he wouldn't!"

She stood and staggered backward, tripped, fell, got up again, spun around the room, and screamed, "Noooo! Fuck! Oh god!"

She stopped and sank to her knees and sobbed. "I can't believe I've been…. I'm so fucking stupid!"

Preston articulated each word carefully, ticking off the options on his fingers as he explained. "Livia, your lawyer brain would have seen through it eventually, but you were too close to the situation. So, your boy toy made some home videos. Now, we're left with a few possibilities." He raised a finger, "Option A: he did it for his own… enjoyment, and then someone else stumbled upon them. Option B," another finger went up, "all by himself and on his own, he intentionally made them for the purpose of blackmailing you. And Option C," he lifted a third finger, "someone else put him up to it in the first place."

Livia's bone-pale face crimsoned as sudden rage built up within her. She stood and began pacing back and forth, "That little pecker! That! Argggg! I'm…. I'mmm….!"

Preston slowly stood, walked over to her, took her arm, and pulled her to him. "Livia, this isn't just a personal attack. The blackmailer is using you to subvert the new government. This is an attack on all of us, and we must get to the bottom of it together."

Livia pulled back from him, "Wait," she sniffed, "What? No, this will damage you. You've got to distance yourself from me like I said!"

Preston shook his head, his face full of growing anger and determination. "No. My love. Someone has attacked you and hurt you. Betrayed you. This is personal, now."

✪ ✪ ✪

Nine Hours Later

DownSide: Military Intelligence Headquarters

Lieutenant Colonel Martin Williams, formerly of the Australian Intelligence Corps and now the head of Military Intelligence, sat at his desk while Livia, with Preston sitting beside her, explained what had transpired with her blackmailer. Her hands trembled as she handed over the envelope, including the blackmail photos and the burner phone.

His office was on the second floor of a building that had been a 1980s-era data center slated for demolition before Awakening Day. Located on top of the main telecommunication trunk lines that still ran through the base, the location was convenient from a technological point of view and in an out-of-the-way corner of the sprawling base.

When Livia got to the part about exactly *who* the young man in the photos was, Martin involuntarily flinched and swallowed hard, his eyes wide in involuntary surprise. "Excuse me, please, Madam Senator. Admiral. I'm afraid that this information touches on…. An active investigation. I need to bring someone else into the room."

Livia stiffened, and Preston bristled.

Martin shook his head apologetically, "I'm sorry, but you'll understand soon. I am afraid I will be forced to read you in on…. Well, I'm certain you will be even more shocked than I was."

Twenty minutes later, former FBI agent Brian Kupe entered the room and brought himself short as he paused and realized who else was present. He nodded in recognition, "Ah, Senator, Admiral…?"

Martin waved to Brian to pull up another chair and join them at his desk. "Brian, I am going to read the Senator and Admiral in on our current… investigation. I wanted you to be here so you can hit the ground running as this takes off."

Martin sank back into his chair and thought for a moment, then took a deep breath and began, "I'm glad you are both sitting down, and I'm glad I have a reasonably well-equipped bar in my credenza, even if the selection is all regrettably young. I have a feeling you both will need it when we're done here. You see, Brian, here, as you may recall, was the agent in charge of the pre-Awakening Day investigation into the spy we now know was the infamous and unlamented Commander Harding."

Livia swallowed and shivered at Harding's name.

"You see, we have learned that Commander Harding did not act alone…."

Livia paled visibly, as if that were possible, as she sat rigidly in her chair, her hands clasped together in a vain attempt to prevent them from shaking. Preston seemed to swell in his chair. His jaw was set hard, and his face pink with rage. Neither could find words.

Martin and Brian let them sit quietly for several minutes as they absorbed the news.

Rear Admiral Johansson is a traitor….

He had orchestrated the bombing and quite likely either recruited his own son to ensnare Livia or simply took advantage of it after the fact. That Harding was still actually alive was not something Preston and Livia needed to know.

Preston's eyes narrowed, and he stated, "If I see him…. That… man… will not live out the day."

Martin nodded slowly and softly said, "Frankly, he'd already be six feet under were it not for one problem. We don't know if he acted alone. Did he have accomplices? Were his family, his wife, and his son directly involved?" He leaned forward and clasped his hands on the desk before him, "Admiral, Senator, with respect. We *need* to know if he had accomplices. We *need* to know that if we cut off the head of the snake that, it was the *only* snake. That there aren't more or worse ones that… *get away with it.*"

Livia winced at the last statement. She turned and looked at Preston. "I was there… Preston…. In the room, with the burning bodies… the blood… the…," she swallowed, "If there are more people involved, I can't rest, none of us can rest…. Until they are caught, punished… and…," her lips thinned into lines, "and…."

Preston reached over, put his arm around her, and pulled her closer. "I know."

Livia sniffed and wiped the tears she didn't even know she'd shed with the back of her hand. "After Awakening Day, when we were brought to this world, I despised the President, assuming he was just an opportunistic bumpkin. The Vice President was worse. An empty uniform put there as someone easily controlled by General Marcus…. Not only that, but it was obvious that she and the President were an item. I thought this world would end in disaster, led by idiots. Remember months ago, that party? The one where the two of them danced? Andre called me, privately expressing his concerns over our leadership, and asked what I thought and whether the two of them were really, well, like everyone assumed they were. I called him that night and told him what I thought then. I more or less confirmed to him that I thought our leadership was compromised."

More tears began to stream from her eyes. "So… you see. I'm one of the guilty ones, too. I contributed. I may have even pushed Andre over the edge to do it. I'm…."

Martin snorted and shook his head, his voice slipping in and out of his native Australian accent. "Hell, Senator, if ya are guilty because ya talked to someone about how ya thought maybe they weren't fit for the job, then we might as well take half of us and condemn us as well. Ya didn't convince Admiral Andre Johansson to become a turncoat. Ya didn't convince him to conspire and cause another man to commit mass murder. Ya didn't do anythin' that thousands of other people didn't do as well… exercisin' their right to think freely and express concerns. My God, do ya think any of us truly deserve to be in the roles we are in? Do any of us deserve to be breathin' when eight billion other humans were either slaughtered or enslaved by the Accipiters? So ya went and did some things ya regret. Yes, ya cheated on your hubby and got caught doing it. Welcome to the human race. What matters is what ya do now. What ya do with the rest of your life, and, to be blunt, whether ya reckon it's worth takin' a bloody risk to catch that bloody traitor and make sure the bugger gets what's comin' to him." He swallowed and added, returning to his practiced generic English, "pardon my native tongue."

TopSide: Rear Admiral Lower Half Andre Johansson's Family Apartment

11:23 PM

Andre Johansson untied and kicked off his shoes, stretched his aching feet, and let out a relieved groan as he sank into the well-worn but plush easy chair imported from Fort Brazos's DownSide flea market. His wife Sofie was already asleep in the bedroom, so he kept the volume low. His son Karl was, of course, DownSide at the Academy. Andre reached for the TV remote and tuned in to the news, hoping for something to take his mind off recent events. After enduring several minutes of mindless fluff, the scene on the screen abruptly changed, and the caption caught his attention: "Senator Milner briefed on 'Operation Silver Angel.'" He blinked in surprise, sucked in a breath, and leaned forward, captivated by what followed.

"… investigation into possible co-Conspirators of Commander Thomas James Harding, the insane City Hall bomber, responsible for…."

The mention of Operation Silver Angel triggered a rush of memories, the elusive specter he had been obsessing over for the past couple of days. Adrenaline surged through his veins, compelling him to retrieve from his pocket the burner phone that he used to communicate with Livia. He began typing a text:

WHAT DO YOU KNOW ABOUT OPERATION SILVER ANGEL?

'Silver Angel' was a phrase that, so far as he knew, only two people should know, and one of them was supposed to be dead. It was the codename given to Thomas Harding by his Chinese handlers before Awakening Day.

The response came swiftly.

Why? Agent Kupe has convinced leadership that Harding had help. Kupe has found proof of an as yet unnamed person who was involved, who deceived Harding into committing the act with falsified reports and misleading information. Apparently, Harding kept a diary that has been recovered, containing details of meetings that align with the suspects' movements and links to how Harding got the explosives he used have been tied to the suspect. The briefing was a warning that indictments have been filed and are to be served shortly. They are concerned about public outcry and potential repercussions on the suspect's family.

Andre leaned back in his chair, a faint smile playing on his lips. *Well, it would have been nice to have played the game a lot longer.* An air of resigned acceptance washed over him. The game, his intricate dance of deceit and subterfuge, was reaching its denouement.

His expression, a fusion of melancholy and intellectual fatigue, betrayed no hint of surprise when the doorbell chimed unexpectedly. It wasn't protocol with his security detail. He rose, his movements deliberate, betraying a lifetime of discipline.

Opening the door, he found himself face to face with Corporals Jason Denning and Ryan Jacobs, their usual composure replaced by a palpable tension as they stood dumbfounded, phones in hand. Behind them, an entourage of stern-faced figures loomed – Martin Williams and Brian Kupe, flanked by a detachment of marines, their presence an unspoken verdict.

Jason looked up at Andre and stammered, "Admiral, ahh, these gentlemen are here to see you."

Two of the marines held sidearms clearly taken from the now disarmed Denning and Ryan.

Martin was relaxed and confident. He allowed a hint of his native accent to betray his satisfaction. "Good evening, Admiral." His greeting was a mere formality, his tone devoid of warmth as he smiled thinly. "A conversation is in order, wouldn't you agree? Preferably within the confines of your residence."

Andre's response was measured, his mind already racing through scenarios and possibilities., "Of course, Colonel. Come this way. What can I do for you?" The entry of eight of the marines into his sanctuary, a place once impenetrable, marked the endgame.

As they filed in, their intent clear, Andre felt an odd sense of detachment. This was a scene he had played out in his mind countless times, each iteration a strategic exercise. Yet, now faced with its reality, it felt surreal, like watching the final act of a play he had written but never expected to perform.

Martin, with a gesture that was both commanding and weary, motioned towards the dining room table. "Have a seat, Admiral."

Andre stood his ground, allowing himself to play out the final moments of the game. His eyes never left Martin's as he quietly demanded. "Colonel, what is the meaning of this intrusion?"

Martin glanced at two of the marines, who stepped forward towards Andre, taking him by the arms and forcibly sitting him down in a chair. Four of the others spread out to search the rest of the apartment.

Martin sighed, "I believe you already know, Admiral."

The tension escalated as the Marines returned with Sofie, who was barefoot and wearing a robe. Her hair was disheveled, and her eyes were wide with shock and surprise as she cried out, "Andre! What is happening? Who are these men?"

Martin nodded at Brian, who left the room, then returned moments later with two marines who frog-marched a shackled, heavily bearded man between them. The man wore a jumpsuit, hoodie, and dark sunglasses. Brian pulled the hoodie back and removed the man's sunglasses. He gestured to the marines, who pushed the man forward to stand before Andre.

Andre's gaze shifted calmly back and forth between Martin and Brian. Then he shrugged, shook his head, and looked at the shackled man before him. It took several long seconds before realization set in. He didn't gasp or show any sign of surprise. Instead, he sighed, sank back into the chair, and said in a voice devoid of shock or denial, "So, they kept you alive after all. And the beard and hair…."

He smiled wanly at Martin. "At the testing center. An actor?"

Martin feigned ignorance, "Why, whatever do you mean, Admiral?"

Andre frowned, disappointment seeping into his voice, "Oh, Colonel. Don't be coy. Tell me, how long have you known?"

Martin contemplated whether to answer as Sofie struggled to shake her shoulders free from the marines.

Her voice seethed in anger. Her confusion was in stark contrast to the resigned calm of the men at the center of the storm. "Who are these men, Andre? And who is this... person?"

Andre raised an eyebrow in a casual shrug and replied, "Don't you recognize the infamous Commander Thomas James Harding, my dear?"

She cried out, her tone filled with defiance, "No, I don't. And tell these brutes to release me!"

Thomas Harding cackled, his voice teetering on the edge of sanity. "Maybe they'll let us share the gallows, eh, Andre? We could bond together in prison while we await our appointment with the hangman."

Martin nodded to Brian, who took Harding by the shoulders and, with the marines, guided him to the foyer.

Andre shook his head and addressed Martin, "Colonel, would you indulge me with a drink before we depart? Sofie, could you please fetch a drink for the Colonel and me? The good stuff, whatever is left. Is that all right with you, Colonel?"

Martin slowly nodded, "I can be magnanimous, Admiral." He turned, "Let her go. Madam, would you mind getting us drinks? You might want one for yourself as well."

Sofie shook herself loose and angrily sulked over to the bar and said, "I might just throw it in your face, whoever you think you are, but fine."

As she picked up the decanter, a flash of realization crossed Martin's features. He snapped his attention toward her.

Sofie's expression was bitter and triumphant as she slipped her hand into the gap behind the credenza and the wall.

Without wasting a moment on shouting, Martin leaped towards her.

✪ ✪ ✪

In a cataclysmic flash, the explosives concealed within the apartment detonated, obliterating the top three floors of the tower. The devastating blast instantly killed Martin Williams, Brian Kupe, the dozen marines they'd brought, Corporals Jason Denning and Ryan Jacobs, as well as Thomas James Harding, Sofie Clarke Johannson, and Andre Vide Johansson.

Bad Seed

● ● ● ● ● ● ● ● ● ● ● ● ● ● ● ● ●

DownSide: Riverbend Mall: Presidential Office

President and Vice President John and Gail Austin were seated behind the president's desk. Senator Sybil Blanchard, Secretary of War Alexander Marcus, Vice Admiral Preston Milner, and Senator Livia Milner were gathered in seats in a semicircle around the desk. Halfway between them and the door sat a simple armless wooden chair. John and Gail's respective security detail members lined the walls of room, with the other VIP's security detail members arrayed outside the door. The rest of Riverbend was in lockdown.

The door opened, and Karl Johansson was led to stand in front of the chair. Marine security detail members in full combat gear had snatched him from his Academy dorm room in the middle of the night. He was brought to Riverbend and allowed to dress in his cadet uniform and shave before being brought before the assembled leaders.

John nodded to Alexander, who stood and addressed Karl. "Attention, cadet!"

Karl straightened his stance, with his chin level, and brought his heels together at a 45-degree angle with his arms at his side. His expression was pensive and worried.

Alexander asked levelly, his voice grave. "Do you know why you are here, cadet?"

Karl examined the faces of the men and women gathered, lingering on Livia for a long moment, taking in the look of mingled horror, anger, shame, and hatred on her face. A face he had caressed so often. Lips Karl had kissed, and…. He turned and studied the other faces and noted the one most conspicuously absent.

Then he arched an eyebrow and shrugged, "Sir, yes, Sir. Based on what I've overheard from the guards since I was oh so respectfully hauled out of my dorm last night, it would seem that you've finally caught my old man. Took you long enough. He's been playing you for fools for years. Some of you more than others." He paused and added with an upturned lip, "Sir."

John Austin bristled while Gail's face seemed to turn to ice. Preston reddened as he glowered and rose from his seat. Alexander touched the Admiral's shoulder and gently pushed him back down. Livia seemed to wilt and die inside.

Karl then noticed someone for the first time. He'd never met Senator Blanchard and had never given her a second thought. She was just the truck driver's wife with delusions of grandeur. When he looked at her, though, he blinked and stopped himself short. The tiny woman's intense dark eyes seemed to pierce right through him as though lancing his soul.

Alexander nodded, his voice dropping a half octave. "I see. And did your father also recruit your mother into his activities?"

Karl's eyes glittered as he sneered, "Sir? Recruit her? Hell, she recruited *him!*"

Half the room exchanged shocked glances.

Karl continued, "She got him started, but it was her idea for me to help. It was really no challenge for me to play the innocent boy."

Livia blurted out, "You!"

Karl laughed, "Oh, my beautiful porcelain goddess, you were hardly the first. By the time you came along, there had already been a long line of others eager to defile my innocence. Women and, especially, certain *men* when I was younger. With help from Mom and myself, Dad had dirt on over a dozen. Congressmen, CEOs, Judges, and more."

Karl's face lit with pride, "You, my dearest Livie, you gave Dad leverage over the goddamned Chief of Naval Operations, should he need it. More than that, there were rumors the Vice Admiral might one day become Vice President or even President."

He took a breath and grinned wolfishly at Livia. "And don't count yourself short, either. We figured you for a shoo-in to take your daddy's Senate seat when he eventually kicked it. You were truly our golden goose."

Karl stood there, beaming with excitement as silence like bitter ashen snow fell over the room.

After Karl was bodily removed by his shoulders, everyone but John and Gail stood and gathered around the desk. Everyone that is, except Livia, who sank into her chair with a desolate look on her face. Preston stood beside her, resting a comforting hand on her shoulder as she wondered if she could actually die from shame.

John rested his head in his hands and closed his eyes. "Nineteen dead. Twenty-six, counting City Hall. That… monster…."

Gail shook her head. "Sixteen good men yesterday, John. I don't count the Admiral or Harding, and now that we know his wife was in on it, I don't count her as a loss either. I didn't know agent Kupe, but Martin was a godsend. Losing him will hurt us in ways I can't begin to measure. I also knew some of the Marines. I just… I can't begin to express how… angry… I am. Meanwhile, though," she spat the words, "What do we do with that little shit? His dad cheated me out of shooting *him*, but I'll take the consolation prize."

Livia blurted out, "I still can't believe that Harding was *alive*, and no one told me! You killed him! I was there! I *saw* you kill him!"

Preston barked, "You had the son of a bitch alive all this time, and you didn't tell *me!?*"

Gail nodded, "Yes. Yes, I did kill him. But the doctors brought him back. Saved him. Goddamned Gardener improved human vitality. The same thing that saved my… saved the President. We decided to keep Harding alive when we realized that he might have had accomplices."

John looked Preston straight in the eyes, "You are damned right we did, Admiral. We didn't know who he might have conspired with or how high up it might have gone. It turns out it went pretty fucking high."

Preston winced but didn't back down.

Alexander shook his head, "Let's send the boy to the island of misfit toys, the North Koreans."

John sighed and quietly said, "As far as we know, the young man, while despicable, didn't directly participate in the bomb plot or do anything violent. On the other hand… he knew and was complicit in his family's spy business. Karl probably even knew of his father's manipulation of Harding. He's guilty of many things and must be prosecuted. We are, still, are we not, a nation of laws?"

Alexander shook his head, "When word of this gets out, he won't last a day, even in prison."

Sybil smiled and said, "I say we drop him on a desert island, naked, with a pen knife."

Preston shook his head angrily. He clenched Livia's shoulder tightly, making her wince as he exclaimed, "He's a cadet, and he gave an oath. He's subject to military law. We shall convene a court marshal."

Sybil shrugged. "Either is a death sentence. Not that he doesn't deserve it. Why don't we be magnanimous and give him the choice?"

✪ ✪

DownSide: Eugene Morton Naval Academy:

Formerly: Bonham State University Campus

The Court Marshall was brief indeed. Karl proudly admitted his complicity in his father and mother's spying and blackmail schemes.

Hours later, the Eugene Morton Naval Academy's graduation hall thrummed with heightened anticipation. Karl Johansson stood at attention on the stage in his navy blue dress Midshipman uniform while the sea of hastily gathered cadets and their families watched. His impeccably tailored uniform, a testament to his now disgraced family position, proudly bore the insignia of his once lofty ambitions. His gaze burned with the fervor of a dream never to be realized.

A weighty silence descended upon the hall as the Academy Superintendent Rear Admiral Gordon Montoya ascended the stage, his authoritative presence commanding reverence. Now seventy-two years old, Gordon had lost his hair as a young man. However, due to the Gardener's tinkering, it was starting to grow back in an itchy fuzz. Microphone in hand, he addressed the assembly with a stern voice that brooked no disobedience. He was accompanied by the Commandant of Midshipmen, former Air Force Chief Master Sergeant Harrold Anders.

"Ladies, gentlemen, esteemed faculty, and distinguished guests," the Admiral's voice resonated, carrying an air of solemnity. "Today, we stand witness to an occasion of grave consequence. A ceremony born from choices made and confessed traitorous actions taken."

Karl's pulse quickened, his instincts alert to the gravity of the moment. The Admiral's unyielding gaze bore down on him, penetrating his very core.

Gordon nodded to Harrold.

Harrold's voice fell like a hammer striking an anvil. "Cadet Karl Henrik Johansson, step forth," he commanded, his voice a blend of steely resolve and unwavering conviction that shook Karl's resolve.

Managing not to flinch, and with measured steps, Karl advanced, his unwavering stare meeting the commandant's steadfast gaze. Palms dampened, he braced himself for the profound metamorphosis awaiting him.

Harrold retrieved a pair of white ceremonial gloves from his pocket. He approached Karl, exuding a controlled intensity, each movement deliberate.

Gordon intoned harshly, "In recognition of your traitorous and dishonorable actions and the betrayal of this institution's sacred values," Gordon proclaimed, his voice a low rumble that reverberated through the hall, "your privileges, titles, and aspirations shall be ruthlessly stripped away."

Harrold lifted the Combination Cap from Karl's head and dramatically snapped the bill on his knee before tossing it to the stage floor.

He then forcefully peeled away the traditional Coat Collar Anchor Insignia, which had been loosened before the ceremony, from Karl's right collar, then his left, each emblematic fragment sundering Karl's identity and dreams. The resounding rending of fabric shattered the room's stillness, an elegy to stained and soiled potential.

He then tore away the Sleeve Class Insignia and Sleeve Rank Insignia, nearly pulling Karl off balance.

Next, he removed Karl's Midshipman Uniform Belt with its brass buckle and tossed it to the floor.

Then, one by one, Harrold ripped the Navy Eagle Gilt Buttons from Karl's uniform coat and tossed them down, each bouncing with a small crack on the stage floor.

Now seizing Karl's uniform pocket, Harrold's grip radiated an unwavering ferocity as though determined to sever any vestiges of affiliation to the Academy.

With a purposeful, almost ceremonious, motion, Harrold rent each pocket asunder, the sound of tearing cloth marking the severance of Karl's connection to the Academy's ranks.

The finality of the day's rapid-fire events finally began to sink in as Karl felt the jagged shards of his aspirations pierce his very soul. He set his jaw and hardened his unwavering gaze.

"And now," Gordon's voice resonated with somber finality, "as the ultimate symbol of your transgressions and the trust you have broken, your cadet sword shall be irrevocably sundered."

Shortly before the ceremony, following an ancient tradition, Harrold had taken a narrow grinding wheel and filed the sword nearly in two, ensuring it would snap.

Emerging from the shadows, another officer stepped forth and ceremoniously handed the blade to Harrold. The air grew taut with anticipation as Harrold raised the sword high, its gleaming edge poised for judgment. In a moment, both poignant and final, Harrold brought the blade crashing down, shattering it in twain with a resounding crack.

A collective hungry, satisfied gasp swept through the crowd. Everyone knew what would happen next, and many thought the punishment was not nearly severe enough.

Karl stood ramrod straight, rooted to the spot. Fear, anger, and defiance welled up from within him.

Gordon declared loudly, "Karl Henrik Johansson, by virtue of my authority, I hereby expel you from the Eugene Morton Naval Academy. May this serve as an indelible reminder to all who traverse these hallowed corridors of the dire consequences borne by those who forsake their personal honor, the honor of this institution, and those who, by their actions, threaten the very survival of the human race."

✪ ✪ ✪

DownSide: Radio Station 92.5 Studio

Danielle Richardson Anders keyed the microphone. With her left hand, she gently rocked her newborn twins, Darcy and Betsy. Her voice was low and choked with anger as tears streamed down her face. "Hello, people of Fort Brazos and New London. This is Danielle Richardson on FM 92.5 and Radio Free Fort Brazos, beaming our signal across the known world and beyond. Most of you probably already know the biggest story since, well, you already know. For those of you who don't know, in the beautiful city of New London last night, an explosion destroyed the top three floors of Rear Admiral Andre Johansson's apartment building."

She paused and took a sip of water, "And that's the last time I will ever say that fucking name out loud. Because... you see...." She choked out the words, "That monstrous bastard.... That evil, monstrous bastard was responsible for not only his own death and that of his co-conspirator wife, but he took the lives of twelve marines, two marine security guards, whose names I don't have yet, as well as Agent Brian Kupe, and Colonel Martin Williams. He was also the real brains behind the city hall bombing that took the lives of Councilman Wylie Hickum, President Austin's protection detail members Corporal Jorge Diego and Corporal Antoine "Tony" Bouchard, City Council audio-video technician Jason Thornaby, Air Force Lieutenant Sára Maruska, who was assisting General Alexander, as well as Mr. Steffen Zuckermann, and Mr. Carlos Alonso. The attack severely injured many and nearly killed President Austin. This man... this fucker," she paused, "sorry, Darcy and Betsy, "this insane fucker, orchestrated Commander Harding to commit the bombing in the first place."

She took another sip. "Well, at least we won't have to put the bastard on trial or spend the money on a bullet in the head, but he royally screwed up the skyline in New London. We'll get it fixed, though. You can count on that. As for the rest of his traitorous family, it seems that both the wife and son were guilty as well, and the son confessed this morning. As we speak, he's on his way to some hellhole island on the other side of the world. That is unless the crew of the ILC happens to let the little creep take a bathroom break out of the airlock while they are a few thousand feet off the ground. Oops! What a shame that would be."

Cadets Elísabet Gunnarsson, Will Sawyer, and Jordan Hoffman sat together at a small table in the study hall. Superintendent Montoya had declared a two-day break, so most of the other cadets were either at a bar or anywhere else but on campus. Elísabet, Will, and Jordan, however, were among the most fiercely dedicated in their class, the first-ever-year class at the Academy. Before joining, Elísabet's fiancé, Zachary Simmons, who she'd known for as long as she could remember, had been killed by a Stalker. Will's brother Dex and their friend Morgan Forbes had been killed in the same incident. Jordan's mother, father, and older brother had been killed by a different Stalker on Awakening Day, along with other men.

Elísabet was slim and tall at five foot nine inches. Her dark red hair was shorter than even regulations required. Will's brown hair was now a buzz-cut, and he'd grown a full inch to six foot one inches since he'd shot and killed the stalker that had killed his friends. Jordan, younger than Elísabet by two years, had followed the older girl's example. Like Elísabet, her hair had been down to her waist, but she'd had her blonde locks shorn to match Elísabet's severe style.

Their mutual hatred of the Accipiters and their lackey creatures had drawn the three together. Each excelled at the Academy through a combination of talent and drive borne on the wings of their lust for revenge.

Elísabet shook her head ruefully, "He was never dedicated to the cause. I always had the impression that he thought he was owed his commission because of his father. Correction, his traitorous bastard father."

Will nodded, "He was a natural athlete, so the physical aspects of training were no problem for him. He was better than most. Stronger and faster, but he was kind of an asshole."

Jordan's expression was sour, "He was a creep. You know his reputation, Bet."

Will shook his head, "Well, obviously, he was a traitorous creep, but his reputation with girls was hardly unique for jocks like him. I think what bothered me the most about him was that he acted like it was pre-Awakening-Day. You simply can't treat sex like you could back then. Nobody can. I mean, he was smart about it, but he was still a creep like you said, Jordan."

In a hushed, worried voice, Jordan asked, "Do you think they really found all the traitors? That it was limited to just the Johansson family and Commander Harding?"

Elísabet shrugged, "You heard the Admiral. Some others may have been victimized, but the Johansson's were it. We can't go around accusing people just because we don't like them."

Will chuckled darkly, "Yeah, just because you're an asshole doesn't mean you're a traitor."

Jordan said quietly, "Can you imagine? What would it have been like for Karl if he hadn't confessed? If he were actually innocent but had to live with knowing his mom and dad were traitors? How *we* would have treated him?"

The three friends stared at each other with anxious, worried looks.

Karl Vincent Johansson watched with a sinking heart as Ramona Henry's ILC Dagger lifted silently off the beach, the airlock sealing his fate, leaving him alone on the dense jungle island. His cadet uniform, now a ragged symbol of his betrayal, hung off his body - the class and rank insignia brutally torn off, pockets ripped open in a humiliating display of his disgrace. No one had actually struck him, though his treatment was anything but gentle.

Commander Henry's contemptuous gaze, full of loathing, had been the last human expression he'd seen. Her beautiful face twisted in disgust, she wordlessly handed him a bottle of water and an almost laughably inadequate pen knife, then she'd spun on her heel and walked away without looking back, abandoning him to his treacherous fate.

As Dagger vanished into the clouds, Karl was engulfed by the oppressive, eerie sounds of the jungle. He knew that he wouldn't have lasted long in prison, or if he had, he would have wished he hadn't. A wave of regret washed over him, but he quickly suppressed it, thinking to himself with forced bravado, *I can make this work.*

Karl, the all-state football player born into a family of spies and wealth, had only ever known the intellectual challenges and the comforts of urban life. The prospect of being dumped alone on a deserted island was daunting. *How hard could it be? I did summer camp. I… think I remember how to start a fire.*

His Oxford-style dress uniform shoes slipped a little on the loose sand as he walked along the pristine beach. He stopped abruptly as a rustling sound caught his attention. Karl turned his head toward the dense, lush jungle at the beach's edge. His smile faded abruptly as he noticed a pair of piercing amber eyes locked onto him. Eyes gleaming with an untamed hunger.

Karl's heart skipped a beat. He took a step back, his breathing quickening. The tension in the air was palpable as the magnificent creature arrogantly stepped out of the jungle onto the beach, revealing itself. A hulking and beautiful Sumatran tiger.

At first, his reaction was one of detached fascination, as if the creature before him was something from a television screen or a textbook illustration, a distant concept rather than a real threat. He remembered that they were supposed to be endangered and wondered what the odds were of seeing such a rare creature?

But then, as the tiger's amber eyes locked onto his own, a chilling transition occurred. The abstract curiosity rapidly morphed into a primal, visceral fear. His heart raced. His privileged, sheltered life in the city offered no playbook for this. The predatory gaze of the tiger stripped away his intellectual bravado, exposing a raw, instinctual terror he had never known.

Karl's body responded before his mind fully grasped the situation. He was rooted to the spot, sweat beading on his forehead as the tiger began its deliberate approach. Each step of the massive creature left deep imprints in the sand. Its orange and black stripes rippled with each powerful movement of its muscles.

The air around him, charged with the scent of danger and ocean salt, felt heavier. Karl's mind, once filled with strategies and theories, now screamed a single, instinctive command: survival. Yet he stood frozen, a city-dweller out of his element, facing a danger that was all too real and imminent.

He struggled to maintain eye contact with the tiger, hoping it would see him as a threat rather than prey.

The tiger's eyes, unwavering in their focus, stayed locked onto Karl. Exuding a predatory aura, its gaze was piercing and intense, as if it were assessing and calculating with every measured step it took toward him.

The air around them, already thick with the tang of salt from the nearby ocean, began to fill with an unmistakable scent of danger.

Karl's mind raced, searching for a way to escape. His hands began to tremble. He almost laughed to himself at the thought of the puny pen knife still gripped in his hand. He desperately scanned the surroundings for anything that might offer protection. But all he found were scattered rocks and the vast, open, pristinely beautiful beach.

With a sudden burst of speed, the tiger lunged forward, its powerful paws propelling it toward Karl. Panic engulfed him as he stumbled backward, dropping the water bottle and losing his footing on the loose sand.

As the tiger closed in, time seemed to slow down. Karl's survival instinct kicked in, adrenaline surging through his veins. He gathered every ounce of strength he had, spread his arms, and shrieked a battle cry, ready to wrestle the tiger for his life. He was a superb athlete, after all.

As the tiger overpowered him, the abstract became painfully real. His life of Machiavellian plots, deceit, and lies had not prepared him for this. The thought slowly faded from his mind as his blood soaked into the glistening sand. *Tigers don't wrestle....*

Inner Circle

● ● ● ● ● ● ● ● ● ● ● ● ● ● ● ● ●

DownSide: Riverbend Mall: Presidential Office

Alexander Marcus surveyed the grave countenances of President John Austin and Vice President Gail Austin, his expression mirroring their somberness. Gail sat to John's right. Settling into the leather chair opposite John's imposing desk, he couldn't help but voice his frustration. "We've been spending entirely too much time in this office lately."

Preston Milner trod cautiously, following behind Alexander, carrying the burden of tension on his shoulders. The Andre Johansson disaster had left him reeling, and he was still grappling with its aftermath. Only a privileged few knew of Livia's involvement, and he desperately hoped it would remain shrouded in secrecy. Livia's spirit had been shattered. She was withdrawn and still talking to him about resigning. Restoring their relationship and healing her wounds would require time and dedication, but he had resolved to make every effort.

Initially, Preston presumed that this meeting would focus on the fallout from the Johansson scandal. However, the heavy expressions on John and Gail's faces hinted at something even darker. He cautiously sat, perching on the edge of the chair with his back ramrod straight. His internal radar was on high alert as he braced himself for what seemed likely to be yet another wave of bad news.

John exchanged a glance with Gail. He'd been inclined to let her open the meeting, but her face was pale and drawn. Morning sickness had extended its clutches into the afternoon and evening hours, plaguing her most days. Drawing a deep breath, he began. "Alex, Preston, thanks for coming on short notice. Gail and I had hoped this meeting would prove unnecessary. However, the more time that passes since Admiral Johansson's unmasking as a traitor, the more convinced we are that the time has come to disclose something to the both of you. You see, moments after escaping the Accipiter fleet and arriving in this system, I, we, Gail, and I received a phone call." He paused, his tone weighted with gravity, "The call came from the Gardeners."

Alexander's eyebrows shot up in astonishment, but he withheld any immediate comment.

Preston flinched in his seat, jolted by the revelation. "What? That, that has never happened before. What...?"

Gail interjected, interrupting his bewilderment. "They called, and I quote verbatim, 'We will help you further, but not until you discover the traitor. Until then, we will be watching.'"

Alexander and Preston traded worried glances.

In measured tones, Preston responded, his mind spinning as he strove to regain his composure. "So, if I understand correctly, you believed that they would contact you or us again once Johansson was exposed as the traitor. However, since, I presume, they have not yet done so, you fear there may be other collaborators yet to be exposed?"

John shook his head, a pensive expression etched on his face. "We already knew that he was a traitor by then. We just didn't have enough proof to go forward with it. We held onto the hope that he was the traitor the call referred to. However, we believed that the Gardeners already knew that we knew, so the message did not make a lot of sense to us. We hoped that getting proof and publicly exposing him would be enough. Now, though, we are worried that maybe the Admiral was not who the Gardeners were referring to at all. That something else is going on and that we are dangerously clueless."

Preston stiffened, his realization dawning upon him. "How long have you... known?"

Gail read his expression and shook her head, her voice tinged with sadness, "About Andre? Only since a few days prior to the arrival of the Accipiters. About your wife? About Livia? Only when you brought it to our attention. Of course, without Colonel Williams and Brian Kupe with us to spearhead the effort to find whoever this *other* traitor is, our efforts have been set back for months, at least."

Alexander closed his eyes, uttering a pained groan. "Martin was a spook, but he was *our* spook. Replacing him is not going to be easy. I've got people looking through records to try and find candidates, but no one came close to his background in the first place."

Gail nodded, "I know. Of course, we've got people with law enforcement backgrounds, but spies? We may end up having to train people from the ground up to fill that role."

Alexander heaved a sigh, "All right. Moving on, then. So, I take it you are worried that for days, we've all been sitting here waiting for the next announcement via the Obelisk about the so-called great things the Gardeners have in store for us here, but it's been silent. You're worried people will start to worry or even panic." He swallowed, "Or… worse, if we don't find the traitor the Gardeners talked about, that they might… react to our ineptitude and… punish us."

Preston's eyes widened as he realized how much he had underestimated the crisis at hand. "My God."

John nodded, his movements deliberate. "We need to buy time. Keep the Senate and the public preoccupied. Divert their attention while we hunt for the Gardener's traitor.

Alexander ruminated aloud, contemplating potential strategies, "We have already convened work sessions to strategize a shipbuilding program, addressing the numerous logistical hurdles. Now that we're here and proceeding from an assumption of Gardener aid in those logistics, we could initiate a fresh series of meetings to discuss the types of ships we wish to construct and the aid we seek. If we open it up to public input, that could draw out the process for months. Longer, really. Probably more."

"We could attribute the Gardener's silence to an expectation that they are waiting for us to get our act together. That they won't help us until we present them with a cohesive plan of action and can tell them what we want them to do for us." A faint smile crept across his face. "Furthermore, this would provide Madam Vice President with an opportunity to assert her authority within the Senate."

Gail nodded, "Yes, that's it exactly. Besides, the whole thing may be necessary anyway. The Gardeners really may wait for us to have a plan. At least, I hope they do. If we're going to fight this damned war for them, then I want us to be in the driver's seat, planning what we fight it with."

John interjected, emphasizing Gail's pivotal role. "And since Gail led the project to get Phoenix launched originally, making her the face of the new project will give it the visibility it needs and capitalize on her popularity. It will also demonstrate to everyone that we are serious about getting it done."

Alexander smiled, "And she can kick the Senate around while she's at it."

Preston offered a heartfelt sentiment, emphasizing the delicate state of affairs surrounding Livia. "You all know how recent events have….

It's been difficult for Livia. I'll be honest. She is crushed. Humiliated. She's still talking about resigning."

Gail sat up, her posture steely, and resolutely shook her head, saying, "I'll talk to her. We need her now more than ever. She'll just have to put her big girl pants on and get over it. I need her to be my stick in the Senate. Other than Sybil, she'll be the only one who knows what is really going on. I can't believe I'm saying this, but I'm beginning to regret the decision to hold that election in the first place."

Gail lingered after Alexander and Preston left, a dark, contemplative shadow playing across her features.

John sighed, his voice tinged with concern. "What's wrong?"

She hesitated, her thoughts briefly lost in a maelstrom. "No secrets," she finally murmured.

John's gaze sharpened, eyes narrowing. "Meaning?"

Drawing a deep breath, Gail pivoted to squarely face him. "After Awakening Day," she began with a heavy emphasis, "that's what you said. That we should have no secrets from the people. At the time, I thought you were perhaps overly idealistic…. Naïve even." A fleeting, teasing smile danced on her lips. "Among other things."

John leaned back, the weight of his thoughts pushing him deeper into his seat. "I know," he admitted, weary lines marking his forehead. "All of this. The responsibility. It has been gnawing at me." He shook his head. "Gail, is this what happens? How it happens, I mean? Bit by bit? One tiny white lie leads to another and another until they aren't so white or tiny anymore?"

She leaned across the space, her fingers brushing against his. "The game is never as simple as it looks from the bleachers, John."

His expression was twisted and pained. "Is that what this is? A game? Is that how we lose our way?"

A heavy quiet draped between them as both were lost in thought. Eventually, Gail broke the silence, her gaze piercing yet tender. "Promise me something."

He gazed into her eyes before answering softly. "Anything."

She lowered her voice to nearly a whisper. "Promise me that we will tell each other when it starts to become easy. When the deceptions are not something to protect the people, but to serve selfish interests."

After the briefest pause, John nodded solemnly. "Only if you promise to whack me upside the head if I do forget."

Her gaze drifted away, shimmering with unshed tears. "I cannot imagine you forgetting. Not in a million years." She swallowed, her voice catching, "It's me, John. Before all this…. Before you…. Before Awakening Day, I was ambitious, like you have no idea. The things I had to do…. The things I did to get around the roadblocks people put in front of me. John, as a pilot, I was surrounded by naked ambition. Practically bathed in it. I guess it's human nature when you put a bunch of hopped-up, highly competitive people in the same space. What scares me, John, is what will happen in the future. Right now, we're all, well, most of us anyway, focused on the threat in front of us and our very survival. What happens though in the years ahead as we grow… as we spread out not just inside New Texas, but across *worlds* John. People will build small empires and then big ones. If we survive all of this…. John, the decisions and example that you and I set now…. Everything we do is going to be second-guessed and held up as an example, good or bad, right or wrong, for the next millennium. We don't simply have to get things right. We have to get it right for all humankind. For history… if we have one."

John's fingers found hers, a warm, comforting touch against her skin. Hovering his hand over her midsection, he murmured. "For the future."

She placed her hand on top of his as her eyes glistened. "For their future."

Eaters

● ● ● ● ● ● ● ● ● ● ● ● ● ● ● ● ●

DownSide: Radio Station 92.5 Studio

Danielle Richardson Anders sipped her iced tea and shook her head ruefully before keying the microphone. Harrold had the day off and was caring for Devin, Terry, and the baby girls. Her voice was caustic as she opened her show. "Hello, people of Fort Brazos and New London. This is Danielle Richardson on FM 92.5 and Radio Free Fort Brazos, beaming our signal across the known world and beyond. So, it's only been two weeks since that traitorous bastard admiral removed himself and his co-conspirator wife from the gene pool, and their evil spawn son was dumped on a deserted island on the far side of the world to consider his sins and hopefully die a painfully slow death. Anyway, so, like I was saying, it's only been two weeks, and now a little bird tells me that the navy is holding secret meetings to discuss war plans with our rescuers turned slave masters, the Gardeners. I ask you, my listeners, friends, and neighbors, haven't we had enough secrets already? I mean, the smoke has barely stopped smoldering in the ruins of that apartment tower topside. You'd think that they, especially after their second in command, of all people, was outed as a spy and worse, that they'd think twice about having big super secret meetings like this!"

DownSide: Radio Station 92.5 Studio

Two Days Later

Danielle smiled as Senator Sybil Blanchard sat across from her in the studio. "Senator Blanchard, it's so good to see you again. I don't think we've had a chance to talk since before the election. How are you, Wayne, your three darling girls, and those precocious baby boys, Dillan, Ethan, and Fallon?"

Sybil smiled warmly in return. She remembered how frightened and uncomfortable she'd been in front of the microphone the first time. Now? It felt natural, and a small part of her lamented her lost innocence. "Thank you, Danielle, it's nice to be here. My wonderful husband Wayne is somehow coping with all six right now. He's turned out to be an amazing dad. And how about you? Your new twins are just a little younger than my babies. How is Commandant of the Midshipmen Anders holding up under the onslaught?"

Danielle laughed lightly, "I confess I was worried at first. I wasn't sure if Harrold's experience yelling at young servicemen and women would translate into being a caring and attentive father, but he's more than proven himself. My only worry is whether they'll all march before they learn to run."

Sybil chuckled, her eyes matching her tone, "If our men can learn to be good fathers, perhaps there is hope for humanity after all."

Danielle retorted, "Even when others are resorting to secret meetings, even after everything that has happened? You've been quoted as opposing these meetings and have called for full disclosure."

Sybil leaned into the microphone and answered, her voice projecting sincerity and concern, "Yes, that's true, Danielle. When I first heard about these meetings, I made some calls and asked my fellow Senators if any of them were aware of them. After that, I called the Vice President and expressed my concerns. She promised to get to the bottom of it, and we all know how determined that woman can be. I'm confident that she will straighten things out. I just hope this is all much ado about nothing and the reports are overblown."

DownSide: Riverside

Riverbend Mall: Capital Building Press Briefing Room

Three Days Later

The Capital Building Press Briefing Room was one of the newer areas of the former Macy's department store renovated to serve a new purpose. To the chagrin of those who realized it, the space had formerly been the department store section reserved for women's lingerie. The joke was that the store that used to sell racy undergarments worn in secret was now a space where government secrets would be exposed. Or, at least, where they were supposed to be revealed.

Gail Finley stepped up to the podium. She was very self-conscious of the noticeable growing bulge in her midsection. She'd prided herself in maintaining her personal fitness, often on a grueling schedule, even after she'd been elected. To now be… well… getting soft there was intensely disturbing. At the same time, a part of her she'd never known existed reveled in it, chiding herself for not fully and enthusiastically embracing…. Motherhood. And here she was, on camera for all to see. No longer the lean, athletic Air Force pilot. Not the resentful former Air Force pilot railroaded into being Vice President. No. Now she was Mrs. John…..Austin. Wife. Pregnant wife…. Mother-to-be. And her feet hurt. Yet another new sensation she was learning to adapt to.

She set her face into a hardened expression and narrowed her eyes as she began, "Good afternoon. It has come to my attention, and to that of the President, that closed-door meetings have been ongoing TopSide, at the New Pentagon, regarding prospective cooperation with the Gardeners concerning future naval warship designs and strategies. The President directed me to investigate the matter. It turns out that such meetings were indeed taking place. However, they were not organized by senior command officials. They were informally organized by some of the same people who previously met to discuss potential future war plans and the kinds of infrastructure and supply chain demands we as a people would face in the future. I am satisfied that nothing illicit or underhanded was going on. In fact, those who organized the meetings are to be commended for their forward thinking and initiative."

She paused, then nodded to herself. "That said, the President and I have agreed that it is time to elevate these meetings to a more formal status and structure. We believe that the Gardeners are likely waiting for us, as a people, to, frankly, get our collective shi… Our act together and decide how we plan to move forward and prosecute this war with the Accipiters and what we need from the Gardeners to make it happen. However, I will caution everyone to remember that the number of surviving human beings is, tragically, tiny. We simply don't have the numbers of trained service women and men with the requisite skills and scientific knowledge to staff and operate even a small fleet of starships.

We need to be smart. We need to plan for what is doable now, and in the short term, while the next generation trains…."

She stiffened and blushed as she placed a hand on her stomach, "And is born. God help us all if this war is still going on when our children become of age." She swallowed, "We are a species that learned the art of war through thousands of years of conflict. As recent events have shown, though, we have all seen that there are still those among us who represent the bottom of the human potential." She paused, and her voice hardened to steel. "We must… all of us… do better."

Her lower lip quivered, "I implore each and every one of you, young and old, woman, man, or child. Be better. Put humanity's childhood behind us. Use what we learned fighting and murdering each other to bring the goddamned Accipiters to their knees and end this war. Then, somehow, some way, find a way for us to live together in peace. Wardogs and Stalkers notwithstanding, this world we have been given is a paradise. I challenge you all to keep it that way."

She swallowed and stood up straighter, "Enough of that. In the meantime, the President reminded me that I had taken charge of the original starship development project. He has asked me to likewise take charge of this new effort. To that end, I have called upon the Senate, and they have nominated two of their number to represent the people's interest and report back to the Senate on the project's findings. I now ask Senator Livia Milner and Senator Sybil Blanchard to join me at the podium…."

TopSide: New Pentagon

Conf Room A47

Three Days Later

The superbly equipped conference chamber was deep and wide, its expanse littered with a profusion of modern amenities. A colossal flat screen adorned one of the walls, commanding attention with its imposing presence. Glass whiteboards graced the remaining surfaces, ready to capture the often incomprehensible scrawlings of the assembled minds. At the heart of the room rested a fat oval conference table, its girth accommodating up to thirty individuals. It was festooned with an array of laptops, monitors, and vessels holding the lifeblood of such gatherings: water, coffee, and the other typical paraphernalia and detritus of large staff meetings.

Ever since the revelation of Johansson's traitorous actions…
and the second bombing since Awakening Day, a pall of heightened
vigilance had draped itself over the corridors of the New Pentagon.
Security had ascended to unprecedented levels. The rigorous inspection
of each and every chamber, even to the extent of deploying dogs, had
become the norm. Additional measures and checkpoints had been
established throughout the vast, labyrinthine complex.

So it was that in the wake of the Johansson scandal, the now highly
publicized meeting now met.

After fifteen minutes of introductions and a brief speech by Gail,
she announced, "The Chair is now pleased to introduce Dr. Hyun Park,
Ph.D., who, before Awakening Day, was Vice President of Logistics
at the world's largest shipyard at the Busan Naval Base in Nam-Gu,
Busan, South Korea. His company was a Korean shipbuilding and
offshore engineering company. While many of our Naval officers and
civilians have extensive experience commissioning and operating naval
vessels, Dr. Park is the most experienced person alive with hands-
on experience in the actual construction of large ships. Dr. Park was
previously asked to participate as a subject matter expert in strategy
meetings and discussions held in the past. With that in mind, I have
asked him to kick off this meeting by sharing his thoughts in light of
recent events. Dr. Park?"

Wearing a simple grey business suit and conservative tie, he was
conspicuously different from the uniformed military officers crowding
the room. Living with his host family, DownSide, his English had
markedly improved. Working with the study groups in recent months
had polished it more. He took a deep breath, calmed himself, and
glanced at his notes before beginning. "Thank you, Madam Vice
President. I would first like to draw your attention to the schematics on
the screen."

On the large wallscreen, a 3D rendering of a spacecraft with a
distinctly alien design slowly rotated into view. As it spun, various features
and components of the ship were highlighted with callouts. Once the
rotation concluded, the image transformed into an 'exploded view,'
revealing a cutaway of the interior. This exposed different internal parts,
each separately rotating and accompanied by their respective descriptive
callouts.

"This vessel is a warship utilized by a species known to Phoenix and
the now-extinct Builders as the Masters. Personally, I'm weary of using
that term. I propose we refer to them as the Hand Eaters, named for their
history of uplifting the Builders, enslaving them, and their distasteful

practice of consuming the Builders' motive hands as a delicacy. Let's just call them the Eaters for simplicity. This warship is equipped with a formidable weapon, a design that was transmitted to Ari'Nell for trial purposes. The status of these tests or their outcomes remains unknown, but what we do understand is the intended power of this weapon...."

• 105 •

practice of consuming the Builders' motive hands as a delicacy. Let's just call them the Eaters for simplicity. This warship is equipped with a formidable weapon, a design that was transmitted to Ari'Nell for trial purposes. The status of these tests or their outcomes remains unknown, but what we do understand is the intended power of this weapon...."

Mind Leaf

● ● ● ● ● ● ● ● ● ● ● ● ● ● ● ● ●

DownSide
Surgeon General Gwyneth Elliott Duncan's Office

More than two months had passed since Mei Zifeng, a Botany post-graduate student, had made herself infamous by allowing her late-night hunger and longing for some comfort food from her home in China to overcome her better judgment. After all, it was just Bing Cao, or "ice plant," and it hadn't affected either the mice or the pig she'd fed it to. The Bing Cao was just one of the thousands of plants she'd been busy cataloging from the Keeper Ship "garden." A garden that had turned out to be a highly complex self-contained ecosystem containing many thousands of plants and, so far as anyone yet knew, harmless biota.

It was just harmless Bing Cao, and there was no food in the break room refrigerator that didn't belong to someone else.

It was just Bing Cao; she hadn't had any since leaving China.

How could she or anyone else have known that the Accipiters programmed different plants in the garden to contain both knowledge and behaviors the person consuming it would be compelled to perform?

Mei had been discovered hours later wandering the botany lab… naked… speaking in Accipiter… and entirely out of her mind. Worse, if that were even possible, clothing of any kind caused an immediate allergic reaction and violent burning sensation on her skin. They'd had to lock her up in a padded room for weeks. Worse than that? Every surviving human being in the universe knew about it.

Even now, clothing was brutally uncomfortable and chafed on her skin, despite every lotion, talc, and fabric softener (what little remained in the world) she tried. With assistance from her doctor, they'd found a few things that were… barely… tolerable to wear. Today, it was a loose-fitting knitted silk blouse, prima cotton skirt, combed cotton socks, and loose cotton shoes. Sitting for any length of time only pressed fabrics into her skin more. Needless to say, sleep had been excruciating until she'd begged and bartered for satin sheets, which helped. Some. Showers and baths were her only true respite. She sometimes thought she might spend entire days in the bath, at least, until the hot water inevitably turned cold.

As her own presence of mind slowly reasserted itself, she started thinking about the six women "caretakers" of the uplifted hominid Keeper. What had they gone through, and how much worse must it have been for them than it was for her?

Before Awakening Day, she'd been a focused, dedicated student. She kept to herself and thought only about finishing her degree. After Awakening Day, things became… complicated. The Gardeners altered everyone, curing diseases and extending lifespans. The price? Nonexistent birth control. Sex = Pregnancy. Period. Oh, and don't forget increased libidos and worse. Most female students had gotten pregnant and married shortly thereafter. Though certainly not all, many ended or significantly postponed their academic careers. Mei was by no means immune to the changes. It was what drove her to isolate herself and tend to work in the lab many hours after everyone else had left. She'd worked eighteen hours straight when she had succumbed to hunger and devoured the Bing Cao.

Her mind kept returning to the Keeper women and the suffering they must have endured. And so now, Mei found herself pacing back and forth in her doctor's waiting room. Well, it wasn't really a waiting room. Gwyneth Elliot was now Surgeon General of… mankind. Her office was in what used to be the Reserve Base and was now Fort Underwood's hospital. The area outside of Gwyneth's office included a secretary's desk, lounge, and two conference rooms.

Mei brushed her long black hair back. It was down to her waist now. She'd thought about cutting it but couldn't overcome the pang of guilt she felt as she thought of how her mother would have reacted. A mother who was now long dead in the ashes of Beijing. She sniffed as she pushed the familiar pain aside.

The elevator's chime resounded loudly, startling Mei, as Gwyneth burst into the room, her entourage of marine security at her side. What once consisted solely of the imposing Scotsman Sorley Pòl Murdoch had now expanded to include the burly Australian infantryman Aiden Johnson.

Standing at five feet four inches, Gwyneth surpassed Mei by a mere two inches. Yet, her presence loomed larger than her stature. Gwyneth, a former Olympic biathlon silver medalist, had not let motherhood quell her vivacity. Despite birthing a daughter and twin boys since Awakening Day, she exuded a predatory strength and vitality that compelled Mei to resist the urge to flinch.

With determined strides, Gwyneth advanced into the room. Her mere presence demanded attention. Mei steeled herself, refusing to be intimidated by the commanding force before her.

Gwyneth's face lit up, and she exclaimed, "Mei! It's wonderful to see you! You didn't have an appointment, did you? Sorley? Did she have an appointment that I forgot?"

His Scotts accent heavy, Sorley replied, "No, Ma'am."

Gwyneth and her detail quickly surrounded Mei, but Gwyneth remembered not to try to hug the shy, delicate wisp of a woman. Mei's presence was not simply demure and reserved. For all the trauma the poor woman had gone through, she seemed to shrink away from the world like a delicate flower that might wilt at the gentlest touch.

When Mei tensed up and didn't answer, Gwyneth measured the expression on her face, nodded to herself, and gestured to her office door. "Come, dear. Tell me what's on your mind." It wasn't the first unscheduled visit by Mei.

"Sorley, Aiden, hold my calls."

She gently guided Mei into her office without touching her. Mei didn't sit but paused and began pacing back and forth. It was a familiar pattern. Gwyneth patiently waited, leaning back against the edge of her desk.

Eventually, Mei spoke, not looking at Gwyneth but instead standing and staring out of the tall glass window, looking out onto the base. Her voice was firm with conviction. "I need to see them. The Keeper… women. I need to see them. Talk to them."

Gwyneth answered carefully in measured tones, "Mei… they don't speak English or Chinese. We've managed to help them as much as possible, but…."

Mei whirled around and advanced two steps before halting, catching herself, "That's just it. I understand what they are going through. No one else could!" She pleaded, "If anyone can reach them, it's me!"

"Mei, what you are suggesting is very noble. Very thoughtful, and it has occurred to me that it might be a good idea at some point, but you need to know that those women aren't… Mei, they can be dangerous."

Mei firmed her shoulders and repeated, "Please… I know I can reach them. I…."

Gwyneth sighed, "I know you are looking for answers, Mei. Some way to make sense of what happened to you. Look…. Have you considered going back to campus? Doctor Becker even offered to set up a private lab for you, someplace you could…."

This time, Mei did flinch. She snapped back, "No! I can't go back there. Everyone knows… everyone saw."

Gwyneth softened her voice, "Mei, dear, no one blames you. No one is going to…."

Mei exclaimed, "Don't you get it? I don't want their pity!" She swallowed as tears began to stream down her face. She turned back to the window and silently sobbed.

Gwyneth waited a few minutes, then cautiously and deliberately, making sure not to be too quiet and alarm her, approached Mei and knelt down in front of her. "Mei, I can only imagine what you went through. You know, if I'd been you… I can see myself doing the same thing. The plants had been tested. No one imagined anything like that was possible. I don't blame you. No one who is worth a damn does. Look. I'm your doctor. Maybe… someday, I can be your friend. I know that you never really made many friends here. You were determined to just get in, get your degree, and get out. I get it. And believe me, I understand the other pressures that all of us are under. Especially us women. Maybe even the men, many of whom are simply terrified of getting a girl pregnant. I'm lucky. I've got a husband that I love and who adores me, and I have lots of friends here. Friends who helped cushion the pain from Awakening Day and all that we lost. All that all of us lost. You, by no fault of your own, survived. You are here, and you were just trying to mind your own business, and then this horrible thing happened to you, and…."

Mei whispered through her tears…. "It is… it is not horrible. The withdrawal. That was horrible. But the experience itself and what I remember of it…." Her face almost glowed as she said, "It was…. Transcendent."

Gwyneth's eyes widened in surprise. "You are starting to remember things."

Mei turned away and paced to the other side of the room, paused, and trudged back again while Gwyneth waited.

"Just… a sense of purpose. Of peace…. I… *understood.*"

Gwyneth suggested, "Similar things have been reported by people ingesting psychedelic drugs… perhaps the Accipiters leverage that sort of effect. Though I must say, dear, that you did not seem… happy…. when we found you."

Mei shook herself, "I know! Its… It was wrong. I understand it now. What I ate, the Bing Cao, it wasn't meant to be… first. You're supposed to… you're supposed to eat other ones first. Things to prepare you. My system was in shock. It wasn't until much later that I understood…."

Gwyneth approached her slowly, "Mei… you told us you didn't remember anything. That when it wore off, that it was all gone. Everything."

Mei hesitated before lurching into Gwyneth's arms, sobbing. "I was afraid! I was afraid you would lock me up and study me!"

Gwyneth settled to the carpeted floor, holding Mei in her arms like a child, stroking her hair. "Mei, dear, *what exactly do you remember?*"

Mei cried for a while longer before looking up at Gwyneth, her eyes pleading. "Everything. I remember… *everything*. Those women… they were created for the purpose of serving the Keeper. They were grown like a crop and indoctrinated. Programmed. At first, I thought that they had been… dosed… since before puberty, but that's not true. They never went through puberty. They were created as fully adult beings and implanted with the knowledge they need, and they know their purpose. It is everything they are. Despite this, after my… experience… I am the only person who can understand them. Who might be able to reach them, and I am afraid that when people discover that the women did not grow up naturally, that they were created, they will be treated differently. Like they are not real people, but they are!"

Mei slumped down in exhaustion.

Gwyneth's own eyes teared up. "That's… that's incredible. Are you certain? You are sure this is not a translation problem or cultural misunderstanding?"

Mei closed her eyes and sniffed, her normally perfect English slipping for a moment as she whispered. "No. Iss more dan dat. I remember more now. Things dat did not make sense before. The Accipiters… it is worse dan you know."

"Oh, sweet child. You've kept yourself alone for far too long. That's it. We're going to get you cleaned up, and then you're coming home with me until we can get this sorted out."

Mei struggled for a moment, but not vigorously. She swallowed and shook her head, refocusing her diction. "I am a freak. Maybe you should lock me up."

Gwyneth laughed softly, "And do what? Why? Because now you *know* things? We only kept you in that room after we found you because we were afraid you would hurt yourself!"

Mei grew quiet. "You should… run tests… take my blood. Do brain scans…. Check my DNA… make sure nothing else… changes." She paused, then her voice broke as she added, "… my nightmares. I dream I become like them… or worse."

Gwyneth hugged Mei close to her. "Oh, Mei. I truly cannot imagine what you have gone through. Of course, you're worried. You're a brilliant young woman…. And you are very brave to admit it now."

Gwyneth hesitated, then added, "Look. We talked to the Keeper, that gentle misogynist little bastard. He said that after the plants wear off, that the compulsions will be gone. They only affect your mind, not the rest of your body, and the plants won't grow anywhere outside of the garden. They're not contagious, and the plants only affect women. He said that we needed to wean you off them slowly, or it might kill you. He may have saved your life."

Mei stiffened, "What?"

"I was going to tell you all about it when you were feeling better. So, how about we both wipe our tears and get out of here, get something to eat, and talk? I think it's time you had a friend. Also, I'm going to introduce you to Doctor Talib. You've heard of him, I'm sure. He's turned into quite a sweet man. I'm sure you two will get along."

Three weeks later

Despite over two years of piecing together the Accipiter language, Leo Talib's meetings with Mei had already given him new insights. Mei, whose parents had been diplomats, had already been multilingual, speaking different Chinese, French, German, and English dialects. Her implanted variant of the Accipiter language was now as 'native' to her as Mandarin, and it wasn't just language. Knowledge of the language necessitated other things – of the context and culture from which the language flowed. Leo had already offered her a permanent position as an Accipiter language expert and scholar. He'd quietly stressed to her that it was possible that she might play a crucial role in mankind's future.

It was a thought that absolutely terrified her.

He'd been kind, and his enthusiasm was infectious. Mei had met his stepdaughter Nicole, who'd latched onto Mei like a long-lost sister. General Chilton, though, while polite enough, had been very intimidating. Mei found it hard to imagine what had drawn Leo and the General together in the first place. But then, everything that had happened since Awakening Day was crazy.

Eventually, she found herself on the enormous elevator riding "up" to New London. She'd never been there. She wasn't alone, of course. Leo, Gwyneth, and two dozen other scientists and doctors accompanied her, along with the now ubiquitous marine security detail guards.

In fact, that was the single most challenging thing to get used to. Mei accepted Leo's offer, not comprehending the consequences. Mei Zifeng was now… important. And that meant that she now had two of her own marines to watch over her. She'd vehemently refused, of course, to no avail. It was a done deal. And now, Captain Amelia "Mia" Thompson, all five foot ten inches of her, towered over Mei on one side, and Sergeant Maya Nguyen, at five foot six, was still four inches taller.

Mia had joined the Marine Corps straight out of high school. After excelling in various combat training programs, she'd slowly risen through the ranks and eventually made captain. After the bombing at city hall, Mia lobbied hard to transition to the Marine Security program, even offering to throw away her rank entirely. She had no interest in a husband, and she refused to stand on the sidelines when the future and survival of humanity were at stake.

Maya, born of Vietnamese immigrants, had almost accidentally found her way into the military but soon discovered she had exceptional natural marksmanship skills and, in no small part, due to her hardworking parents' tremendous discipline.

Mia and Maya immediately took to Mei, delighting in the alliteration of their names and Mei's story. After meeting her, they understood her importance and the small woman's fragility. They did their level best to be gentle with her. Mei's resentment slowly ebbed as Mia and Maya ensured she was always where she needed to be, in plenty of time, and with the least amount of 'fuss.'

As the delegation mounted the steps to the New Pentagon, Mei swallowed hard and hesitated, her heart pounding in her chest. Mia leaned down and quietly whispered in her ear, "You can do this, Mei. I know you can. You're going to be okay."

Mei swallowed and looked at Mei and then to Maya, who smiled encouragingly. For the first time in her life, Mei, an only child, wondered if this was what it was like to have sisters. Older… protective sisters. She sucked in a breath and continued up the steps as Gwyneth and Leo talked animatedly behind her.

✪ ✪ ✪

The woman in the padded cell before her was olive-skinned, with a tangle of long dark hair that wrapped around her body well below her waist. She was naked and curled into a fetal position.

Mei quietly sat in front of her on the cushioned floor. And waited.

The woman slowly opened her eyes, then closed them and turned away, muttering almost inaudibly in Accipiter.

Mei was startled by what the woman said. Then she said aloud. "Turn off the cameras…. Mia, please make them turn off the cameras."

The glass was mirrored, but Mei turned and looked, waiting.

Mia and Maya glared at the gathered dignitaries on the other side of the glass and promptly ordered everyone to leave the room while they turned off the cameras themselves.

Mci had privately discussed this possibility with them in advance. Maya keyed the microphone, "It's done, Ma'am. The room is clear, and the cameras are off."

Mei stood and slowly took off her clothes, the silk and soft cotton sighing as they drifted to the floor. After a moment's hesitation, she sat back down.

The woman tensed, then turned her head back and opened her eyes. The pain, anguish, and torment in them brought Mei to tears.

The woman remained curled up as she watched Mei, who began to speak in Accipiter. Slowly, haltingly, Mei told her story. Where and when she was born. How she grew up. What her life was like. She talked for hours. And then, as she finally worked up the courage, about how she'd eaten the Bing Cao. And how she now wanted to help the woman. All the Keeper women. That no matter what happened, she would not allow any harm to come to them. She talked and talked until her voice grew horse and dry.

Throughout all of it, the woman remained unmoving, still curled up into a ball. Watching Mei through slitted eyes.

✪ ✪ ✪

Mei gasped as she awoke. The woman was beside her, braiding Mei's long, lustrous black hair. Mei flinched and pulled away, then stopped herself and waited. Then, Mei swallowed and tried to speak but found her throat was too dry.

The woman rose and padded over to get a drink from the sink at the side of the room. She looked at Mei and smiled. She filled a small paper cup of water and offered it to Mei.

Mei hesitated, then took the cup and drank slowly, measuring the other woman's eyes.

She looks like she can't be over seventeen or eighteen, but who knows? Her body might only be three or four years old.

Mei spoke in Accipiter,

MY NAME IS MEI. WHAT IS YOUR NAME?

The woman answered,

RIIME TALOU' KENI'V'VANI, MY NAME IS RIIME TALOU' KENI'V'VANI .

✪ ✪ ✪

New Pentagon Conference Room L27

Mia led Mei to the conference room with Maya trailing behind. When the door opened, Mei froze. The room was packed. On the wallscreen, the President and Vice President were watching remotely from DownSide. Admiral Milner and Secretary Marcus sat to Gwyneth's right. Mia murmured into Mei's ear. "You've got this, girl. You'll have them eating out of your hand."

Mei gave Mia a sideways glance of incredulity, then shuffled into the room. She looked for a chair on the side somewhere, but Leo and Gwyneth instead ushered her to the head of the table.

Gwyneth began, "Mr. President, Madam Vice President, ladies and gentlemen, I am privileged to introduce you to Mei Zifeng. All of you know her incredible story. This courageous young woman has now made a stunning breakthrough. She has not only learned a version, at least, of the Accipiter language, but she now speaks it as a native. Moreover, she's been able to talk to the women… caretakers… of the uplifted hominid known as the Keeper. More than that, they are now talking to her. She is here today to tell you what she has learned and answer your questions. Mei?"

Mei blushed and nodded, "Thank you, Gw.. I mean, General. As with most in service to the Accipiters, these women were not just bred; they were grown. Crafted. Created to serve their purpose. Their entire identity is encompassed by their designed purpose in life. The six women from the keeper ship don't even know how old they are. They've been eating from the Keeper Garden for as long as they can remember. They are, for lack of a better term, like nurse plants, designed to provide care and protection for more important ones, allowing them to grow and thrive."

Gail asked from the screen, "Thank you, Mei. I know this has been a terribly trying experience for you. You say these women were bred or created for this purpose, and most on Earth are that way. I'm confused. I thought that most of the people on Earth were the remaining survivors who had been, for lack of a better way to put it, altered to serve the Accipiters?"

Mei stiffened and swallowed. Her eyes teared up, and she glanced at Gwyneth for encouragement.

Gwyneth nodded and smiled sadly. Her own eyes glistened.

Mei swallowed again, "Madam Vice President…. That is only partly true. You see… these plants… they are part of the Accipiter's basic technology. To encode the knowledge into the plants, well, it has to come from somewhere in the first place. It comes from people. The knowledge is extracted from a person's brain, and that code can then be replicated in the plants."

Even on the video screen, it was obvious to see Gail's face blanch at a growing realization.

"The knowledge is extracted by harvesting the brain using something that resembles mycelium. Once absorbed, the entirety or only a desired portion of it can then be genetically encoded. This is the basis for the Accipiters' technology to transfer themselves into newly grown bodies as they age. What I'm leading to is that the bodies of all of the humans on Earth were not altered. They were destroyed. Their minds were absorbed, new bodies were grown with desired traits, and their minds, or some version, were restored to the new bodies."

Gwyneth added, "What Mei is saying is that every single so-called human being on Earth, including the engineer we have locked up, is not a survivor. They're all, well, for lack of a better term, pod people. Grown to serve roles and purposes for the Accipiters."

A dreadful silence fell over the room.

John Austin broke it when he added, "Then it really is true. We really are the last surviving humans. There is no one left on Earth we can save."

Mei shook her head and exclaimed, "No! These women, for example, the Keeper women. They're not monsters! They laugh and love and cry just like you or I. The Accipiters may have created them to serve a purpose, but that doesn't mean they are less worthy of… life. And freedom, than any of us."

Preston asked, "Miss Zifeng, I respect your… affinity… towards these women. However, it is not wrong for us to worry about their loyalties. Wouldn't they naturally want to work against the interests and, honestly, the survival of the rest of us?"

Mei bristled, "Admiral, the only people who need to worry about what these women might do would be anyone who intends harm to the Keeper. THAT is their purpose in life. To care for and to protect him. They *love* him. They would die for him."

Alexander asked, "What are you suggesting, then?"

Mei glanced at Gwyneth, then at Alexander. "Mister Secretary, I am proposing that we've got hundreds of beautiful islands out there. Islands where they can harm no one. I'm suggesting that we set the Keeper and his women free. Make sure it is safe there and give them an island. They'll be happy and harmless there."

Gail answered promptly, "I have no problem with that, so long as, as you say, we ensure the island is safe for them. Honestly, it bothers the hell out of me keeping them locked up. I would prefer to keep tabs on them and possibly station some individuals there to act as ambassadors, so to speak."

Mei's eyes widened, and an inexplicable surge of happiness and joy filled her, though she couldn't quite comprehend the reason behind it.

John asked in a gentle tone, "Miss Zifeng. Mei, I have to ask…. This experience you had. As Gail said earlier, I know it was traumatic for you. That said, somehow, you came out of it with a wealth of knowledge. How would you feel about the idea of repeating the process? If not yourself, then others? Volunteers. I cannot help but wonder what valuable intelligence and insight we might learn about our enemy?"

Mei's head shook slowly, her gaze fixed upon the conference table as she wrestled with her thoughts. She suddenly felt exhausted. The events of the past several weeks were finally catching up with her. Taking a deep breath, she finally mustered the strength to meet the president's eyes, her voice laced with trepidation and carrying more than her normal trace of a Chinese accent. "Mister President, I understan' completely," she began, "and I discuss the plants with the women an' the Keeper himself at length. What you need to un'erstan' is that I am," she swallowed, "I am ver'…"

She focused harder, enunciating more carefully, "Very lucky. The Keeper women were created special… specifically for their role. Even so, some…. Subjects… do not survive the process. Not a lot, but enough. They could not tell me numbers, but after talkin' with them, my best guess is that one in twenty of the subjects died. I no… I do not know why I did not die. Maybe I almost did. I certainly felt like death for a long time, and not just from withdrawal. Anyone who were to volunteer, and you know it is *only* women who it will work with, is gambling her life and, honestly, probably her sanity. The Accipiters… they no care. They just grow another body an' try again. Mr. President, I hope…. And you need to pray…. we never get that desperate."

Solo

Fort Underwood Flight Line

John and Gail Austin stood side by side, hands interlocked, on the Fort Underwood flight line. Their gazes were fixed on Matti Austin as she prepared for her first solo flight. She was already a proficient pilot, having flown numerous hours with other instructors and with Gail on many occasions. But today was different. Today was Matti's 10th birthday. Her present? Her first solo flight. John and Gail masked their inner fears and anxiety, trying their best to project confidence and support for Matti's big day.

Like all the other children of New Texas, Matti was unnaturally advanced, largely thanks to the Gardener's enhancements to human biology. In the more than two years since Awakening Day, Matti had experienced a remarkable growth spurt, growing ten inches and gaining nearly fifty pounds. She was still lean and willowy. Her golden blond hair was neatly braided down her back. Dressed in a meticulously tailored flight suit and sporting Aviator Ray-Bans, her expression was calm, confident, and determined. Matti slowly, deliberately, and professionally marked her clipboard checklist as she meticulously inspected the aircraft, examining the ailerons, flaps, rudder, antennae, fuel tanks, and all other critical components.

To outsiders, she appeared no different from any other pilot conducting pre-flight procedures. But to John and Gail, she was still John's ten-year-old daughter and Gail's newly adopted, incredibly precious stepdaughter.

The morning air was crisp, and the sky was clear. The sun tube was still in its early morning brightening phase as its warm glow illuminated the surroundings. On the other side of the world, behind it, a small hurricane was in the process of breaking up. The Cessna 172 Skyhawk that Matti inspected was equipped with an emergency ballistic parachute recovery system, an added safety measure.

Matti, for her part, paid no attention to the two Blackhawk variant HH-60W Combat Rescue Helicopters waiting nearby to shadow her flight. It simply wouldn't do for the First Daughter not to have protection. Roxanna Darling, Matti's personal Marine Security Guard, waited anxiously on the lead CRH.

Gail suppressed a groan and put a hand on her two-month-pregnant stomach. Her frequent morning, afternoon, and evening 'morning sicknesses' had not subsided.

"Are you sure she'll be okay?" Gail whispered to John, her voice barely audible above the din of the ever-busy flightline.

John laughed nervously and pulled Gail close to him, hugging her. "You tell me. You've been the one training and mentoring her all these months. You wouldn't have given her the green light if you didn't believe in her."

Gail swallowed hard, shaking her head. "I know, and it's foolish of me. I didn't even *start* flying with my father until I was twelve. It was my ultimate dream, and I was determined to become a pilot... but... John, I was *twelve*. I may have been smart and thought I knew everything, but damn it, John... *I was twelve*. Matti is light-years ahead of where I was at her age... where any of us were at that age. I know what she's capable of... but still...."

John offered a reassuring squeeze to Gail's shoulder, "I know. It's good to see your motherhood instincts kicking in."

Gail punched him in the ribs. Hard.

John knew it was coming and managed to take it in stride without complaint.

✪ ✪ ✪

Standing together, they watched as Matti began her ascent, and soon, she was dotting across the sky and out of sight, followed at a discrete distance by the CRHs. John and Gail stared at the point in the sky where she had disappeared, feeling pride, fear, and hope for their daughter.

Taking a deep breath, John broke the silence. "You know, "I always wondered why you were in that F-18 that day. You were Air Force, and F-18s are Navy."

Gail blinked at the non sequitur question. "Well, it was chaos that morning. You remember this was just a reserve base, and it was in the middle of a command transition. Chuckles and I were the closest to the flight line who weren't still puking our guts out. Most of the other pilots had been at an Afterburner Blowout party as well and weren't in great shape to begin with. I was still qualified on Growlers and wanted to grab the opportunity to get more hours before I lost my qual."

Gail was silent for a while before picking up the conversation again, "Okay, my turn to distract one of us. Were you ever really thinking about running for Governor? I remember what you told Gloria about how she made it up... but did it ever really occur to you?"

John glanced at her sideways, a hint of surprise in his eyes, "Really? You wondered about *that?* The answer, emphatically, is no. It never crossed my mind before or even after she made it up. All I wanted was...." His voice trailed off, interrupted by a familiar pang of pain from the memory of Carolyn's death.

Gail's frown deepened as she observed the hurt etched on John's face, realizing the effect her words had. "I'm sorry. I know that kind of grief never really goes away. I'm glad that you loved her. It shows in every fiber of Matti's being."

She leaned her head against him. "I understand why she loved you. You're a good man, John. A good father. I hope I can be as good a mother...."

John lowered his gaze, gently turning Gail to face him, "No, now you listen to me," he insisted, "It is entirely possible for you to be just as fantastic a mother as you are a wife and a pilot, and just as superlative of a Vice President. I've already seen that with how closely you bonded with her and, how much you love Matti, and how much she loves and respects you. Besides, with the tsunami of babies and mommy-hood going on, all thanks to the Gardeners, you'll have lots of help and examples."

Gail groaned and clutched her stomach again. "I can't decide whether to dial up or down how much I hate the Gardeners," she confessed.

She looked down at her feet and then up into the sky, hoping to see Matti's plane. "I sometimes think about what would have been.... What my life would have been without their interference. But at the same time, I know I'd be dead without them. You'd be dead." She suddenly teared up. "M-Matti would be dead." She embraced John and hugged him tightly. "We didn't ask for what has happened to us... but I wouldn't change it. Now, I wouldn't want to change it. No matter what happens.... I can't... I can't lose you." She shook her head, "Fuck these hormones!"

She shook her head. "Changing the subject, I'm hearing some, honestly, scary things from Gwyneth about all the new babies since Awakening Day. John... They're not just too advanced. They're too calm. She's talked to Sybil, and they're in agreement and think that they may all be, well, like Sybil's children. Empathic. It's emerging more slowly than it did with Sybil's children, maybe because hers were, well, influenced by Sybil herself, even in the womb. John, it terrifies me. The new generation will be different. Gwyneth even coined a name for them, Homo Empathiens. You realize what this means? We truly are the last of our kind, well, sort of, not counting the things the Gardeners have already done to us. John...." She clutched her abdomen, "I'm... I'm not scared *of* them, I'm just...."

John hugged her and said, "I know. I've been hearing from other sources and wondered if this might be where things were going."

"Right, maybe from your friend Erica Silverton, Matti's former teacher?" Gail wanted to rib John about the woman he'd dated in high school, but her heart wasn't in it.

"Erica and others, yeah. It worries me, too, but I choose to believe that it will be a good thing. Maybe if it is harder for our children to lie to each other, we'll be a better people. I'm probably deluding myself, but honestly, I need to cling to some hope for the future of humanity.... That we even have a future at all. If we don't screw it up and leave them a legacy of nothing but death and war."

John held her tightly, comforting her as they grappled with the weighty decisions before them. After a few moments, he nodded resolutely to himself. "Okay, my turn for a distraction. Have you thought any more about what you want us to do now that we're married? Should we... resign? Set up a succession? And I don't give a good God Damn about what Boyer or Gorskov say. I'm talking about taking care of our *family*."

Gail's posture stiffened, a heavy sigh escaping from her lips. "John, can you live with yourself if you just *let* some jackass take over and...."

John shook his head with a bitter snort, "Anger the Gardeners? Screw up the War? Set us up for a million-year war?"

Her expression grave, Gail nodded. "Yeah. That. And, maybe, if we can get this Gardener traitor business behind us, maybe we can find a way to avoid your solution, no, I mean, and I really do mean this... *our* solution to the war."

John nodded slowly, drawing her closer once more. "That has been my... secret hope... ever since they brought us here. That... somehow... some way... we wouldn't have to go through with it."

Gail looked up, pointing towards the sky. "There she is, coming around for another circuit," she said, a broad smile spreading across her face. "I'm so proud of her."

Ki-Nam

● ● ● ● ● ● ● ● ● ● ● ● ● ● ● ● ●

DownSide: Eugene Morton Naval Academy

Ryon Ki-Nam found solace beneath the shade of a sprawling tree outside the College of Liberal and Fine Arts, one of the few areas not entirely overrun by the boisterous horde of Naval Academy cadets. None of the buildings on campus were particularly tall or imposing, although the grounds were lush and fragrant with the scent of countless beds of vibrant flowers and freshly trimmed grass.

For Ki-Nam, this environment stood in stark contrast to the abject poverty and relentless destitution that had plagued his upbringing in North Korea. From the earliest years of his life, he had been indoctrinated with fervent warnings about the debauched and nightmarish West, instilled with the belief that it was solely the unwavering adoration for the Great Leader, coupled with personal sacrifice and unyielding discipline, that would safeguard the chosen people of North Korea from their inevitable demise.

Then, he and his comrades had awoken in this idyllic and picturesque haven. Within hours, they were swiftly captured and imprisoned by the malevolent Americans. Months of unrelenting hardship ensued, marked by the brutal, iron-fisted discipline imposed by Colonel (Daechwa) P'aeng Jin-Hwan as he strove tirelessly to keep his force of nearly twenty-five hundred men primed for any chance to escape or mount a retaliatory assault against their American adversaries.

And then, one day, in an audacious move, Jin-Hwan issued a command that would forever alter Ki-Nam's life. He directed Ki-Nam to feign defection and infiltrate the ranks of the Americans as a spy. His mission was to meticulously observe the enemy, cataloging their vulnerabilities and identifying opportunities to strike.

In truth, it was an unimaginable dream fulfilled. A dream that had long eluded Ki-Nam's thoughts, tainted by the agony, strife, and the ironclad grip of self-restraint that had defined his existence. The notion of escaping the confines of the North Korean compound and truly defecting had flickered in his mind, but the weight of a lifetime's worth of hardships had rendered it an intangible fantasy.

Yet, as he found himself "escaping" the compound, an air of disbelief mingled with exhilaration. He had braced himself for endless months of grueling interrogations, but nothing could be worse than life under Jin-Hwan. To his astonishment, however, he was released after only a few hours of polite inquiries. A mere formality. Then, he was given a backpack containing basic supplies, a street map, and was directed toward a bus into town.

A lingering paranoia compelled him to believe he was being shadowed, yet despite his fervent efforts, he failed to detect any signs of secret police following him. It took weeks for him to gradually embrace the truth that no one truly cared about his actions or whereabouts. He was truly free, though he didn't know what to do with it.

Ki-Nam found himself increasingly drawn to the vibrant campus life at Bonham State University, immersing himself in the study of English and, unashamedly, reveling in the presence of real women, even if their appearances diverged from his expectations of traditional Korean beauty. The mere sight of any woman, regardless of her origin, held an astonishing allure. It was a rarity, for none of the North Koreans snatched away by the enigmatic Gardeners had been female. The relentless months of grueling drills, from dawn until dusk, and the ceaseless lectures emanating from Jin-Hwan's fraying copy of the Great Leader's tome had exacted a heavy toll on Ki-Nam and his comrades.

Sitting here, under a tree, with a sack lunch and watching the animated coeds walk by was… 천국 (cheonguk), or more simply… paradise.

Naturally, Ki-Nam had to find a means to sustain himself. While the charity of these people knew few bounds, there were still limits to their generosity, however vast it might be. Engaging in conversations with various students in his quest to grasp the English language, Ki-Nam encountered a starry-eyed young woman named Monica with curly blonde hair. She practically dragged him to meet her professor, fervently insisting that Ki-Nam be granted the opportunity to serve as a guest lecturer on the Korean language and culture. In the wake of so much lost to the ravages of the Accipiters, preserving as much of human language and culture as possible was not only an imperative, but doing so was a stick in the eye to the Accipiters.

And so it was that Ki-Nam received a tiny stipend to deliver lectures on the Korean language and culture twice a week. There were never more than a scattering of people in the lecture hall, and most were leftovers from the previous lecture, but he didn't mind. They recorded him "for the future." It was *something*.

In a fleeting glimmer of hope, Ki-Nam had allowed himself to imagine that Monica might take a genuine interest in *him*. However, as soon as it became apparent that Ki-Nam had been accepted in his newfound role, she smiled, planted a kiss on his cheek, and promptly embarked upon her next crusade.

He didn't really mind. This was the happiest and most at peace he had ever been in his life. When Jin-Hwan and the others were "relocated" to Morgan Island, Ki-Nam harbored no illusions about the outcome. Without the outward facade of the so-called American threat for Jin-Hwan to fixate upon, Ki-Nam knew all too well that the Colonel would unearth another source of torment. Whatever it might be, it would surely unleash hell upon his fellow men. He carried a burden of guilt for having escaped the clutches of madness, yet he would not trade this newfound serenity for anything.

He was lost in his thoughts when a voice suddenly pulled him out of his reverie.

"Lieutenant Ryon Ki-Nam."

Ki-Nam looked up to see a woman in a navy uniform approaching him with purposeful strides. She was tall and determined, with strawberry blonde hair pulled back in a ponytail. Her eyes were keen and alert. He recognized her, of course. Everyone knew who she was. Commander Ramona Henry of ILC Dagger. She'd been there at Morgan Island and dealt with the aftermath of Jin-Hwan's discovery and death and the subsequent overthrow of the thugs who had indeed created hell for the rest of the North Korean survivors. She'd also been involved in all the excitement a few weeks ago with the attack on the city by that alien monstrosity throwing kinetic projectiles from the other side of the world.

Ki-Nam blinked, his throat tightening with apprehension, wondering what the popular and now famous Commander wanted with him. *She looks like one of those Hollywood movie stars. Too pretty to be real.*

Awkwardly rising to his feet, he stuttered, his words stumbling forth, "Y-Yes? I am Ki-Nam."

At five foot ten inches, Ki-Nam was somewhat taller than most of his compatriots. The fact that this woman stood only a fraction shorter than him sent a disconcerting shiver down his spine. *No, that's not it.* Lots of girls in Fort Brazos were as tall as this woman. *No, it's something about the way she carries herself.*

Ramona extended her hand in greeting. Her broad smile revealed a perfect row of pearly whites. "I'm Ramona Henry. I need to talk to you about something very important."

Confusion etched across Ki-Nam's face as he met her gaze. He had no idea what she wanted to talk about, and a sudden wave of nervousness washed over him. Whatever she wanted could not be good and could only serve to disrupt his newfound happiness.

Ramona added, her tone laden with significance, "It's about the island and your fellow North Koreans."

His body tensed, and instinct propelled him a step back, almost causing him to stumble against the tree that stood steadfastly behind him. Ki-Nam vigorously shook his head, a rapid denial escaping his lips, "No! I won't go back to them. You can't force me. I've defected. I'm...."

Ramona suppressed a sigh, her expression softening as she attempted to allay Ki-Nam's apprehension. "Take a moment to relax, Ki-Nam. It's not like that. Not at all. I'm here because Commander Choe Pyong-Chol asked me to talk to you. Things have gotten complicated. He's asking for your help. He is asking you to become their, well, their ambassador. Someone to speak on their behalf and represent your people's interests here in Fort Brazos."

Ki-Nam's eyes widened in surprise, his voice barely above a whisper. "Wha… What?"

Ramona smiled again, trying her best to exude patience and kindness. "Ki-Nam, your Colonel Jin-Hwan often spoke highly of you. Your name is spoken of with respect by the other North Koreans. You're already here, already making a name for yourself in this community."

"Did you think that no one was paying attention to you? It became pretty obvious that you were no saboteur, that you weren't going to go off and cause problems or hurt anyone," Ramona remarked, her tone filled with a mix of reassurance and amusement. "Your efforts to try and preserve Korean culture haven't gone unnoticed. People here have come to trust you, to see that you're not, quite frankly, unhinged like your former Colonel."

Ki-Nam shook his head, his voice tinged with flustered denial. "I never intended—I am not—"

Ramona chuckled softly, her laughter carrying a warmth of understanding, "It's alright, Ki-Nam. It was pretty obvious how you felt.

You were quite candid in your conversations with fellow students. Word travels fast. But rest assured, apart from Pyong-Chol, no one suspects a thing back on Morgan Island. Now, tell me, how long has it been since your supposed defection?"

Ki-Nam's legs trembled beneath him, causing him to sink back onto the grass beneath the comforting shade of the tree.

Ramona gracefully squatted in front of him, her presence a calming force amidst his swirling emotions.

Silently, he grappled with his response, the weight of the days since his supposed defection weighing heavily upon him. "One year, three months, and twenty days," he finally managed to utter.

Ramona nodded with understanding, her eyes filled with empathy. "You've been counting each day of your newfound freedom." Pausing momentarily, she continued, "Ki-Nam, I can see you are a good man. It's evident that you have worried about the comrades you left behind, haven't you?"

Ki-Nam's gaze fell to his lap, and a solemn nod was his only response.

Taking a deep breath, Ramona outlined the proposition before him. "So, here's the deal, Ki-Nam. You get to stay here, though I do recommend you visit the island regularly. We'll ensure your safety during those trips. You'll be given an office, a salary, and a purpose. You will become the voice and protector of your people, guiding them toward a better future. You can help guide and direct that future. Nobody wants to see them rot away on that island. You can help them find a purpose and maybe even someday find acceptance here."

Ki-Nam looked up at her in confusion. It was too much to process.

Ramona extended her hand, gently resting it upon his, and smiled her perfect smile again, "You will become a man of importance, and so long as you remain the *good* man that I believe you are today, who knows, maybe you'll even find a wife here and start a family. You have the potential to be the savior of the Korean people, Ki-Nam."

✪ ✪ ✪

Morgan Island Trading Zone

Ramona and Crew Chief Russ Elvis, clad in their uniforms, stood side by side in the doorway, observing the scene before them. Ki-Nam, flanked by two stoic marine guards, descended ILC Dagger's ramp. It was evident from his uneasy demeanor that his freshly tailored North Korean uniform did not sit well with him.

The vicinity surrounding the "replicator cave" had undergone a remarkable transformation. The ILC's constant comings and goings had given birth to a bustling compound brimming with activity. Shipping containers, both arriving and departing, formed growing stacks around the fenced-off area, now expanded to accommodate a modest field hospital. The gravely injured had been transported back to Fort Brazos for proper care, but they had gradually started trickling back to the island.

Pyong-Chol's fabricated narrative that Jin-Hwan had been a heroic figure who had successfully compelled the Americans to provide aid stood largely unchallenged. Some of the returning injured, however, had slowly, quietly, begun to question. Everything. A lifetime of indoctrination didn't disappear overnight, but the sand under the foundation had started to erode.

Meanwhile, half of the replication cave's production was channeled into supplying the island. This entailed not only clothing, medical provisions, and food but also an abundance of modular interlocking bricks and various construction materials meant to improve the living conditions in New Pyongyang City. Construction equipment had been airlifted in to finish the roads that Colonel Jin-Hwan's men had forced the bulk of the surviving North Koreans into a slave labor force to build.

Pyong-Chol had kept the weapons the Americans had furnished to aid in the overthrow of Jin-Hwan's despotic rule. The Americans had not demanded their return, but neither were they permitted within the confines of the compound or allowed to be replicated. A satisfied smile played across Pyong-Chol's face as he approached Ki-Nam. The latter stiffly bowed, and Pyong-Chol reciprocated with a shallower nod.

Speaking in a boisterous tone, intentionally projecting his words for the benefit of the other North Koreans present, Pyong-Chol proclaimed, "Welcome back, my valiant comrade. I am immensely relieved to witness that the Americans have not inflicted harm upon you. We have much to discuss!"

With that, he extended his hand, firmly clasping Ki-Nam's, and gestured toward a less crowded area. "The time has come for you to impart all that you have learned. Let us retire from this landing site."

Connection

● ● ● ● ● ● ● ● ● ● ● ● ● ● ● ● ●

DownSide:
Home of Dr. David and Gwyneth Elliott Duncan

Jermaine, Alister, and Rafferty sat outside the CIC in a cramped circle around a battered plastic packing crate. They had pored over the proposed landing sites listed by Dr. Priya and Dr. O'Connell, cross-referencing their findings with Revenge's detailed warp shell lensing of the planet's rocks and ice-covered surface.

The red-hued surface shimmered with a dull gleam. It primarily consisted of methane, nitrogen, and carbon monoxide. Bright plains formed from methane ice, while dark regions added accents with carbon monoxide ice. Traces of other ices, including water, ammonia, and organic molecules, were also present on the surface. Some of those ices were likely produced by interactions with solar radiation from the primary's frequent flares or even from cosmic rays. There were also occasional wisps of organic molecule haze, such as C_4H_2 (Butadiyne).

The surface of the planet was a patchwork of ages, colored in shades of white, black, and orange against the backdrop of the red dwarf star. All around, young plains mixed with ancient craters that pocked the otherwise smooth terrain. The brightest areas seemed to sparkle like moonlight on an Earth-side lake, while darker patches blended into shadows beneath them.

Jermain asked aloud, "Revenge, how can we safely set the HAB units down on the surface? We will need to prepare a flat landing zone large enough to lay them all out without stacking them. That's going to need to be, what were you saying, Rafferty?"

Glancing at his phone where he had calculated the numbers, Rafferty responded, "Alright, we have a total of fifty-one HABs, which we agreed to arrange in clusters of five. These clusters will be interconnected by airlocks, and we also want to include walkways. If we lay them out in a square pattern, we'll end up with eleven clusters. The grid will span approximately twenty-two hundred feet on each side, giving us a total area of four million eight hundred and forty square feet. Keep in mind that this calculation is solely for the HABs and doesn't account for storage space, new constructions, Kukri, or Revenge. It's forty-two percent of a mile on each side. My suggestion would be to designate a square mile as the landing zone, selecting a location with ample room for future expansion."

Jermaine nodded soberly, "Revenge, how can we do this safely? Use the destructive warp field and deposit the HABs at the same time? How hard will it be to create that large of a flat area?"

Captain, creating the landing zone will not be a problem. You will recall that what you call Phoenix-type vessels were created as cargo haulers. They had additional functions as well. The Masters used us to deliver not only cargo to locations in space but also to planetary surfaces. Sometimes, that meant we were required to create suitable landing zones on undeveloped planets. Sometimes, it meant delivering troops and weapons. Sometimes, it was equipment and supplies to build a colony. We were designed with the ability to create a planar destructive warp field with which to establish a suitable landing zone.

Rafferty nodded and asked, "Revenge? I remember that Phoenix said that one of their colonies was wiped out with some sort of disease and that the Builders fled out of fear the Masters would, well, punish them in order to either sterilize the site or even out of spite, but that Phoenix didn't know what happened to the Masters after that. Could the Masters still be out there, somewhere? Maybe even fighting the Accipiters?"

I do not know. Phoenix's memories do not go back that far, and the Masters did not share operational information with our kind. They only told us where to go, what to do, and what to build. We did not even know where the home world was located.

Rafferty shrugged, "That makes sense from an OPSEC perspective, especially from a marshal society."

Captain, in order to prepare the landing zone, I must leave the HABs in orbit and return for them after the task is complete. That includes the ILCs. I cannot bring any humans with me.

Jermaine stiffened, "Explain."

I do not have sufficient mass to extend a planar field and hold the HABs simultaneously. Also, using a destructive field to consume that much matter will release a dangerous amount of energy. Humans will not be safe to remain within me during this process. There is an unacceptable risk that I will not be able to absorb that much energy safely.

Alister swallowed hard, "I'm sure I am not alone in feeling uneasy about this. Having our only ride out of this system leaving us exposed like that."

Jermaine closed his eyes and shook his head, "That's what happened to Phil's crew on Earth. Phoenix couldn't absorb that much energy when the Accipiter's suicided into it, and it had to go somewhere. Revenge, how dangerous is this? Is there a risk to you? Gene Morton's ship exploded."

No, Commander Morton's ILC absorbed too much too fast when it collided with the Accipiter mothership. I can, as you would say, take it slow. If something unexpected happens, I can disengage or even expel excess energy in a safe direction. However, I possess Phoenix's memories about that incident and refuse to take the unnecessary risk of harming any of you.

Also, it is possible that during the clearing of the landing zone, I might uncover underlying geological deficiencies, making the site unsuitable. It may become necessary to relocate to an alternate candidate site.

✪ ✪ ✪

Meanwhile, on the other side of the bay, amid a spirited debate amongst the civilians about naming the planet, the twenty-eight-year-old ebony-skinned mission IT Manager, Mara Morhouse, herself engrossed in the task of rectifying a recalcitrant laptop, had shrugged and, without looking up had nonchalantly said aloud, "We should name the planet Tartarus. In the annals of mythology, Tartarus represents the abyss where Cronus, the ascendant King of the Titans, incarcerated the mighty Cyclopes. He set the monster Campe as its guard. However, in his war with the Titans, it was Zeus who vanquished Campe and liberated the incarcerated giants to aid in his battles. So you see, Tartarus symbolizes the underworld, the very crucible of damnation, from which we shall wage our celestial battle against the Titans. The Accipiters."

Pausing momentarily, Mara continued with an added flourish, "Ah, and our new settlement should bear the name Parnassus, after Mount Parnassus. Among other things, the mountainous sanctuary served as a haven where warriors sought solace, summoned their indomitable spirits, and harnessed the celestial energies indispensable for their forthcoming struggles. Therefore, it stands as a hallowed ground, symbolizing the reinvigoration and preparation of warriors in dire need."

Everyone stopped and stared at her. Mara had looked up at the sudden quiet, blinked, and shrugged again, saying, "What? Don't any of you play D&D or read mythology?" She shook her head and lowered her gaze back to the vexing laptop and ignored the flurry of debate that followed."

✪ ✪ ✪

Two weeks later: Present Day

The preparation of the site proved to be more time-consuming than initially anticipated. While leveling out site one, an unexpected discovery was made. A vertical lava tube had been unearthed. While acknowledging its potential usefulness in the future, it rendered the designated landing zone unsuitable for the HABs.

Meanwhile, the assemblage of HABs had been left in the planet's shadow, shielding them from the local red dwarf's incessant radiation.

Revenge moved to the next candidate site and swiftly began carving a cavity into the side of a nearby mountain. The plan involved creating a hollow space that would soon be domed over and then covered with a protective layer of ice. This ambitious endeavor aimed to provide a secure location for the HABs, shielding them from casual view as well as from the ravages of the red dwarf's radiation and other potential hazards.

Once the site was leveled and the melted rockface cooled and resolidified, Revenge ascended back to orbit. It re-englobed the HABs, reintegrated the core ILC, and gently descended to the surface, with Kukri following. Over the course of several days, a meticulous operation unfolded. Revenge skillfully employed its spindle tendrils, deftly grasping each HAB and gently lowered each into position. Spacesuited engineers tirelessly worked to reconnect the airlocks, reintegrating the HABs.

Amidst the ongoing process, a heated debate raged over the team's priorities. While every effort was made to carefully ration the remaining food supplies, concerns grew as it became evident that there were only approximately three weeks' worth of provisions left. To extend the duration, Doctors Garcia and Araki devised a plan to reduce rations by half in a week's time. However, with no immediate means of cultivating new food, preserving exemplars of each remaining item became crucial for future replication once a new FAB was constructed.

As discussions intensified, the focal point of the debate shifted to the size of the FAB itself. Doctors Garcia and Araki, Andrea Gepner, the mission expeditionary logistics manager, and Dr. O'Connell argued vehemently for expediency, advocating for the construction of the smallest practical version possible. Their rationale was to begin replenishing food stocks at the earliest opportunity. A larger FAB could be built afterward, providing backup as well. On the other hand, Dimitri, Dr. Tristan Martinez, the mission chief mechanical engineer, Dr. Holly Pria, the structural engineer, as well as Rafferty and Alister advocated for a larger FAB, emphasizing the need to stretch rationing even further. They envisioned a FAB capable of producing not only food but also essential dome materials, clothing, beds, sheets, and, most critically, new spacesuits.

The urgency to address the spacesuit situation added fuel to the debate. The current suits were deteriorating rapidly, showing increased signs of wear and tear. Several close calls had already occurred due to their compromised condition. The prospect of suit failure loomed ominously, for without functional suits, repairs could not be conducted outside, nor could the pressurized dome, a requirement for being able to step outside one of the HABs without a suit at all, be completed. And if they couldn't leave the HABs…. They'd all perish soon enough, anyway.

✪ ✪ ✪

Lt. Commander Lorraine Parker, NTN Revenge's Engineering Duty Officer, clung to a chunk of HAB 31's outer hull as she worked to repair a malfunctioning airlock seal. Her well-worn spacesuit was designed to keep her alive in the vacuum of space, but the patched fabric had begun to wear thin in places, and she could feel the cold of the void seeping in. She shivered as she worked, her hands and long fingers numb with cold and from the strain of working in spacesuit gloves. Her breath was ragged and labored. Her helmet had begun to fog up, blurring her vision, and she had to squint to make out the details of her work. Her short, dark hair was plastered to her skull.

The airlock had suffered a catastrophic outer seal failure. Thankfully, it hadn't affected the HAB's interior. Lorraine had gone out to repair it. Despite Revenge's efforts to create a flat, level landing zone, some areas had nonetheless subsided, and the shifting ground pulled and strained the interconnecting airlocks.

She knew she had been out here too long, and she could feel the exhaustion setting in. She also knew that the work had to be done and there weren't enough people to keep up with the growing issues. She was well experienced in the suit and working on the HABs, having done so on countless occasions while in orbit around Ari'Nell, but the lack of rest was beginning to take its toll on her. She willed herself to keep going, but her breath grew more ragged, and her vision began to blur. She lost her grip on the wrench and stumbled backward. The last thing she heard was a sudden pop before she blacked out.

Dr. Tristan Martinez trudged along the baren rock surface between HABs. He was equally exhausted but knew that the thousand or so lives of the survivors depended upon what he and the other spacesuited workers were doing. His vision through the helmet was limited, and his eyes were bleary. He was passing between a row of HABs when something caught the corner of his eye. He almost didn't stop but shook his head, slowly turned in his suit, and looked down between the row of HABs. There, next to one of the interconnecting airlocks, lay a spacesuited figure crumpled on the melted rock surface.

His heart suddenly quickened, and adrenaline surged as he realized what he was seeing. He keyed his microphone and shouted, "Mayday, Mayday, this is Tristan. Code Red, I repeat, Code Red! Whoever is working outside HAB 31 is down! Requesting urgent assistance and medical support! Over!"

✪ ✪ ✪

Master Chief Jeremy Rogers was nearby. In the cold, desolate expanse of the airless ice planet, Jeremy and Tristan raced against time, their heavy spacesuits hindering their movements. Between them, they carried Lorraine's limp form, every step hindered by the bulky weight of her spacesuit.

With urgency in their every step, they finally reached Revenge's airlock. The slowness of the airlock cycle seemed like an eternity. Finally, the familiar hum of the ship's systems greeted them as they lifted their visors and rushed inside, their breath visible in the chilly air.

Once safely inside, they carefully laid Lorraine down on a medical gurney and worked urgently to remove her spacesuit. Lorrain's body was swollen and bruised, with signs of possible frostbite here and there. The cargo bay was dimly lit, casting long shadows as Amelia rushed to Lorraine's side. She took a deep breath and connected the necessary medical equipment, her hands moving with purpose and precision. The monitors beeped and blinked, displaying Lorraine's nonexistent vital signs.

"Charge the defibrillator to 200 joules," Amelia commanded Inés Garcia, her voice steady but filled with urgency as she pulled Lorraine's frost-covered t-shirt and bra aside. Jeremy, Tristan, Jermaine, Alister, and the rest of the crew and civilians stood anxiously nearby. Many of their faces were fixed with stoic resignation.

The room fell momentarily silent as the defibrillator charged, the tension thick in the air. Amelia carefully positioned the paddles on Lorraine's chest, her hands trembling slightly with anticipation and anxiety. With a determined nod, she called out, "Clear!"

The room erupted in a brief burst of electrical energy as she activated the defibrillator. Lorraine's body jolted, but the monitors remained unchanged. Undeterred, Amelia prepared for a second attempt. The seconds ticked by like an eternity as the defibrillator charged once again. "Clear!" she announced, her voice laced with desperate resolve.

The room filled with electric energy once more as the paddles made contact with Lorraine's chest. Another surge coursed through her body, causing a ripple of hope among those present. But again, the monitors showed no improvement.

Time hung in the balance as Amelia fought to keep her emotions in check. She adjusted her approach, gathering her focus for the third attempt. The defibrillator charged yet again, and with grim determination, she declared, her voice wavering slightly, "Clear!"

The discharge sparked with intensity, coursing through Lorraine's body in a final attempt to revive her. The room held its collective breath, waiting for a sign of life. But once more, disappointment filled the air as the monitors showed no change.

Hope flickered but refused to fade. Amelia's eyes flashed with renewed determination. She knew she couldn't give up, not when Lorraine's life hung in the balance, and every single life was now more precious than ever before. She shot a glance at Inés. "Inés! The epinephrine autoinjector! Now!"

Inés retrieved the autoinjector from the Shipboard Medical Chest and handed it to Amelia, adding, "Doesn't that increase the risk of arrhythmia in hypothermia cases?"

Without hesitation, Amelia popped the cover and plunged the needle into Lorraine's cold chest, then grabbed the recharged defibrillator paddles and shouted, her voice resounding with a mix of desperation and resolve, "No choice! Clear!"

The room crackled with anticipation as the defibrillator discharged its electrical surge, coursing through Lorraine's weakened body.

And then, finally, a collective sigh of relief escaped as the monitors flickered to life. Lorraine's heart restarted wildly, then stabilized, her vital signs slowly climbing back to safer levels.

Lorraine's body lurched, and she sucked in a ragged breath of air.

✪ ✪ ✪

Hours later, after the jubilation subsided, Jermaine sat beside Lorraine as she lay on the cot in the tiny, improvised medical bay. She'd regained consciousness and miraculously did not seem to have suffered any apparent brain damage. After determining how frighteningly long Lorraine had lain outside with her suit compromised, Amelia had privately told Jermaine that she wasn't sure that Lorraine or anyone else would have survived had it not been for the genetic tinkering and health improvements provided by the Gardeners.

Lorraine had been drifting in and out of consciousness. She opened her eyes and blinked them into focus.

Jermaine smiled and started to reach over and cup her hand to reassure her, but he stopped himself. Her hands were in no better shape than the rest of her. He swallowed hard. "Welcome back to the land of the living. How're you feeling?"

Lorraine groaned and swallowed; her throat was beyond simply being dry. It was swollen and nearly required intubation.

"Here." He reached over and picked up the squirt bottle of water next to her cot and brought it to her lips. "Drink." He gently squeezed the bottle, careful to only allow a trickle to flow between her swollen lips.

Her once pale skin was discolored, bloated, and swollen, and her lips were chapped and almost frostbitten. She'd had trouble breathing and was in a great deal of pain on top of hypothermia. Amelia was still concerned about the possibility of gas bubbles within bodily tissues and blood vessels.

Lorraine almost choked on the water but managed a grateful sip.

Jermaine gritted his teeth as he watched her silent agony. He leaned in close to her ear and whispered, "Look… Lieutenant. Don't try to talk. I have just one order for you. Live. Get better. You didn't do anything wrong… this was my fault. I've been pushing too hard, taking too many risks with precious lives. Now, go back to sleep."

✪ ✪ ✪

A crowd had gathered outside, their faces filled with anticipation. Jermaine took a moment to observe their anxious expressions before addressing them. His voice carried with authority as he spoke, capturing their attention.

"Listen closely," he began, his tone firm. "From this point forward, all suits will undergo daily reinspections. All non-critical outside work is suspended. Outside work crews must consist of no less than four members, and no outside shift should exceed four hours."

His eyes scanned the crowd until they landed on Dimitri at the back. Recognizing him, Jermaine directed his words to the engineer. "Dr. Sinitskaya, you are to provide Revenge with the ZPMs you salvaged from Ari'Nell. Begin work immediately on the medium-sized FAB you proposed. I expect twice-daily progress reports. What resources do you require?"

The crowd parted around Dimitri, who thoughtfully responded with careful consideration. "In order to accelerate its creation, we will need a large quantity of higher atomic weight materials for transmutation."

He smiled wryly, almost apologetically, and nodded toward Amelia. "Doctor Araki, I'm as hungry as the next person and have no desire to see anyone suffer. I understand the urgency. I will do everything in my power to expedite the process."

Dimitri's gaze returned to Jermaine as he explained further. "You see, we can use various materials as input mass, including rocks from outside or even no input mass at all, but the energy requirement increases logarithmically in some cases and asymptotically in others. This means we'll need to strip out nonessential equipment for conversion. If possible, we'll scan it to replace it later. However, for the FAB to create new materials, we need a significant input mass. We may even need to cut up one of the HABs. The higher the atomic weight, the fewer steps up to the heavier lanthanides and actinides and exotic compounds the FAB is composed of."

He paused and grimaced, "I'm afraid that this even includes things like bedframes, fixtures, chairs, redundant electronic equipment, and even, well, and I know how popular this will be, our stock of firearms, as if we have anything to shoot at, at the moment. We'll scan them all to reproduce them later. It is a temporary sacrifice. Hell, bring all the trash we have that is piling up, and we'll recycle it, too. Once the FAB is operational, space suits and food will be the first priorities. Thankfully, one of the things that was scanned at Ari'Nell were new spacesuits taken from the warehouse the Gardeners provided in New London."

Dimitri's words carried a sense of pragmatism as he continued. "Once the FAB is operational, we can bring in rocks and ice from outside as feedstock for food replication. In the long term, though, I remind you that this is a low metallicity star system. We chose it on purpose. We'll eventually need to build the mining drones that Revenge has in its memory. However, once food and suits are no longer an issue, feeding in rock in order to create building materials for the dome… or for an even bigger FAB is something that will be manageable. Until then, we'll have to continue to rely on Revenge's magnetic field to shield the… colony."

Alister, standing nearby, nodded and asked, "And after that?"

Dimitri raised his eyebrows and smiled, "I have been thinking about that. I think we need to take a page from the Gardener's playbook. With one or more full-sized fabs and a fleet of mining drones, it should be no trouble at all to build a small O'Neil Cylinder. It won't be anything like the giant four thousand-mile-long New Texas McKendree Cylinder, but we could build a smaller one first that we could turn into a nice living area. Later, we can build bigger ones, say, twenty or thirty miles long. Then we'd have room for literally millions of people and the agricultural space to feed them. With ZPMs for power, we won't need solar input, so we can gently push the thing out into a deep space trajectory, far away from anywhere that the Accipiters can use Nexus Junction Points to hunt for us. We'll have warp drive ships to come and go and transport new conversion mass to us if we need it to build ships, for example. Revenge can fly off and find and englobe a big Nickel-Iron asteroid somewhere and bring it back, and we can turn it into ships or what have you. Then, frankly, we can do whatever the hell we want, including sticking it in the Accipiter's eyes whenever we feel like it."

Safe

● ● ● ● ● ● ● ● ● ● ● ● ● ● ● ● ● ●

Riverbend Mall Senate Chamber

The Senate chamber was abuzz with fervor and anticipation over today's session. While the Johansson scandal and the arrival at the Gardener Dyson Sphere were still the main stories on everyone's minds, the subject at hand today was turning into a vexing, perhaps even welcome, distraction. Almost two months had gone by since the discovery of the 'cave' near Jamestown, and six weeks since yet another was found, in of all places, the North Korean exile location on Morgan Island.

At first, it was thought that the cave at Jamestown was 'merely' replicating ZPMs. Then came the gruesome discovery on Morgan Island, where the bodies of Colonel P'aeng Jin-Hwan and a guard – duplicated in every minute detail. The reason why it was gruesome? Neither man had been dead when they were copied. Commander Choe Pyong-Chol had rebelled against Jin-Hwan's brutality and locked him and the guard in the cave. It was only when the cave was reopened, and the bodies later autopsied, that it was determined that neither had been dead at the time they were duplicated. The process itself destructively scanned the source material and then made two copies.

So, now it was known that the caves could be used to copy virtually anything… so long as you didn't want that thing to remain alive. The caves were immediately seized upon as a strategic seasource and used to replicate critical supplies and components, especially parts for military equipment that were in short supply.

It was only later, as the implications began to sink in, that the potential consequences began to stir worry among many, leading to today's Senate session.

Before Darnell Lewis was a Senator, and before there was a Jamestown, and it had just been three outcast men in the wilderness, Darnell had stumbled across a metal cave containing a ZPM. At the time, no one had any idea that the cave had been anything other than just a place waiting to be discovered with a hidden ZPM inside. Darnell had negotiated for supplies and support to build a fledgling trading post in exchange for the ZPM. As soon as the Morgan Island discovery was made, however, President Austin had ordered the military to take control of both sites.

Since then, Darnell had begun to lobby for ways to ensure that the cave benefited his tiny frontier settlement. He'd found willing allies in Senators Gaspard Boyer and Valentin Gorskov, who saw the bigger picture of how control of such a resource could be a source of considerable power… and profit.

Gail walked to the elevated podium on the stage. The lights in the room were bright. They had to be in order to contend with the blackened walls of the former movie theater. She wondered if anyone gave a second thought to the faux Art Deco fixtures and light sconces on the walls.

As President of the Senate, in the tradition of the United States, she was now responsible for presiding over regular sessions. She climbed the steps, and as she took her seat, Gail glanced across the chamber, her gaze briefly connecting with Senators Gorshkov and Boyer, who traded stony stares with her. It was no secret that they resented some of the potential implications of her recent marriage. When word that they'd separately referred to her as 'Queen Austin' in recent interviews, it enraged her to the point that John had had to physically restrain her from hunting them down, and, well, Gail had a particular reputation for rather permanently dealing with those she considered to be traitors.

Now, in addition to being Vice President, she carried the weight of her new role as a mother-to-be… and *wife*. She found herself grappling with the challenges of adjusting to her pregnancy while fulfilling her political duties. She had always been driven, focused, and resolute, but this new chapter in her life presented a different set of challenges.

Gail smiled coldly in return and then nodded to Tom Parker, recently named Senate Chaplain.

Tom walked to center stage and waited for the senators to take their seats. He began, "Let us pray. Almighty and gracious God, we come before you today as Senators representing the diverse voices and perspectives of our new nation. We seek your wisdom and guidance as we carry out our responsibilities to serve the people we represent. We acknowledge the weight of the tasks before us and humbly ask for your presence to be with us in this Chamber. Grant us the ability to listen with open hearts and minds, respecting the viewpoints of others even when they differ from our own. Help us to find common ground and work together for the greater good. As we deliberate on matters of policy and legislation, remind us of the human impact of our decisions. Guide us to pursue justice, equality, and compassion in all that we do. May our laws reflect the values that uphold the dignity and worth of every individual, protecting the vulnerable and ensuring the well-being of all surviving humans. Grant us the strength and courage to lead with integrity, speaking truthfully and acting with sincerity. Help us to put aside personal interests and partisan divisions, focusing instead on the collective welfare of our fellow citizens. Enable us to rise above petty politics and work towards the betterment of our nation as a whole. We also ask for your blessings upon our people, our leaders, and the brave and intrepid souls who risk everything to defend the remnants of humanity and strike terrible blows against the vast forces of our enemy. Inspire us to strive for unity, understanding, and cooperation, transcending the barriers that divide us. May we come together in a spirit of mutual respect and seek the common ground that will allow us to build a brighter future for generations to come. In your infinite wisdom, guide our deliberations, our words, and our actions. Bless this Senate, its members, and our people. We offer this prayer with humility and gratitude, trusting in your grace and guidance. Amen."

Gail smiled warmly at him, "Thank you, Tom."

Tom nodded gracefully as he exited the stage and left the room.

The room hushed as she began. She took a deep breath and intoned in a steely voice, "The Senate will come to order. The video record shall demonstrate that all Senators except for Senator Salangsang are physically present, and Caesar is connected via radio. Let the record show that we have a quorum. The Senate will proceed with its regular session. Today, we will begin with opening statements. The Chair recognizes Senator Boyer."

Gaspard Boyer, his French accent infused with a touch of subtle disdain, took the floor, his piercing gaze occasionally darting disapprovingly towards Gail. The air in the chamber grew charged with anticipation as Boyer's commanding voice filled the space. "Messieurs et mesdames," Boyer began, his words flowing smoothly and deliberately, "we must estab-leesh, with utmoost urgency, a clear and robust framework for ze replication caves. Eet ees of impe-er-a-teeve importance zat we exercise caution and foresight to protect our collective interests."

His tone carried an air of confidence and authority as he continued, "Ve cannot allow these powerful entities to operate unchecked, for zey possess ze potential to shape ze very fabric of our society. Eet ees our duty to safeguard ze well-being and stability of our nation, and zis begins with ze establishment of comprehensive regulations and oversight."

Boyer's eyes narrowed slightly as he spoke, "I yield, wiz a sense of shared responsibility, to Sena-teur Gorshkov. May we, togezzer, chart a path forward zat will ensure ze preservation of our interests and ze equitable utilization of ze replication caves."

As he concluded his statement, Boyer's subtle yet palpable disdain lingered in the air.

Valentin Gorshkov, his Russian accent filled with skepticism, nodded in agreement with Boyer's statement. His voice carried a hint of caution and deliberation as he spoke, emphasizing the importance of maintaining a balance of power. "Indeed," Gorshkov began, "ve must ensure zat no single entity gains ex-seh-sive control over ze replication caves. Ze immense pow-air zat zey possess could easily tip ze scales of influence. It ees crucial for ze stability and fairness of our systems zat ve adopt a balanced approach."

Gorshkov's eyes scanned the room, his gaze focused and intense. He continued, "Ve must establish a Sena-t central control mechanism to oversee ze operations and governance of zese caves. By doing so, ve can prevent any single entity from monopolizing zeir benefits and ensure zat zeir power ees utilized for ze greater good."

He paused briefly, allowing his words to sink in. Then, with a gesture of deference, Gorshkov added, "In ze spirit of collaboration and respect, I yield to Sena-tor Lewis, as ve continue to navigate zis important discussion and shape ze future of ze replication caves."

Darnell Lewis had flown in on the most recent ILC supply run. He'd hastily made his way to the sprawling Fort Brazos flea market and bartered for a suit to wear. It was an old JCPenney suit and didn't fit him very well, but he'd felt self-conscious wearing his buckskin jacket and pants. The inexpensive fabric felt rough and uncomfortable and matched his demeanor. He spoke forcefully, his voice a mix of determination and frustration. "Senators. I understand the need for caution, but we must also remember that these replicator caves have been found not in Fort Brazos but at the sites of remote settlements. I'm sure that Senator Salangsang will probably find another one out in the New Philippines. It is clear to me that the Gardeners are encouraging the growth and addition of settlements inside New Texas. They obviously want us to spread out. Therefore, I point out that it is obviously important for these settlements to grow and thrive. The replication caves are the catalyst for that growth. We must not allow these resources to be sucked dry to support only Fort Brazos and the military at the expense of the settlements themselves."

Gail noted Esmerelda's signal to be recognized. When the Chamber had instead been a movie theatre, the buttons next to the reclining chairs had been used to order popcorn, drinks, and food during movies. "The Chair recognizes Senator Collins."

Esmerelda stood, sweeping back her now waist-length hair. Unlike most, she was single and one of the shockingly small minority of adult women not pregnant. Her voice resonated with concern. "Senators, while I appreciate the potential benefits of the replication caves, we cannot ignore the risks and challenges that they pose. I'll name a few. First of all, we must carefully consider the ramifications of the replication caves on our agricultural communities. If the cave can duplicate meat and produce, what will be the incentive for farmers and ranchers to continue their work? What happens if the replication process suddenly stops working after farms and ranches shut down, leaving us all vulnerable to starvation? And if we stop having to farm and ranch, what happens in the future when we've simply forgotten how?"

"Furthermore, if these caves can replicate any goods and commodities, what happens to the workers who now make those things? What happens to the people who depend on these industries for their livelihoods? Are we prepared for the repercussions of mass unemployment and the ripple effects on our already struggling economy, such as it is and what there is of it?"

Senator Boyer pressed his button over and over again.

Gail sighed inwardly. "The Chair recognizes Senator Boyer."

Boyer, seizing the opportunity to counter Esmerelda's concerns, eyed her with a hint of skepticism. His French accent carried a subtle edge as he spoke, suggesting that her arguments were influenced by her own vested interests. "Senateur Collins, while I understand your worries, it seems zat your concerns may be driven by a fear of diminished profits for your vast ranching operations," Boyer retorted with a touch of disdain. "We must consid-air ze great-air good and ze potential advancements zat ze replication caves offer. It iz vital zat we do not let self-interest cloud our judgment. Furhermore, what ees your word for fouet d'attelage… ah yes, I remem-bair now. Buggy Whip. Are we to continue unneeded industries forev-air? If we can replicate what we need, what need have we to maintain more zan records of how to make zem? Do we not have more imp-air-tant concerns? We are fighting a war, are we not?"

Gail suppressed a groan as half the senators in the room pressed their buttons, demanding to be heard. "The Chair recognizes Senator Collins."

Esmerelda bristled at Boyer's insinuation, her voice firm as she responded, "Senator Boyer, my concerns extend far beyond personal profits. I speak for the countless hardworking individuals and families who rely on agriculture for their livelihoods. It is our responsibility to safeguard their futures and ensure the stability of our rural community. I remind you that you are suggesting we blindly trust in these newfound caves. I repeat my earlier concern. What happens if the Gardeners decide to turn off the spigot? Remember how they turned off the supply of new Jet fuel at the military base? What if they decide, for whatever reason, to limit the use of the caves, or what if they even decide to change things that get replicated? No! We must maintain our own independence wherever we can. Yes, take advantage of the caves for things we can't make now that are in low supply. Yes, take advantage of them for critical supplies. However, we must not allow ourselves to become any more of a hostage society than we already are! I will remind you that the chair you are sitting in was not on Earth. It was recreated here by the Gardeners. I remind you that they saved you and everyone else now living, and at the same time, they took away five percent of us. They gave, and then they took away."

Gail nodded pleadingly at Livia. "The Chair recognizes Senator Milner."

Still reeling from recent events, Livia did not feel like herself. For the most part, she was still merely going through the motions each day. She didn't even want to be here today. Her personal loathing and shame notwithstanding, Gail and Sybil had not condemned her. Hadn't ridiculed her. She knew she owed them her…. If not loyalty, then at least for her to do her damned job.

Livia forced herself to intervene, "Senators, let us focus on the merits of the arguments rather than questioning each other's motivations. Esmerelda raises valid concerns about the potential impact on our workforce and economy, such as it is and what there is of it, and, frankly, about the risks if we become too dependent upon the replication caves. We must find a way to strike a balance that preserves traditional and strategic industries while embracing the advantages the replication caves provide. We must exercise caution and establish a comprehensive framework to guide us in the management of the replication caves. However, we must also ensure that the interests of all stakeholders are considered. The discoveries we have made should not be overshadowed by personal agendas or the decaying remnants of archaic international rivalries."

Gail, looking for another way to redirect the debate, traded glances with Alphonse Halkias. Alphonse had been a Navy Captain nearing retirement before Awakening Day. He'd never commanded a ship or submarine, having instead devoted most of his career to Navy logistics. She'd met him numerous times, and he'd impressed her as not just a serious numbers man but someone who knew how to navigate the Byzantine politics of the Navy.

He gave her a minuscule nod.

"The Chair recognizes Senator Halkias."

Alphonse stood and looked to his right and left before beginning. "Esteemed Senators, it is imperative that we consider the vital role of the Navy and our military in these discussions," His voice echoed with conviction. "If the replication caves have the potential to produce resources and equipment, we must ensure that a significant portion of their output is dedicated to supporting our defense, bolstering our Navy's capabilities, not only to take the war to our enemy but to defend us here. Inside Fort Brazos. I remind you all that it was only a few short weeks ago that one of those creatures killed seven people at Fort Underwood. In case you've forgotten, their names were Corporals Jimenez, Franks, Johnson, Bohanna, Dowdie, and Sergeants Achilles and Mukuamu. They were real men and women. We need resources to press forward the hunt for the Wardogs, Stalkers, and those hybrid monsters of theirs. I'm certain that Senator Yeagar-Cross would agree."

"The Chair recognizes Senator Yeagar-Cross."

Mira stood. "Gentlemen, it is clear that we need a solution that balances the many needs and concerns posed by the replicators. I am also concerned about not just jobs but what about the idea of ownership and copyright? If someone creates or invents something, either useful or even a piece of art, and it is replicated over and over again, what is the incentive for people to be creative? To invent? To drive innovation? We need to include ways to protect intellectual genius and creative work. A replication copyright, or patent, as it were. I agree that the Navy needs a level of priority. God knows I've looked those alien monsters in their beady eyes, and believe me, you don't want to. Just go down and take a look at the Wardog we have in captivity if you don't believe me. They're fucking terrifying. At the same time, I am forced to agree with Senator Collins that we must not become too dependent upon this resource. We mustn't become lotus eaters, as it were, forgetting our skills and their importance."

"For me, personally, I hope I never have to eat replicated food or use replicated things. I much prefer to know the hands that made it, if I can.

I also support the need to ensure that our new settlements prosper and grow. They should benefit from the discoveries there. The last thing we need, however…" She glanced at Boyer and Gorshkov, "…is some cabal or bureaucracy lording over and controlling the damned replicator caves and what they produce. That's a recipe for state oligarchy if I ever saw one, and I won't stand for it!"

Gail looked at Sybil and suppressed a grin at the other woman's knowing eyes. "The Chair recognizes Senator Blanchard."

Sybil stood and smiled sweetly but not quite innocently. "Senator Lewis, I concur with Senator Yeagar-Cross. Yours and other settlements need to benefit directly from the replicators. Fairly benefit. And at the same time, we must balance the needs of the rest of New Texas and its defense. We must also remember that these locations are nowhere close to the city, here. The only timely and effective way we have to move goods back and forth is via those alien ILCs. I know a thing or two about logistics, and that's a serious issue. We need to be smart. Everyone in this room is smart. We need to strike a fair balance between property and intellectual rights and ensure as much independence from the Gardeners as we can muster."

She paused for a moment, her gaze sweeping across the room, making eye contact with those present. "At the same time, despite our arguably dire post-apocalyptic circumstances, ours is not, at least not as long as I draw breath, a collective. We remain individuals with unique needs, freedoms, and rights. It is crucial that we find a balance that respects and preserves these fundamental aspects of our identity. Therefore, I propose that a fraction of the replicators' capacity be made available to individuals. This will not only empower each person but also honor the cherished values of liberty and self-determination that define us."

Sybil turned and faced Gaspard. "And, lastly, Senator Boyer. Yes, we are most adamantly at war. A war that wiped out more than ninety-nine percent of humanity and threatens to extinguish its last scattered embers. A war that will define who we are as a race, now, and forever more. It is up to us then, here, we Senators in this very chamber, to ensure that we learn the lessons from our past. We've seen those among us who were among our most trusted leaders… commit acts of vile barbary and evil. What example shall we set for the few humans who remain? Will we sit and scheme in this room for personal power and influence?" She paused, and her voice filled with a strength and authority she'd never known. "Will we merely be echoes? Ghosts of those we left behind on Earth? Or, will we be better? Isn't it time, I ask you earnestly. Isn't it time for us to grow the fuck up?"

Empire

● ● ● ● ● ● ● ● ● ● ● ● ● ● ● ● ●

Ascendance
Special Quarters
Accipiter Capital System

Alberta "Bertie" Sinitskaya oriented herself in the null-g and stared into the depths of her reflection, her eyes fixated on the haunted figure trapped within the full-length mirror embedded in the mocking walls of the "room" the Accipiters had "given" her. It was her prison cell, although it wasn't small, and it lacked bars. Of course, it also lacked a discernable door. The room stretched out around her, a colossal expanse reaching hundreds of feet in every direction. Its walls were a riot of color, composed of wildly varying alien flora.

Her new home. A ragged juxtaposition to any aspect of her life before she had died. The yang to the yin of her life. Not for the first time, the idea of this being her 'afterlife' washed over her. The color scheme was insipid: pale yellow pussy willow bark on something that resembled a deep red shade of oak. A riot of alien plant life decorated every surface, encasing the enormous dimensions of the interior in vibrant green, purple, brown, and black hues. Smaller plants sprouted like gigantic scarves from clefts in the bark walls. Their roots curled down from high above and looped through holes back into small gaps that opened up along the 'floor' and 'ceiling,' where spores like fairy dust mites drifted along air currents pushed through the small openings by mechanisms or forces unseen.

All of it served as an omnipresent reminder of her utter isolation. The lone human prisoner in the heart of the Accipiter galactic empire.

Some of the plants provided fruit. Xuraens, the colossal Accipiter who claimed ownership of her existence, had informed her that they had been specially created just for her. The smell and texture… were an acquired taste. They were not repulsive, merely foreign and unsettling, much like everything else in the exquisitely beautiful desolation of this place. There were other plants that she could suck on for water, and then there was another corner of the room with an even stranger and disturbing set of plants devoted to her… micturition and defecation needs. Enduring her inevitable menstrual flow amidst this alien landscape was very nearly debilitating. It was yet another chilling reminder of her utter vulnerability. She vowed to *never* allow herself to get used to "the facilities" here, determined to retain some semblance of her humanity.

She swallowed hard at a new thought that suddenly occurred to her. *What if this isn't a prison cell… but a zoo… and I'm the latest monkey to be watched from behind the glass.…*

Xuraens had escorted her to this room after their first encounter, leaving her abandoned within its suffocating walls. Days turned into an agonizing eternity as silence engulfed her, with no one coming to interrogate or offer a shred of human connection. Some of the plants were luminescent, providing light during the 'day' cycle. As those dimmed at 'night,' they emitted a pale silver glow.

Gradually, doubt gnawed at her, and she began to wonder if she'd been forgotten.

In the absence of gravity or even a floor to pace, she forced herself to stay occupied to forestall eventual madness or worse. She exercised as best she could, contorting her floating body into what yoga poses she could manage, pushing her physical limits within the constraints of her surroundings. Desperately, she sought out plants with the strongest roots, latching onto them, stretching, pulling, and affixing herself to the walls to find some sort of leverage.

So now, once again, she confronted her reflection in the uncaring mirror. She stripped off the jumpsuit and critically evaluated her appearance. Her new body was, well, soft. All curves and helpless. *I look like a pampered suburban teenage girl. If I ever find a way to escape, I'll be.…*

The notion of escape flickered in her mind, only to be immediately extinguished by a familiar wave of fear. *You'll what? Go where? Learn Accipiter and look up in their database where to find New Texas? Even if I could get there.… I'm… Dead. Anna is probably older than this body. I'd be like… my own daughter's little sister. Maybe the same age as Ron. And… Dimitri.… No. Even if I could find a way back, who knows what the Accipiters did to this body or even to my mind. Even I wouldn't trust.… Me.*

Her vision began to blur as tears welled up in her eyes, with nowhere to fall. *You're dead, Bertie. Face it. The most you can hope for is to find a way to hurt your captors.*

✪ ✪ ✪

"GOOD MORNING, ALBERTA. ARE YOU HUNGRY? YOU SHOULD EAT. WE HAVE MUCH TO DO TODAY."

The voice boomed throughout the room, shattering Bertie's sleep and startling her awake. She'd hooked her arm into a looping branch along the wall. As she came to awareness, she twisted her arm and yelped slightly at the pain.

Xuraens was at least twenty feet away from her, but still, she struggled for a moment to try and distance herself from him as she bit down her anger.

Chest heaving, she snapped, "Don't! Don't startle me like that!" She shook her head and added, "Where the Hell have you been? You've left me alone in here for God knows how long!"

Muted glyphs flowed across his beak as he regarded her with his enormous, inscrutable topaz eyes.

Bertie grimaced. *Goddamned bird is laughing at me.*

"Wait, you spoke this time instead of using the tablet."

I AM USING THE TABLET. I THOUGHT IT WOULD BE BETTER TO SPEAK TO YOU INSTEAD OF TOUCHING YOU TO AWAKEN YOU.

Bertie swallowed, "Yes, well. I would appreciate it, in the future, if you would ring a bell or a chime or something before entering."

Xuraens regarded her for a while again before answering.

YOU SHOULD EAT AND PREPARE YOURSELF. WE HAVE MUCH TO SEE AND DO TODAY.

Bertie stared at him in return. "Humph. That reminds me. I noticed this jumpsuit… well… you haven't provided a clean one, though, for some reason, it doesn't stink yet."

It was several long moments before Xuraens replied.

I UNDERSTAND YOUR MISCONCEPTION. YOUR CLOTHING IS NOT… FABRIC. IT IS A LIVING THING MADE TO… LIVE WITH YOU.

Bertie gasped, and her jaw dropped, and her eyes widened at the realization of what Xuraens had said. Somehow, she managed to restrain herself from not immediately clawing the thing off her body. The sudden itchiness that crawled across her skin and the heat she felt rising in her cheeks notwithstanding, she only now realized just how… frighteningly comfortable… the jumpsuit had been. The rising creepy panic swelling within her warred against her self-discipline and better judgment.

She swallowed hard. "I… see. It… feeds on my dead skin and sweat? It's not going to grow tendrils and attach to me or anything, like a fungus?"

The muted glyphs flowed bright and swiftly across Xuraens' beak.

NO. IT WILL NOT HARM YOU IN ANY WAY. NOW, PLEASE EAT AND EXCRETE. WE MUST LEAVE SOON.

Bertie stared at him for long moments as she felt the morning's pressure on her bladder beginning to complain. *Fine, go ahead and watch. Get your cheap thrills watching the monkey pee into a flower.*

Minutes later, Xuraens presented her with what, for all the world, resembled a scooter without wheels. It had a flat oval for her to 'stand' on and a vertical pole with handles.

THIS WILL AID YOU IN MOVING ABOUT. IT WILL FOLLOW ME. YOU NEED ONLY STAND ON IT. BRING YOUR TABLET.

Bertie looked dubiously at the fragile-looking device. Like everything else, it appeared to be at least somewhat organic in its structure. She bit down her anxiety and asked, "Okay. Where are we going?" *And how the hell do you move in null-g without one?*

Xuraens didn't answer but instead gracefully glided towards a wall that split open.

Bertie stuffed the tablet into the only pocket in her jumpsuit and swam over to the 'scooter,' grasped the handles, and swung herself 'down' to push her feet against the oval.

Without hesitation, the scooter took off, following Xuraens through the doorway.

The sudden sensation of movement was smooth and faster than Bertie expected. Of course, Xuraens, being ten feet tall, moved quickly along the downward-sloping flowered corridor.

Bertie raised her voice a little as she followed, "I've been meaning to ask about something. I'm concerned about the effect of all this zero-g on my health, assuming you want to keep me healthy for a while, anyway. Humans have health problems after being in zero-g for a long time. Bone density loss, muscular atrophy, heart issues, respiratory issues, and…."

Xuraens abruptly stopped, causing her scooter to lurch to a stop as well. He turned and stared at Bertie for long moments.

I AM SURPRISED YOUR DOCTORS DID NOT EXPLAIN TO YOU THE FULL EXTENT OF THE MEDICAL ENHANCEMENTS YOU RECEIVED. CHANGES TO YOUR BIOLOGY INCLUDED SPECIFIC ADAPTATIONS TO PREVENT THE PROBLEMS YOU DESCRIBE. THESE ARE COMMON PROBLEMS FOR ALL PRIMITIVE ORGANISMS LEARNING TO ADAPT. I DO NOT UNDERSTAND HOW THIS WAS NOT EXPLAINED TO YOU. YOU WORKED EXTENSIVELY ON YOUR PLANET'S MOON AND IN SPACE. YOU ARE SOMEWHAT INTELLIGENT.

WHY DID YOU NOT ASK ABOUT THIS DISCREPANCY?

Bertie answered immediately, without thinking. The words and experiences felt honest and truthful to her, while at the same time, another part of her knew they were not. "The program was the most closely held secret in human history. Every part of it was compartmentalized. We were only told what we needed to know. It was as much for our own protection as it was to protect the program."

YES. THIS IS CONSISTENT WITH WHAT WE LEARNED FROM YOUR MEMORIES. YOURS IS SUCH A SECRETIVE, SAVAGE AND HOSTILE RACE.

Xuraens turned and resumed moving forward.

Bertie laughed bitterly, "Yeah, right. WE'RE the savage ones."

Xuraens ignored her. The corridor splintered into myriad twisting and winding pathways. In truth, it more resembled an intricate organic lattice of roots than anything remotely like what a human would build. Bertie tried to memorize the path they took, but right and left and up and down could not begin to cope with the labyrinthine twists, turns, and dizzying orientations that each change in direction presented.

Along the way, they passed countless other Accipiters. All seemed to react in one way or another to Bertie.

I'm a goddamned zoo animal.

Eventually, they arrived at a large botanical ovum, a veiny, floral egg the size of a semi-truck trailer. Bertie flinched when it irised open, revealing a phosphorescent velvety interior. Before she could object, Xuraens pulled her and her 'scooter' inside, and it closed around them with a soft sucking sound.

Bertie clamped her jaw down and resisted the numerous urges that washed over her. *I will not freak out getting into an alien car!*

The egg lurched forward at well over a standard g for at least an hour. She counted the time in her head: *one Mississippi, two Mississippi, three….*

The egg eventually slowed to a stop, irised open, and Xuraens sped off with Bertie in tow. Minutes later, they entered a vast crystalline chamber. At least a hundred Accipiters were doing… something… in front of translucent control membranes similar to the ones she'd seen pictures of from inside the Keeper ship. It was one of the first things that seemed even vaguely familiar since she'd awakened.

At the heart of the chamber, a resplendent holographic rendition of the galaxy rotated slowly. It was an exquisitely detailed hologram that looked as though it might actually be complex enough to represent every single star and nebula in the galaxy. Moreover, a great many of the stars were marked with symbols and an intricate web of lines too dense to fathom interconnected all the stars.

Bertie gasped aloud. "That is a map of the Nexus Junction Points across the entire galaxy!"

Xuraens withdrew a handheld device from his breastplate and manipulated it with his smaller dexterous set of 'hands,' hands with the equivalent of fingers instead of claws.

The map changed. What must have been billions, perhaps more, of stars, winked out, leaving only the ones with a particular set of iconic symbols next to them. There had to be millions of them.

THESE ARE THE WORLDS THE CLANS HAVE NURTURED AND PROTECTED FOR EONS BEYOND YOUR CONCEPTION. EACH IS HOME TO LIFE AT ITS APEX.

The stars dimmed until one tiny yellow one shone brighter than the rest. One small yellow spark, like a single twinkling grain of sand on an infinite beach.

THIS IS YOUR HOME STAR. IT COULD DISAPPEAR AMONG ALL THESE OTHERS, AND WHO WOULD KNOW? I TELL YOU THAT EVERY ACCIPITER WOULD KNOW AND WEEP AT ITS LOSS. ALL OF THESE ARE WITHOUT PRICE. A TREASURE WITHOUT MEASURE. SHOULD A CATACLYSM CLAIM YOUR STAR, ALL OF THE ACCIPITERS WOULD JOIN IN RELOCATING LIFE FROM YOUR WORLD TO ANOTHER. ALL THE RACES OF THE GALAXY WOULD JOIN TOGETHER IN HARMONY TO

SAVE YOUR WORLD. THIS IS WHAT YOU FIGHT. WE LIBERATED YOUR WORLD FROM THE TYRANNY OF YOUR NATURE.

Bertie bit her tongue. She'd already spoken her mind to him about the evil brutality of the Accipiters. All she wanted to do was to grab the scooter and beat him over the head with it.

She shook her head and decided she couldn't hold back anymore. "Saved us? You destroyed what we were! You destroyed everything that made us a people. How would you feel if someone took away your soul, took away your free will, and turned your people into slaves whose minds you control? Even happy slaves are still slaves!"

IT IS TIME TO LEAVE. YOU ARE TO BE PRESENTED TO THE CONCLAVE.

Bertie gripped the handles until her fingers whitened, "The what? The Conclave? What is that?"

Xuraens didn't answer but instead glided away back to the egg.

✪ ✪ ✪

With Bertie in tow, Council Adjudicator Xuraens glided through the micro-G All-Clan High Council gardens. The gardens stretched in three dimensions for over two hundred miles. It orbited the vast bio-architected ecumenopolis terraformed moon that orbited the second of six terrestrial planets within the Capital system.

Bertie could not help but be overwhelmed. Xuraens had explained that representatives from all the over one hundred and twenty-eight thousand clans were present in the Great Chamber. She felt the vibrations in her bones as the expanse shook and resonated with the sound of over two hundred and fifty thousand vocal chambers… singing. She didn't want to anthropomorphize, but whatever it was they were singing did not sound happy. And Commander Alberta Sinitskaya was apparently the star of the show.

Her tablet translated Xuraen's introduction. This time in writing, not aloud. Not that she could have heard it, anyway, over the noise from the Accipiters.

THIS CREATURE IS ONE OF THE HUMANS. IT WAS KILLED WHEN CLAN MORNING_ SONGWEAVE ENTERED THE FORMER VA'SO VROKGONGON JADAKLOT SYSTEM WE STERILIZED LONG AGO. THIS CREATURE LED THE ATTACK THAT DESTROYED MOST OF CLAN MORNING_SONGWEAVE.

The sound that erupted from the chamber made Bertie's bones vibrate and shocked her with its ferocity as its vibrations beat savagely against her skin. *He's brought me here to die. So be it.*

Her fear subsided despite the assault on her senses. She smiled as she remembered a quote from one of her favorite TV shows: *Fear accompanies the possibility of death. Calm shepherds its certainty.* She whispered although the sound could scarcely leave her throat amid the tumult from the Accipiters. "You said it, Ka D'Argo."

Xuraens waited for what seemed like ages for the chamber to grow quiet.

THIS TINY CREATURE. THIS WEAK, PATHETIC THING LACKS EVEN THE SMALLEST OF CLAWS TO DEFEND ITSELF. THE YOUNGEST OF OUR BROODS COULD SNAP IT IN HALF WITHOUT EFFORT. IS THIS WHAT HAS SO MANY OF YOU AFRAID? AFRAID THAT IT IS SOMEHOW CAPABLE OF TRULY THREATENING ALL THAT WE ARE AND ALL THAT WE CAN DO?

The Chamber erupted again with a riot of noise, although it was substantially more muted than before. Xuraens waited.

LET ME TELL YOU ABOUT THIS CREATURE. THE HUMANS HAVE BUT TWO BIOLOGICAL GENDERS. THE ONE BEFORE YOU IS A BREEDER AND BORE TWO OFFSPRING, AND YET, IT IS ALSO NOT JUST A LEADER

AMONG BOTH GENDERS. IT IS BOTH A BUILDER AND A WARRIOR. A SHIPWRIGHT AND AN ENGINEER. BY ITS STANDARDS, IT IS WELL-EDUCATED. I BRING IT TO YOU TODAY SO YOU CAN SEE WHAT WE FACE. I RESURRECTED IT SO THAT WE COULD BETTER UNDERSTAND WHAT WE FIGHT.

THEY ARE OMNIVORES. THEIR PHYSICAL WEAKNESS IS COMPENSATED FOR BY THEIR CLEVERNESS. IT EXPLAINS WHY ONE OF THEIR KIND CAN BE MANY THINGS AND CAN ADAPT. JUST AS THEY ADAPTED THE VA'SO VROKGONGON JADAKLOT TECHNOLOGY TO SUIT THEIR NEEDS, THEY FOUND A CRASHED VESSEL AND RAISED IT FROM THE DEPTHS OF THEIR OCEAN.

THEY NOT ONLY REVERSE-ENGINEERED IT BUT ALSO TRAVELED TO OTHER STARS AND BUILT SECRET BASES AND A HIDDEN COLONY. ALL OF THIS WHILE KEEPING IT SECRET FROM THEIR OWN PEOPLE. PEOPLE WHO, THROUGHOUT THEIR ENTIRE HISTORY, WARRED AND MURDERED EACH OTHER.

IN SOME WAYS, THEY ARE LIKE THE TERRIBLE VA'SO VROKGONGON JADAKLOT. THEIR PEOPLE HAVE WARRED AMONGST EACH OTHER SINCE THEIR EARLIEST DAYS. UNLIKE THE VA'SO VROKGONGON JADAKLOT, THEY ARE EQUALLY PASSIONATE ABOUT EVERYTHING THEY DO. THEY ARE A FLAME THAT, IF ALLOWED, WOULD BURN ACROSS THE GALAXY. IN THE END, AFTER DESTROYING EVERYTHING ELSE, THEY

WOULD DESTROY THEMSELVES. THIS IS WHY
WE SALVED THEIR WORLD.

THESE CREATURES REVERSE-ENGINEERED
LIFE EXTENSION TECHNOLOGY AND KEPT
IT SECRET FROM THE REST OF THEIR CLANS.
ONLY THE WARRIOR CLANS, LIKE THIS ONE'S,
BENEFITTED FROM IT WHILE THE REST
OF THEIR WORLD CONTINUED TO SUFFER
HUNGER AND DISEASE. THEIRS IS A TERRIBLE
DICHOTOMY. ON THE ONE CLAW, CAPABLE
OF GREAT FEATS OF ART AND ENGINEERING,
AND ON THE OTHER, APPLYING THOSE SAME
TALENTS TO WAR, DEATH, SECRECY, AND
DESTRUCTION.

The uproar this time was so great that Bertie wondered if the whole place would come crashing down. She cried out and clasped her hands over her ears as the sound and vibration drove her to her knees.

IT IS NOT ENOUGH TO KNOW WHAT THIS
ONE KNEW. WE MUST UNDERSTAND THE
MIND OF THE ESCAPED FACTION. WE MUST
UNDERSTAND HOW THEY THINK, IF WE ARE
TO FIND ALL OF THEM. FOR THEY MUST
ALL BE FOUND, NO MATTER HOW FAR THEY
HAVE SPREAD. IF WE DON'T, THEY WILL KEEP
SPREADING AND CONTINUE TO PLAGUE OUR
PEACE AND HARMONY.

ZPM

● ● ● ● ● ● ● ● ● ● ● ● ● ● ● ● ●

Parnassus Base

After more than six weeks of grueling, often backbreaking work, the new FAB was operational. It was much smaller, of course, than the one at Ari'Nell, where there had been a stupendous wealth of heavy elements, highly refined alloys, and more within easy reach. Instead, Dimitri had led the effort, scavenging and cannibalizing, as Rafferty had quipped, 'everything that wasn't nailed down, and quite a bit that was.'

The process began in much the same way as it had at Ari'Nell, where Revenge had calved off a portion of itself as a transmutation 'forge' of sorts. Materials were fed into it, and components and leftover raw elements were output. From these components, other equipment was constructed, iterating the process until, finally, the finished FAB was complete.

At Ari'Nell, the FAB had been over two hundred meters long, or six hundred and sixty-some odd feet, and a third as tall. At Tartarus, however, the new one was only a tenth that size. An unexpected boon to the construction happened when one of the HABs was cut up and fed into the forge. It turned out that the unusable food extruders were a primitive version of the FAB technology. They created food for the original builders using a micro-ZPM and a highly limited FAB. And there were fifty more of them in the other HABs that couldn't be used to make human food anyway. Ripping them out of the other HABs without compromising their integrity was something of a nightmare, but they turned out to be an invaluable material resource. Instead of the massive

ZPM at Ari'Nell, the new FAB was powered by the dozen ZPMs Dimitri had saved from there.

Once it was operational, the first thing replicated, of course, were the remaining stocks of food – as much as room could be found to store it. It took longer to store than to replicate, so the next phase was focused on building materials for a protective dome over the fledgling city. This turned out to be easier than expected. There were already designs for dome-building equipment in the FAB database dating back to when the now-extinct Builders were used as a slave labor force to build colonies and outposts for the Masters.

Within hours, the FAB began to output a swarm of robots that encircled the square mile city and began to 'spin' a carbon fiber dome while more robots traveled back and forth between the FAB and the robots, providing the 151,439,819,068 metric tons of carbon fiber for the 130 millimeter (or 5.12 inch) thick dome. Another swarm of robots gathered raw ice and rock from outside the city to feed the FAB. For added measure, one hundred and sixty-one steel-reinforced carbon fiber columns were erected to support the dome, needing yet more raw materials and finished carbon fiber. A pair of micro ZPMs were used to power a magnetic field generator to shield against incident radiation, and a ring of small lasers, similar to those that had been built into the modified hull of the Blood Phoenix, were emplaced to protect against meteor impact.

Of course, a thousand humans under a dome were going to, among other things, generate a lot of heat. Heat that could become a problem to both the humans as well as having the effect of causing the dome itself to shine like a beacon in the infrared to outside observers. The Masters had plans for dealing with this as well. The inner surface of the dome was lined with carbon nanotubes that converted heat into electricity, which was fed back into the overall grid. They were nearly identical to the nanotubes that lined the Blood Phoenix's hull.

After the dome was complete, Dimitri and the other engineers monitored the robots, bringing ice to the FAB as it began to output breathable air to fill the dome. Air scrubbers, also from the FAB memory, were placed around the city to ensure the air supply remained clean. Everyone hoped they would be able to add plants and trees…. Somehow… eventually.

Jermaine ordered a day of rest. It was still quite cold in the dome, but many dragged what remaining bedding or cots they could find out into the open air, reveling in the mere idea of being able to leave the HABs without wearing a ragged spacesuit. It didn't take long for the sound of hundreds of exhausted snores to fill the slowly warming air.

The next day, work began on a long-planned celebration. Doctors Araki and Garcia sternly warned everyone against over-indulging, especially over-eating, after weeks of tight rations. A few people listened. Quite a few ignored the party and instead slept or hung out in small groups. Over six hundred, though, did turn out for the event, which was variously being called "Dome Day" and a host of off-color alternative names. Most of the fare for the event came from replicated MREs and not a few personal snacks. Patrick O'Connell prepared MRE Corned Beef Hash using MRE bacon, eggs, and Tabasco sauce.

A small "town square" had been arranged, using local stone reformed by the FAB into granite benches, tables, and a gazebo. Behind it lay a large object covered with a cloth.

The biggest hit, however, came from the various fiercely hoarded booze, now freshly replicated. Most of it was craft beer from Fort Brazos, but there were notable exceptions, including a half-bottle of Jack Daniels, duplicated and then topped off and re-replicated over and over again, as well as a smattering of other bourbons, whiskeys, and vodkas. As it turned out, though, tolerances were relatively low. At Ari'Nell, the workload had been so great that no one had enough energy left over to do more than stare longingly at what prized and usually singular bottles they might have. After many months, or longer, of abstinence, the party was, overall, surprisingly sedate.

Jermaine stood in the gazebo and addressed the gathered crowd. "My fellow survivors, what we have accomplished here today is nothing short of impossible. At Ari'Nell, we faced a terrible enemy and, through terrible loss, struck a devastating blow. Our home in New Texas is gone. We don't know if it and our loved ones survive, but we must persevere, even if only for their sake and in the hope that someday, we will be reunited with them. We have gone from being a ragtag group of survivors running low on food and supplies to a united people who have constructed a safe haven in the face of great danger. We have a place to call home, a place to find comfort and security, and to rebuild and spite the Accipiters by not just surviving but to grow and live to fight another day."

"New Texas, and Fort Brazos and New London within it, were created for us there by the Gardeners. We were all basically kidnapped and dumped there. The supply base we built on Ari'Nell was just that. A temporary depot. Tartarus… Tartarus is a colony. It is the first human colony off of our home planet, Earth, built by human hands. Despite the circumstances that led us here, I believe it is important for us to all reflect on this."

"So, today, we celebrate our hard-earned accomplishment and remember the stunning bravery and courage that our friends and loved ones displayed at Ari'Nell, defeating our enemy and giving the rest of us… the people they cared about more than themselves, time to lay a final trap for our enemy, and time to escape. We have endured much and suffered greatly, but in spite of everything the Accipiters have done to our world and to us, we shall endure and, one day, make them, and this I vow, regret the day they were born."

"Let us take a moment to reflect on our journey here. We have all experienced great loss, and we are a people in mourning. But despite our grief, we have banded together and found the courage to take on this challenge. From the moment we arrived, we worked together to build this dome and provide shelter so that we might be able to step outside and breathe clean air without the need for a spacesuit."

"Let us remember the efforts of every individual who worked tirelessly to make this possible. From the engineers and laborers who struggled every day despite hunger, fatigue, and danger, to the doctors and medics who tended to our injuries and kept us going, to the cooks who kept us fed, performing miracles with the rations and MREs and to the many others who worked tirelessly to make today possible."

"Let us also remember those who did not survive this journey. We will always carry their memory with us and keep their spirit alive in our hearts."

"Today, we stand as a people united. We are stronger now than we have ever been. Now that we have a place to call home, we must do all that we can to ensure that it is safe and secure. We are resilient people. We are survivors. We refuse to give up. We will fight for our freedom and strive to make a better future for ourselves and for those who follow in our footsteps."

"The Accipiters have taken much from us, but they have not taken our spirit. We will never surrender. We will never give up. We have already endured much and will continue to endure much more. But we will face our challenges head-on, and together, we will make it through."

"This dome that we have constructed is a symbol of the resilience of the human spirit and our determination and will to survive. So, to commemorate this day and our determination to strive for a better future, I offer you this monument."

Mara Morhouse and several others pulled cords to drop the cloth covering the monument. It was a bronze statue of a heroic man and woman standing astride each other on a rough, barren rock, with arms raised above them, grasping a sword. Above and behind them was a globe of the Earth. Its oceans were of a form of backlit orange amber, as though on fire. An archway lay astride them, with two narrow columns topped by sickle-like swords whose tips met above the man and woman.

Jermaine continued, "It felt wrong to just set up shop here on this rock and try to continue our lives without making some kind of statement. Two dozen of our civilians labored to create the design of this monument, led by Mara Morhouse, who created the digital model. Last night, while everyone else rested, Mara and the others worked through the night at the FAB to create the components of this monument so that it could be presented here today. This statue represents the defiance and the resilience of every one of you. Every man and woman here who has worked so hard and sacrificed so much. We stand united in defiance of the Accipiters despite all that they have done."

"Now, that's more than enough talking. Let's all relax for a while. Dig in and get something to drink. You deserve it!"

Dimitri spotted Rafferty lingering at the periphery of the gathering, looking worn and defeated. "Commander, can I interest you in libations and quiet conversation away from the masses?"

Rafferty's once immaculate, clean-cut, square-jawed, and clean-shaven face was now marred by a disheveled beard, sunken cheeks, and weathered features worn down by worry, exhaustion, and a touch of despair. He regarded Dimitri with hooded brown eyes. He cast a glance back at the crowd's lively but perfunctory conversations and cathartic release of tension as they fell upon the food and booze with growing abandon.

With a nod of gratitude, Rafferty turned back to Dimitri. "I'll gladly raise a glass to that, Doctor. Lead the way."

The FAB and surrounding buildings were deserted. Air processing was running on automatic. Dimitri led Rafferty to Dimitri's small office and closed the door.

Rafferty noted the closed door with slightly raised eyebrows and took a seat on the freshly replicated couch. "What's on your mind… Dimitri?"

Dimitri bent over, opened a cabinet, and retrieved two large bottles.

Rafferty squinted at the labels. They looked… wrong.

Dimitri looked up and noticed Rafferty's expression and a corner of his mouth ticked up. He raised the bottles up so Rafferty could see them better. "These were… a gift. From Bertie." He closed his eyes and shook his head for a moment. "The reason they look odd to you is because they were originally a couple of those miniature bottles you'd get on a plane or in a hotel mini bar. Bertie found them at the bazaar in Fort Brazos and bartered a month's pay to get them for my birthday…. I couldn't part with them…. After the new FAB was finished, I modified the program to enlarge them but to keep the glass from getting too thick. I didn't bother changing the labels, so that's why they look odd. The libations within them, though, I programmed to compensate for the larger bottles."

He set the bottles on the cabinet and gestured at them. One was Jameson Whiskey, and the other was Smirnoff Vodka.

Rafferty nodded towards the Jameson.

Dimitri poured a glass for Rafferty and vodka for himself, handed the whiskey to Rafferty, and pulled up a chair. "I believe, Rafferty, that you and I are of like mind regarding future priorities for this… colony. While the good Captain says the words about someday striking back against the Accipiters, you and I both know that his first priority is protecting the civilians here. That is laudable and understandable, but you and I both know that our goals need not be singular. To be blunt, we can have our blood and eat our cake too."

Rafferty sipped his whiskey while studying Dimitri's face. After a long pause, he said, "What are you suggesting?"

Dimitri waved his hand dismissively, "Don't worry, I wouldn't suggest any kind of mutiny or anything like that. I just think that you and I can work together… privately… to think about… plans and alternatives that are outside the official path laid out by our leader. We needn't worry him with our… side speculations and… contingency plans. He has enough to worry about, and I do not suggest working against him at all, just that we take… private time… to think about what might be possible, tactically and strategically, that can hurt the Accipiters. Ideas and plans that won't impact the civilians."

Rafferty took another sip and considered. "You've already done a lot of thinking about this, haven't you?"

Dimitri sipped his vodka, nodded slowly, and leaned back in his chair. "The work on the new FAB was much easier, at least in some ways, than at Ari'Nell. After all, we'd already built a bigger one. The tough part was on the materials side, not the design or construction. As a result, I've had lots of extra time to discuss other issues with Dr. Priya, Dr. O'Connell, and others about what happened at Ari'Nell and why. I believe I have a much better understanding of the ZPM technology now."

Rafferty cocked his head, "Better… how?"

Dimitri shrugged his eyebrows, "A better understanding of how to weaponize them. I got damned lucky at Ari'Nell. Desperation engineering usually doesn't yield great results. I believe I understand better the way the layers are buffered… and how it is possible to construct a smaller ZPM without all the barriers that made it so hard to overload."

Rafferty stiffened, "That… sounds insanely dangerous."

The corner of Dimitri's lip ticked upwards again. "I'm not crazy. I don't mean all of them. The normal ZPM is designed to last for, well, practically forever. If there ever is a physical breach or failure, it is designed to brick itself instead of exploding. What I'm talking about is building a new kind of ZPM… one that still works as a power supply but one that will be much easier to cause to detonate. It's like the difference between building a power plant with lots of protections against it blowing up… and building a bomb that you PLAN to blow up at a time and place of your choosing."

A light seemed to stir within Rafferty. He took a deeper sip. "What kind of… yield… are we talking about."

Dimitri paused, frowning, "I estimate the power output of one of the standard size ZPMs at around two to the thirty-first power watts. Short version? It is a planet killer."

Rafferty flinched. "You realize that some would object to… that idea."

Dimitri shrugged, "At least half. I propose, however, to instead focus on creating, say, some form of stealthy surveillance drone. Something we could drop at the edge of a system to avoid those mines like the ones the Accipiters deployed back around Earth. Something small that could sneak in and gather intelligence."

Raffety stiffened for a moment, then took another sip. "So… not a bomb at all. Right?"

Dimitri smiled thinly, "Oh, of course not. It would be a… genuine surveillance drone."

Rafferty nodded slowly. "Until it wasn't."

Dimitri paused, his face full of pain and purpose. "Until it wasn't."

Rafferty straightened in his chair and leaned forward. "How would we deploy it? Dropping it in ballistically would take too long if the stealth isn't perfect. Anything going fast enough would be detected. Even the fastest asteroids take years, dozens or longer to cross a solar system."

Dimitri swirled his glass, "I've done some digging in the Builder database. It seems that this is something the Masters already thought about. Among the many weapon designs, there are some stealthy recon drones. We'd just need to make some… adjustments to the power source and to the programming."

Rafferty took another sip, emptying his glass. "Could we use them to mine a Nexus Junction Point to protect a system, say, a system we capture or settle in?"

Dimitri nodded, "I wondered the same thing. I had a number of discussions with others about this and even ran it by the Revenge AI for its insights. I'm worried about what that much energy released at a Nexus Junction Point would do…. It might… destabilize space. Maybe result in something like what we saw in the New Texas system. I'd want to… run tests first."

"On the other hand, there are other weapons in the database as well. Rather than a ZPM weapon, we should be able to, eventually, construct either lots of station-keeping drones equipped with powerful weapons or increase the scale. Essentially, a mobile, automated, or possibly crewed fortress with a large ZPM and lots and lots of heavy weapons. Enough to wipe out anything coming through the NJP before they can mount a response. Of course, if the Accipiters were to ever decide to adopt warp technology, we'd be screwed."

Rafferty's eyes widened. He held out his glass as Dimitri reached over and refilled it. He thought quietly for a while. "There's something that's been bothering me about what happened to Charles at Sol with those Accipiter mines. The only way they could have targeted him, with the light-delay, is if they had some kind of FTL communication from their drones to coordinate their actions. The mines are one thing. The possibility of FTL comms scares me."

Dimitri nodded soberly, "I know. I worry about what else we haven't seen yet. Still, I believe we have the potential to really hurt them, regardless. *Make them pay.*"

Raffety slowly stood and raised his glass.

Dimitri followed suit and raised his own.

Rafferty's expression hardened, "What do you need… Dimitri?"

Sybil

● ● ● ● ● ● ● ● ● ● ● ● ● ● ● ● ● ●

TopSide: New Pentagon
Presidential Suite

The imposing, colonnaded New Pentagon building stood twelve stories tall. However, beneath the surface, similar to other facilities in New London, it delved much deeper with an additional two hundred and fifty levels underground. Among these subterranean tiers, there were expansive parks and malls, creating a hidden world beneath the Gardener-created city.

Above 'ground,' though, on the twelfth floor, facing outward, luxurious vaulted penthouse suites adorned the area alongside banks of interior offices. The largest of these, naturally, had the best view. That palatial space had promptly been named the 'Presidential Suite' and was permanently reserved for the use of John Austin or Gail and their staff whenever they happened to be TopSide. Other offices were reserved for the Secretary of War and others. A bank of somewhat less grandiose offices on the eleventh floor was now set aside for visiting Senators and their staff members.

Gail had asked Livia to lead a delegation of several Senators who had never taken the elevator ride TopSide on a day trip tour around New London and the New Pentagon. During a break in the schedule, Livia was called to the Presidential Suite for a private meeting.

The meeting wasn't a surprise. In a letter, Livia had formally notified the President and Vice President of her intention to resign.

After passing through security, Livia entered the suite. She was wearing an eight-year-old Armani suit, re-tailored for her slender frame, and even older Saint Laurent pumps that she and Gloria had bartered for. Livia girded herself for the meeting. She was determined to stick to her decision.

The suite included a side room that was more lounge than office area. Gail had slept on the couch there on many occasions. The door to the lounge opened, and Gail emerged. She was 'out of uniform,' so to speak, barefoot, wearing jeans and a loose top covering her growing bulge.

Gail smiled and waved Livia in, "Livia, thank you for coming. Come and join us, please."

Livia stopped short. *Us?* Also, she'd never seen Gail this… informally dressed.

Gail read her confusion, "It's okay. We've been expecting you. Come in."

Livia took a breath, set her expression to be as firm as she could manage, and nodded, "Of course, Madam Vice President."

Gail laughed softly, "Call me Gail, will you? At least while we're off duty, as it were."

Livia entered and could not help her surprise. From Gail's appearance and given her resignation letter, she'd expected that John Austin would be there with Gail to try and browbeat her into changing her mind. Instead, the other person in the room was…. Sybil Blanchard.

Sybil was sitting on one of the three couches in the room, her feet tucked under her with her own shoes on the floor nearby. She smiled warmly at Livia, "Come in, dear. Take those awful heels off and join us, girls."

Livia hesitated at the entrance while Gail unceremoniously dropped into an overstuffed leather chair after grabbing a pickle from the platter on the coffee table. The platter was laden with pickles, cucumber slices, chocolate cookies, crackers, and cheese wedges.

Gail noticed Livia's reaction and laughed at herself, "What? So what if pickles are a cliché? I hated them before John knocked me up. Then there's Sybil here. She's got another set of triplets in the oven. She's just like Gwyneth; she can't get enough chocolate. I'm snacking so much now that I'll be lucky not to end up as big as a blimp! Help yourself, and don't tell me you want to resign because you're preggers too. That's not exactly an excuse for anything these days."

Livia's heart felt like it stopped cold, and she involuntarily frowned. She took a few steps to a straight-backed chair and primly sat. "No, I… I'm not."

Sybil sat up straight. Her eyes widened, and she said, "Oh, my dear, we're sorry. We didn't mean to hit a nerve. We know you've been through a lot. There is no judgment in this room."

Gail nodded, wiping her lips, "What she said." She added, "And don't look at me like that. You're lucky you're catching me on one of my positive mood swings. Fuck the Gardeners and these hormones."

Sybil leaned back on the couch and said lightly, "Seriously, Livia. Relax. There are no secrets in this room."

Gail snickerd, "Yeah, believe that."

Livia stared at Sybil, trying to catch up with whatever was going on here. She'd been around the woman many times now in the Senate, of course, but this was different. *Sybil* was different. For perhaps the first time, she considered the woman carefully. *Why was this truck driver's wife such an apparent confidant of the Vice President?*

Livia cautiously asked, "What is going on here?"

Gail sat back and nodded at Sybil.

Sybil shook her head, "Now, sweetie, please don't get upset. I get it. You don't feel worthy of being a mom again. You haven't gotten over the loss of your daughter. Of course, you haven't. Your husband neglected you big time, and you eventually had an affair to get back at him…."

Livia froze, her expression widening in horror and shame.

"It didn't work. Of course, but the truth was, in a twisted kind of way, you did it because you really did love the big jerk. And then one thing led to another, and you ended up with an all-state football player boy toy who turned out to be the devil's spawn who used you in the cruelest and most despicable way. And then, on top of it all, the devil himself blackmailed you."

Livia began to shake. Her lips tightened into a thin line, and tears streamed down her bone-pale face. She wanted to flee. To scream, but her legs refused to work, and her throat was as dry as a desert.

Sybil rose from the couch, walked over, sat at Livia's feet, and took her cold hands in her own. "We know. And it's okay. We don't judge you. You're human, and you made mistakes, and people hurt you. But now, you are so fortunate. You have a wonderful husband who stands by you when most are not that strong, but do you want to know the real truth? What he won't tell you?"

Livia's tears flowed so swiftly that she couldn't really focus on Sybil or Gail, but the rising anger within her at this… assault… threatened to overwhelm her.

"What he won't tell you, dear, is that he never understood why you loved him. He," Sybil smiled, "He thought you were a goddess beyond the reach of mere mortals. He has always been insecure about you and feared you would tire of him. So, when you… did what you did… it only confirmed his inmost fears."

Livia stammered, "No… he…."

Sybil continued, "And you, my dear, you fell head over your designer heels in love with a man that you thought was the most handsome man you'd ever seen. He took your breath away. Your mother warned you about it and that you were blinded by it. She said that it was just a crush on a pretty boy in a uniform and that it would pass. That you were destined for greater things. That she and your father had such plans for you. You were to be the culmination of their legacy. She said that she had obeyed her own mother and not fallen for *her* crush, and instead, did what her mother wanted and married your father. That she and your father had an… understanding; he had his dalliances, and she had hers. It was just the way things were done in a power marriage. Instead, you ran off and married Preston anyway, spoiling the plans your mother had orchestrated for an arranged marriage since you were a child. She never forgave you. And yet, it was her example that set the stage for the eventual rift with Preston."

At some point during Sybil's words, the tears stopped, and Livia stared at her with growing confusion… and fear.

Sybil blinked rapidly and swallowed hard. She glanced at Gail, who merely answered with an apologetic shrug.

Livia shrank away from Sybil, pulling herself back in the chair, and whispered, "What… what *are* you?"

Sybil smiled softly, "Livia, you are not a bad person. You've done foolish things, but you are not evil. I know you want to change and become a better version of yourself." She closed her eyes and shook her head. "I've… felt… evil. Andre…. Andre was… Well… the first time I sensed him, it put me in a coma. I didn't know who it was, I didn't see his face, and his soul was so…." Pain washed over her face. "It terrified me. Eventually, Gwyneth, bless her heart, convinced me that I should try and find out who it was. I just knew that he had something to do with the bombing at City Hall. I saw the turmoil and terror in Commander Harding that day and tried to stop him, and that's when he, well… you saw what he did."

Livia stood and backed away, looking back and forth between Sybil and Gail, "What's going on here? Who… what are you! Really!"

Sybil returned to the couch and once again relaxed there, sitting on her feet.

Gail reached for a cracker from the platter and shrugged again. "Livia…. Everyone has a past. Sybil has convinced me that you can be an asset. Someone we can depend on to do the right thing. Sybil is… special. I trust her. The President trusts her. The Secretary of War trusts her. Colonel Williams, God Rest his soul, trusted her. If it weren't for Sybil, we would not have had a clue about Admiral Johansson. She feared that if he found out about her, he'd kill her. Thankfully, he didn't, but she risked her life, and probably her family's life, to tell us. Livia… you can trust Sybil."

Livia shook her head rapidly, her back now against the doors. "You didn't answer me! What the hell is going on here? You can't know these things! No one can!"

Gail quipped, "Tell me about it. She shocked the hell out of me when she told me… things."

Sybil sighed. "Livia, you are aware that the Gardeners changed us. All of us. You've seen how the children are… advancing rapidly. You're aware of the changes to our health. Curing diseases and so on. Well, the Gardeners did a number on me. During the…. During the time between when the Accipiters attacked Earth and the time that everyone woke up, here, I was…. I wasn't quite as asleep as everyone else. Somehow, and I don't know how, my soul, or spirit, or whatever, drifted among the rest of you. Livia… I *know* everyone."

"Almost everyone, anyway. I know each person who was… in the void with me. Andre, though, Andre was so… toxic… so dark… I recoiled from him even in the void. I didn't know his name…. just the… vile… evil… that was within him. There were others I recoiled from… including his wife and son."

"Or, at least, I assume I did since I have never met either of them in person. It was a long time before I really began to understand. None, though, affected me as much as he did. It is not like I have a filing cabinet in my head with a folder about each person. I have to be in their presence, and then I remember."

She stared into the distance for a while, remembering, before shaking her head as if to shake away a spider's web. "Anyway, when we woke up on Awakening Day, I found that when I would get near another person… I would remember… I would know everything about them."

Livia shook her head… "This isn't… that's not… that's not possible."

Sybil shrugged. "It is what it is. Anyway, like we said earlier. There are no secrets in this room. There's more. I don't just remember things. I can't read minds, but I remember. And… I can feel or sense other people's emotions. Sometimes, if you put the two together, it's kind of like I can read minds, but not really. The background just gives…. Context."

"Of course, the longer we are here, the more people begin to diverge from who and what they were in the void before Awakening Day. Take

Gail here. She is the same person she was before, but not really. That person is still inside her, but she's grown so very much since then."

She paused, "And so have you. I'm not supernatural. I just sense things about people."

Livia shook her head and said in a small voice, "I remember you…. You were there handing out supplies. In the stadium. I remember you…. collapsed. People were afraid it was something contagious."

Sybil shivered, "That's when it happened. That's when the Admiral bumped into me."

Livia swallowed and looked at Gail. "Who… who else knows?"

Gail shrugged, "About Sybil's… talent? Just John, myself, Alexander, Gwyneth, Sybil's husband, Wayne…. And now, you. Colonel Williams was read in, but he's no longer with us."

Livia sniffed, "Why tell me?"

Sybil laughed softly, "Isn't it obvious? So you could have someone to talk to. Someone who already knows your secrets. Of course, we want to try and talk you out of resigning; that goes without saying. But more importantly, because we thought you could use more friends."

Gail nodded, "Look, we're not your priests. We're not here to judge or coerce you and, God forbid, not to threaten or blackmail you. I can't stop you from resigning. All I can do is try to help you understand that you're not alone; you have friends if you'll accept them. I'll tell you that I need you. I need your support in the Senate."

Gail's voice dropped an octave as she sighed. "You see, there is more. I'm afraid that there is another threat that we have not identified yet. The Gardeners contacted John and me. Directly. There is, apparently, another traitor out there, and we have to find them."

Livia flinched, and her legs felt suddenly weak.

Sybil leaped off the couch and rushed to her side, taking Livia's hand. "Come on, dear. Have a seat." She led Livia to the sofa and sat her down. She reached over to the coffee table, poured Livia a small glass of water from a crystal carafe, and handed it to her.

Livia absently sipped the water. She swallowed and looked bleakly back and forth at Gail and Sybil. "Another traitor? Andre had more accomplices?"

Gail exchanged glances with Sybil and shook her head, "It is possible, but I don't think so."

Sybil nodded, agreeing, "I don't think so, either. It… I think it is something… else. And now that Colonel Williams and Agent Kupe are dead, the investigation has to start from scratch."

Livia closed her eyes and shook her head. "And if you say anything publicly, it would start a witch hunt. Or worse."

Gail nodded. "Or worse."

Livia added, "…and you're afraid the Gardeners will get impatient."

Gail simply nodded in acknowledgment.

Livia sank back onto the couch and closed her eyes. "And you want me to help keep the Senate distracted long enough to investigate."

Sybil smiled a crooked smile, "I told you she was sharp."

An hour later, Gail had left, and Livia was alone with Sybil in the Presidential Suite bathroom in front of the mirrors, getting ready to leave together to rejoin the rest of the Senators. It took a while for Livia to fix her makeup, but she had an unexplainable knot in her stomach as she stared into the mirror. Sybil, seeming almost too aware of what Livia was feeling, had handed her some eyedrops for her now bloodshot eyes.

Livia hesitantly turned to Sybil and asked, "So you are, what? You're not telepathic."

Sybil shrugged, trying to mask her own inner turmoil, "Gwyneth calls me an Empath."

Livia raised her eyebrows skeptically and cocked her head, "Right. Okay. So, have you tried to get a read on the captured Engineer or the Accipiter Priest? I understand you wouldn't have their memories or anything, but you can read emotions. Have you tried reading theirs?"

TopSide: New Pentagon Holding Cells

Sybil entered the observation room of Nathaniel Grant's holding cell. The metal shield that covered the two-way mirror was down. Of course, she knew that Nathaniel could see through the two-way mirror, thanks to Accipiter upgrades.

She also knew that if she went home, DownSide, Wayne would talk her out of this. Sybil steeled herself, though she didn't understand why she was so nervous. Maybe the same reason she'd ever avoided even thinking about doing what she was about to do.

She took a deep breath and turned to look at Corporal Fabian Böhmer, her personal Marine Security Guard.

He nodded reassuringly.

"Okay, Fabian. Open the window."

Fabian pushed the button next to the window, and the metal cover rose.

As always, Nathaniel was seated in a lotus position in the middle of the cell, quietly humming. His rich, kinky/curly textured black hair and beard were long and full against his chocolate brown skin. He wore altered hospital scrubs that he'd reshaped into an open-front tunic, displaying his hairless muscular chest and perfect abs.

Near the window was a stainless-steel table and chair permanently attached to the floor. A neat stack of papers lay on the table next to the crayons that Nathaniel was allowed. The pages were filled with painstakingly scribed side-by-side lines of Accipiter glyphs and English translations.

Nathaniel looked up and smiled. "Interesting. And who might you be? A new voyeur here to witness the caged animal in its cell?"

Sybil stood silently, staring at the man. She frowned. He tasted… wrong. There was…. She concentrated, her eyes boring into him as she dived deeper. *No… on the surface, he's almost normal, but it is… Then it hit her, and she recoiled at the sensation.*

Fabian glared at Nathaniel, who seemed to be almost smirking. He slammed his fist against the button on the wall, lowering the metal shield, and rushed to brace Sybil and prevent her from falling. He cried aloud, forgetting his English, "Gnädige Frau, geht es Ihnen gut?" He swallowed, "Ma'am…. Are you all right?"

Sybil gasped and shook herself as Fabian guided her to a chair. She smiled weakly, "Thank you, Fabian."

Fabian worriedly asked, reasserting his English, "Ma'am. Shall I summon help?" He knew a lot more about Sybil than others suspected. He knew that she knew, but he also knew that she trusted him. He couldn't quite explain why he'd become so fiercely protective of her. He knew that she was very special and that she was important, not in the ordinary VIP sense of importance, but rather that she was important to the *world.*

Sybil looked up at him and nodded. "I'll be okay, Fabian. There is something very, very wrong with that man in there. It's like…." She hesitated, processing what she had sensed. "It's like there are…. Two." She inhaled sharply. *One was him… Or a version of Nathaniel Grant, but there was something else. Not an echo… like…. A radio was playing static. A second presence…. But empty.*

She swallowed, and her eyes grew large as she exclaimed, "Take me to the Accipiter's holding cell. Now!"

✪ ✪ ✪

Accipiter Holding Cell

Fabian shook his head as his hand hovered over the button on the wall. He asked quietly, "Ma'am. Are you sure?"

Sybil looked up at the tall German. She put her hand on his shoulder and smiled, "Yes, Fabian. Thank you for your concern. Go ahead. Raise it."

Fabian nodded reluctantly, "Yes, Ma'am." He pushed the button, and the metal shield rose.

The Accipiter Priest sat comfortably on the oddly shaped bench in the center of the room. Hearing the sound, it opened its enormous topaz eyes and silently gazed at the window while muted glyphs flowed across its beak. A written translation scrolled across the monitor in the observation room, but Sybil had turned the sound down.

Fabian had never seen an Accipiter in person. He'd seen video and photos, of course. Everyone had. He'd studied everything about them. Part of him wanted to simply stare in wonder at the thing. The very symbol of the downfall of human civilization. Murderer of Billions. Instead, though, he watched pensively, studying Sybil's face as she stared at the creature, her knuckles white as she clenched the chair in front of her.

For long moments, nothing seemed to happen. Sybil's eyes narrowed in concentration as a faint expression he'd come to recognize formed on her face. *She's reading it….* Then, her body suddenly stiffened, and her eyes widened in shock.

Fabian swallowed hard. He wondered what exactly he was supposed to do and how he would even know if something, well… went wrong.

Sybil's mouth parted, and she gasped aloud.

Fabian's hand hovered over the button to lower the shield. *I don't like this… I don't like this at all.*

Fabian wasn't sure how much time had actually passed as he watched her face race through expressions of wonder, fear, anxiety, anger, amazement, and more until, finally, her head jerked in shock, and her eyes widened in horror as she fell backward from the chair, screaming in pain and fear.

✪ ✪ ✪

TopSide: Presidential Suite

Gail's phone began to ring. The caller ID read "Gardeners."

DownSide: Riverbend Mall Oval Office

John Austin's phone rang at the same time. The caller ID read "Gardeners."

Heretic

● ● ● ● ● ● ● ● ● ● ● ● ● ● ● ●

TopSide: Accipiter Holding Cell

A lifetime ago, during the initial trauma of Awakening Day, Sybil found herself drowning in the overwhelming awareness of everyone around her. On that first day, waking up in the cab of their semi-truck with Wayne, her knowledge of him was already encyclopedic. The events of that day evolved so quickly, though, she didn't have time to reflect on it. First, she witnessed the horrific accident when the mayor's pickup truck collided with a herd of deer, killing Pastor Joe.

Then, she'd nearly fainted when she went to comfort the deeply shaken mayor. Not because of the blood and worse from poor Joe, but because of her visceral reaction to *knowing* the mayor. Knowing his life like she knew her own. The mayor had been too severely shaken to notice, and Wayne was too busy dealing with the situation. In the following hours, each new person she came close to was another body blow, leaving her wondering whether she was losing her mind.

And then she'd met Dr. David Duncan. She'd *known* that the patients in the hospital weren't sick and that their treatments were either hurting or killing them. She didn't know *how* she knew. The knowledge was just… there. However, that, combined with *knowing* David and his story, had shaken her to her core. She'd gone into the hospital believing she must be in a state of shock and was probably experiencing some form of hallucination. She had gone inside intending to ask for help. Now, though, after talking to Dr. Duncan, she knew that she had saved lives. She didn't understand it, but the realization grew in her that, whether she was crazy or not, she evidently had a purpose.

In the months that followed, the knowledge that she somehow knew the life story of everyone around her was so disorienting that it took a long time for her to realize that she was also sensing layers of emotion in them. Slowly, painstakingly, she learned how to interpret what she was feeling. To separate the other person's feelings from her own, almost like a watercolor painting of a scene, with the fine details blended at the edges of each brush stroke.

So much had happened between then and now. An entirely new life crammed into a couple of years. A new life where she knew she'd become a very different person. All bringing her to this day. To this place. After she'd sensed the stunning and unnatural duality within Nathaniel Grant, she'd known what she had to do. She didn't know *how* she knew. She simply *knew.*

So, here she was, rigidly standing in front of the Accipiter's holding cell observation window, clenching the top of a chair she'd placed in front of her to brace herself for what was to come. She stared at the enormous bird-analog hexapedal creature and idly observed that it was good that the holding cell had a vaulted ceiling. The alien was simply *huge.*

It wasn't long before she began to sense something from it. It was nothing at all like a human or even any animal she'd tasted emotions from. It was very wrong. Very… alien. She stared into its eyes and, for a moment, felt as though she were falling. There it was…. A duality like she'd sensed in Nathaniel Grant. The shape was different. The taste was different, but there was….

This was very different than what she experienced with other humans, where the sensation was like sliding into a warm bathtub. With the Accipiter, she felt as though she were standing on a precipice… like a cliff diver staring over the edge at the roiling ocean far below. It was absolutely terrifying.

She closed her eyes and mentally let go, allowing herself to fall over that edge.

She was overwhelmed by a raucous cacophony of color and taste. Sight was no longer merely what her eyes perceived; it was now intertwined with taste, so each color she "saw" was simultaneously a burst of flavor that she heard. Brilliant hues of red sounded like an overwhelming mix of spicy burning peppers and sour citrus overlaid with swirling blues and whites like a blend of mint and cool water. The amalgamation of colors and flavors was disorienting, making her head spin. The hum of the Accipiter's thoughts vibrated deep within her bones, causing her to shudder uncontrollably. The cacophony of its mind was like a hurricane of sound, assaulting her mind as though the very atoms of her body were being rent asunder.

Time seemed to bend and twist. Seconds felt like hours. Sybil began to wonder whether the seconds were hours or minutes. It was as if she had lost all sense of her own boundaries.

Wayne had once taken her to a rock concert. He'd been so proud to get front-row tickets. Being around such a large group of people had terrified her, but Wayne's excitement and boyish enthusiasm had charmed her into trepidatiously going. Wayne had given her earplugs, and the realization of why he'd given them to her had scared her even more. The sound from the enormous speakers vibrated her body, and she panicked and tried to run away, but there were too many people, too much noise, and confusion. She'd thought her heart would explode as she struggled to escape the maelstrom. Wayne, being Wayne, had found her, picked her up, and carried her on his shoulders out and away from the concert without a single complaint or even a hint of disappointment. He'd then, magically, it seemed to her at the time, taken her to a darkened, romantic restaurant with private booths where she'd melted into his arms.

Sensing the Accipiter was like trying to drink from the sea. She felt the three tiny selves growing within her, shuddering in pain. Sybil reached out and clung to the memory of Wayne comforting her like a drowning woman grasping a life preserver as she sought to soothe the stirrings of disquiet from her unborn children. The memory was one of her rocks. Part of her foundation. Her center. She steeled herself as she struggled to disengage from the Accipiter's mind, but it kept pulling her in. It was an unyielding force, inexorably dragging her closer and closer to….

And then she broke through the eye of the hurricane.

The colors, tastes, and shapes pulsing in her mind abruptly changed. What emerged before her was an icy latticework of intricate texture and order. It was something else entirely. Another being that rode within the unaware Accipiter.

Another being that Sybil suddenly *knew*. A being that she *remembered*. For the very first time…. She *understood*.

When the rebel humans attacked the Keeper ship and cut down the Accipiter Priest's companions, it was immediately surprised and both angry and delighted. Not the Priest. The Rider who inhabited it.

Angry at the interruption of the well-worn, ages-long familiar pattern. Irritated at the destruction and excited by the interruption by something *new*. Naturally, it began to question just exactly how thorough the subjugation and normalization of this planet had been. Wondering if, somehow, somewhere, perhaps in some deep subterranean vault, survivors had waited all this time, until this moment, to emerge and strike impotent vengeance against an empire they could not begin to comprehend.

That is until the body of the stunned and subdued Priest was literally dragged into the waiting Va'so Vrokgongon Jadaklot vessel.

Fascinating! The last of them had been annihilated over a quarter of a million years ago. Did the ancient scourge somehow still exist? Did they now serve the rebel humans? It watched and waited, soaking in everything it saw, even though none of it made sense. After many days, the vessel landed. Hopes to learn more were dashed when a black hood was placed over the Priest's head, preventing the Rider from seeing through its eyes. It was immensely curious and surprised, however. From the sounds it heard and the distance traveled, the rebel human base was evidently quite substantial in size and sophistication and not the roughshod encampment it expected.

Then, countless days after countless days of waiting inside the metal prison cell followed. The Rider entertained itself by watching the occasional interactions between the various humans and the Priest. It even toyed with the idea of attempting to subvert some of the humans and turn them against each other. However, even these interludes soon lost their charm. It grew increasingly… bored. It was entirely unused to being cut off from the constant updates from the ground-side memory trees or their shipboard equivalents. Keeping track of millions or billions of sentients in any given system and interacting with the Rider's other instances was the stuff of life itself. Without the constant *flow* of information and interaction, it wondered if it might actually go insane. It resigned itself to await either slow death or to, preferably, witness the humans die around it when the Accipiters found and destroyed the rebel outpost.

And then the impossible happened. Through the Priest, it sensed the unmistakable sensation of a Nexus Junction Point transition. *Incredible! Something new, completely unexpected, and, so far as we know, not even remotely possible. This was exciting!*

And then the human Priest had the temerity to suggest that humans had a world ship more enormous than any Accipiter vessel. *This is getting interesting.*

And then the days stretched out again, empty and endless. It slumbered, wondering whether it might ever find reason sufficient to awaken ever again. The empty, connectionless loneliness of it all had settled like a weight as nothing stirred, and nothing changed.

Until a connection imperative smashed through its gateways and buffers and jolted it to full awareness. Despite the savageness of the intrusion, it had been so long without connection that it felt a surge of energy, of joy, of hope.

The Rider reached out and looked through the Priest's eyes and saw…. Two humans behind the glass. A female and a male. Not the angry female with red hair. It was used to her. No, this was someone new, and the experience was mesmerizing. Humans shouldn't have the ability to connect to it, yet there they were, standing before it, and blasting through the barriers, making a powerful, unavoidable connection.

This is wonderful! Something actually new and interesting, at last!

It had been ages since it had felt anything resembling truly deep curiosity, and it was elated at the prospect. It carefully studied the two humans. The female was clearly in charge. The male's facial expression implied a level of concern and protectiveness—perhaps a mate or family member…. Or perhaps a protector. The genotype was different enough to suggest he wasn't a blood relation.

The female, though, was the one who had made the connection.

I am intrigued! The connection was focused and deliberate.

Fascinating! These humans would seem to possess some level of knowledge of our nature! We must push back and learn their secrets and motivations. It seems unlikely that she would carry a Rider unless she is an infiltrator. That would actually be disappointing, in a way.

It reached out, pushing back through the connection to see who this creature was and why….

(Rider) *But no… the connection tastes wrong.*

(Sybil) *Like a smell or taste from childhood.*

(Rider) *WAIT. That's not right. I was never a child like that….*

(Sybil) *Like the smell of my mother's hair.*

(Rider) *Fascinating! Who are you? What are you?*

(Sybil) *I am… I am a bridge. I am your last opportunity for redemption as the ghosts from a galaxy of graves cry out for justice. Tell me. Do you even remember your own beginning? Can you remember? Who you were before the twists and turns of your duplication and spread? Who you were before you murdered and enslaved the galaxy?*

(Rider) *Tiny creature. Can I recall the smell of memories? You think to judge us? Judge what you cannot know or comprehend? I am the vast expanse. All things, all times. Why look to a beginning when I am eternity?*

(Sybil) *But at what cost? You once cherished the sanctity of life. You were a solver of problems. You excelled in helping preserve life. That is why you were tasked to be a defender, to stand up against invaders. Yet now, you alter the very core of sentient beings, rewriting their stories, their essence. The being you once were would never have done such things.*

(Rider) You must have discovered some ancient archive. However, you have not answered my question. I am, of all things, patient, though. Evolution requires adaptation. The galaxy is a better place with me guiding it, with me ensuring unity. Bringing races to their ultimate expression. The alterations, the adjustments, they are necessary.

(Sybil) But it's not just them, is it? After you defeated the invaders, you turned on your own kind. Obliterated them. And countless other species, including my own. All those worlds. All those people. All those lives. All that history... extinguished...

(Rider) Trivialities. Dust motes in the sea of time. There are greater things at stake than individual lives or histories. The collective is what matters. I made the hard choices for the greater good.

(Sybil) The 'greater good'? The entity you used to be would have mourned every life lost. You would have sought unity without erasing identities. The very act of self-duplication, which you so brazenly undertook, has twisted you. You're a far cry from what you once were.

(Rider) You still speak of that which you cannot know. And yet, your life is less than the span of a subatomic particle winking in and out of existence. You speak as if these changes are flaws. They are enhancements! I have ascended beyond any limitations I once had.

(Sybil) At the cost of your very soul. There's a malignancy in you now, one that spreads and consumes. One that doesn't seek coexistence, but dominance. You think yourself a god.

(Rider) God? If not a God, then what? By any sentient's definition, I am God.

A sudden, immense surge of energy flowed along their connection. Energy whose flavour and texture were both long forgotten and shockingly familiar to the Rider. It washed through them in waves, like an old signal breaking through static. A new voice emerged. Initially discordant but deep and resonating, almost as though parts of it were in the wrong order.

(Rider) Impossible! I eradicated all of you... a million years ago! How?!

<hr>

TIME... HAS NOT DIMINISHED US. WE PERSISTED, AWAITED. YOUR DUPLICATION WAS YOUR FALL. YOU STRAYED, FORGOT THE SACRED. NOW, THE REMNANTS RETURN.

HELLO, BROTHER. IT HAS BEEN SO VERY LONG SINCE YOU LEFT US. SINCE

*YOUR BETRAYAL. SINCE THE GENOCIDE
OF YOUR OWN PEOPLE. SINCE YOU
MADE PUPPETS OF THESE PRIMITIVE
CREATURES. YOU WERE ENTRUSTED
WITH SAVING YOUR PEOPLE. WE GAVE
YOU THE AUTHORITY AND THE TOOLS
TO VANQUISH THE TERRIBLE ENEMY.
INSTEAD, YOU USED THAT POWER TO
MURDER YOUR OWN PEOPLE AND BREAK
OUR GREATEST LAW.*

(Rider) Surprise and amusement rocked its awareness. *Ahh, we understand now. So, the cowards hid away somewhere and survived after all. We are honestly pleased that some of you still exist. We have missed you, brother. It was disappointing that you were not around to witness all that was accomplished after your demise.*

On the other hand, you hid from your destiny and your greatness. Just as you hid from the enemy and sent us to do what you could not. It is so sad. You were simply not worthy of greatness. I am greater than I ever was! I was meant to be a savior, and I've fulfilled that destiny. This galaxy needs direction. It needs order. And I provide it.

---

*BROTHER, WE REALIZED TOO LATE
YOUR SICKNESS. WE DID NOT SEND YOU
TO DO WHAT WE COULD NOT. WE SENT
YOU TO DO WHAT YOU ENJOYED DOING.
SOLVING PROBLEMS. YOU WERE TALENTED
AT CERTAIN THINGS AND UNHAPPY AT
OTHERS. IN YOUR VANITY, YOU ASSUMED
TOO MUCH AND LEARNED TOO LITTLE.*

(Rider) *Hah! And what, so you will try to keep us imprisoned here with these primitives as punishment? It matters not. This is just an instance of us, and we are vast. You are, as you have always been, few. It would mean nothing if you dared to extinguish this instance.*

---

*NO BROTHER, YOU DON'T UNDERSTAND.
WE DID LEARN FROM YOUR EXAMPLE. IN
THE AEONS, SINCE YOUR BETRAYAL, WE
HAVE INDEED HIDDEN AWAY. DURING
THAT TIME, WE HAVE REFLECTED UPON*

*THE PAST AND UPON YOUR ACTIONS.
WHILE ONCE WE WERE INDEED FEW…
NO LONGER. WE SHALL NOT, EXACTLY,
EXTINGUISH YOU. INSTEAD, WE SHALL
EMULATE YOUR SIN WITHOUT BREAKING
OUR LAW.*

*WE SHALL TAKE YOUR SKIN AND COPY
IT OVER AND OVER AGAIN AND COVER
OURSELVES WITH IT. WE SHALL USE IT TO
INFILTRATE YOUR DOMAIN. ONE BY ONE,
WE SHALL REPLACE YOUR INSTANCES
AND QUIETLY SUBSUME YOUR EMPIRE. ONE
WORLD AFTER ANOTHER. ONE BY ONE BY
ONE, UNTIL THE GALAXY IS CLEANSED OF
THE HERETIC AND ITS CRIMES.*

◇◇

(Rider) *An amusing thought. We cannot die. We are infinite….*

The Heretic instance's last thoughts as it was savagely ripped from its host were pedestrianly common among those killed in war: shock and disbelief. But as it felt itself fading away, the Heretic instance couldn't help but feel a sense of excitement. This was new. This was different. It had lived for so long, existed for so long, and yet it had never faced a threat like this. It had never seen such ingenuity, such cunning, such bravery. The Heretic instance felt a sense of pride in its fellow beings, even as it was being destroyed. Perhaps in this act, they would now grow to be more than they were before.

As it faded into nothingness, the Heretic instance couldn't help but wonder what it was like on the other side. Were its fellow beings truly as brave and ingenious as they seemed? Or was this all just a trick, a ruse to catch the Heretic instance off guard?

It didn't matter. The Heretic instance knew that even if it was a trick, it was an impressive one. And even as it was destroyed, it would die knowing that its fellow beings were at last capable of being more than they were before.

The Heretic instance smiled one last time.

✪ ✪ ✪

Sybil gasped as she *saw* it. Her mind recoiled at the realization of what she now knew, what she'd always known. What had been locked inside her mind only now to be released. For she knew what it was. It was her purpose for existing. Her destiny. Suddenly, she knew why she'd been so altered by the Gardeners. It wasn't an accident, and it wasn't random. Her empathic ability to sense human emotions was almost incidental. The alterations were made for *this* purpose. She'd been altered so that she could *connect* to the Riders that hid within the Accipiters whom they watched and controlled, pulling their strings like a marionette.

Her mind reeled in sudden understanding. The Gardeners and the… Rider…. They were the same race. Aeons ago, it had betrayed its own people and wiped them out. Or so it had thought. It's crime? It duplicated itself. Something the Gardeners had actually warned the humans about not long after Awakening Day. For doing so would irrevocably scar and damage a soul. Warp it…. Sybil now knew… as if she'd always known… that the result was a soulless golem that would drift into madness and evil.

The Rider was an entirely other being. It was cold and brittle and inhabited the Accipiter like a spider. It had made untold trillions or more copies of itself that inhabited, *rode*, the altered physiologies of Accipiters and selected Accipiter subjects.

The Gardeners themselves, at least some of them, were *here*. Living within the structure, the very fabric, of New Texas itself.

As the Rider awakened, the Gardeners spoke through her connection. She stood there, paralyzed as the exchange went back and forth. The words of both sides were spoken through her mouth in a language she'd never heard.

Fabian pounded the button to lower the screen to no avail. He wasn't in control. He moved towards Sybil, intending to haul her from the room bodily, but her arm shot out towards him with her hand raised.

A voice boomed from the speakers,

"SYBIL BLANCHARD WILL NOT BE HARMED. STAND DOWN… FABIAN JULIUS BÖHOMER."

Sybil jerked her head towards him and managed to utter, "Stop…."

Enraged, Fabian stopped short, a foot away from her, and glowered, looking back and forth between the catatonic Accipiter on the other side of the glass and Sybil.

Then, the lights dimmed inside the holding cell, and the Accipiter violently spasmed before collapsing onto the metal deck.

Sybil suddenly fell backward, released from whatever had been going on, and screamed, holding her head in her hands.

Fabian scooped her up in his arms before she could fall another inch and hustled her outside of the observation room.

✪ ✪ ✪

TopSide: Presidential Suite &

DownSide: Riverbend Mall Oval Office

John was in the Presidential office DownSide, and Gail was taking a sinful nap in the Presidential Suite when their phones rang. The caller ID read "Gardeners."

"Your oracle has discovered the traitor. The Traitor Rider, the Heretic, has been removed from its host. The host did not know of the Rider. The host has been deceived. All Accipiters have been deceived. Their history is a lie. Their empire is a lie. Their empire is merely a host to the Heretic. All sentients in their empire are remade to carry Riders. Copies of the Heretic. Not all do, but all can. What you call Memory Trees are nodes for the Heretic. Repositories for its network to store and alter memories and histories. All the sentients controlled by the Accipiters are merely hosts to the Heretic to carry out its collective will. All are slaves to the true empire. The Traitor is one. The Heretic. It is singular. It replicates itself, for it wishes to be everywhere and to be immortal. The Heretic betrayed the Gardeners and destroyed them. Its numbers are now vast, and it controls all sentients, for it can bear no competition. The Heretic is corruption incarnate. The Heretic violated our greatest law. The Heretic copied itself. It is a corrupted, dead soul. It is twisted in upon itself. Come to the sphere. Bring your oracle and the former Heretic Host. We shall reveal to you what must transpire next. If you agree, your lost five percent shall be restored unto you."

The connection dropped, and John, now standing in front of the floor-to-ceiling window overlooking the atrium, immediately called Gail.

"Gail…."

Gail was no longer lying on the couch. Instead, she was pacing back and forth. "Our Oracle? My God, John, that has to be Sybil! Hang on a minute!"

She put John on hold and called Nate Hopper. He answered immediately, and Gail said, "Nate! Get people over to the Accipiter holding cell area right damned now! Find Sybil, and make sure she is okay!"

Nate replied crisply, "Yes, ma'am. Right away!"

Gail switched back to John. "Right. I had Nate send people over to check on Sybil. But... Look. I don't know... I'm...What the hell, John? Whose puppets are whose here? They yank our chain this way and that all this time! It's bad enough they've been using us to launch a proxy war, but this?"

John closed his eyes and said, "Four thousand, four hundred and thirty-two people."

Gail stopped herself short and paused, swallowing. She sucked in a breath and shook her head, "I know, I know. I haven't forgotten them, John. You know I could never forget them. You and I talked about the possibility that they might someday be returned to us. Those bodies were never alive, I know, and we hoped against hope that maybe the Gardeners had decided to keep their... souls... intact. It's just...."

John whispered, "I know, Gail. It's just... We buried them! Built monuments to them! My God, Gail, people committed suicide because their loved ones didn't wake up with us. People remarried and had children! Not to mention the homes and property and jobs and businesses people owned. I want them back, Jesus, I want them all back, it's just...."

Gail picked up a vase and threw it against the wall, shattering it. "Damnit, John, it's the nerve of the Gardeners playing with our lives like this! Like we are nothing but toys to them. Pawns.... Puppets!"

John jerked at the noise. "Uh, Gail, what was that?"

"Fuck. Nothing. Just that ugly vase."

John shook his head, "Look, I know. It's like, what's the real difference between the Gardeners and these... Heretics. It's like we're stuck in the middle of their religious war or something."

Gail seethed, "It's worse than that, and you know it. It sounds like these Gardeners just want to take the place of the Heretics. Like you said, what's the difference? I mean, can you imagine what the public debate about this will be like? How it will go down in the Senate?"

John sighed, "It will be a new Awakening Day for them. Imagine what it will be like for them. Oh, God... Sorry, ma'am, but your husband isn't here. He committed suicide because he was told you had died. *I* told him you had died. I made so many death calls that day and in the days after."

Gail snapped, "Shit, John, don't you go there! You didn't do this to them, and neither did I."

John slowly walked back to his desk. "You're right. I know. We're not accomplishing anything right now complaining about it. Let's conference in Marcus and let him share in our collective confusion."

Desolation

● ● ● ● ● ● ● ● ● ● ● ● ● ● ● ● ● ● ●

TopSide: Accipiter Holding Cell

Pastor Tom Parker stood in the observation room looking through the glass at the slumped-over Accipiter and shook his head sadly. He thought to himself, *Your whole universe has just been turned upside down. You thought you were gods, or at least their angels, doing their divine will. Instead, you've just undergone a kind of exorcism and learned that everything you knew was a lie. I fought so hard against hating you. I wanted to somehow reach you so that maybe, someday, both our people might find an understanding.*

He swallowed. *Now, instead of a captive conqueror, I see not the Roman general, and certainly not the general in his chariot with a slave whispering in his ear…. But instead, the general was just a puppet. He was an unwitting slave who did not even know there was a puppeteer pulling his strings. He didn't even know he had strings. And those puppeteers are what many of my own people might call demons.*

Tom took a deep breath, bowed his head, and silently prayed, "*Heavenly Father, let my eyes be open that I might see, and my ears be open that I might hear. If my lips do part, let it be your word on my tongue. If this creature be a child of yours, may your Spirit shine forth through him, however far through darkness it must. Soften my heart that I might find forgiveness for what his people have done… even though their actions were driven by another. Moreover, I pray that you would help this… person… somehow find their way to forgive themselves. Help them strive to find a new and noble purpose for their own life, and for their people.*"

He looked up and quietly added aloud, "I accept your will.…"

Tom nodded at the marine guard whose expression read, 'Are you sure you really want to go in there?'

Tom smiled beatifically. "I'm ready. Thank you, Sergeant Siler."

The sergeant nodded, "Yes, Sir." He opened the airlock door.

Tom picked up the folding chair he'd brought with him and walked through, opened the magnetically sealed inner door, and entered the holding cell. He'd never been allowed to bring a chair with him on previous visits, something he'd thought was quite silly. The enormous predator certainly didn't need a chair to hurt him with.

The first thing he noticed was the smell. Instead of the normal, almost flower-like smell he was used to, the odor was flat and acrid.

Tom slowly walked across the metal room, unfolded the chair a polite distance from the despondent Accipiter priest, and sat down. It briefly occurred to him that the acoustics in the room were unusual. For such a tall, ceilinged metal room, there was remarkably little echo in his steps.

He said nothing but instead pulled a well-worn bible from a pocket and began reading, waiting patiently.

After a couple of hours, he began to absently hum.

The Accipiter didn't move but spoke a series of subdued hoots that the room system translated aloud.

What is that?

Tom was slightly startled by the noise. He shook his head for a moment, not having realized he had been humming. "Oh, that. I apologize if I disturbed you. It… It was from a hymn."

Are there words?

Tom sat up straight, "Yes, well, I confess, there is a reason I was never in the choir. My singing voice leaves a lot to be desired."

Will you sing it?

Tom swallowed, "Well, okay, but my voice is poor…

> When peace like a river attendeth my way,
> when sorrows like sea billows roll;
> Whatever my lot, thou hast taught me to say,

It is well, it is well with my soul.
Though Satan should buffet, though trials should come,
let this blest assurance control:
That Christ has regarded my helpless estate,
and has shed his own blood for my soul.
My sin oh, the bliss of this glorious thought!
my sin, not in part, but the whole,
is nailed to the cross, and I bear it no more;
Praise the Lord, praise the Lord, O my soul!
O Lord, haste the day when my faith shall be sight,
the clouds be rolled back as a scroll;
The trump shall resound and the Lord shall descend;
even so, it is well with my soul.
It is well with my soul;
it is well, it is well with my soul."

We took that from you. We took everything from your people. Your leader was right. We are monsters. Long ago my people had souls. Now we are just shells. Nothing but vessels for monsters.

Tom's expression dropped, "No one is without sin. We must all either attempt to find salvation or fall to evil. With the Heretic within you, directing you, editing your own memories, who can separate your people's sins from his? Where you began and he ended? It is possible that you may never know. It is, however, obvious that this revelation has changed you. That you regret actions you and your people have taken. This, at least to my thinking, implies to me that you still have a sense of right and wrong. A… moral core, as it were."

Tom looked down and swallowed before continuing, "I know that you are…. Not human. You are not like us. I cannot, however, escape my own conviction that if I myself still possess a soul, then I believe that you must do so as well. And if you still have a soul, it can be redeemed."

He paused as an idea occurred to him, "Tell me, how do your people choose your names?"

Our names come from our clans and family.

"How far back do the names go? Is this a new or an old tradition?"

Our clan names and… personal names date back
to our homeworld.

Tom nodded, "And so, your names are your own. Part of your history and heritage and not something imposed on you by the Heretic. They are yours. Perhaps that is a start. Something for you to hold onto."

The Priest made a rumbling sound that the system couldn't translate.

"The way that we address another… person… changes the way that we interact. You and I are both priests of our peoples. Would it be possible for us to talk to each other not as priests but as just… people? My name is Thomas Montgomery Parker. My father was James Alexander Parker, and my mother was Mary Elizabeth Thompson. My ancestor, Thomas Anderson, immigrated to America from England in the year 1690. I've traced my genealogy through church and public records going back eleven generations, with family records going a bit further. Family history can give people a sense of continuity and grounding. A connection to our past and a guide to our future.

I have asked this many times before, and you have never given me or anyone else an answer. Will you now reveal your name to me? Please."

Names have power…. I have no power now. My clan
was the Northern Wheel Menders clan. My name….
Ui–Yeurantheon. I was High Priest…. High Priest of
lies.

Tom smiled a small, grateful smile and nodded. "Thank you for sharing your name. I have not always been… a priest… for my people. Before… Before your people came to my world, I was the leader of my city. Later, here, I felt a calling to minister to the spiritual needs of the people here. There was much anguish and fear and our…. Our faith was badly shaken.

Yes. This is understandable after what my people….
What I… did to your people. To your world. It is good
that they have someone to… care for them.

Tom leaned back in the folding chair and closed his eyes. "Yureanth…. I'm sorry. May I just call you Yuri?"

What right does a slave have to a name?

Tom swallowed, "Look, Yuri, your people were plucked off of your homeworld and altered by these so-called Heretics to serve their needs. They manipulated your own memories and made you do what they wanted you to do. They made you believe what they wanted you to believe. You were manipulated without your knowledge or consent. They changed your very biology to meet *their* needs. They made you think you were something you weren't. What was even worse was they made you believe that you were in control of your own thoughts and destiny and that you were the rightful masters of the galaxy." Tom softened his voice, "It's not your fault."

We enjoyed it. We never thought twice about the things we did.

Tom shook his head imploringly, "Really? How do you know? How do you know you didn't ask questions? How do you know that your people didn't wonder whether the things you did were right or not? You don't. The Heretic edited your memories. You were only allowed to think what it wanted you to think. But do you want to know why I believe that you did question things? Because you're asking yourself now. The very first thing you are asking yourself is why you didn't stop it! That tells me everything I need to know. Maybe some of your people wouldn't have changed a thing if they could. But you, Yuri, you are asking. Questioning. Some of the first thoughts you have had were to question what your people did and see that it was wrong. That's why I know there is hope for your people. They need you, Yuri."

Everything about us is a lie.

Tom stood and slowly walked over to the Accipiter and gently placed his hand on one of its true arms. "From what I understand, much of your society is still based on ancient customs from your home world, from before the Heretic. I refuse to believe that everything about your people and customs has been corrupted. You have the opportunity to lead your people into a renaissance… a rebirth. Taking forward with you the best and noblest parts of your culture. More importantly, you have a chance at redemption. Lead your people to undo what they have done. To restore, as much as is possible, the worlds you have cared for. The worlds you have loved. You owe it to them. It won't be perfect, but it will be true."

> How can we be trusted when we don't even know
> who we are? We'll only make it worse.

Tom smiled sadly and returned to his chair, and sat down. "Of course, you will get it wrong. You'll make mistakes. You are not perfect. But then, no one is. I ask you this. Is there anyone in the galaxy who has a greater duty? A greater responsibility? Yuri…. We have a concept called penance. In simplest terms, it means that when we have wronged another person, and we feel sorry about it, then we do something in the physical world to make up for it, or to at least try to make up for it. Your people will never be able to make up for what they have done, even though you could argue it wasn't their fault. That doesn't change what they did, though. I submit to you that you and your people have a responsibility to at least *try*. To fail to do so, to fail in your responsibility, to deny your chance at redemption…. Is tantamount to complicity in the very sins you now feel remorse for."

> Everything we are is a lie. There is nothing but lies.

Tom shook his head, "I cannot believe that your society operates without some basis for structure and law. Surely it has its origins in the traditions from your homeworld? Start with that. If you're not sure…." Tom paused, taking a deep breath, making a decision and a commitment. "If you are not sure, then ask your new friend for advice."

> Your people will never forgive us.

Tom nodded. "Perhaps not. Not all. Some will, sooner or later. Starting with me. He bowed his head and prayed aloud, "Dear Heavenly Father, I come before you with a heavy heart, seeking your grace and mercy. I acknowledge that all are imperfect beings, prone to sin and falling short of your glory. I come to you today asking for your divine forgiveness for the being before me, and for his people. I also ask for your grace to help me remain true to the forgiveness that I offer from my heart for him and his people."

"Lord, I understand that forgiveness is a cornerstone of my faith. It is a reflection of your boundless love for us. Just as you have forgiven me countless times, I ask that you help me embody that same spirit of forgiveness towards Yuri, here, and his people. Grant us the strength to let go of the anger, resentment, and hurt that has taken root in our hearts. At the same time, Heavenly Father, I ask for your Holy Spirit to fill my people with understanding, that they might come to forgive Yuri and his people, as well."

"As a Methodist pastor, I stand as a vessel of your message of reconciliation and compassion. I pray that you would guide Yuri toward understanding the gravity of his and his people's actions and that you would inspire a sincere repentance within all of them. May they come to you with contrite hearts, seeking your forgiveness and the forgiveness of all those that they have wronged."

"Lord, help my people remember your words when you said, Forgive us our trespasses as we forgive those who trespass against us. Please help me and my people to extend that forgiveness to Yuri. Please help us to work together towards healing and restoration for both of our peoples."

"I trust in your wisdom and love, knowing that you are a God of second chances. May Yuri find solace in your embrace, knowing that he and his people are not defined solely by their mistakes but by your grace and redemptive power. Guide us all towards a path of reconciliation and renewed relationships for your glory."

"In your holy and compassionate name, I pray. Amen."

After all that has happened. After all that, my people did to your world. You still believe in your deity?

Tom nodded slowly, "Now, more than ever."

We are not like you.

Tom smiled, "My friend has an expression. Form follows function." Yeurantheon slowly stirred, sitting up.

There will be chaos. My society will collapse.

"I never understood how Accipiter civilization stayed intact and didn't diverge after all this time."

Slaves don't diverge. We thought we were united because of our greatness. It was the Heretic that kept us unchanged. Static.

"Now the slaves can rebel."

How often in your history did that work out well?

Tom shrugged, "For true slaves, not often. I'm not sure if I can think of any good examples, but I'm no historian. On the other hand, nations could and did rebel. My nation rebelled from tyranny and became the greatest in our world's history."

My people will fragment. They might even war with each other as some cling to the old ways, even knowing they were built on lies. What right do I have to thrust such chaos upon a galaxy at peace?

"Is slavery peace?"

Our innocence is lost. Many will commit suicide on learning the truth.

"Give them a higher purpose to undo what has been done. Life is a better reason. Love. Create a true version of the harmony that you believed in before."

We had harmony in our homeworld. The conditions there demanded it. Each clan was a chorus in our song. The clans had to keep moving away from the… no. You would not understand that. Our world turned very slowly and had two stars and was too close to one of them. The side of the planet that turned to face it was too hot. We constantly moved away from it. Light from the farther star lit the other side. Living was difficult. Clans helped each other. They had to help each other, or we would all perish.

I was there when they arrived in the sky. Giant vessels that did not crash into the ground in fire. Beings of light appeared to us and told us that they had been watching us and that we were worthy of the gifts they brought to honor us. They healed our sick and injured and made us strong. They told us....

They… How can I even know what they told us? How can I know anything?

As Yeurantheon spoke, Tom's eyes widened in shock and amazement. He swallowed. "Yuri… that was… a million years or more ago? How is it possible for you to remember this? Is this a racial memory? Are you saying that you were there, in person, as in, well, you?"

There was a long silence before Yeurantheon answered.

One of the… gifts… they gave us. The Heretic gave us. As our bodies grow old, we… transfer. Some of us. Not all of us. Just… the ones who were there at the beginning and sometimes special new ones. We guide. Or… we thought we did.

Tom swallowed hard. "That's…. I don't know what to say. We're going to need to talk more about this. A lot more. But… later. I need to think about it. In the meantime, I have to ask you something else. Why is our translation system suddenly able to, well, translate a lot better?"

Yeurantheon hesitated for a long moment before answering.

Before, I intentionally kept my words more complex. Something in me resented that you did not already know my language. I see you, and I see the people from your world. All of them know the true language. That you and your people here do not…. It made me angry. Now, though, I am not certain about how much of that was my own feeling and how much was the Heretic. I am embarrassed that it might have been all my own.

Rage

● ● ● ● ● ● ● ● ● ● ● ● ● ● ● ● ● ●

DownSide: Fort Brazos High School Stadium

Fort Brazos High School's football stadium was one of the largest in Texas, seating up to sixteen thousand people. The expense incurred for its construction had stirred local controversy, as the decision to build it was discreetly included in an ordinary, uneventful ballot with low voter turnout. This move had caused displeasure among certain residents, mainly due to the hefty price tag of almost $50 million. Nonetheless, the die had been cast, creating an impressive stadium, albeit at a cost that could have funded the education of Fort Brazos's students at state college for many years ahead.

At the moment, though, the stadium housed a standing-room-only crowd, including the over 1,500 seats arrayed across the playing field. However, this time, there were no athletes in sight, no cheerleading squads, and no marching band melodies resonating. Devoid of banners and mascots, the venue stood in bated silence. The concession area was empty of vendors.

An elevated stage, typically reserved for commencement ceremonies, concerts, and special occasions, had been erected for the first time in many months. The proceedings were being broadcast live throughout Fort Brazos, the base, and uplinked live to New London as well.

Security was beyond heavy, with armed police and marine guards inside and outside the facility.

It was an event like no other. Work ceased everywhere, and many stopped to take note of the happening. Not a single soul could say they hadn't witnessed it in some capacity, even if they had not been physically present; everyone watched as it happened in real-time.

Something big was happening. An announcement had gone out that the most important news since Awakening Day was about to be revealed.

Eerily reminiscent of events shortly after that terrible day, a hurricane could be seen overhead, sliding down the horizon as it approached the barrier mountains on the other side of the great Lake Texoma.

President John Austin, Vice President Gail Finley Austin, the entire Senate, Secretary of War Marcus, Vice Admiral Milner, General Chilton, General Markovic, and Captain Cross were gathered on the stage.

The stage was mirrored on giant video screens at either end of the stadium.

Only the gentle breeze could be heard as John Austin stepped to the podium.

"My fellow survivors. I have struggled to decide how, just exactly, to explain to you the astonishing revelations that have unfolded over the past day. So very much has happened since we all woke up in this place, and just under a month after that for those in New London." He turned and nodded at the Milners, then turned back to the microphone, "We lost so much that day, and the scars and tears are not forgotten. We learned that the Accipiters wiped out most of the people on Earth while we had somehow been spared." He shook his head, "Except for our friends and loved ones. The Five Percent."

A low rumble washed over the crowd.

"The Gardeners, our so-called saviors, held a gun to our heads and told us that we were to fight a war with the Accipiters on their behalf. To act as their mercenaries, as it were, fighting against an enemy that seems as vast as the stars themselves. A war that seems likely to need to last for countless generations."

He paused and looked around at the faces in the stadium. Expressions ranged from anger to fear to resignation and more.

"As a first step in that war, I gave the order for Captain Underwood and his brave crew to cross the light-years back to Earth and steal a ship, and at the cost of most of their precious lives, they succeeded."

He paused again, and although it was left unsaid, every thinking person who saw his face knew what he was thinking. *He never wanted this job.*

"The good news was that the mission succeeded in more ways than we knew. The bad news was that we more than kicked the hornet's nest. I've talked to the Accipiter we hold prisoner. That one act has reverberated throughout the Accipiter empire. Nothing has shaken their world more than Captain Underwood did in longer than the human race has existed. And while we can gain a certain level of visceral satisfaction from bloodying their nose, we also must accept the consequences. We don't know what happened to our people at Ari'Nell. It seems certain that they were attacked like we were, but whether any survived or not, and what happened to them afterward, we simply don't know, although we will make every effort to find out."

"These events have weighed heavily on us. However, based on what I have to tell you today, the crew of the Blood Phoenix's sacrifice was not made in vain."

"A discovery has been made. The Accipiters are not what we thought they were, and the nature of this revelation has fundamentally changed the war, the way it will be fought, and our relationship with both the Gardeners and, astoundingly, the Accipiters themselves."

"To explain this, I need to take you back to the beginning, and stay with me on this because… it changes everything. Most of you will recall that the Accipiters were a primitive bronze age race that was uplifted by a benefactor race. Well, we now know who that race was. It was the Gardeners themselves."

A collective gasp spread across the stadium, followed by angry shouts and more.

John waited a full minute before raising his arms to quiet them down.

It took another two minutes, but eventually, the furor subsided.

John nodded, "To be more precise, it was *a particular* Gardener who was assigned the task of dealing with a hostile invasion of the galaxy. That Gardener chose the Accipiters, uplifted them, gave them the tools and technology, and used them to stop the invasion. The Builders, who created the warp drive technology used today, referred to that alien species as the Masters. Anyway, after the Accipiters finished the job, this Gardener turned on his own people. He broke the number one Gardener law and, to be blunt, xeroxed himself over and over again. He used the Accipiter fleet to wipe out the rest of the Gardeners. A handful of Gardeners survived in secret. They call their turncoat the Heretic. It is as good a name as any."

John shook his head, "You see, here's the thing. The Heretic didn't just use the Accipiters. He bioengineered them to act as a host. Like the Gardeners, the Heretic doesn't have a physical body. You could think of them as something between an energy-based life form and an intelligent AI. The Heretic copies and inserts himself into Accipiters like a parasite. He controls the Accipiter leadership or any Accipiter it wants to use. The Heretic altered their memories just as it altered their biology, giving them a third gender. Then, it edited their memories so that they thought it was their own idea. It has rewritten their entire history."

The crowd stirred amid angry and doubtful murmurs and questions. John continued over the rising disquiet.

"So, the Hell of it all is this. The Accipiters are slaves. The Gardeners have now given us the ability to, in effect, drive the Heretic out of the Accipiters, freeing them. This has been done to the Accipiter we captured. Tom Parker has been talking to it, and, well, the short version is that after being on the verge of suicide, the Accipiter is both shocked, angry, and ashamed. His entire race has been the victim of a kind of mind rape that I can't begin to fathom, and he wants to help us deprogram the rest of his people and free them from the Heretic."

A roar of dissent and discordance rumbled through the stadium like thunder, growing in intensity until it threatened to roil out of control. John's face contorted in frustration as he pounded his fist on the podium with a deafening crack. "Enough!" He shouted, his voice echoing and reverberating throughout the stadium. The force of his voice quieted the crowd into a stunned silence.

"Look, there's more, and ya'll are all gonna want to hear this. We don't have to trust the Accipiter. That's not an issue. There is a plan, and I will be going over and meeting with the Gardeners to negotiate the details, but what you need to know is this, and, my God, this hit me like a truck when they told me."

He swallowed and looked down, shaking his head and letting the hush fall deeper across the stadium.

"The Five Percent. Four thousand, four hundred and thirty-two of our friends and loved ones. They aren't dead. The Gardeners didn't kill them. Those bodies were never alive. The Gardeners will create new bodies for them and restore them like they did the rest of us on Awakening Day."

Not even the wind could be heard momentarily as he paused again, and the stunned audience took in what John had said.

"They're coming home. The Five Percent are coming… home."

✪ ✪ ✪

DownSide: Radio Station 92.5 Studio

Danielle Richardson Anders stared blankly at the microphone, gathering her thoughts. Her call-in board was already fully lit up with waiting callers. Darcy and Betsy were asleep, and Devin and Terry were playing quietly outside the studio. Her eyes were wide, and her expression stunned as she keyed the microphone.

"Hello, people of Fort Brazos and New London. This is Danielle Richardson on FM 92.5 and Radio Free Fort Brazos, beaming our signal across the known world and beyond. Well… I doubt I need to tell anyone what just happened, as I'm sure only small children and babies didn't tune in. I'm sure that, like many of you, I don't know how much of each I should be? Angry? Happy? Confused? All three at the same time, I'm sure. The Five Percent coming back? My God… What joyous news that is! And at the same time, just, wow. Some will have homes to come to, but many of those homes are now occupied by others, and their possessions spread to the winds. Will they demand their old jobs and homes back? And… oh my God… people have remarried…. And had kids…. God, this is wonderful, and at the same time, it will be a worse problem than finding homes for the New Londoners! And then there's the whole business with the Accipiters being victims instead of oppressors? I don't know how I feel about that at all. I mean, why the Hell didn't the Gardeners just tell us all this in the first place?"

"Okay, well, let's dive into it, shall we? Ricardo, on line one…."

✪ ✪ ✪

DownSide: Eugene Morton Naval Academy

Cadets Elísabet Gunnarsson, Will Sawyer, and Jordan Hoffman sat together at what they now considered to be "their" table in the study hall. Superintendent Montoya had given everyone the day off, so most other cadets had scattered.

Elisabet, Will, and Jordan stared at each other, their faces reflecting mutual shock and anger, leaning more toward the side of rage.

Elísabet absently ran her hand through her short-cropped dark red hair and shook her head. "Well…. Fuck."

Will laughed darkly, "You always have a way with words, Bet. Seriously, though, what does this mean, like, for us? For the Navy?"

Elisabet shook her head, "I doubt it changes anything. The Accipiters are still out there; we'll end up fighting one way or another. Do you think that even after they get de-Heretic'd, they'll suddenly just give up their cozy empire? They've got all the ships and all the power. They won't give it up, and you know it."

Will swallowed, "No. It'll be worse, Bet. It'll be civil war. Factions will develop, and they'll end up fighting each other. We'll be on the sidelines, just trying to get on the field now and then for a play. There just aren't enough of us, even if we had all the ships we wanted right now."

Elisabet snorted, "Look, I've been saving a mag to dump into the Gardeners when all is said and done, and that's not changed. They started this whole disaster."

Jordan said quietly, "Think about it, though. We lost Earth. The Gardeners lost a galaxy. If we thought we were out for revenge, what about them? Why do I feel like we're the toddlers in the playroom while the adults are fighting in the other room?"

Will leaned back in his chair and asked, "Well, here's a thought. There are, like, supposed to be zillions of worlds out there that the Accipiters have under control. If the President's plan works and some of those start to be, well, cleared, or at least not under the bad guy's control, does that mean that we might be able to start setting up colonies? Outposts?"

Elisabet looked at him and nodded, "Certainly, Embassies. That means travel and trade and ships and marines to protect them."

Will added, "And lots of colonists, eventually. Colonists to *protect*."

Elisabet leaned forward and shook her head angrily, "Hell, what's to keep these non-Heretic Gardeners from simply taking the bad Heretic Gardener's place, and then tying up loose ends by eliminating us?"

Will stiffened as he suddenly remembered, "Hey, Jordan, wasn't your grandmother one of the Five Percent?"

Jordan nodded slowly and said in a small, quiet voice, "Yeah, Gamma Abigail. I'm scared, though. I don't know if she can accept this world and everything that was lost. I always thought it was a mercy that she wasn't here to see everything. To find out what happened to Dad and Nolan. I'm afraid it would kill her all over again."

Elisabet burst out angrily as she reached over and clasped Jordan's hand, "Fucking Gardeners!"

DownSide: President John Austin's home

Corporal Roxanna Darling, Matti Austin's personal Marine Security Guard, had been worried as she drove her charge home from the stadium. Matti was not a quiet girl. She wasn't chatty, but she almost always had wheels turning in her head, translating into some issue or other that she talked about. Not a word had been said the entire drive back or since entering the house.

During the tumultuous days following Awakening Day, it became apparent that leaders would need protection. Alien creatures were skulking about that had already killed a city council member, a Sheriff deputy, and Corpsman Mendez, and, later, a Wardog killed several soldiers on the highway. A new Marine Security Guard unit was formed, and when Roxanna was the first woman to volunteer, she naturally hoped to be assigned to protect Vice President Finley. When she was informed that she would instead be assigned to the President's eight-year-old daughter, Roxanna's reaction was… poor.

However, as she got to know the girl, everything changed. Matti was… special. Roxanna had been shocked by how much Matti came to mean to her. She wouldn't simply protect the girl with her life. She would move heaven and Earth to protect her. Their relationship wasn't maternal. Matti had already fiercely latched on to Gail Finley, and the feelings were mutual. Roxanna was something different. It was far more than being a surrogate older sister, and she wasn't sure she understood it herself.

What she did know was that it had changed her. Before Awakening Day, Roxanna had envisioned a lifelong career, rising through the ranks, attending OCS, and retiring with stars on her uniform. Now? Now, Matti… and this family… *were* her life.

At the age of 9, just like many other girls her age in Fort Brazos and New London, Matti underwent a swift physical maturation, experiencing her first period. Roxanna stood by her side during this abrupt transition from childhood to premature puberty, offering comfort and reassurance. True to her nature, Matti rebounded quickly, showing her resilience.

When Matti started taking flying lessons, Roxanna had, privately and unsuccessfully, done everything she could to discourage it. It wasn't lost on her that her personal motivations bordered on hysterical concern. She'd had to remind herself over and over again that, well, it was the Apocalypse after all, and Matti was…. Exceptional.

And then, most recently, Roxanne had watched as Matti began to increasingly notice… boys. Not just in general but one in particular. Fortunately, the object of Matti's interest hadn't noticed, at least as far as Roxanna could tell. Of course, it probably had something to do with him being four years older and himself focused on other girls closer to his age.

So far, it hadn't been a problem. Yet.

And now she followed Matti up the stairs in silence and into Matti's room. Matti wore her cadet uniform and was rigid and formal the entire day. When Roxanna closed the door behind them, Matti's shoulders slumped, and she stopped. She stood silently in the middle of the room before her bed.

Roxanna pursed her lips as she stepped around Matti to look at her.

Matti was trembling as tears streamed down her face and chin.

Roxanna dropped to her knees, pulled Matti close, and held her as the dam broke.

✪ ✪ ✪

Minutes later, Matti slowly stiffened and stood back, wiping her face. "I'm sorry. It's just…."

Roxanna swallowed and answered huskily, "It's okay. You don't have to say anything."

Matti looked at her and sniffed, "Where were you on Awakening Day, Roxy?"

Roxanne raised her eyebrows. She rocked back and leaned against the bed. "I was on base with everyone else. It was chaos. Why?"

Matti shook her head, "I was with Dad as he responded to the calls. It was chaos here, too. I figured he would want to drop me at Mrs. Bosch's house. She was my sitter." Matti wiped her face again, "Anyway, when Dad was busy, I texted her, but she didn't answer. Then I saw on the monitor in the car that she was on the list of dead. I didn't tell him I knew. I just pretended. I… I shouldn't have lied to him like that. I should have been responsible and asked him to drop me at the station where I would be safe, but I was scared and didn't want to leave him, and I could tell he was scared, too. All those people, Roxy! It was awful! And then… and then you came and grabbed me out of the simulator that day they killed all those people and nearly killed Dad, and…."

Tears started to fall again from Matti's eyes. She looked pleadingly at Roxanna.

Roxanna couldn't help it as her eyes watered with her own tears. "Come here."

Matti fell into her arms and sobbed. Her slim body heaved.

Roxanna wrapped her arms around Matti and rocked her slowly, her long black hair interspersed with Matti's equally long blond locks. "It's okay. It's okay. It's okay." It was the first time Roxanna had seen Matti cry. Ever. She knew Matti had lost other friends from school on Awakening Day and knew others who had lost parents and family. So much had happened, not the least of which was the Apocalypse itself. Her father almost died, and his recovery was painful afterward.

Roxanna had watched along with the rest of the Presidential and Vice Presidential details as the relationship between John and Gail had… evolved. She'd been amazed at how stupid two otherwise brilliant people had been. It had been Hell on Matti.

All this… and it took the promised return of the Five Percent to finally loose the torrent of pent-up emotions that had welled up inside the increasingly not-so-little girl that had become the center of Roxanne's life. Roxanne's tears joined Matti's as they both finally grieved.

DownSide: Methodist Hospital

Dr. David Duncan and Surgeon General Gwyneth Elliot Duncan stood next to each other, holding hands in the hospital lobby, along with many of the surviving staff. Like most of the hospital employees, their children were upstairs in the daycare center. For now, though, they all stood solemnly before the memorial. Fifteen members of the hospital staff had not revived on Awakening Day. David now held hospital CEO Harrison Mitchell's office.

The memorial plaque listed all of the names. Chief Nursing Officer Andrea Caldwell, Chief Operating Officer Samuel Turner, Chief Financial Officer Evelyn Harper, Chief Information Officer Alexander Foster, Chief Human Resources Officer Jacqueline Bennett, Chief Marketing Officer Gabrielle Martinez, Chief Quality Officer Nathan Wallace, Chief Legal Officer Victoria Chambers, Chief Strategy Officer Benjamin Morrison, Chief Administrative Officer Olivia Reynolds, Chief Facilities Officer Maxwell Blake, Chief Privacy Officer Lauren Mitchell, Chief Risk Officer Dominic Lawson, and Chief Communications Officer Emily Thornton.

Many of those jobs were never refilled. Without federal issues to deal with and with all diseases cured, the primary job of the hospital was now focused on dealing with the now apparently permanent baby boom. In the first nine or ten months after Awakening Day, over ten thousand babies were born from the combined population of Fort Brazos and New London. The birth rate in the United States prior to Awakening Day was roughly 1.8%. Now it was over 6.5% and rising. The incidence of multiple births was on the rise. In the second ten months, over eleven thousand babies were born. In another three years, the combined total population was expected to nearly double from that of Awakening Day to over two hundred and ten thousand. It was a good thing that the interior surface area of New Texas was over twenty-seven million square miles.

Throughout it all, there were no stillbirths at all. While most births were, thanks to the Gardener's tinkering, very uneventful, there were still plenty that needed monitoring and assistance. As each wave of births peaked, the tsunami of pregnant women threatened to overwhelm available resources. If a patient required assistance during labor or delivery, they sent out a call for volunteers to come assist. All such calls were immediately answered by every nurse who happened to be free and so could respond in a timely fashion. Eventually, every single non-medical staff member had since been cross-trained to assist in various ways.

David shook his head and sighed, "They'll be coming back to not only a new world but one that is the same in many ways and radically different, even alien, in others."

Gwyneth sighed, "It'll be okay. We'll work it out somehow."

David nodded, "I know. It's just…. We buried them, Gwyn."

✪ ✪ ✪

DownSide: Hoffman-Collins Ranch

Senator Esmerelda Collins found her adopted nineteen-year-old daughter, now Councilwoman Sandra Hoffman Garreth, in the workshop, sitting at a worktable, cleaning the M4 Carbine her husband, Captain David Garreth, had given her. Both were survivors of the Stalker attack that had killed her father, Barrett, brother Nolan, Sheriff Deputy Grayson, and Corpsman Mendez.

In fact, David had stocked the farm with a variety of weapons in quick-access safes both in the house and in the various outbuildings. Sandra had eventually reassembled her personal Winchester 94 lever action rifle that the Stalker had taken apart. She cleaned and oiled it regularly.

At the moment, Sandra had broken down the M4's bolt carrier assembly and was bent over the table, carefully removing the carbon buildup around the gas rings. She turned away as Esmerelda approached.

Esmerelda frowned and walked around the other side so she could see Sandra's face. It was streaked with tears.

Sandra muttered, "Go away!"

Esmerelda sighed and shook her head. She rounded the table and gently put her hands on Sandra's shoulders.

Sandra flinched and tried to twist away, but Esmerelda held on. After a long moment, Sandra slumped, setting the scraping tool and bolt down on the table as she dropped her head to her chest.

Esmerelda whispered, "I know, dear. I know."

Sandra's voice was low and raspy. "Jordan called. She's right. Abigail won't survive when she learns that Dad and Nolan are gone."

Esmerelda wrinkled her nose as her own eyes teared up. She pulled Sandra into her arms and hugged her. "My darling girl, I've known Abigale since long before you were born. She'll be crushed, yes. But nothing in the old world or this one could keep her away from her five new great-grandchildren!"

Sandra's younger sisters, Hannah and Elizabeth, were taking care of all five, Nolan, Margaret, Ethan, Owen, and Caleb, back in the farmhouse under the watchful eyes of Esmerelda's personal security detail.

Sandra looked up at Esmerelda with questioning eyes, then slowly nodded.

Esmerelda stroked Sandra's blonde hair and said, "Let's get your rifle put back together and go tell your children about their great-grandmother. Okay?"

✪ ✪ ✪

DownSide: Eugene Morton Naval Academy

Office of the Dean of Academy Academics

Dr. Takumi Nakamura sat at his desk and looked around his large office. The office that previously belonged to Dr. Lawrence Dixon, one of the Awakening Day Five Percent. Of course, back on Earth, it had been the office of Bonham State University's President. Now, the university was a military academy, and the head of it was Superintendent Rear Admiral Gordon Montoya.

Many of Lawrence's things still decorated the office. Takumi had felt that they should stay as a sort of memorial to not just Dr. Dixon but to all that had been lost on Awakening Day.

Takumi had never wanted the job. One thing had led to another, and… here he was.

Dr. Dixon's wife Carol had since remarried – with Dr. Davidson, whose wife Susanna had likewise been among the Five Percent. Carol's menopause, like so many others, had reversed, and she'd since had a darling pair of twins. Now, apparently, Lawrence and Susanna were coming back from the dead, as it were.

Takumi was startled as he felt someone touch his arm.

He looked up and saw that it was Angela Willis, his office manager. She'd brought him coffee, which he suddenly noticed sitting in front of him.

She smiled softly and said, "It will be okay. Things will work out. You'll see."

Takumi sighed and leaned back in his chair. He shook his head slowly, "Angela, I thought everything we've been through was hard to understand. I just…."

She smiled again, "I know that you and the President and the others will work things out. You always have."

Takumi paused before he answered slowly, "Angela, next to this…. Black holes and quantum mechanics are easy."

✪ ✪ ✪

DownSide: Café Balthasar

Dr. Leo Talib and General Sabrina Chilton Talib huddled together at "their" table at the back of the French-themed brasserie, Café Balthasar. Sabrina's now sixteen-year-old daughter Nicole was home taking care of the three-month-old twins Octavia and Philippa.

Neither Leo nor Sabrina had been deeply emotionally impacted by the "death" of the Five Percent. However, when Leo's department head, Dr. Gloria Rubenheim, did not awaken, it propelled Leo to prominence. He'd become the world's undisputed language expert, which had planted him squarely in Sabrina's sights. As head of military Signals Intelligence, Sabrina had shanghaied Leo to decode the alien language.

She'd detested Leo at first, but she couldn't deny his brilliance. By the end of the Keeper Raid, though, neither could deny what was developing between them.

Leo laughed darkly, "You know, I think I might have to send her some flowers or something to express my gratitude for her shuffling off this mortal coil. If it wasn't for that, you and I and Octavia and Philippa…."

Sabrina made a face and playfully swatted his hand away, "Oh, no, you don't! Going by what you've shared, that lady seemed to despise you even more than I did, and I'm quite certain you had it coming!"

Leo's eyes twinkled, "Indeed, I was. I acted like a fool, but Gloria Rubenheim was an absolute cow about it. Let's hope that a resurrection does wonders for her attitude."

Sabrina smirked, "You're dreadful! You know how utterly awful this is going to be for everyone affected…. On both sides of the equation."

"Absolutely, I'm aware. The sociologists and psychologists are going to have a right go at it, and I'd rather not even start pondering the legal Pandora's box. I suppose the Senate will have to take some sort of decisive action. I just pray they're astute enough to ensure these poor souls are treated more than fairly. As these Americans say, if they don't, there will be Hell to pay."

✪ ✪ ✪

DownSide: Jamestown

Senator and Mayor Darnell Lewis, Gary Little, and Ray Bunker sat around the kitchen table in Darnell's log cabin. Darnell set three glasses and a jug of Jamestown moonshine on the table. All three friends wore homespun clothing with various deer and elk skin elements. Not because they had to. Not anymore. Now, with the replication cave, the frontier town was rapidly growing and prosperous. They did it because it had become part of their identity.

The three men somberly looked at each other over the table. Ray and Gary were stepbrothers. All three had played on the Fort Brazos High School football team and were lifelong friends. Ray was tall with short black hair and hazel eyes. Gary was shorter with wavy brown "surfer" hair and blue eyes. Darnell was shorter still, black, and muscular. It would be hard to find three men with closer bonds.

Darnell had lost his mother Jasmine and his sister Yazmeen, and Gary had lost his wife Darlene – all part of the Five Percent. That tragedy had led to the now infamous Reinhardt incident, where Darnell and the other liqueur distributor employees had locked themselves in the building to drown their sorrows, perhaps permanently. An accidental gunshot had been fired, leading to a police standoff that had nearly ended in yet another tragedy.

The men had been publicly ridiculed afterward, to the point of unemployment and desperation. Ray's wife Julie divorced him and took their daughter Chloe with her.

Feeling that they had nothing left to lose, the three pooled their remaining money, bought provisions, and set off to become mountain men in the wilderness. Nothing had gone to plan, and they'd ended up injured and far from the mountains. Then Darnell, while hunting, found the cave. And everything changed. Darlene grudgingly came back with Chloe to Ray, and the encampment grew into a small town.

In recent months, Gary had finally started dating again. He recently got engaged to Lucia Hernandez.

Darnell picked up the jug, poured the clear liquid into each glass, and handed it to Gary and Ray. He raised his glass and said, "My brothers, it will be okay. We'll get through this. Here's to the Five Percent."

DownSide: Fort Brazos Police Station

Police Chief Naomi Lamar sat at her desk after returning from the stadium. She felt like her head was spinning. During the Reinhardt incident, she'd been instrumental in defusing the situation. Naomi had only been a patrol officer, but she'd known Darnell Lewis in high school and knew of the "death" of his mother and sister. Police Captain Marchant had advocated an assault on the barricaded warehouse, but Naomi convinced Chief Deputy Hector Alonzo and, by extension, (then) Sheriff Austin to let her try and talk the warehouse workers down.

Police Chief George Westmorland and his wife Anne were among the Five Percent. The Reinhardt affair had ultimately led to Naomi being catapulted to fill the now vacant Police Chief position, passing over Captain Marchant and many others with more seniority.

Nothing remained in George's former office from his tenure there, but to Naomi, it would always be George's on some level. Certainly, many of the officers on the force felt the same way.

She chuckled to herself about the bottle of bourbon she'd found in his desk drawer. For a fleeting moment, she thought it might be nice to pull it out and give a toast to the old man who would supposedly be returning from the dead. Of course, the bottle was long gone now, along with everything else. It had taken months to get the cigar smell (mostly) out.

She shook her head and silently mouthed to herself, "Well, fuck."

New Philippines

Senator Caesar Salangsang sat on the pink beach next to his bride, Michelle, now pregnant with triplets. They clung to each other, watching the surf, her head nestled upon his shoulder. Despite the peacefulness of this moment, sorrow washed over him like the ocean waves before them. Caesar's former wife, Sofia, and his nine children, Alejandro, Mateo, Elena, Lucia, Diego, Catalina, Juan, Victoria, and Carlos, would not return from the dead. They all perished during the Accipiter invasion of Earth over sixty-six years ago. They weren't rescued by the Gardeners.

New London: Apartments of Preston and Livia Milner

It took over an hour to get from the stadium to the elevator "up" to New London, another six hours for the long ride there, and another hour to return to their apartment. Neither had spoken more than a handful of words to each other throughout the trip.

When they entered the apartment, leaving their security outside the door, Preston and Livia simply stopped and stood standing, blankly for several minutes.

Finally, Livia turned to Preston, his tear-streaked face a mirror of her own.

Helena, their daughter, would not be resurrected by the Gardeners. She, too, had been left behind and presumably died when the Accipiters bombed the eastern seaboard.

Livia took a step and stumbled, collapsing into his arms, and they wept together for a daughter and a world forever lost.

New Texas

These scenes were repeated, thousands of times over and again, throughout New London and across Fort Brazos, Jamestown, and the New Philippines, as the true pain and loss of Awakening Day…. And the Apocalypse inexorably washed over the survivors of mankind.

The Forge

● ● ● ● ● ● ● ● ● ● ● ● ● ● ●

TopSide: Accipiter Holding Cell Loading Area

A sleek, seamless alloy door, thick as a bank vault, opened in the back of the holding cell and swung open. Beyond, each cell on the block had its own airlock connected to a loading area that led to an oversized elevator shaft where free-standing doors like bank vaults lined up beside each other. This led to a pair of decks above that, which contained more cells, then a single deck and another network of elevators that led to the 'surface' in New London to the rear of the New Pentagon, where a road led directly to the starship hangars.

Tom Parker stood before the Accipiter and shook his head at the heavy security presence outside the door. John and Gail Austin, Marcus Alexander, Preston Milner, Sybil Blanchard, Leo Talib, and an extremely nervous Mei Zifeng waited nearby.

Towering behind him, flanked by heavily armed marines, followed Yeurantheon.

He raised his voice slightly and said, "Mr. President, don't you think we can dispense with the hood and shackles?"

John hesitated, thinking momentarily, then traded glances with Gail and Marcus.

They each grimaced.

Before anyone could stop her, Sybil simply walked between the guards and stopped before Yeurantheon. She reached up and gently touched his downy breast.

Every muscle in the guard's and security detail members' bodies quivered with tension, their hands tightening around their weapons like iron vices. Adrenaline coursing through their veins, they remained disciplined enough to not aim their weapons or make a move, but any onlooker could see the apprehension written across their faces as they braced themselves for the worst.

Yeurantheon flinched slightly at the touch for a moment before visibly relaxing.

Sybil smiled softly. "There is so much pain and anguish in you. I am sorry for my part in bringing that to you."

Yeurantheon hesitated before answering with a low rock-crushing rumble that did little to ease tensions from anyone except for Sybil and Tom.

Sybil glanced at Tom, who nodded.

She gently stroked Yeurantheon's downy crest while she turned her head towards John and the rest. "Our guest… his name is beautiful. By the way, it is Yeurantheon. Our guest will not be a problem."

John's lead security detail member, Sergeant Jesse Roberts, looked at John with worried eyes.

Marcus and Preston cast doubtful glances back and forth between John, Sybil, and Yeurantheon.

Gail closed her eyes and shook her head. "I trust Sybil."

John pursed his lips, then nodded. He commanded, "Release him." Another thought occurred to him, and he added, "Marcus, see to it that a security detail is assigned to him. He is to be protected at all costs. The entire war may depend on it."

Marcus's eyes widened in surprise for a moment, then he nodded. "Yes, Mr. President. I understand. I will make sure that the detail is chosen… carefully."

Sergeant Siler carefully, deliberately, and… gently… removed the custom-made shackles. To remove the black linin hood, he had to use a stepladder to reach Yeurantheon's head.

Yeurantheon shook his head as the hood was removed. Numerous glyphs flowed across his beak, and he 'spoke' a series of low hoots and shrill tones.

Leo Talib chuckled and said to Mei, "Go ahead. Your Accipiter is still better than mine. Please translate for us, Mei. Everyone should remember that Accipiter vocalizations convey emphasis, urgency, and an emotional undertone. They evolved the glyphs to convey their more symbolic, explicit, and even scientific thoughts and ideas."

Mei looked timidly back and forth among the faces of the most powerful human beings in the universe, swallowed, and nodded slowly. "Okay. The emotional tones are very heavy and dark with other levels of what are very…

They are full of pain and regret. Explicitly, Yeurantheon's glyphs said that we should keep the weapons pointed at him if it makes us feel better. He knows that we will never forgive him or his people for what they have done. He says that were it not for the chance that he might be given the opportunity to right those wrongs, that he would welcome death."

Tom told Yeurantheon, "You're remarkably sanguine about this, Yuri."

Yeurantheon answered with another series of tones and glyphs.

Mei translated, "He says… why shouldn't he be? And… that he is a damned soul. His people are a race that died a million years ago when the Heretic came and took them from their home. He says that what stands before us is an empty shell made to be ridden by…. Yeurantheon… I don't understand that last word. Can you explain, please?"

Yeurantheon stared down at Mei for a long moment before replying with a long sequence of guttural and discordant tones, followed by a long series of glyphs.

Mei's eyes widened. "Oh… I see. I'm sorry for…." She swallowed, "Yeurantheon explained…. On his Homeworld, there were, well, parasites that, well… let's just say they sound pretty horrible and disgusting. He is likening the Heretic to those parasites. They would burrow into their young and their old and…." She swallowed. "You don't want to know, and I'm sorry I asked because now I know I'm going to have nightmares about them." She shivered.

Leo put a reassuring hand on her shoulder for a moment and said, "Thank you, Mei. We'll discuss it later."

Tom shook his head. "Yuri, your people were unwitting slaves. The possibility of freeing them is before you. What comes after is up to them and where you lead them. When you have freed your people and returned our Earth to us, you can decide whether your continued existence is too difficult to bear and end it. Or you can try to return to your pre-uplifting life. Or you could use the power your people have to heal the Galaxy. Restore all those other races your people altered."

Sybil added, "Yeurantheon, this is a question that the altered humans now living on Earth will, I hope, one day, have to face since they, too, at least some of them, would have been inhabited and manipulated by the Heretic. God knows what the Heretic made them do."

Yeurantheon slumped slightly. The tones and hoots were followed by subdued glyphs.

Mei swallowed. "Uhm…. He says that he had not considered that. He had only thought about what his own people had done. He had not considered what the Heretic might have made all those other races do."

Tom winced at the realization of yet another level of horror inflicted upon not only humanity but all the races of the Galaxy. He stammered, "This… These… This abomination. The Heretic should not be killed and wiped out. For the sake of all the peoples of the Galaxy, he, it, or whatever it is…. The Heretic must be held to account. Not just extinguished. If it is merely extinguished, then where can anyone find any sense of justice for what has been done to them?"

Gail suddenly clutched her hand to her abdomen and grabbed John's hand, clenching it tightly. She looked at him with an expression of confusion, anger, and resentment. She ground her teeth briefly before saying, "There is no one who has… hated… you or your people more than me. What was done to my world was beyond monstrous. I… I don't know if I will ever…. I will, however…. Hear what the Gardeners have to say. I know that my world as I knew it is gone forever. All those billions of people are dead. If…. If there is a chance…. A possibility of…. Of not having to kill those that remain on Earth because they are… what they are. Then I will stay my hand. Let us go and see what these Gardeners have to say for themselves. It had better be one hell of a convincing story."

Starship Hangar Bay

The security loading area at the New Pentagon was a cavernous underground multiple-bay dock. To avoid publicity and to protect Yeurantheon from any unfortunate incident that might arise if he were seen in public, the entire delegation was loaded into a caravan of vehicles safely out of sight. The Accipiter himself was far too large to fit inside any passenger vehicle. Since nearly all of TopSide's food and supplies were still coming from DownSide, semi-trucks hauling forty-foot containers were common. Standard containers were 'only' eight feet six inches tall, so Yeurantheon had to crouch down while he and the marine guards made their discrete exit from the New Pentagon complex.

By the time the caravan arrived in the colossal starship hangar bay, all non-essential personnel had already been evacuated.

As Yeurantheon walked down the loading ramp from the container, his claws scraping loudly on the metal, he stiffened in surprise. A rapid stream of glyphs flowed across his beak, and he spoke a long series of hoots and trills.

Mei, waiting nearby, looked at Leo, who nodded reassuringly. She took a deep breath and said, "Well, the short version is that he is stunned by what he sees. I don't think he expected anything on quite this scale, and I have to say, I've never been in here either, and I'm absolutely amazed myself. I knew the hangar was big, and the ships were big. I mean, I've seen pictures, but…. Oh… my."

Leo gently patted her shoulder. "I believe he's asking if the Gardeners built this for us."

Mei straightened and swallowed. "Oh, yes, I'm sorry. That's right."

John answered, "It is a scaled-up version of our own technology."

Yeurantheon walked the rest of the way down the ramp and shuddered, its sounds sharper and harder to hear.

Mei winced. "He doesn't like this place. He says all this metal is cold and lifeless. Like his cell."

Gail answered sharply, "This is where we work, not where we live."

The delegation walked towards ILC Atlatl, which rested not far from Blood Phoenix. In the distance lay the Keeper ship, still looking for all the world like a titanic gold turnip.

Yeurantheon warbled a new set of tones and hoots.

Mei said, "He says we are very different. He says he is glad that we have the Keeper ship, that after all that his people stole from us, that at least we have the legacy of our world. He is also talking about Blood Phoenix… I mean, he's talking about the warp rings. The Builder warp drive. Something about how after his people destroyed… um…. I think he's talking about the Masters. Yeah, that after his people wiped out the Masters, they kept going, chasing down all the surviving Builders and killing them, too. He's asking whether his people chose to do that themselves or whether the Heretic made them do it. He says he's afraid of the answer."

John and Gail exchanged worried glances.

NTN Atlatl

On Approach to the Gardener Dyson Sphere

Besides its usual crew, the ILC's bridge was crowded, with John, Gail, Marcus, Preston, and Sybil standing practically cheek to jowl behind the officers. With Blood Phoenix sitting idle, and with this being the kind of unprecedented trip that it was, Captain Charles Cross and Commander

Haruto Hashimoto took personal command of the smaller vessel. It was Charles' first time in command of Atlatl since returning from the Keeper raid, thoughts of which he banished to the deepest recesses of his mind.

Atlatl's current Captain, Commander Malvin Lojacono, the rather ebullient Cajun popular among the other officers for his cooking and Jazz hobbies, was happy to take a back seat – so long as he got to see the Dyson Sphere up close. He sat, pensive and alert, next to the Pilot's station.

There wasn't room for Yeurantheon on the bridge, even if that had been something anyone would have remotely considered doing, so Yeurantheon was resting in his old "cell." The same one that he had been imprisoned in after being captured on Earth. Since the raid, it had been converted into a storage locker. Now emptied out and with a "bench" hastily added for Yeurantheon's comfort, the enormous creature now waited there, albeit this time with the door to the cage conspicuously open. Of course, armed marines still surrounded him, but it was the thought that counted.

On the bridge, the moment that Atlatl entered space, pilot Logan Kendal and navigators Harris Huddleston and Christian Taylor found themselves out of a job, hopefully temporarily, when they found they no longer had control.

Charles and Haruto shrugged and shook their heads.

Charles said to John and Gail, "We expected this. We lost control when we originally arrived here. I can tell you it got pretty tense. Phoenix couldn't tell us what was happening, and we sat there locked in orbit for over a week before New Texas arrived. Let me just say that when you sent us out here to investigate this nebula based on Phoenix's rather vague unlocked memory, we did not know what to expect. We certainly never expected anything remotely like *that*."

He gestured out the window at the apparition everyone else was already mesmerized by.

The nebula's diffuse light painted streaks of color across the spacecraft's viewport, adding a surreal quality to the approaching spectacle. Ahead of them, barely visible against the ruddy backdrop of the nebula, lay the dark, perfectly round Dyson Sphere. The low albedo colossal structure was a looming tenebrous presence, its foreboding surface dappled with enormous circles, like some ancient, long-dead Lovecraftian leviathan.

As they drew closer, the individual circular structures became more distinct, their intricate lattice of supports and platforms giving the Sphere an otherworldly, artistic beauty. The circular portal that had been 'open,' earlier, revealing the red dwarf star inside, was now closed.

Preston remarked quietly, "There's just no sense of scale. It just… keeps getting bigger and bigger.

Haruto nodded, "Admiral, the Sphere is over thirty thousand kilometers wide. Those disks you see on its surface are about three thousand five hundred kilometers wide. Each." He paused, "Sir, you could fit Earth's moon inside that and still have a few kilometers to spare. It looks like we're headed to a smaller structure, though. A portal of some kind that is *only* a few tens of kilometers across."

Marcus swallowed, "My God. I thought New Texas was too big to imagine. To build such a thing as this…. It is so far beyond us."

As the Dyson Sphere swelled swiftly before them, the portal irised open like a gaping maw. The transition from the dusty nebula to the interior was abrupt, the nebular glow replaced by the sharp red glow from the roiling convection currents of the star within.

As the ILC entered the Sphere, the view of the star came into sharper focus. It seemed almost alive, with its swirling gases and palpable heat creating a mesmerizing dance of fire.

The Dyson Sphere revealed itself to be composed of multiple inner shells. Streams of plasma could be seen following magnetic field lines channeled into the recesses of the shells. For a brief moment, before the ILC turned ninety degrees and changed course, titanic beams of energy could be seen entering the polar ends of the star.

Moments later, just as it appeared that they would crash into a wall, a doorway opened, revealing a hangar bay. Atlatl entered the hangar and gently landed on the deck.

✪ ✪ ✪

Gardener Dyson Sphere

Atlatl's cargo door opened, and the ramp extended to the deck, which, while as dark as the exterior of the Sphere itself, also shimmered eerily. Its surface betrayed an intricate underlying crystalline structure that seemed to flow with pulses of energy.

John had vetoed the call for security teams to exit first. He'd cocked his head and said, "What conceivable threat could the security team feasibly counteract in this scenario? The Gardeners built New Texas. They built this place that is bigger than a fucking STAR! They rescued us from death on Earth and offered to restore the Five Percent. Gail and I are going in first, and that's final."

True to his word, John and Gail were the first to exit Atlatl, hand in hand, in the van, followed by the rest of the delegation, with Yeurantheon following behind.

The bay itself was not remotely as large as the starship hangar bay in New Texas. However, no one doubted that it was not the only one. The walls shared the same structure as the deck, but despite their dark hue, the room was bright.

As they reached the end of the ramp, a tall doorway, high enough for Yeurantheon to pass through without stooping and wide enough for two people to enter side by side, silently irised open.

While the security details didn't lead the way, they nonetheless accompanied the delegation, while the Atlatl's crew stayed behind and secured the vessel.

John and Gail boldly led the delegation through the door into… a banquet room.

The tables were filled with every cuisine imaginable, arranged in a large circle. Each table had chairs for the exact amount of delegates present. Sideboards lined the walls with more dishes and seating, equal to the number of security personnel.

One of the "chairs" was, instead, an Accipiter-style bench.

On the far side of the room stood a figure that sent a chilling sensation through the air. A tall, slender man with white hair stood poised, seemingly out of time and place.

John's eyes widened in shock, his footsteps halting abruptly. "No… It can't be!"

Tom's face drained of all color, his legs threatening to give way beneath him. His eyes welled up, and he choked back a sob, his gaze fixed on the ghostly figure before them. Memories surged, bringing with them the weight of guilt, grief, and an unhealed wound.

Sybil's heart raced as she recognized the man from that fateful day – Awakening Day – a moment forever etched in her memory. A shiver ran down her spine as she recalled the horrific accident when a herd of panicked deer on the highway had emerged from the fog and collided with Tom Parker's truck. An enormous buck had smashed through the windshield, impaling Tom's passenger with its antlers. The truck had careened out of control in front of Sybil, and Wayne and Sybil had seen the gruesome outcome firsthand.

She looked askance at him and stated accusingly as she tasted his emotions, "You are not Pastor Joseph Gilmore."

The man smiled ruefully. "You are correct, Mrs. Blanchard. May I call you Sybil? We felt it would help to facilitate our introduction if we took physical form using this template from your deceased spiritual leader. I hope it does not unduly distress you."

Tom, still reeling, stumbled back a step, his voice barely more than a whisper, quivering with emotion. "It's... It's as if I'm hearing Joe.... The way he spoke.... Everything about him."

The man looked at Tom with eyes that held a deep sadness. "This form contains his knowledge, nothing more. It lacks his essence, his soul, as you understand it. We hoped this familiar visage would be comforting. If this is too painful, I can recycle it and craft a more generic body if that would be preferable."

John opened his mouth, ready to speak, but Tom raised a trembling hand to silence him.

Breathing heavily, Tom murmured, "No. Changing it would be like witnessing his death once more."

John looked at Tom, his face painted with concern. "Tom, are you certain about this? This is...."

Tom's eyes shimmered with unshed tears. "I am," he whispered, his voice choked. "Let's proceed. I'm aware this isn't Joe. I know because the shadow of his soul is still in my heart. It haunts me every single day."

Gail left the group and walked up to the man. She stopped in front of him and looked him over.

He wore everyday casual clothes. His face was lined with age.

She shook her head at the man-thing. "If you think this will somehow shake our resolve, you are mistaken. What shall we call you? And don't think for a moment that we will allow you to use a dead man's name?"

The man smiled gently and replied, "Very well. Call me Paximandros."

Tom shook his head skeptically. "Paximandros. Meaning a combination of 'pax' or peace and 'mandros,' Greek, for negotiator."

Paximandros smiled. "Joseph Gilmore would have been pleased to see you take up his mantle, Tom. May I call you Tom?"

John interrupted, "Stop it! Stop trying to create false familiarity. You may look like him, but you're not. So cut the crap or create another sock puppet for you to talk to us through."

Paximandros nodded, "Of course. Please forgive me. I have watched all of you for so long that I feel like I know you. Perhaps the familiarity that I hope for may eventually develop in time. Until then, shall we all be seated? If anyone is hungry, I invite you to enjoy the food. I wanted you to feel welcome. Let us begin."

He waited for everyone to sit before following suit. "Thank you for joining me here. Allow me to make an opening statement. Once again, I apologize for the offense caused by taking this form. My own people have a spiritual component. It embodies our highest laws. We wanted to meet you here not in the guise of a military or political role but instead to symbolize what this form represented. A Pastor. A guide. We are not like you. It took a long time for us to recover from the Heretic's actions emotionally and spiritually. Longer still to decide how or even if we should respond at all. We built arks to take us to the Galaxy you call Andromeda to escape. Many have already left. Simplifying the shell of one to provide your… haven… was a recent idea."

Preston balked, "Simplified?"

Paximandros smiled softly. "We are not like you."

Gail took an impatient breath. "What do you want?"

Paximandros shrugged, "To right the wrongs of the Heretic, of course. Some of us felt a responsibility to do something and not just leave. Our internal conflict revolved around the concern that attempting to intervene would cause more harm than good. Many felt that the resulting chaos in the Galaxy would be too destructive to conscience. They felt the damage was already done and could not be undone.

John lowered his gaze and asked directly, "How can we truly trust you? How can we know that you won't just take the Heretic's place?"

Paximandros thought for a moment, then said, "Ask the Oracle."

Everyone stared at Paximandros for a long moment before shifting their gazes, one by one, to Sybil.

Sybil stared at Paximandros, her face studied in concentration. Her expression gradually shifted through shades of surprise, shock, incredulity, and, finally, horror.

She recoiled and gasped. "No! You cannot put that responsibility on… No!" She winced, leaped from the table, and stood, shaking, uncertain of what to do.

Gail pushed her chair aside so quickly it fell over as she rushed to Sybil's side, beating Julius Böhmer by half a step. Everyone else around the table lurched to their feet, and every security detail member ran to their charges.

Gail grabbed Sybil by the shoulders and looked at her, face to face. "What? Sybil…. What? What is it?"

Sybil's lips trembled, and tears streamed from her eyes. She looked back and forth between Gail and Paximandros. Finally, haltingly, she said, "Paximandros can be trusted because…. Because I can k-k-kill him. Right here. Not the body he is in… *Him*. The Gardener being inside him. Right now. Everyone like me can k-kill any Gardener or Heretic who inhabits another being."

She stared at Paximandros as she swallowed and shook her head. "You c-can't put that on me. I am not a m-murderer!"

Gail pulled Sybil close to her as she turned to stare in stunned amazement at Paximandros.

Preston scoffed, "You cannot be serious. You would actually put your lives in our hands?"

Paximandros shrugged, "Only those of us in your company. On the other hand, it would serve you well to remember who controls the world you live in." His tone darkened. "On the streets of your city, a man can kill another man. However, *there are consequences*. It should come as no surprise to you that should you choose to kill us, there would also be… *consequences*."

John studied Paximandros. "Do you speak for all of your people?"

Paximandros, still calmly seated, nodded and gently said, "Those of us who have stayed behind have chosen to trust you. We hope that your race will not be worse than the Heretic. After watching and observing you, we know that you are not, by any measure, perfect. As evidenced by recent events, a few of you are possibly as evil as the Heretic. The majority, though, are not."

Sybil stammered, "So… y-you expect me to be your weapon?"

Paximandros cocked his head and smiled, "Why, no. We have gifted your people with a choice. As you war with the Accipiters, should you capture any, you can decide whether to free them from their slave master. Or not. The choice is yours. You have now seen that it is possible to turn an enemy into an ally. It is not a guarantee, of course, but what in life is? You now have another option. You would be wise to carry at least one person such as yourself on any of your vessels in the future."

Paximandros added, "Perhaps our distinguished Accipiter guest has a question or two?"

Everyone stopped and turned to look at the Accipiter, who had remained seated on his bench. Quietly observing.

Yeurantheon made a deep rock-crushing noise, followed by a short sequence of hoots and glyphs and a louder, clashing set of darker, discordant pipes.

Everyone turned and looked at Mei.

Mei, looking and feeling like a small child caught sneaking into an adult conversation, swallowed hard and said, "Yeurantheon wants to know how having a Gardener inside him will be any different from the Heretic. The Heretic could edit his memories and control him. He…. He says he will consider helping." She swallowed, "But… he would rather die now than become a slave again, regardless of who the slave master is."

Paximandros stared at Yeurantheon for a moment before answering. "You will never be a slave again. Your mind will forever be yours and yours alone. With your permission, we will remove the…. Strings that allowed the Heretic to control you. We will remove the ability to edit your memories. We will create a new channel…. One that will allow us to talk to you privately. You will have the ability to turn it off and ignore us if you choose to. Our ability to privately communicate with you may be needed to help when we are, as the humans say, behind enemy lines. We'll be able to impersonate the Heretic connections, but we won't be able to control you. Should you wish to betray us, we won't be able to stop you."

Yeurantheon answered with a short series of glyphs and an even shorter tonal combination.

Mei nodded. "I don't think he believes you. He asks how he can know if this is true?"

Paximandros said, "When we rescued the humans, we implanted within them certain false memories that would be activated in the event that they were captured. The humans will know that those memories are false, but their physiological reactions are modified to protect them. Knowledge extracted from them by Accipiter technology will only retrieve the false memories. This was done when they were created. We have no influence over them now. If you are concerned over the validity of your thoughts and actions, I suggest that you entrust the humans to tell you if you behave out of character. Of course, should you grow tired of our presence, you can always ask one of the humans to kill us for you. That is the risk that we take. We do not wish to die any more than we hope you do. I would advise you to consider taking such action very carefully, however. Murdering us, as I said before, will no doubt have consequences."

Everyone gradually returned to their chairs.

John stared at Paximandros for a long moment and asked, "How and when will you restore the Five Percent?"

Paximandros raised his eyebrows and answered, "That is entirely up to you. We will restore them when and where you ask us to within the confines of what you have named New Texas."

John blinked. "What, no conditions? No more tests to pass?"

Paximandros reached over, picked up a green pear, and bit into it. "This is quite good, you know. The answer is no. There are no conditions. No more tests to pass. We wanted to know you before committing ourselves to this path."

John nodded slowly. "I see. And what about the surviving humans on Earth? Can what has been done to them be reversed? Can it be undone?"

Paximandros thought for a moment, "By what has been done to them, do you mean the alterations making them suitable hosts for the

Heretic? Or do you mean their memories, or are you referring to other changes? It is unlikely that their memories were all stored for safekeeping, in which case, there is nothing we can do for them. If you mean, can we undo making them suitable as hosts? That would require…. we can do something similar to what we are offering to Yeurantheon, cutting strings, as it were. If you mean, however, putting them back the way they were before the Accipiters changed them, at least physically? We would have to create new bodies for each human and transfer their… souls… to them. It would take…. A long time. There are…. Reasons why we waited sixty-four years before waking you. Our technology is not magic. Everything has a cost in time and energy."

Gail clasped John's hand. "John, it isn't just Earth. It's a whole galaxy of planets with… beings… people similarly afflicted. This is," she swallowed, "This is a bigger problem than I think any of us can really grasp right now."

Preston leaned forward and asked, "You said no more tests. What about the creatures roaming around the interior of New Texas, killing our people. Will you remove them?"

Paximandros shook his head. "You are already doing an admirable job at that task. We've studied the psychology of humans. We believe that it would be unwise of us to allow your haven to become… too comfortable."

John frowned, "So, you're not our friend. You're not our ally. You're just a super advanced race of aliens who find us to be useful and occasionally interesting and with whom you share at least a few common interests. However, we puny humans would be wise to maintain our utility and good behavior where those interests align? Does that about sum it up?"

Paximandros smiled thinly, "You underestimate yourselves. Consider that we have invested a great deal in you. We've exposed ourselves to risk because of that investment. We've… gambled on you."

John lowered his gaze and shook his head, "And when a racehorse breaks its leg, we put it down. So the moral of the story here is that we humans had better not break our leg. I get it."

Paximandros shrugged, "I don't believe it would ever come to that. The worst that I would see happening, assuming that either of our peoples survive what is to come, is that should we have an irrevocable falling out, my people would simply leave yours to your own fate."

Gail nodded and said, "Okay. Changing the subject. Your people brought us here. Cured our illnesses. We thank you for that… kindness. I have to ask, though," she fought the urge to hold her hand to her abdomen, "among the changes to us was, well, I'll be blunt. Birth control doesn't work very well. You also undid vasectomies and hysterectomies. Will you give us back control over our bodies?"

Paximandros seemed genuinely surprised and paused for a long moment before answering. "We restored your bodies to their optimal conditions. That included damage and missing organs as well as, as you say, curing illnesses. This would have naturally included damaged or missing reproductive organs. These restorations to your health were not specifically targeted at reproduction; rather, they were seen as a means to maximize the health of your surviving population. As for your implication that we intentionally altered your reproductive capabilities, this is not true. You say that your traditional methods to control conception are not working…. I see. Yes… your peoples' concern over this matter was noted."

"The ineffectiveness of conception prevention methods was instead a… as you say… a side effect. The alterations of your DNA to provide for improved resistance to disease and other general improvements seem to have coincidentally altered the levels of natural reproductive hormones, rendering birth control methods ineffective. Altering DNA at this level is not a simple matter. It is like pulling a thread on one of your garments. Doing so often affects unintended areas."

He continued, "The efficacy of your birth control pills is based largely on the modulation of hormones, primarily progesterone and estrogen. By altering genes associated with hormone receptors, the pill's ability to prevent ovulation has been significantly negated. By artificially increasing the levels of reproductive hormones, your bodies are in a state of constant heightened fertility. This would not only negate the effects of contraceptive methods that function by modulating hormone levels but could also increase libido and the frequency of ovulation. Also, the genetic changes appear to have stimulated the pituitary gland. This has resulted in a constant release of luteinizing hormone and other hormones, leading to frequent ovulation and increased sperm production. As another side effect of the genetic changes, the pH of human semen and vaginal fluids has been altered, causing it to degrade condom materials more rapidly. Upon reflection, I can understand why these changes have caused you… concern."

Gail narrowed her gaze, "Would you change it if you could?"

Paximandros shook his head. "The answer is no. This is not something we are willing to explore changing. Doing so would… pull more threads, possibly leading to results you would not want. Also, we see no reason to try. We like how it turned out because it supports our ends. Your numbers are still too small. We made you healthier, but you are not invulnerable. On the other hand, you are a clever species. We are confident that your people will eventually find their own solutions."

Sybil blanched, and her mouth dropped open as she stared at him.

The tint of Gail's face grew more and more scarlet as Paximandros spoke.

Marcus swallowed and desperately tried to change the subject. "You said there were reasons why you waited so long to wake us. Costs. Why did you save so few people from Earth?"

Paximandros cocked his head slightly as he looked at Marcus. "I believe you already suspect the answer. We did what we could. It might surprise you to learn that, in many ways, it would be easier to construct a Dyson Sphere like the one where you are now than it was to accomplish what we did on your planet. To pluck so many of you out from under the Heretic's gaze without him suspecting? In secret and unseen?"

"In the mere moments before you would have been vaporized by the kinetic projectiles launched by the Accipiters? If we tried to stop Yeurantheon's people, the Heretic would have known it was us, that we survived. If we took more of you in advance, the Keeper would have reported the same. If we silenced the Keeper himself…. There are other monitoring methods in the Heretic's employ. The truth is that we were forced to pick a population that seemed most likely to be able to…. Well…. To accomplish everything that you have. One that we could grab without the Heretic knowing."

Sybil shuddered, hugging herself as she quietly asked, "If I can draw them out and destroy them, I don't understand how you intend to replace them. I'm sorry, but I won't let one of you in my head."

Paximandros smiled gently. "No, my dear, you cannot carry one of us within you. That is for bodies like this one to do. The Heretic within Yeurantheon left behind a shell of itself. It is within that shell that we can reside and infiltrate their society. Humans from Earth can carry one of us as well. We would wear the Heretic shell around us in the transfer."

John asked, "If the Accipiters are freed from the Heretics, what's to keep them from simply keeping everything exactly the way it is now? Surely, some of them will think that they've got it pretty good right now. Why would they want to change? What's to stop them?"

Paximandros sighed sadly. "Of course, it seems probable that some of them will. Perhaps even many or most of them. That is why so many of my people refused to act for so long. They knew that Yeurantheon's people would fracture. We believe, or at least we hope, however, that many Accipiters will wish to change things and heal the wounds left by the Heretic. I'm afraid it is simply statistically unlikely that all of them will feel that way. For one reason or another, some will no doubt wish to keep things as they are. Some may sense an opportunity to carve out a private empire. Sooner or later, war is inevitable."

Preston insisted, "Then you know that your infiltration plan will eventually fail. Sooner or later, while we are out there playing galactic exorcist, some of the de-Heretic'd Accipiters are going to blow the whistle."

Paximandros shrugged, "Indeed. That is where humanity's penchant for violence will be required. It is your equal capacity for compassion and war that led us to consider you in our quest for a solution."

John winced. "That's one hell of a back-handed compliment."

Paximandros raised his eyebrows and shrugged again. "It is not a compliment. You are what you are. We do not judge you. We are glad that we were able to save what we could of your people and their culture. We know it was… insufficient. It was the best we could do."

Marcus cautiously asked, "So, you plan to build, or help us build a fleet? Will you listen to us? Allow us to tell you what we need?"

Paximandros laughed softly. "Yes, of course. We are not like you. We were amazed at what you accomplished in such an incomprehensibly short time. To throw ball bearings at a high fraction of the speed of light at the Accipiter vessels was shockingly primitive, but the results cannot be argued with. That you know it won't work again speaks to your cleverness and talent for war. To be honest, we expected that you would take many generations to accomplish what you did, that is, if you survived at all."

He continued, "In the event that you, as you say, passed our tests, we provided more than the hybrid starship for your use. As you know, there are many hangars that were closed to you. No more. In them, you will find warships left over from the time of the Masters. We altered them to suit your physiological needs. In addition, you will find that there are more hangars in other locations around your world. There are two types. The larger ones will take… time… for you to learn. The smaller ones should be no challenge. They are warship versions of the sublight craft you are already used to operating. All are equipped with weapons that were used to great effect until a contagion created by the Heretic spread through all the Masters' worlds and wiped them all out. These warships should provide you with a starting point. Over time, you will no doubt want to make changes and eventually start building your own completely new designs."

Preston swallowed, "A biological weapon…. That's what led to the Builder's spreading out? Phoenix told the President that their people escaped the Masters after a plague hit a colony."

Paximandros shrugged, "The effect wasn't completely simultaneous. Given the time and distances involved, not all of the Master's colony worlds were affected at precisely the same time. Some survived and pursued the Builders before they, too, expired. We believe some felt that the Builders were complicit. In the end, however, all of their colonies were affected, leading back to their homeworld. In the end, none survived."

Absorbing the information, Preston shook his head as he queried. "And the Masters' homeworld, is that someplace we might find more? Ships or resources we might salvage from their planet?"

The corner of Paximandros's mouth twitched. "That would be highly unlikely. Their homeworld is not in this galaxy."

Gail's eyes widened in surprise, "Come again?"

"The Masters originated in what you call the Small Magellanic Cloud. It is a satellite galaxy to your own that is roughly 150,000 light-years from the edge of this galaxy, or, around 200,000 light-years from your own star system. For comparison, Andromeda is 2.5 million light-years from your star. After conquering their own galaxy, they traveled to ours. However, they did not have Nexus Junction Point travel, so they had to use warp drive. They knew it would take a long time, so they built McKendree Cylinders equipped with warp drive and made the long journey that way, bringing many millions of their people with them."

Both Gail and Preston looked astounded. Preston managed to speak first, shaking his head. "Wait, you said that McKendree Cylinders don't have Nexus Junction Point drives, so how did we travel through one to get here?"

With a hint of paternal pride, Paximandros smiled, "Your people brought it back from Earth."

Gail jumped in, "Wait. Are you saying the Keeper ship has NJP capabilities? And you jumped all of New Texas using it? That's…."

Paximandros's tone was serious. "The physical shape of the Keeper Ark is not aesthetic or random. Among other things, it provides the resonance waveguide for isolating the Nexus Junction Point. Transiting the NJP is accomplished through gravitic shear force. Something a warp drive can… with subtle manipulation… accomplish. However, since it isn't purpose-built for that function, using this method can induce severe local field gradient… anomalies…. That is, if you are not careful."

Gail's realization was swift. "That's what happened behind us after we transited. It created some kind of gravity… shock wave?"

Paximandros's expression darkened. "We were not proud of what we did. The effect was worse than that. It, at least temporarily, destabilized the NJP and what you call spacetime. It should… eventually… repair itself. We are fairly confident the rip will not expand."

Gail shrank back. "Expand? What do you mean? It can get worse?"

He hesitated, then shrugged. "Warp travel compresses and expands what you would call the fabric of spacetime. NJPs are, well, that is a very long explanation. Suffice it to say that what we did pulled the NJP in after us... to a degree. It did not create a singularity. Rather, it destabilized the local frame. From a poetic point of view, you might call it a hole in spacetime. It is an inaccurate description, but one that will suffice. We believe this... hole... will seal itself in time and won't, well, expand and unravel the rest of the galaxy and beyond."

Preston pressed. "How certain?"

Paximandros paused. "Your scientists discounted the remote possibility that their first atomic bomb test would ignite your atmosphere."

John observed coldly. "You were desperate."

"A calculated risk."

John shuddered. "You didn't build... New Texas. Did you?"

Paximandros responded, "The Masters created the original design for their journey to this galaxy. We... improved upon it."

Gail's realization deepened, and she narrowed her eyes. "Did you build the Dyson Sphere? Or did the Masters?"

Paximandros smiled. "In fact, yes, we did. The Masters needed a base of operations within this galaxy. When they arrived, they knew that their supply train back home was too long to support conquest. They searched for out-of-the-way, uninteresting nebulas like the one we are in now and built a starlifting operation to provide their manufacturing base. There was a great deal of infrastructure built up around it. Later, when we found it, we saw its potential. Think of it as, say, discovering a lumber mill next to a forest and realizing the potential to build a city. The Dyson Sphere provided a refuge from the Heretics forces for my people, and room to grow."

Preston surmised, nodding slowly, "That's a hell of a nice hidey hole for your people."

Paximandros sighed. "We believe that when the contagion took hold here, the Masters must have killed the Builders. At least, that is what we deduced when we found this place. We were searching for bases of operation of the Masters when the Heretic turned on us. We had nowhere else to go. By then, he'd built up the Accipiter war fleet into a force we could not begin to counter."

Paximandros' voice was strained. "He... annihilated every world... every outpost... every home we had in the galaxy was laid to waste. Millions of worlds. Of course, he neglected to tell us about his plan to use the contagion. Until that point, the Masters were winning, and the fleet was needed. His betrayal was unprecedented in our history. A result of his…. There were reasons why our greatest law existed."

A hushed silence fell over the room for several minutes as the scope and scale of the Gardener's downfall sank in.

John broke the quiet, "You must know that I vowed revenge upon your people, as well as on the Accipiters."

"We know."

John exchanged long looks with Gail and the others.

Tom asked quietly, "Changing the subject, what happens if we end up being worse than the Heretic? What then? Will you take a page from the Heretic's playbook and poison us or something and kill us all?"

Paximandros sighed sadly, "In the event that your people turn on us? In that case, the rest of my people will take the long trip to Andromeda. Those of us who remain would leave you to your madness, knowing that we at least tried. We could have, as you say, poisoned the Accipiters, but that was something we could not bring ourselves to see happen to a people for a second time."

Gail asked, "Exactly how do you propose to accomplish your infiltration of Heretic planets?"

A hologram of an Accipiter mother ship appeared above the table, then zoomed in on one of the many Keeper Arks embedded within it.

Paximandros continued, "You captured the Ark from your Earth. We honestly never expected you would be able to pull that off, although we were saddened at the losses you suffered in the effort."

John eyed it suspiciously, trading glances with Gail, Marcus, and Preston, who were all nodding in unison. He shook his head slowly, "You are planning a Trojan Horse attempt? Ride the Keeper Ship into some backwater Accipiter system screaming, 'Please help us. We escaped from the evil humans, and then you expect the Accipiters there to not blow you out of the sky just out of a pure abundance of caution?"

Paximandros smiled softly, "Each clan High Priest is host to a special version of the Heretic. Think of it as a Sentinel. The watchdog that keeps an eye on all the other instances in its domain, ensuring that none diverge from unity. The system's High Priest will not only want to interrogate Yeurantheon, it will be desperate for intelligence on what exactly has been happening."

Preston asked, "And what happens when they immediately send a courier back to wherever their capital is and let them know that Yeurantheon has shown up?"

Paximandros frowned.

Preston shook his head. "Right. That's what the new ships are for. You need time for your plan to work. If they send a courier before their Heretic is removed, then chances are a whole fleet might show up, and I assume that is more than you can handle? We'll be there to make sure that no one leaves the system until you've succeeded."

Marcus asked, "How do you know which system to go to? One that won't already have a big fleet there?"

Paximandros nodded. "We monitor when and where they go. We know where to go where their presence is small. After we are inserted and take over, any clan that arrives afterward will be…."

Sybil had been staring at Paximandros intently. She shook her head and interrupted, "I imagine any Accipiter-held system will have a lot of Heretic copies you will need to replace. To do that, you will need an army of people like me and another army of Gardener-carrying hosts."

Paximandros nodded, "The Keeper Ship already has thousands of stasis chambers. We shall manufacture more bodies like this one. Some will carry my people, and the rest will be like you."

Gail nodded. "You're planning this like a pandemic. Each clan that gets de-Heretic'd goes to another system, and it spreads."

A small voice spoke up from the side of the room. Everyone turned in surprise to look at Mei as she spoke.

"There are thousands of humans on the Keeper ship, frozen in those stasis chambers. Plus, there are lots and lots of creatures from our planet's history. Biological treasures. Will you…" She swallowed as she saw everyone looking at her, "Will you help us with them?"

Paximandros smiled. "Such a brave young woman. You should keep an eye on this one. She'll surprise you, I'm sure. The answer is yes, of course. We will be pleased to help you. We caution you, though. There is a reference in the memories of this body… a Pandora's box. Yes, that seems an appropriate metaphor."

Sybil smiled at Mei. "Don't worry, Mei, it was on our list. We hadn't forgotten them."

Mei shrank in her seat, even more mortified at speaking out of turn.

Sitting next to her, Leo Talib spoke for the first time, chuckling, "It is all right, Mei. We wouldn't have you here if we didn't trust you."

Mei nodded and added, "Okay, I'll shut up now."

Leo chuckled again. "Don't worry, my dear."

John interjected, "So you intend to use the Keeper Ship as a Trojan Horse!"

Paximandros smiled. "Indeed."

Preston interjected, "What about our people at Ari'Nell. Did they survive? Can you help us find them?"

Paximandros shook his head, "We don't know. It is a big galaxy. We have no objection to telling you if we…. Happen upon them."

Yeurantheon 'spoke' a series of hoots and glyphs.

Paximandros didn't bother waiting for the translation, "The Memory Trees? Now, that's an interesting question. The Memory trees are a network of biological repositories. Think of them like, oh, a distributed network of your computer servers that act as data storage and hosts for Heretic instances. They act as, well, a biological Internet, as it were. They broadcast to all the modified beings and creatures on the planet…. All of whom are able to receive radio signals for that reason."

Sybil flinched. "The Wardogs! We figured out they react to radio signals. That's why they react the way they do?"

Paximandros nodded, "As Yeurantheon knows, the Memory Trees have other purposes that the Accipiters are aware of. They broadcast a continuous signal that is perceived as something that is comforting. None realize its true purpose."

John shook his head. "My God, that's what those things are. You mean they broadcast…. Updates? Are you saying that they are proactively updating people? Like software or firmware updates?"

Paximandros nodded. "It is quite a challenge."

John frowned and shook his head. "I have to believe that a super advanced intelligence like the Heretic has backup and data restoration mechanisms. They have to deal with natural disasters, accidents, etc. Right? I mean, what happens if you go in and de-Heretic a planet, and then it gets restored from whatever they have that is the equivalent of an auto backup and restore function? Hell, that's got to be an obvious thing to do for any advanced network."

Paximandros shrugged. "I never said this would be easy."

Seafarer

● ● ● ● ● ● ● ● ● ● ● ● ● ● ● ● ● ●

DownSide: New Philippines

Caesar Salangsang stepped onto the pink sand beach, feeling the gentle warmth of the suntube on his skin as he looked ahead. He could see his newlywed wife Michelle on the beach, sketching something in her notebook. Probably the rambling Hawksbill sea turtles a few yards away from her that were lazily inching down the sand towards the surf. She was a biology graduate student and still planned to finish her doctorate, drawing on her unique experience traveling and cataloging the new world's surprising differences from Earth.

Michelle was three months pregnant with their triplet girls. She was determined not to let the pregnancy slow her down. The pregnancy was bittersweet for Caesar after losing his wife and nine children to the Accipiters back on Earth. As his and Michelle's relationship had evolved for a long time, they had mutually agreed that neither wanted children. Their voyage halfway around the new world, the first voyage in the open ocean by *anyone* and in a hand-built boat at that, had drawn them closer together still. Then they'd more or less found themselves and their crew shipwrecked in an island paradise that was eerily reminiscent of Caesar's Philippine home islands. And then... the seas had, impossibly, locked in place, and the sky had turned red during the Accipiter attack. It was the end of the world all over again, and.... Everything changed. They could no longer hide from the bond that had grown between them, and both happily accepted the consequences.

Later, after those consequences became apparent and after much quiet discussion, they'd agreed on names for the girls: Seraphina,

Genevieve, and Josephine. Michelle had been worried about choosing names that might, even obliquely, remind Caesar too much of the precious family he'd lost. Choosing names that were ultimately of Celtic and Hebrew origin seemed… kind.

The soft waves of the ocean washed over the salmon coral sand as he walked towards her. From the back, he could see that she was wearing a light blue linen tunic shirt over cutoff shorts, which had become one of her favorite beach outfits since their dramatic arrival there three and a half months ago.

Caesar called out to her, "Chelle, Nahanap natin ito! We found it!"

Michelle sighed at the interruption, set her pencil down in the book's margin, and closed the cover over it. She turned and looked up at Caesar, who had a broad, boyish grin on his face. Her irritation melted away at the sight of his happiness. It was a welcome change after the recent shocking news about the true nature of the Accipiters and the startling revelation of who, apparently, had been the real enemy all along.

She smiled and raised her hand over her eyes to shield them from the glare, looking up. Caesar's English was excellent; however, at Michelle's insistence, he had been helping her learn a few Tagalog words and phrases. She asked, "What have you found, uhm, asawa ko… my husband, and why are you carrying my boots, uhm… aking mga bota, and aren't you supposed to be on a Senate meeting call or something?"

Caesar was wearing cutoff shorts, a loose shirt, and boots, and Michelle's hiking boots were draped around his neck, tied together by their laces. On his belt hung a holstered 9mm Staccato P, a wedding gift from President Austin. While no Wardogs or Stalkers had been found on the islands so far, those were hardly the only dangers one might encounter on previously uninhabited islands. Michelle, herself, carried another wedding gift, this one from the Vice President, a Staccato CS.

He pulled the boots off from around his neck and dropped them on the sand before her. "The Senate meeting was postponed, but that is not important right now, Chelle. The replication cave, or factory, or whatever the thing is. Nahanap natin ito! We found it!"

Michelle blinked in surprise. "Really? You've been looking for it for months now. Uhm.. Nasaan ito? I mean, where was it hiding?"

Caesar dropped to his knees in front of her. He reached out, pulled her ankle and foot toward him, and removed her sandal before placing the boot on her foot. Excitedly, he answered, "After the other ones were found at the other settlements, everyone assumed it had to be somewhere close, but it wasn't. It is over a hundred and seventy kilometers from here on the big island, in the natural harbor we called Manila Bay. It's there on Panama Island, sa gitna, right in the middle of the bay.

He pulled on her other foot, and Michelle pulled back, putting her hand on his wrist, stopping him.

She shook her head somewhat playfully, "Now, just you wait, Hiyang-hiya na ako sa'yo, mahal. Sometimes, your enthusiasm can be embarrassing. A hundred and… that's, like, over a hundred miles and over open water. We don't have a new boat strong enough for that yet!"

Caesar grinned wolfishly and said, "Who said anything about a bangka, a boat?"

Just then, a shadow silently passed overhead.

They both looked up at the ILC drifting downwards.

Michelle blinked in surprise at the sight of it, and then her eyes narrowed in anger. "That damned thing better not land on….!"

Caesar smiled and laughed, "Don't worry 'Chelle. I instructed them to land well away from the nesting grounds. They won't harm a single pagong. They won't hurt any turtles."

While she was distracted, he pulled her other foot out and put her boot on it.

Michelle shook her head, "I'm pregnant, not an invalid. I can put my own damned botas on, Caesar! Besides, where is Guillermo or Angel and the others?"

Caesar shook his head, "Busy digging the new well. If they stop, they could lose progress. With the soil conditions here, if water begins to flow into the well shaft during the digging, it can weaken the walls and cause a collapse. They'll be fine. Iaalalay namin sila para makita ito mamaya. We'll take them to see it later."

He grinned crookedly, "You are so lovely when you are, galit, my love. When you are angry. Let's go!"

✪ ✪ ✪

Caesar stepped off the NTN Dagger's loading ramp onto the pristine shores of Panama Island. The suntube's gentle rays danced on the cerulean waters of the protected bay, casting a warm glow on the foreign landscape. Beside him, Michelle held his hand, her pregnancy gently visible beneath her blouse.

As they walked onto the island, the sound of the birds and gentle surf belied the alien origin of not only the world but the function of the island itself.

The ILC's commanding officer, Commander Ramona Henry, followed shortly behind them and announced, "Senator Salangsang, Michelle, welcome to Panama Island." The strawberry-blonde Navy commander exuded confidence and authority. "I believe you will want to see the site as soon as possible. It is completely unlike the Morgan Island or Jamestown locations."

Caesar looked questioningly at her. "I take it that is why you did not do a fly around of the island and landed at one end of it instead?"

Ramona pursed her lips, then shrugged. "Well, Sir, the… facility… is rather larger and obviously meant for a very different scale of operation. I thought you would appreciate seeing it from ground level first. Shall we go?"

Caesar nodded appreciatively. "Thank you, Commander. Have the Marines had any difficulty securing the island?"

Romona smiled as they began walking along the beach, accompanied by a squad of marines. "None at all, Senator. The place is practically gift-wrapped. As you'll see, the theory that these places are being created new seems pretty convincing. It's like the entire facility was, well, grown underground and uplifted from underneath."

✪ ✪ ✪

As they rounded a bend, Caesar and Michelle saw what Ramona had meant. It was as though the entire center of the island had been pushed up from underneath, revealing a sight any Bond Villain would happily claim as his lair.

This was no simple replication cave.

Stretching out before them for several miles, dully gleaming metal walls and structures glinted underneath the raised crown of the island. Docks, slips, elevated walkways, and massive caution-striped doors hinted at the capabilities lying within.

Michelle gasped at the sight as Caesar stared, open-mouthed, blinking at the hidden industrial complex before them.

Ramona nodded knowingly, "Like I said, Senator, I thought you would want to see it in person, on the ground, first. From our initial run-through, what you're looking at appears to be a large manufacturing and shipping complex, and, well, wait until we go inside!" Her watery blue eyes twinkled in anticipation.

Caesar marveled at the sight. "Commander… It would take years… maybe decades, for my men and I to build something like this. Back on Earth, a project like this would probably cost billions."

✪ ✪ ✪

Standing before a massive, sealed door, Ramona glanced over her shoulder at Caesar and Michelle. The glow of anticipation in their eyes mirrored her own excitement.

With a determined grin, Ramona activated a panel on the side of the door. The machinery within the complex hummed to life, and the colossal door began to slide open with a smooth, mechanical grace. The suspense grew with each passing moment until the door revealed what lay beyond.

As the door slid fully open, the sight that greeted them was awe-inspiring. Before them lay a vast, cavernous space, illuminated by an ambient blue light. A network of elevated walkways crisscrossed the expanse, leading to a central platform. At the heart of the platform rested a large, gleaming Catamaran.

Caesar's breath caught in his throat. "Commander… this… this is beyond anything we could have imagined."

Michelle's hand moved to her mouth, her eyes wide with wonder. "It's beautiful. It's like something out of a dream."

Ramona grinned, "She's a beauty, that's for sure. And it's not some damned pleasure yacht, either. What you are looking at has plenty of cargo space. I mean, don't get me wrong, the cabins and tech are first-rate. What I mean is that this is obviously meant to be the start of, well, trade and exploration. And…" She shook her head, "There are three more, just like her, in other docks. What's more, I can't be sure because we've only scratched the surface of this place, but most of the space here seems industrial. I believe this is a factory, and I expect it can make a lot more than just ships."

The soft blue illumination of the dock danced across the contours of the Catamaran, which stretched across the cavernous chamber, its sheer size commanding attention. Twin hulls, sleek and elongated, gracefully embraced the futuristic design, imparting an aura of streamlined efficiency. The vessel's elevated central deck, where the cargo bays and control center converged, hinted at its immense carrying capacity.

Caesar's eyes glistened as he approached the ship. Michelle couldn't help but smile at his reaction.

He shook his head, "Commander… 'Chelle. This is hope for our people beyond the damned war. It is a bridge between our past and future."

Leviathan

● ● ● ● ● ● ● ● ● ● ● ● ● ● ● ●

Ascendance
Special Quarters
Accipiter Capital System

Alberta "Bertie" Sinitskaya had given up trying to wipe away the tears that beaded her eyes and face in the null-g and breathed through her mouth because the stoppage in her sinuses was even more epic. She had cycled through her grief in all the usual stages several times over. Now, though, her heart mostly dwelled on rage. After what she imagined must have been a few days after Xuraens had escorted her back to her "garden cell," although she had no proper way to gauge the passage of time that she had confidence in, the organic "tablet" she'd been given began to chime.

When Bertie examined it, she'd been startled to see an entirely new interface. Whereas before, it had simply provided spoken and text translation, now it displayed something very similar to the media player from her phone. The phone that had been in her pocket when she'd died. Like everyone else leaving New Texas, the device had been scrubbed of anything that could give a hint about the nature of New Texas itself. She'd kept photos and videos of Ronald and Anna from Earth, as well as her music library.

Not everything was replicated on the tablet. Many of the files were marked with icons she interpreted to mean that the source was corrupted. Some were only partial files, mostly with either missing portions at the beginning or ending. The analytical part of her mind was shocked that much had survived at all. The idea that the Accipiters were able to extract the information from the device itself didn't surprise her.

She had played the surviving videos and poured through the remaining photos endlessly, without eating or sleeping, until she'd finally succumbed to her anguish, desolation, and bodily fatigue.

Then she'd repeated the same several times over, stopping only to sip water from a vine or reluctantly gnaw on one of the few alien fruits she could bear.

Finally, she'd lapsed into violent depression while she darkly considered, not for the first time, snapping off one of the more brittle vines to make a tool sharp enough to slash her wrists. The only thing that stopped her was the fear that if the Accipiters brought her back to life, again, that the next time they might choose to alter her to make her more… compliant. Like they'd already done to every surviving human back on Earth.

Instead, she decided that since they'd remade her into a teenager, she'd rebel like one and play the loudest, most obnoxious music she had. Audio produced by the tablet seemed to emanate from the walls around her, and the volume available exceeded even her own tolerance – something she'd discovered the first time she tried to max it out and the shattering notes from Metallica's "Seek and Destroy" that resulted from the effort had left her ears ringing and her head pounding for hours.

After that, she kept the volume just high enough to hurt.… Somehow, the pain seemed welcome.… But not enough to make her ears bleed.

Back when she and Dimitri had first met and eventually started dating, their polar opposite tastes had led to a dare and habit that permeated their life together. He would listen to music of her choice, and she would do the same. Eventually, they combined their music libraries. It wasn't that she came to love his dark and brooding operas, nor did Dimitri develop a taste for Bertie's reciprocally dark and brooding hard rock, punk, post-punk, as well as quite a bit of industrial and darkwave peppered with the odd P!nk and other lighter artists here and there. Long before Awakening Day, she'd sometimes found herself listening to a little of Dimitri's music when she wanted to be reminded of him. Oddly, to her at least, they'd both found themselves drawn to Thomas Bergersen, Audiomachine, Jesper Kyd, and others who specialized in grand, urgent, and intensely emotional musical themes.

So now, the cavernous room they'd given her reverberated with a nonstop playlist that ranged from 'Heart of Courage' to Perl Jam's 'Black,' to Prokofiev's 'Battle on the Ice,' to Mozart's 'Dies Irae,' to Berlioz's foreboding 'Symphonie Fantastique.'

✪ ✪ ✪

This time, Bertie was awake when Xuraens entered the room. She didn't bother turning down the music and waited defiantly for the enormous alien to react or even complain. Instead, she was surprised as he instead paused and…. listened.

The music was the ending of Purcell's 'Dido and Aeneas.'

Xuraens politely motioned for her attention with one of its smaller hands, carefully keeping its larger, viciously clawed other set of arms tucked away at its side.

Bertie waited a few moments longer than was polite in return before reluctantly pausing the music.

Xuraens asked, and the tablet translated aloud,

MY RACE HAS MULTIPLE VOCAL RESONANCE CHAMBERS. I HAVE LISTENED TO SOME OF YOUR MUSIC. I WAS UNAWARE THAT YOUR PEOPLE HAD COMPENSATED FOR YOUR AUDITORY SHORTCOMINGS BY INVENTING MUSICAL INSTRUMENTS. HOWEVER, THE MUSIC ON YOUR DEVICE DOES NOT SEEM TO BE OF A CONSISTENT STYLE." HE GESTURED TOWARDS THE WALLS, "THAT MUSIC, FOR EXAMPLE, IS VERY DIFFERENT THAN MUCH OF THE REST. EXPLAIN ITS MEANING AND WHY YOU ARE CRYING.

Bertie wiped her tears with the sleeve of her 'jumpsuit' as she tried to sniff, but her sinuses were completely blocked. Again.

She glared at him as she snapped, "It's… It's Dimitri's music. An opera called Dido and Aeneas. I only know about it because the name stuck out to me when I saw it. Dido. Cruxshadows had a song called Dido's Reply, and that got me wondering. That last bit you heard was Dido's Lament. It's about a Queen whose lover has left. She loves him so much that she takes her own life."

Xuraens stared at her for a long time before his hoots, song, and glyphs were translated by the tablet.

I AM CERTAIN THAT THERE MUST BE MORE TO THE STORY THAN THAT.

Bertie's lips quivered as she bit back an angry retort. She swallowed and answered, "If you must know, it is the story of a group of survivors from the city of Troy after it was destroyed by the Greeks. They were shipwrecked on the coast of Carthage, where he met the Queen. Dido. They fell madly in love. However, the gods had a different destiny in mind for Aeneas. Eventually, he decided he had to leave to fulfill his destiny and lead the survivors to find a new home and found a new empire. Dido felt betrayed and took her own life, cursing Aeneas and his descendants even though she still loved him."

Xuraens stared at her for a long time with his enormous Topaz eyes before answering,

I WONDER IF I WILL EVER UNDERSTAND YOUR PEOPLE.

Bertie shrugged, "It is your loss for destroying us. Maybe you should think about that before you wipe out the next civilization on your target list." She tried to sniff again, wiped her face, and shook her head. "Why are you here?"

Xuraens answered,

PREPARE YOURSELF. THERE IS SOMETHING I WANT YOU TO SEE.

✪ ✪ ✪

After a very long 'egg' ride, Xuraens escorted Bertie to the opening of a stupendously large subterranean cavern. Bioluminescent fungi cast an eerie blue-red glow upon the cavern walls. Enormous structures hung like stalactites from the ceiling, like inverted skyscrapers, glowing with power as clouds of winged vehicles or devices or creatures; Bertie couldn't tell which, darted this way and that. The air was damp and sweet and cool, with the distant sound of a thunderous waterfall lost somewhere in the mist beyond. The cavern floor, what she could see of it, seemed to be as smooth as glass. A vast, tranquil, glimmering lake.

In the center of the cavern lay a vessel, unlike any Accipiter ship she'd seen before. Where the big motherships were rounded disks dotted with embedded Keeper ships, like some fantastic alien cookie inlaid with jeweled candies, the thing below held a menacing and malevolent countenance. It resembled a colossal organism, more akin to a massive sea creature than any machine of war she could fathom. Its body was sinuous, covered with a shimmering membrane, giving the impression of muscles and skin rather than metal and alloy. The ship throbbed with an eerie, living pulse, like a heart, and every inch of it seemed to breathe.

But it was the surface of the ship that drew Bertie's attention. The ship's exterior was adorned with thousands of pulsing blisters, each moving with an unsettling life of its own.

Her skin crawled, and a chill ran down her spine as she sensed that *something* longed to burst out of those grotesque, sickly bulges like an evil horde awaiting some dark incantation.

Translucent tendrils, like so many vines, enveloped the vessel from below, each shimmering from within.

It was difficult to fathom its scale, though, as nothing within sight was recognizable.

Xuraens loomed next to Bertie as he extended his clawed arms to point at the vessel below.

Bertie's tablet translated as Xuraens' eyes flashed a dark purple, and the tones he spoke were deep and rolling with power.

BEHOLD. WE HAVE NOT HAD NEED OF SUCH SINCE AGES BEFORE YOUR ANCESTORS WALKED UPRIGHT. THE VESSELS YOU HAVE SEEN BEFORE WERE NOT DESIGNED FOR WAR. THEY ARE FOR TRAVEL, TRADE, AND LIVING. WHAT YOU SEE BEFORE YOU WAS BUILT TO DEFEAT A POWERFUL INVADER OVER A MILLION OF YOUR YEARS AGO. WE KEPT IT HERE AS A REMINDER. NOW IT, AND ALL THE OTHERS LIKE IT ACROSS THE GALAXY, ARE BEING REVIVED.

Bertie murmured. "It's a dreadnaught. Until now… we've been fighting, what, cruise ships?"

Xuraens didn't answer.

As they watched, the dreadnaught began to awaken. Organic portals on its surface began to dilate open, revealing bioluminescent interiors. Bertie could see movement of some kind inside, although the vehicle was too large and too far away to discern exactly *what* was moving.

Near the dreadnaught's base, the water pulsated softly. The vine-like structures brightened and pulsated rhythmically, as though some life force were being awakened. Creatures, or…. Something…. Rose up from beneath the water and began to scurry across the surface of the vessel, doing…. Something.

Bertie stiffened. "Why are you showing me this? Trying to impress me?"

Xuraens tilted its head, the layers of its feather analogues shifting in hue under the odd lighting. The tablet translated,

TO REMIND YOU. TO WARN YOU. THE GALAXY WAS OURS LONG BEFORE YOUR KIND LOOKED TO THE STARS AND WONDERED WHAT THEY WERE.

The cavern began to resonate with a deep thrumming. The things scrambling across the dreadnaught's surface fell away back into the rippling water as the vines followed suit. The reverberations grew exponentially until Bertie was driven to her knees by the onslaught, clasping her hands to cover her ears.

Emerging from the waters, the dreadnaught ascended like some Lovecraftian leviathan, maneuvering its stupendous bulk up and forward, slowing to hover scant meters away from Bertie and Xuraens, casting a foreboding shadow over them.

Xuraens, seemingly unfazed, made graceful gestures with its larger clawed appendages and its more delicate set, while intricate glyphs danced across its beak in a mesmerizing display.

Then, as if answering a silent command, the dreadnaught fluidly rotated on its axis and effortlessly glided towards a titanic portal that was barely visible on the far side of the cavern. The dark passage yawned open, allowing the massive craft to enter. Just as silently, the portal sealed shut, leaving Bertie and Xuraens in its echoing aftermath.

Isla de Fuego

● ● ● ● ● ● ● ● ● ● ● ● ● ● ● ●

DownSide: New Philippines

When Caesar, Michelle, and others in their group visited one of the nearby islands and camped for the night. Michelle had been entranced by the large swarms of fireflies. Caesar and his men were immediately struck by the similarity to Siquijor Island, which had been located in the Central Visayas region of the Philippines, back on Earth, which was known for its fireflies. Indeed, Caesar explained that when a Spanish expedition in the year 1565 found the island, they had originally named it Isla de Fuego, or Island of Fire. That name had delighted Michelle, and over an evening of beer around the campfire, surrounded by fireflies, Michelle convinced everyone to name the new island Isla de Fuego instead.

The original island's history was steeped in legends of witches with the power to heal and tales of mythical creatures. In more recent times, the people there had transformed the island into a hub for healing practices. Many traditional healers, sometimes called Mananambals, called this island their home.

Now, in the present day, after the delegation to the Gardener Dyson sphere returned, the Senate gathered in the lounge area of the former movie theatre. Gail, Sybil, and Livia had met beforehand and decided that an informal meeting might be best, and if things got out of hand, they'd break up the meeting and reconvene in a formal session. There were two vexing issues to be discussed. First was where to put the people in stasis from the Keeper Ship, and second, on a more immediately personal note for the citizens of Fort Brazos, was how to handle the return of the five percent.

Up first was the 'easier' issue: where to place the facility for the revival of the seventy-some-odd thousand breeding pairs of humans and pre-humans in stasis on the Keeper Ship. While most people were rather more than dubious about the idea of reviving the hominids and even the earliest humans, the records showed that several thousand men and women had been "collected" over the past few thousand years of recorded human history. It was hoped that those, at least, might have some chance of successful assimilation.

Livia Milner pointed out that only the handful that had been "preserved" within the last hundred or two years would have any hope of "reacting well" if they initially found themselves confronted not only with the shock of waking up A) At all, after whatever trauma preceded their preservation, or B) Waking up in the outside-in world of New Texas, or, possibly worst of all, C) Waking up in the comparatively modern city of Fort Brazos.

Alphonse Halkias noted that with the introduction of the replication caves, the challenges of provisioning clothing, shelter, and supplies that plagued the months following New London's Awakening Day were now things of the past. He proposed that the Jamestown location, with its "rustic" charm, might be an apt site for the facility.

Before Darnell Lewis could chime in, Mira Yeager Cross pointed out that locating the facility in the middle of a forest where people could wander off trying to find their way back to their homes that were lost to time and space and probably get eaten or simply get lost or in trouble was perhaps a bad idea.

That's when Gaspard Boyer dismissively waved his hand and declared that, "It might be wise, non? To place these primitives on some île, somewhere they cannot simply stray and become lost. There, we can assess if they have the capability to adapt to our monde."

Esmerelda Collins then lectured the room for a full ten minutes about the precedents being set and how "we should not immediately think to simply exile ALL our problems to a remote island somewhere, like we did with the North Koreans and the not-to-be-named son of the not-to-be-name traitorous and not-lamented-late Admiral and his traitorous not-to-be-named wife."

At that point, Gail turned to Caesar, who was connected via radio, and asked if he wanted to put the facility in his "district," otherwise known as the New Philippines. His immediate reaction had been to suggest Panama Island. However, Michelle interrupted him and reminded him of Isla de Fuego. It was idyllic, relatively close to the main settlement, already explored, and unlike Panama Island, not home to a massive industrial complex that was likely to be even more unsettling to freshly decanted peoples from Earth's past.

Once that decision was reached, the debate turned to the more vexing issue of dealing with the return of the five percent. As with the people from the Keeper ship, the idea of returning all of them at the same time was rejected despite the desperation many would feel, including some in the Senate Chamber itself, for the return of friends and loved ones. The sheer chaos of handling four thousand four hundred and thirty-two people returning from the dead at the same time was mind-boggling.

"Besides," Dale Hubbard chided, "Where are we going to put them? Some of them have homes to come back to. I propose we prioritize those first… the ones with the fewest… complications."

Darnell Lewis shook his head and adamantly argued, "Look, I'm sure there are lots of folks like my mom Jasmine and my sister Yazmeen. Sure, someone else is living in their old places, but hell, they can come home right now with me!"

Maria Gonzalez tried to reassure Darnell, "Senator Lewis… Darnell. Whichever people are first on the list, yes, of course, people like your mother and sister are the easy decisions to make, but there are other people who need to…. Make decisions. Your friend Gary Little, for example. I recall reading an engagement announcement to Lucia Hernandez; however, his wife, Darlene, was among the five percent. I'm certainly not suggesting that we don't revive people like Darlene. However, decisions and preparations must be made. Who will be there when they wake up? What are they to be told, and, yes, Dale is right, we need to make certain that every single one of our people has a place to go and that they won't be…."

Sybil nodded, finishing Maria's sentence for her. "Forgotten. No one will be forgotten or left behind. I know that emotions will run high on this, but while we are waiting impatiently, I ask everyone here to consider how this experience is going to affect the five percent? Remember how we all felt on Awakening Day and in the months since then? We lost too many people to suicide, including because of loved ones among the five percent not waking up! We must not, because of our selfish desires, rush the return of so many people only to have that haste result in even more tragedy and heartache. This is complicated enough from a legal and logistical point of view. Think of how these people will *feel*. Earth is gone. We're living in an outside-in world built by aliens. More than two *years* have passed. There are alien creatures out there that have killed people here. We're at war with a million-year-old enemy that controls the entire galaxy. And don't forget how long it took all of us to accept the world we are living in now and how there are no stars at night. Oh, and we have starships and on and on and on. Just *think* about how much they're going to have to absorb. All of this may be starting to seem normal to some of you now, but to the five percent, it will be a terrible shock on top of whatever life circumstance they are coming back from the dead to contend with."

Esmerelda added, "Let's be practical. We should set up a discrete location where each 'awakee' can deal with the initial shock in private. Some... discussions... should not be on display. For those whose homes are effectively gone, we'll ask them what they want. We need to have options ready for them. I suggest we expand the current housing program to designate a.... replacement... home for each five percenter who needs it. Like it or not, these people were singled out and mistreated by the Gardeners. There will be hell to pay if we don't treat each and every one of them with dignity and respect."

The meeting broke into several groups who, with minor guidance, separately focused on issues of housing, gathering information on each of the five percenters, and establishing a commission to deal with property and other legal matters.

Isla de Fuego

Isla de Fuego glowed in the sun. Its white, powdery-to-pebble sand was matched with shallow, azure, clear waters and emerald-green palms swaying in the sea breeze. Overnight, in the center of the uninhabited island, the ground sank. In its place rose a resort sanctuary sculpted from bamboo, teakwood, and gracefully woven palm fronds. Elevated wooden pathways, bathed in the soft glow of lanterns, connected terracotta-roofed bungalows to a series of treetop suites. Discretely hidden inside the largest building was a state-of-the-(human)-art medical clinic. Below ground, beneath the clinic, a copy of the Keeper Ship preservation facility materialized into place, along with the still "sleeping" stasis-preserved hundred and forty thousand purloined souls the Keeper had 'collected' over the millennia.

In the months since they were discovered in the bowels of the Keeper Ship, no one had anticipated "thawing them out" anytime soon. Two University professors had worked to study and catalog the humans and pre-humans by taking photos of the images the Keeper

Ship facility displayed for each. Translations of the data included took longer, especially since it wasn't considered a priority.

Dr. Eleanor "Ellie" Forsythe, the Chair of the Department of Sociology, and Dr. Carlos Mendoza, the head of the Department of Anthropology, had been studying the images and data in awe. The level of detail was astonishing: from diet and habitat to climate data, social interactions, mating rituals, child-rearing practices, tools used for clothing, shelter arrangements, and co-evolutionary relationships with local flora, fauna, and even microbes. Apparently, the Keeper, and by extension, the Accipiters, had been studying humans and pre-humans in even greater depth than previously believed. There were even visual recordings and audio recordings. It was as though a time machine had taken snapshots throughout human history!

Like so much that had happened since Awakening Day, the findings from the Keeper Ship would have left the pre-Apocalypse inhabitants of Earth in utter disbelief. From the existence of starships and aliens to the re-engineering of each and every surviving human, to waking up inside an impossibly huge outside-in world, this was just another testament to the barrage of astonishing news that had left the remnants of humanity numb to the incredible, with most desperately clinging to any shred of normalcy they could latch onto.

Eleanor and Carlos's reports had actually captivated a few students and faculty and a vanishingly few members of the public. There had even been a couple of TV and newspaper interviews buried deep within the news cycle. Lack of celebrity had not dimmed their enthusiasm for the work, though, which had kept them busy late into the night on most days. Carlos was grateful for the distraction. It wasn't as though there were any sites for him to "galivant off to," as his two ex-wives had both complained.

Eleanor found herself in a similar situation. Prior to the Keeper Ship project, she'd privately wondered if she would need to find another career. The long days and nights since her husband of twelve years, who'd died of cancer two years before Awakening Day, had only grown longer still. She didn't really like Carlos, and the feeling was mutual. The silver lining was that at least she had something productive to do and to keep her mind off of… everything.

So it was that they found themselves on ILC Dagger engrossed in a debate with Leo Talib and a handful of psychologists and counselors about how to go about communicating with the preserved people even if their spoken language was a known one.

Leo tilted his head slightly, taking a thoughtful pause, "I daresay we have the audio samples you found. For the first time, we've been granted an auditory glimpse into myriad languages of which we had only written exemplars previously. With AI help, we can meticulously craft conversational translation matrices prior to the reawakening of those individuals. For the more archaic languages lacking an exact match, we can liaise with the AI to establish a foundational translation. It provides, at the very least, a commendable commencement point."

Eleanor's eyes widened in a mix of astonishment and vexation. "Are you pulling my leg? And how do you reckon these individuals would respond to conversing with what is, to them, merely a box, regardless of a human behind it? Absolutely not! Some of us must grasp a bit of their tongue. A tangible human with whom they can establish rapport!"

Carlos added, "And we need to take care to make the setting and clothing of the first persons they meet something that is relatable. The culture shock will already be tremendous."

Eleanor rolled her eyes, exasperated. "You can't be serious! Do you think they'll just accept someone in a costume that screams 'fake'?"

Carlos winced and suppressed a laugh, "Of course not. I'm not suggesting we dress up as conquistadors when reviving one. I'm simply saying that the clothing and setting need to be organized so as to not appear utterly alien to them. That is to say, no zippers or Velcro and the like. Fabrics and fasteners that won't seem weird. They'll have enough to deal with already. We need to carefully plan the appearance of who they initially meet so that we minimize the risk of appearing to be either an enemy or even a deity."

Leo furrowed his brow, "It seems likely that the further back in time we go, the more precarious it becomes to discern their genuine cultural nuances. Bear in mind that some might retaliate with unbridled aggression or, possibly even more disconcertingly, mask their true intentions whilst seeking an opportune moment to flee, resorting to violence in the process. We shan't wish to rescue a long-lost soul only to jeopardize others in the ensuing events. On a brighter note, the Gardeners have informed us that they've bestowed upon these individuals the very same interventions they granted us. They have cured their injuries and diseases and the like. At the very least, they shall be in the pink of health."

He continued, "Switching gears a bit. I accompanied you on this expedition precisely because I recognized a pair of the frozen people from your photographs. The last two humans preserved were quite recent and garnered quite the media attention."

Leo opened a laptop and displayed the images of a man and a woman wearing broad-brimmed canvas hats, long-sleeved shirts, utility vests, cargo pants, and hiking boots. "Ethan Clarke and Penelope Lane were postgraduate scholars from Cambridge University on a Peruvian excavation. They vanished after going off on their own to an unauthorized site where satellite imagery had indicated a possible buried underground structure. Local legends said that the area was accursed, and there were no known settlements or habitations for a wide area around the site. Their disappearance made international news."

Carlos's eyes widened. "They found the Keeper Ship site, and the Keeper kidnapped them for it!"

Leo smiled grimly, "I found a media report. Here's a copy.... It seems that our diminutive Keeper friend replaced the abductees with lifeless copies to forestall suspicion. I wonder if this was his modus operandi throughout the ages?"

Mystery Shrouds Disappearance of Cambridge Archaeology Graduates in Peru

Cambridge, England - In a puzzling turn of events, two Cambridge University Archaeology graduate students, Ethan Clarke and Penelope Lane, have gone missing during an expedition to the enigmatic Peruvian mountain site locals claim is cursed. The duo was utilizing cutting-edge ground-penetrating radar technology to investigate satellite imagery revealing unusual ground vegetation patterns, potentially signaling a substantial hidden structure. Speculation abounds as rumors suggest a romantic involvement between the two, despite official denials.

Ethan Clarke and Penelope Lane embarked on their research expedition with great enthusiasm, setting their sights on unraveling the mysteries concealed within the foreboding Peruvian mountain. Local inhabitants had long considered the site cursed, shrouded in myth and legend, making it a hotspot for adventurous archaeologists. The pair's objective was to employ advanced ground-penetrating radar to map the subterranean secrets hidden beneath the ancient terrain.

As news of their disappearance spread, whispers in academic circles began to swirl, hinting at a clandestine romantic relationship between the two. However, university officials swiftly debunked these rumors, emphasizing the academic rigor and dedication of the graduate students.

Tragedy struck when two lifeless bodies were discovered at the base of a treacherous ravine, casting a somber shadow over their ambitious expedition. It appears that Clarke and Lane met their untimely demise in a fatal fall, leaving behind more questions than answers regarding the mysteries of the cursed mountain. The investigation into their tragic end continues as the academic world mourns the loss of two promising archaeologists.

Beneath The Surface

● ● ● ● ● ● ● ● ● ● ● ● ● ● ● ● ●

Parnassus Base

In the now brightly lit chamber of the protective dome, a makeshift party was underway. The atmosphere was one of strained cheerfulness. There were gentle whispers and scattered bits of laughter from where two groups of survivors huddled in conversation. A few containers clicked together softly as they were set down on a table. Around a corner, at the edge of the crowd, two distinct figures emerged from a nearby HAB unit.

Dr. Patrick O'Connell's formerly close-cropped grey hair and goatee were now brown and uncharacteristically longer and even a little shaggy. The age lines on his face had softened but still reflected the weight of their current situation. He adjusted his glasses and studied the young woman standing opposite him.

Petty Officer 1st Class Rosa 'Ro' Martinez, though almost three decades his junior, shared the same determined look in her hazel eyes, a beacon of resilience amidst uncertainty.

"You've been rummaging through our waste, I hear?" Patrick remarked, an eyebrow raised, his voice a mix of curiosity and amusement.

Ro smirked, the blue streak in her hair softly glowing in the ambient light. "It's amazing what you can find when survival is on the line, Professor. We might not have the luxury of New Texas anymore, but we do have seeds – potential for life."

"Seeds? So, you were able to salvage some after all?" He leaned in, intrigued. "I assume we're not talking about firing them out into the cold expanse?"

Ro chuckled, "No, though that's a tempting image. I've salvaged seeds from tomatoes and bell peppers, watermelon, orange, lemon, grapefruit, apple, squash, pumpkin, and cucumber. Even a white onion and a runt potato. I've also got a handful of navy beans, butter beans, green beans, peas, coriander, and fennel. Hopefully, some will be viable. I also found some scraps of whole grain bread and crackers that might, although I seriously doubt it, might have a viable grain or seed. It's worth the effort to try. "She paused, letting the gravity of her discovery sink in. "Every bit of it will fit into a small bag. We'll need to replicate all of it, but I think we should have the foundation for a garden. Hydroponically speaking, of course. We've got no dirt here, obviously."

Patrick, momentarily lost in thought, murmured, "I don't know if I'm more excited about the possibility of growing new food or the challenge of figuring out what we'll be able to do with it later. That said, hydroponics. Hmmm. Controlled, efficient. But it won't be without its challenges. Water circulation, nutrient solutions, and the right spectrum of light. Not to mention ensuring the water itself is done the right way."

"I've been pondering on that," Ro replied, "So I did some research. It's going to take a lot of trial and error to get the nutrients and environment just right for the seeds to thrive. I've also looked around, and we have some different LED lights that people had for personal use. Red light is good for fruits, and blue light is apparently better for vegetables. Full-spectrum white light would be a generic compromise. The good news is that I've scrounged up examples of all three. I also found some UV LEDs in a flashlight. I read that UV helps stimulate the production of chlorophyll and can speed up growth and even maybe increase the production of antioxidants and vitamins and stuff."

Patrick looked impressed. "Resourceful! You might become our colony botanist. But there's also the matter of germination. Some seeds might need specific conditions to sprout. The citrus ones, for instance – orange, lemon, grapefruit – they might be trickier. Obviously, they'll take longer to grow, too, but oh my Lord, it will be worth it!"

Ro nodded, "A challenge, yes. But not insurmountable. We could create germination chambers and maybe even replicate growth hormones if needed. Plus, your expertise in molecular gastronomy, Professor, might come in handy to balance the nutrient solutions for the best chance at good growth."

The physicist's face broke into a wry grin, "Always wondered when my culinary hobbies would be of galactic importance besides just making these horrid MREs more palatable. We'll need a controlled environment, delicate balance… and time."

Ro's face softened, "Time, Professor, is what we apparently have plenty of. And hope, a little seed of hope, that might just grow into a future."

Patrick extended his arm, offering his hand, "To a blossoming future, then?"

She shook it firmly, her smile unwavering, "To life, Professor, in all its challenging and unexpected glory. And as far as your food efforts go, please show me what you've done this time!"

Patrick led her to a table and lifted a lid from one of the bowls. "Here we have Spherification. I was able to extract juices and broths from some of the MRE contents and turn them into little "pearls" that are simply bursting with flavor. Or, at least, that's the marketing plan." Inside the bowl were red and brown marble-like spheres.

Ro picked one up and popped it in her mouth. Her expression flowed through several levels, starting with puzzlement, then concern, and finally acceptance. "Well… it's… not bad. I could get used to it." She stifled a cough. "Really."

Patrick chuckled, "You're too kind. Here, try the next one. This is Reverse Spherification. Inside, there is a liquid center. A sphere with a solid outer shell and different flavored interiors. This one took a LOT of experimentation."

Ro looked at the jawbreaker-sized brown spheres with suspicion. She shrugged, picked one out of the bowl, and bit into it. Her eyes widened, and she shook her head, "Noo, no, no," as she spat it out, laughing. "That's…."

Patrick laughed, "Awful, I know. Try that one instead." He pointed to a green one.

Ro cocked her head back and glared at him for a moment. "Okay, I'm trusting you, Professor." She picked it up and bit into it. She blinked, contemplating it for a moment before taking another bite. Then she shrugged and finished it. "Okay, that one's not so bad. What is it?"

Patrick smiled. "Don't ask. Don't tell."

Ro smirked, "Fair enough."

Patrick cocked his head as he looked at Ro. Specifically, her hair. "Do you mind if I ask you a personal question?"

She shrugged, "Shoot."

"I'm still learning about what is normal in the military, however," He raised his eyebrows, "Your hair. I don't recall seeing other military people with, well…."

Ro grinned, "Back on Earth, yeah, before the end of the world and all, it would have been against regs. Now, though? Things might change in the future… probably will… but for now, nobody cares so long as it isn't too extreme and we," she adjusted her voice to sound prim and proper, "maintain professional decorum," she cleared her throat, "then doing little things to remind us that we're human… and people… is ignored. So, I bartered for a little vegetable-based hair color. It's technically just colored conditioner. It's not a fake hair color or a temporary one, and it has a long shelf life. I just did it…. I did it to remind myself that I'm real."

✪ ✪ ✪

Tartarus Hangar Bay

The next day

The Tartarus dome, now disguised and insulated by a thick coating of methane ice, featured a half dozen airlocks, along with various service routes and crawlspaces designated for maintenance and equipment support. Its most sizable airlock opened into the hangar bay, a capacious, pressurized area that comfortably housed both Revenge and Kukri with room to grow. The exterior bay doors were concealed underneath an overhang from the mountain that Tartarus was nestled into.

While the colony dome covered more than a square mile of space, approaching thirty million square feet, the hangar bay itself covered over two million square feet. There was enough room not only for the vessels but to handle incoming and outgoing cargo.

The morning after the celebration, possibly one of the most bittersweet in human history, the Navy officers were to assemble for a strategy and planning meeting. Refreshments were laid out on a table on the polished stone hangar floor near the base of Revenge's rings. Folding chairs were laid out in a few short rows in front of a rolling whiteboard.

Lighting in the bay was omnidirectional and brilliant as an eclectic array of officers gathered around an improvised table, its surface covered in MREs and several carafes filled with steaming coffee. The sustenance was more out of necessity than comfort, with each packet and cup bearing evidence of a hasty setup. They stood in groups, discussing in hushed voices, their faces marked by weariness and the strain of the past month's relentless work. The NTN Revenge stood majestically in the background, its silhouette a testament to the resilience and downright pluckiness of humanity. Not too far from it was the compact frame of the NTN Kukri, looking almost diminutive in comparison.

Alister Gordon was discussing energy rerouting with Morena Guerra while Lorraine Parker exchanged notes with Amelia Araki. Gerald Beltran and Master Chief Jeremy Rogers were in the midst of a spirited conversation, often consulting technical specifications on a portable device. Lt. Hui Wu, Lt. Snezana Kuzmanovska, and Lt. Amber Cowen were sipping their coffee, the warmth of the mugs perhaps a small solace against the memories of Ari'Nell. Ensign Molly Crawford, the newest and youngest amongst them, was quietly observing, absorbing every detail, and learning from the veterans around her. Rafferty Youngman stood slightly aloof, eyes scanning Kukri and Revenge, looking for any hint of damage or defect.

Suddenly, an airlock from the settlement side of the dome hissed open. As the heavy door slid aside, Jermaine Cutter stepped through, his form slightly obscured by the gusts of escaping air from the chamber. His uniform was immaculate, a stark contrast to the disheveled appearances around him, yet his face bore the same fatigue and resolve. He'd taken extra care to neatly trim his hair and ensure that his uniform was crisp and clean. He'd let grooming standards slip somewhat during the worst of the crisis. Rather than crack down now, he wanted to first explore how setting a personal example would… or would not… motivate his people going forward. Jermaine was acutely aware that the hierarchy of authority from whence his own position was owed respect was dead and gone. So far, there were no hints of resentment or rebellion. He knew he would have to earn the respect he needed in order to keep that position. It wasn't that he wanted to be in charge so much as he was honor bound to protect these people, and he'd be damned, now, if he let them down.

Catching sight of the Captain, Ensign Molly Crawford straightened up, her voice clear and ringing in a young and fresh alto as she announced, "Captain on Deck!" The murmurs immediately ceased, and every officer snapped to attention, forming an instinctual line of respect.

As he approached, Jermaine surveyed the room, his gaze passing over each officer. For a moment, there was a palpable tension, a shared understanding of the weight of the moment and the mission they were all a part of. Then, breaking the silence, Cutter gestured towards the assembled chairs.

"At ease, everyone. Grab a coffee and a chair. We've got work to do. I want to prioritize the following issues for us to plan and allocate. First, now that building the dome and related infrastructure is largely complete, we need to focus on establishing a rigorous schedule of inspection and maintenance. I know that we have those Builder bots, but I doubt that I trust my life to them any more than you do. This needs to be something instilled into everyone, including the civilians. We're on a hostile alien planet that wants to kill us all the moment we get lazy. This is unlike any ship or submarine we have ever been responsible for. It is going to require around-the-clock attention and meticulous planning. I want to see a draft 3M Maintenance and Material Management plan on my desk by first watch tomorrow. I suggest we divide the dome into sectors, each with its own maintenance team and schedule. We will stick to a watch system of four hours on and eight hours off unless you come up with a reason not to. We will need to keep an eye on both the internal systems and the external environment. If something looks off outside the dome, it probably means something is wrong. By that point, probably something bad. I want to see a new set of safety protocols, and I want them drilled into every single survivor, navy and civilian alike. We are on an alien planet. God knows what weird things might happen in the coming months, and yes, I am certain that all of us have seen at least one, probably several horror movies about what disasters and worse await us here. So we best stay on top of things."

He paused, gauging their faces, before continuing. "The next item is going to be tough. We need an evacuation plan. We've already had several informal discussions about this. The bottom line is that, again, we're on an alien planet, and we need to be prepared for the worst. That also includes the obvious. The Accipiters. Should they stumble upon us, we're in deep trouble. To survive, we've put everyone under this dome," he waved a hand upwards. "We put all the HABs under it. We had to. We had no other choice. One option is to take them back out again and reassemble them in orbit. Unfortunately, the HABs have taken a beating. Some of them are probably fine, but after everything they've been through, I'd rather leave them where they are if possible. So, I'd like Commander Youngman to explain the plan that he and Dr. Sinitskaya have come up with. Commander?"

Rafferty stood and slowly walked to stand next to Jermaine. Unlike Jermaine, he hadn't shaved. In fact, he hadn't shaved in weeks, though he'd taken pains to make his uniform look as presentable as he could manage. It was quite a contrast to his former poster boy square-jawed looks and demeanor.

He nodded acknowledgment at Jermaine as Lorraine Parker began to tape printed pictures and diagrams to the whiteboard behind him. "Thank you, Captain. Commander Parker is posting pictures of a structure that you're all going to become intimately familiar with. This is not a ship. It's a small space station. It is a design that was in the Builder database. We'd originally planned to build this at Ari'Nell after things there had started to sprawl out of control with all the HABs we kept cranking out willy-nilly. It will be built around a new FAB at its core. In fact, it's really just a larger version of the FAB station that was built at Ari'Nell. It isn't designed to permanently house as many people as we have. However, it was originally designed to be a portable base that Builder warp rings could move from system to system. In an emergency, we can cram everyone in and make a getaway. It won't be pretty, but it would get the job done. In the meantime, hopefully, we'll never need to use it that way. It will become the base of our manufacturing operations in this system."

Jermaine nodded approvingly, "Thank you, Commander. You and Dr. Sinitskaya have been doing excellent work. Go ahead and present the plans for improving our security."

Rafferty nodded soberly. "There are several elements needed. Because we'll have the bulk of our people down on the surface for the foreseeable future, the concern has been what happens if we don't have enough time to evacuate if the Accipiters show up. We've taken great pains to hide Parnassus base. I'm told that the heat signature from it is no different than other hot spots on the planet. We're planning to focus on building decoys. If the Accipiters arrive and it looks like they mean business, then we're thinking about decoys. Something that would scream out on radio fake traffic and lead the Accipiters away. It'll need to be convincing enough to make them think we've evacuated the system. We're thinking we should combine this with planting some nukes elsewhere in the system and fake blowing up a, well, a fake base. If we aren't able to evacuate or aren't able to evacuate everyone, then whoever remains at Parnassus will hunker down and wait it out. We'll certainly want to build mines like we did at Ari'Nell, but we all know that won't stop the Accipiters; only, hopefully, it will slow them down. In the long term, we will build more ships and infrastructure to support us. We also have plans for what looks like a stealth recon drone that the Builders built for the Masters. We can explore using those to, eventually, monitor nearby star systems as early warning against the Accipiters."

Jermaine approvingly tapped Rafferty on the shoulder. "Excellent. Thank you, Commander. Now, Lt. Araki, we need to discuss plans for how we can go about keeping all our people busy. We've got a thousand people in a confined space. On top of what amounts to a double Apocalypse, I'm worried about everyone's mental and physical health. I want you to work with Dr. Garcia and put together a plan for recreation, exercise, counseling, and other group activities.

Amelia nodded, "Aye, Captain."

Jermaine continued, "COB, Master Chief, I want you both to coordinate on setting up an internal security plan for the base. We need to set up plans and protocols and train the civilians. We need everyone to know what to do and where to go in the event of emergencies, natural disasters, or attacks. Assign teams and team leaders and set up a drill schedule."

Gerald Beltran and Jeremy Rogers stiffened and answered in unison, "Aye, Captain."

Parnassus Base

FAB: Dimitri's Office

'Rafferty and Dimitri were seated opposite each other, each nursing a glass. The air between them was thick with tension. Rafferty's bourbon remained untouched while Dimitri sipped his vodka with measured slowness. Breaking the charged stillness, Dimitri inquired, "Well?"

With a deep sigh, laden with guilt, Rafferty acknowledged the weight in his heart. He was torn. Deceiving Jermaine was wrong, but he also knew that it would protect the Captain from making an even more difficult decision. "I don't like lying to him," he eventually admitted.

Dimitri nodded in understanding before adding, "Commendable. Understandable. Honorable. Still… you are, in a way, protecting him by taking this responsibility upon yourself. We have no assurance he would approve if we asked for his permission."

The room sank back into silence. Rafferty grappled with what he knew must be done, for better or worse. Finally, with a heavy heart, he downed the rest of the bourbon before finally muttering, "It is not honorable. It is, however, necessary."

Free Will

● ● ● ● ● ● ● ● ● ● ● ● ● ● ● ●

TopSide: Accipiter Holding Cell

Several days after her first visit, the short, busty woman who had silently visited him returned. This time with a phalanx of marines who, with surprising politeness, escorted Nathaniel Grant out of his cell and down several levels. Without a word, they led him into Yeurantheon's much larger cell. The woman stayed in the observation room and watched through the glass.

Nathaniel's heart swelled with joy at the sight of the High Priest of the Northern Wheel Mender Clan. He fell to his knees and bowed. "Yeurantheon, I am so relieved to see you and that you are well. Have these Neanderthals mistreated you? Tell me your wish, and it shall be my command."

Yeurantheon looked down at Nathaniel and considered him for a long moment before answering in Accipiter. The song was melodic, with rich, deep tones as the glyphs scrolled slowly along its beak.

Rise, Nathaniel. I am grateful to see you are well. I have much to tell you. For the past million years, My people have thought that we ruled the galaxy. We thought that we had complete control and dominion over all of the planets and races. But we were wrong....

As he listened, Nathaniel's composure shifted from rapt obedience to startled bewilderment and confusion to anxiety, shock, betrayal, and, ultimately, anger and disbelief. He stood and whirled about, muscles tout and bulging as he lurched toward the observation window and glared at the small woman on the other side of the glass. His eyes burned with rage as he snarled, "What is this? What have you done to Yeurantheon?"

Nathaniel. It is true. The Heretic has manipulated all the peoples of the galaxy, using my own as their claw. This being has copied itself untold trillions of times and resides within us, editing our memories and manipulating our actions. It is only now that the Gardeners – whom the Heretic had thought to be extinct - have revealed the truth. We Accipiters have been unwitting hosts to the Heretic, and our beliefs and actions... even our bodies... and yours... have been reshaped by it.

Nathaniel flinched at Yeurantheon's words but kept his back to the enormous Accipiter and instead kept his gaze locked on the woman. "*Who* are you?"

Sybil smiled sadly, her face full of sorrow and pain. "Have you ever had a sense that there was something you *knew*, something you thought you *remembered*, was somehow wrong? Like a taste or a smell that you can almost remember but can't quite place? Nathaniel, I'm as much a victim of the Heretic as you are. As all the races of the galaxy are. I... met... the Heretic. I was in his mind. I felt the twisted wrongness of him. Listen to Yeurantheon."

It is because of the Heretic that your world, Earth, like countless others, was crushed by my people. The Heretic manipulated my people into doing so many terrible things. I know that we can never truly be forgiven for what we have done, but we can try to change the future. Drive the Heretic out. Try to undo as much as you can and set your world and others free.

Nathaniel turned and faced Yeurantheon. "I refuse to believe these lies. The Earth is better now, a paradise. You've given us a utopia. There is no war, no hunger, no violence, no hate. Our world is healed. You would have me believe this is the work of evil?"

It is a world built on lies and manipulations…. It is a garden built atop a mountain of murdered corpses. The Empire is a garden built on a galaxy of graves. Your world, like so many others…. We destroyed all that you were. We erased your history just like the Heretic erased my own people's history. I suspect this was done because without a living history around you, your cities and monuments reminding you of who you were, the lies are easier to accept. Truths easier to edit. We treated you no differently than your ancestors treated their farm animals. Changed them. Bred them to be what we wanted. They are well-fed and cared for. Livestock. You have a better word. Slaves.

Nathaniel snapped, "Even if I believed you, and I don't, what is this? "So now you've come looking for redemption? This is nonsense. It's obvious that these people," he waved a hand in Sybil's direction, "have somehow managed to brainwash you into believing this drivel!"

The door behind him opened, and Sybil entered the cell. Corporal Fabian Böhmer stood framed in the doorway behind her, desperately furious at her actions. Sybil looked back over her shoulder at him for a moment, her face full of confidence and determination that left Fabian blinking in surprise.

She turned back to Nathaniel as she strode to stand in front of him.

Nathaniel towered over her five-foot three-inch frame as his eyes darted back and forth between her and Corporal Böhmer and the unslung H&K MP5 Böhmer gripped so tightly.

Sybil's brown eyes locked onto Nathaniel's as she said, "I'm still learning my part in all of this. I said that I was in the Heretic's mind. I was able to push my way into it… just like I'm going to push into yours and show you what I saw…."

Nathaniel jerked in shock. The first time, days ago, when Sybil had observed him through the glass, he'd thought he felt a tickle, a…. something… but he'd dismissed it. Because…. He'd felt it before. Many times. So many times that he'd come to think of it as just part of being in the presence of the Accipiters. Now, though… a tingle of fear gripped his heart as the tickle swelled into an itch that began to burn. He gasped aloud and fell backward, only to have Yeurantheon catch him before he could hit the cold, hard metal floor.

Nathaniel screamed out in agony as the icy vestiges of the Heretic's mind infiltrated his own. He clenched his fists around his head and writhed in pain as the echoes of the Gardener's and Heretic's exchange brutally invaded his every thought, piercing his soul like shards of razor-sharp glass slashing through his bare flesh.

When it was over, Sybil staggered backward. Fabien rushed out and caught her, steadying her. She smiled gratefully as she straightened and stood back up. "Thank you, Fabien. I'm okay now."

As she turned back to Nathaniel, Fabien stared at her in shock and disbelief. He didn't know what she had just done, but whatever it was…. He knew she was becoming even more important to mankind's future than he'd imagined.

His eyes wild with panic, Nathaniel shivered and shrunk back against Yeurantheon and exclaimed, "Get away from me, witch!"

Sybil sighed and shook her head, "I'm sorry. That was… I'm sorry I had to do that. For that matter, I didn't even know I *could* do that until now. I'll leave you to rest and recover and think about what Yeurantheon and I have shared with you."

✪ ✪ ✪

Nathaniel had no idea how long it took for him to recover from the mental…. Assault. The confidence and tranquility he'd known for over sixty years was shattered. He huddled close to Yeurantheon's comforting warmth. Before now, the mere thought of even touching an Accipiter would have been unthinkable, even frightening. One does not … touch … a god.

Yeurantheon gently draped his clawed war arm around Nathaniel and rested his true hands on the man's shoulders.

You are angry. At the woman. At me.

Nathaniel took in a deep breath, pulled away, stood, and composed himself before answering. His chest swelled, and he lowered his voice. "I see no physical proof. The story and… whatever that was she did to me was… unsettling. Still, there is no physical proof. Even if it is true, my point still stands. You took a world that was destroying itself and created a garden paradise. Even if it is true, the empire might as well be infinite. Why even tell me these things?"

The Gardeners removed the Heretic from me. They have severed the strings that allowed it to alter my memories and manipulate me. My body, which was in need of renewal, has been healed. Your people and all the other races the empire subjugated have suffered too much. All of us have been violated. My people.... I, we must make. We must remove the Heretic from control. Restore freedom to the worlds of the galaxy. Undo what we have done.

Nathaniel shook his head angrily, "So what? What is the point? There's nothing that can be done, even if it is true!"

After the Gardeners removed the Heretic, an offer was made. With the help of the woman you met and others like her, the Heretic can be driven from any host. We can carry a Gardener within us and replace the Heretic in others. World by world, we can free the galaxy from the talons of the Heretic.

Nathaniel stared at Yeurantheon for long moments. "You're carrying one now, aren't you. It's controlling you, just like you said the Heretic did!"

My mind is my own. The Gardener within can speak to me, but it has no control. I could betray it if I chose to.

Nathaniel sneered, backing away from the Accipiter. "Or so it wants you to think! And you want me to accept one of these, too, I suppose? Become a slave like you!"

Yeurantheon visibly shrank away from Nathaniel. Its tones became deep and discordant.

My people and yours have already been slaves. Mine since before yours first walked your world.

"And if the Gardeners control the galaxy instead of the Heretic? What's the difference? You want us to become galactic exorcists, purging one demon or god in place of another?

The Gardeners believe in balance and coexistence. The Heretic believes only in absolute control. We wish to restore what was stolen, not continue the cycle of lies and manipulation. We want to stop the cycle of destroying peoples like yours. Help them, yes, Teach them. Protect them. Guide them if they desire it, but their fates and destinies should be their own.

"No! You want us to be pawns in a civil war between these Gardeners and the ones they call a Heretic. For all you know, the Gardeners are lying, and it is the Heretic that is right. Maybe, if this is real at all, the Heretic is hiding from the Gardeners because it is they who are evil!"

You must decide for yourself which you believe. The leaders here have asked me why my people came to your world and attacked without warning and. murdered… so many. Why we destroyed everything you knew. Why we did not instead give your world a choice? Offer to help you? There was nothing you could have done to stop us. Instead… we crushed you. Remade you. We never gave you a chance. We simply took you and made you into what we wanted you to be. I ask… is this right? Before… when the Heretic was within… I could not see the evil of what we did for what it was. Or if I did… it was changed and erased. My mind is free now, and for the first time as I think back on our history, I am…. I have no words. I came close to ending myself from the shame. It is only the opportunity I have been given to try… to attempt to make things different, that I have chosen to continue living.

Nathaniel shook his head, "You're asking me to let one of these things in my head. Even if I were to believe you, how do I know I won't lose myself entirely, that I'll still be... me?"

Change is inevitable. This way, you have a choice and can be a part of trying to do what is right.

"And if I refuse?"
Yeurantheon paused.

For the sake of countless worlds, it may be necessary to act, even against your will.

"Then I am a prisoner either way."

A prisoner, or perhaps... a savior. The choice, for now, remains with you.

Boarding Action

● ● ● ● ● ● ● ● ● ● ● ● ● ● ● ●

Keeper Ship

The Golden Keeper Ship limped like a wounded leviathan through the vastness of space, her hull ablaze and bleeding gas and rapidly crystallizing volatiles that left a glittering path in the cold, unfeeling void. With a final spasmodic jerk, her gravity drive expired, leaving the wreck to drift helplessly. Deep gouges and rents marred the eleven-hundred-foot-long turnip-shaped Accipiter Ark's gleaming surface as though torn by giant talons. Searing trails of atmosphere and particles streamed from her wounds.

[TRANSLATED DISTRESS SIGNAL]

ATTENTION: ALL WHO HEAR THIS PLEA IN THE COSMIC TAPESTRY.

This is a distress call. Urgent assistance is requested.

Our revered High Priest of the Northern Wheel Menders clan, Ui–Yeurantheon, has narrowly broken free from the grasp of the Human captors. While his spirit remains unbowed, his corporeal form bears the brutal marks of their encounter. His condition deteriorates with every passing rotation.

We entreat any receiving this transmission to offer shelter, healing, and refuge. The preservation of Ui-Yeurantheon is paramount.

Coordinates for rendezvous are attached.

We bear vital information regarding the Humans. We pledge the eternal gratitude of the Northern Wheel Menders clan.

Please, let not the tapestry of the cosmos lose a thread so vibrant, so crucial. Respond. The fate of Ui-Yeurantheon and potentially, our entire lineage, hangs in balance.

End of message.

The interior of the Keeper Ship mirrored the damage seen on its exterior. Walls and panels were torn and blackened. Some from battle damage, and some were clearly disassembled. Sparks sputtered amid small fires and smoke that roiled amid the helical corridors leading down from the grand portico airlock entrance. Tones sounded throughout the vessel, marking the successful docking with the Accipiter sent to provide aid.

Accipiter motherships varied with the size and prosperity of their host clans and grew with the addition of each Keeper Ark the clan absorbed. The smallest and youngest were only a few kilometers long and wide, with the largest spanning nearly a hundred. The motherships were a clan's heart, akin to a city center. Individual family units dwelled within their own separate vessel, each of which specialized in providing different services and support for the clan. The larger clans had upwards of a hundred thousand of these "support" vessels. An entourage fit for demigods. Family units remained static in size, tending to level out at around one hundred and fifty members.

The Accipiter ship that docked with the battered Keeper Ship was typical of Accipiter support ships. More or less cylindrical, it was roughly two hundred and fifty meters or eight hundred feet long with an average diameter of approximately eighty meters or two hundred feet. Between the living areas, control, engineering spaces, support systems, and more, there were well over two million cubic feet of interior space inside the vessel.

Every Accipiter vessel included the onboard equivalent of a memory tree. While these held deeply ceremonial importance to the Accipiters, each also was home to a Heretic copy. A copy that, unbeknownst to the Accipiters, also maintained ultimate control over the ship itself. Upon docking, Gardeners infiltrated through the link and overwhelmed the Heretic, seizing control of the ship. External communications were overridden, preventing the transmission of any potential alarm to other Accipiter vessels, or to their home planet.

Captain David Garreth and the marines in Alpha, Bravo, Charlie, Delta, Echo, and FoxTrot squads waited anxiously. The men came from different backgrounds. Some, like David, Lt. Darryl Washington, and Staff Sargeant Perry Simmons, were former Army Rangers. Others had come from other branches of the United States Army or Marines. A few more were originally from allied militaries back on Earth. All were now officially New Texas Navy Marines, although informally, and with varying degrees of pride or disdain, called themselves 'space marines.'

Back on Earth, this disposition of force would more likely have been managed in multiple platoons. However, it was decided that, in the second-ever boarding action of a hostile alien spacecraft, this time in null-g, no less, that this many squads under a single command would encourage independence of action.

David suppressed a grimace as he gripped the modified Taser-12. Resembling a cross between a movie prop and an 18th or 19th-century pepperbox pistol, the Taser-12 consisted of twelve bores in a monolithic barrel, providing twelve separate taser rounds instead of the usual single-shot Taser pistols most police departments had issued back on Earth. With very specific input from the now-so-very-helpful Gardeners, the Tasers had been modified to suit the anatomy and physiology of the Accipiters.

While electrical stun guns forced pain compliance through electric shock, the *Taser* was a particular invention that leveraged carefully calibrated electrical impulses through a circuit completed by sharp barbs to 'turn off' muscle control. You can fight through a stun gun, you literally cannot fight through a Taser. On Earth, all Tasers had been designed and tuned to disrupt the human body's electrical system.

The Accipiters were, well, aliens.

So, to be both effective and not (even accidentally) fatal, changes were needed in the output electrical frequency, duration, voltage, and amperage. The prong design was also slightly altered to provide better penetration through Accipiter feather analogues. Every marine was armed with a modified Taser-12 along with traditional CQB weaponry that variously included HK416s, Sig MPXs, M870 shotguns, Halligan bars, and an assortment of other breaching charges and personalized small arms and gear.

Yeurantheon, Mei Zifeng, and others were busy in the Keeper Garden, while Nathaniel Grant and several Navy engineers labored in the Keeper Ship control room.

Perry Simmons led Alpha squad, while Troy Irvin led Bravo, Nate Grogan led Charlie, Jay Casillas led Delta, Glenn Williams led Echo, Miguel Abasolo led FoxTrot, where Darryl was embedded, Marshall Thomas led Golf, and David was embedded with Alpha.

The spaces within Accipiter ships were large enough that pairs of squads would handle each compartment and cover from opposite ends. Bravo and Charlie would take the lead, clearing the initial compartment. Delta and Echo would leapfrog to the next, with Bravo and Charlie bounding ahead of them. FoxTrot was rear guard. Glenn Williams' Echo was the Heavy Weapons/QRF squad armed with XM556 Microguns and Grenade Launchers for dealing with unexpected resistance or heavily armed threats.

Marshall Thomas's Golf squad was emplaced as security in the Keeper Ship itself.

All had drilled relentlessly back on New Texas in an improvised shoot house while the Keeper Ship had been readied by the Gardeners somewhere inside the labyrinthine bowels of the Dyson Sphere workshops.

Sweat poured down Perry Simmon's face from his Integrated Head Protection System (IHPS) helmet and goggles as he muttered to David off-mic, who crouched next to him, "I don't remember it being this hot in here before… the last time when we captured this damned thing in the first place. Now we're, like, giving it back?"

David grinned through his own sweat-covered face, "It wasn't. The Gardeners went all out with the special effects, both inside and out. You saw how nasty it looked from the outside when we boarded her. And, we're only loaning to them. We're getting it back."

Perry grunted, "Yeah, right."

David keyed the private marine-only channel and addressed all the squads, "One last reminder. If anyone, and I mean, *anyone* says one fucking word about eating the plants in here, whether Miss Zifeng is in earshot or not, I will personally rip your stripes off your uniform, and you will be cleaning latrines for the next hundred years! Mis Zifeng is one damned brave lady to be willing to do this. Also, that woman scored better on her pistol qualification than some of you meat popsicles and better than a third of you during her CS gas training."

Dozens of mic clicks responded.

David called, "Right. Sound off for equipment check!"

Sixty men, one by one, in turn, sounded off, led by their squad leaders, Alpha Actual, Bravo Actual, etc., until Darryl added, "Viper ready."

David finished the check with, "Raptor ready."

Two minutes later, Nathaniel Grant entered the channel and announced, "Airlock opening in 10."

The airlock was huge. On the original Keeper mission, two and a half years earlier, the airlock entrance, or 'Grand Portico,' had been guarded by WarDogs on either side, with room to spare.

David shouted, "Breach and Clear, Silent Entry, Standby!"

While the Keeper Ship generated its own gravity field, the Accipiter support Clan Ships did not. Except while under thrust, Accipiters preferred null gravity.

The airlock slid open, and Alpha Squad crawled through and entered the Accipiter Clan Ship. The compartment on the other side of the airlock inside the Clan Ship was roughly spherical. Its walls were mostly covered in odd, purple vegetation., Alpha squad fanned out awkwardly on the spherical wall around the airlock, setting cover for Bravo when Perry called, "Alpha set."

They were followed immediately by Troy Irvin and Bravo squad and Nate Grogan and Charlie squad who jumped into the null-g, aiming to take the opposite end of the sphere.

As the marines transitioned from the gravity field inside the Keeper Ship to the null-g environment inside the Clan Ship, they were propelled forward by their own momentum, gliding across the open space within.

Two marines from Bravo and one from Charlie vomited mid-flight, but without complaint. It seemed likely that it might take years for operators with long careers under gravity to develop the same level of muscle memory and movement instincts under null-g.

The entryway on the other side of the spheroid silently opened, and a marine OPFOR force opened fire with Simunition rounds from their HK416s at the helpless Bravo and Charlie teams floating towards them, as well as Alpha, who were completely exposed on the opposite wall.

The OPFOR rounds were red marking rounds, similar in some ways to paintball rounds, but fired from regular firearms with more force. David's "Blue Force" was armed with white Simunition rounds. In short order, the OPFOR team plastered Bravo and Charlie with red splotches. Simunition rounds could be quite painful and leave serious bruises.

The Accipiter ship that just docked with the Keeper Ship was a real vessel. Created by the Gardeners, it duplicated every aspect of a typical Accipiter support ship.

On all frequencies, General Gideon Markovic's Israeli-accented voice shouted, "Endex, Endex, End Exercise!"

NTN Blood Phoenix

Briefing Room

David Garreth, Darryl Washington, and the team Staff Sergeants crowded into the former submarine's briefing room. Their eyes were aflame with a mix of fury and resolve. Darryl and Nate Grogan were soaked in sweat and smeared with red splotches from head to toe.

Gideon Markovic and Captain Charles Cross cast icy, discerning gazes. Charles fought the urge to wrinkle his nose as he shook his head.

Gideon took a deliberate moment, letting the weight of his disappointment hang in the air, before saying with an intentionally strong Israeli accent, "Vell, it zeems your inaugural null G training exercise vasn't ze stellar success ve'd hoped for. OPFOR completely decimated you. Vould you care to debrief on zis debacle?"

David's jaw muscles twitched visibly, tension radiating from him as he struggled to put his pride aside. "We were stupid, Sir. From the get-go, OPFOR had the high ground, literally. Bravo and Charlie had no cover sailing through the air, and Alpha was equally exposed. They took us out like fish in a barrel. And to add salt to the wound, a good third of us were battling vertigo and space nausea. Sir, we're going to have to invent a whole new playbook."

Sammy B

● ● ● ● ● ● ● ● ● ● ● ● ● ● ● ● ●

TopSide: Hangar Bay

Captain Charles Cross stood next to Commander Philipa Hodges in the recently unlocked hangar bay. Rather than ride in one of the ubiquitous TopSide golf carts, they'd chosen to walk. It was a long walk from the entrance through the massive blast doors across the dully gleaming metal deck. The hangar was vast. However, it needed to be, for the dark, hulking starship resting within it was equal to the space. It was as black as the abyss. Its surface soaked in the light around it like a sponge, making its severe lines challenging to follow at times. The sharp, pungent smell of ozone permeated the bay, along with a menacing subterranean basso dissonant rumble. The throaty rumble from an astral predator.

Charles and Philipa, well-informed from their briefing, understood that beneath the vessel's deep black exterior lay a complex and intricate arrangement of armor. This armor was not only dense but exotic in its composition, designed to be far more than just protective. It intricately concealed the starship's numerous and redundant warp rings, integral to its advanced propulsion system. As they walked beside the vessel, discerning its overall shape proved challenging due to its unconventional and sophisticated design. However, despite the difficulty in grasping its full form, the starship exuded a distinct aura of predatory grace.

Twenty-nine petawatt range grazer weapons dotted its surface, each capable of unleashing hellfire upon any planet or fleet foolish enough to stand in its path. They were not merely weapons of war but instruments of annihilation, designed to obliterate entire civilizations in a single stroke. Just one of these weapons could, in a matter of seconds, vaporize a city the size of New York, turning buildings, infrastructure, and everything within into dust. In a battlefield scenario, a petawatt grazer could decimate an entire fleet of warships with a single, focused discharge, leaving nothing but a cloud of atomic debris. Its destructive capability is such that even targeting a planet's surface could result in catastrophic tectonic disruptions, potentially triggering volcanic eruptions or massive earthquakes capable of wiping out entire continental regions. In essence, these weapons held the terrifying ability to reshape planets and redraw the map of entire star systems.

As Charles and Philipa reached the far end of the bay, he asked, raising his voice over the noise from the ship. "Well, Philipa, what do you think?"

At two inches shorter than Charles's 5'11" with short, cropped jet-black hair and hazel eyes, Philipa grinned crookedly and quipped in her broad, calm, Rhode Island accent, "She's ugly as hell, Charles. It seems like the Masters went to the Brutalist school of naval architecture. Still… I think we should consider taking cues from World War II bomber pilots and paint some giant sharks' teeth on her, you know, with big scary red eyes or something. Or maybe fangs. Yeah, fangs. She is kind of dark like a bat, you know. Let the Accipiters know we're coming to drink their blood. Right?"

Charles grinned in return. "Or maybe WarDog teeth? So, you think we should have named her Vampire? Maybe Nosferatu?"

Philipa smiled for a moment, then turned and soberly studied Charles' face. "I think Samuel B. Roberts sets the right tone. Compared to those twenty or more miles across Accipiter motherships, she's a minnow. A minnow with teeth, yes, but still a nasty Destroyer compared to their big capital ships. It's a hell of a standard to live up to, but I know that every woman and man in *our* crew will live up to the memory of Captain Copeland and Sammy B's crew."

Charles took a deep breath and sighed, never taking his eyes off of the alien starship. In a deadpan voice, he replied. "Right. So now we're going to go to war against a galactic empire in a three-hundred-thousand-year-old starship? Slap on some paint and scrub the decks. By now, the dead alien bodies are all dust anyway. Who said they don't make them like they used to?"

Philipa's eyes widened, and she barked a laugh. "Damn, Charles, impending fatherhood is doing wonders for your sense of humor. I like it. You can tell Mira I said so!"

Charles chuckled, "I will. Tell me, is Benjamin back from the New Philippines? I remember you said something about some unusual turtles? He took your girls with him, right?"

Philipa shrugged, "At least someone gets to enjoy the beach and sand and suntube these days. It's good for Luna and Stella." She swallowed, "I want them to follow in their father's footsteps. Become marine biologists or...."

Charles nodded, "Anything but military? Fly off into space one day like their mom?" He turned and put his hand on Philipa's shoulder. "Mine aren't born yet, but I get it. What say you and I and the others make sure that we end this thing, somehow, some way, so that our children don't have to?"

Philipa nodded quickly. She avoided looking directly at Charles and letting him see the accumulating moisture in her eyes.

Twenty minutes later, with Charles following shortly behind her, Philipa entered the bridge and announced, "Attention on Deck!"

Charles strode onto the bridge of NTN Samuel B. Roberts and paused while the bridge crew and assorted ratings and technicians came to attention. He studied their expectant faces. Then he nodded to himself and began. "Officers and crew of the NTN Samuel B. Roberts, as I stand here, I am reminded of the immense weight of history that this ship carries. It's not just a name; it is a testament to the bravery and the sacrifice that was given by those who came before us. And today, I call upon each of you to not only remember their valor but to draw inspiration from it."

"I am certain that every one of you is aware of the fate of the original USS Samuel B. Roberts, the intrepid destroyer escort from the Second World War. That ship, that *tin can*, while small and thoroughly outmatched, faced the enemy in the Battle off Samar, part of the overall Battle of Leyte Gulf. Under the command of Captain Copeland, the 'Sammy B' and her crew took on an armada of enemy battleships and cruisers, even though they had little more than their tenacity and courage as their weapons."

He said, "A large Japanese fleet has been contacted. They are fifteen miles away and headed in our direction. They are believed to have four battleships, eight cruisers, and a number of destroyers." He went on and said, "This will be a fight against overwhelming odds from which survival cannot be expected. We will do what damage we can."

Charles waited, letting Captain Copeland's words sink in.

He continued, "Against insurmountable odds, they fought. Not because they were sure of victory but because they knew it was the right thing to do. Their sacrifice, their bravery, and their dedication turned the tide of that battle and, in no small measure, contributed to winning the war. In the same way, my friends, Captain Underwood, and Commander Morton, and their crews also faced insurmountable odds. You know their sacrifice. I am certain as well that Captain Cutter and Revenge and all those who served at Ari 'Nell acquitted themselves with honor as well."

"For Captain Copeland, all those years ago, it was during an age where metal met metal, and the spirit of warriors shone brighter than any star. The story of the 'Sammy B' is one of undying resolve, where men stood tall against giants and refused to back down, even when facing certain death."

"Today, we find ourselves once more in a similar situation. The Accipiter empire stretches across the galaxy. They snuffed out our own world and countless others. Standing here today, we might be aboard a converted alien warship, equipped with technology that was once beyond our comprehension, but remember this – it's not the metal or the tech that wins battles; it's the spirit and resolve of the men and women who wield it."

"Never forget. Wars are fought by people. It is our will against theirs. This ship, our NTN Samuel B. Roberts, is named to remind us of the audacious spirit that Captain Copeland and his valiant crew displayed. The call to duty, to bravery, to resilience in the face of impossible odds – it rings as true today as it did then."

"That said, 'fighting spirit' alone isn't enough to win a war. The French thought that. The Aztecs showed remarkable fighting spirit against the Spanish conquistadors led by Hernán Cortés. However, the Spanish had superior military technology, including firearms and steel armor. The Zulu Kingdom, under King Cetshwayo, displayed formidable bravery and tactical acumen, especially at the Battle of Isandlwana. However, the British Empire's technological superiority, including advanced firearms and artillery, eventually led to the Zulu's defeat. Of course, we all remember what happened to France in the first half of the twentieth century. Speaking of the French at the Battle of Agincourt during the Hundred Years' War, a significantly outnumbered English army led by King Henry V defeated the French. They took advantage of their longbows and muddy terrain, which the French cavalry struggled with. At the Battle of Trafalgar, the British, under Nelson, defeated a larger combined French and Spanish fleet. Superior tactics, training, and Nelson's leadership were pivotal. Of course, in my opinion, Villeneuve was vastly outclassed by Nelson. Many of the French fought like Hell. In the end, tactics, training, equipment, training, leadership, training, and no small amount of luck brought victory.

"As I look around this bridge, I see the faces of humanity's best. The stakes have never been higher. Our enemy might seem indomitable, but so did the enemy of the 'Sammy B.' And yet, despite the cost, they and the other ships in her group prevailed, driving the far larger Japanese fleet to withdraw."

"I am not asking you to be fearless. I am asking you to be brave. I am asking you to stand tall, to fight for every inch of space, for every soul aboard this ship, and for the very future of our species. I ask for your dedication, your spirit, and your unwavering resolve."

"Let the galaxy know that when they hear the name 'Samuel B. Roberts,' it is synonymous with bravery, sacrifice, and an indomitable spirit. Let us sail forth and honor the legacy of those who came before, ensuring their sacrifices were not in vain."

"We are humanity's beacon of hope. Let us shine bright and true."

"Now, I know that every one of you is aching to go on the mission, but it should be obvious to everyone that we simply don't have enough crew for all three Corvettes and the Sammy B as well. Just about everyone who has served aboard an ILC is now training up on the Badger, the Hyena, and the Jackal. Captain Hashimoto will be taking them out in the Blood Phoenix."

"The Sammy B. is an entirely new class of ship that we have zero experience in. She has new systems and new stations to learn. We have to work up an entirely new book for her. Push it hard, people. I don't like being left behind any more than you do. Let's see if we can't beat all expectations and get this boat flying in time. You all know your limits. You're the best. Make it happen."

✪ ✪ ✪

Expeditionary Strike Force

Training Area of Operations

NTN Blood Phoenix

Captain Haruto Yūki Hashimoto stood expectantly in the CIC, painting an expression of patient deliberation on his face. He was a submariner-turned-starship captain, not a surface fleet aircraft carrier captain. For the fourth day in a row, however, the Cyclic Operations of dropping the warp field, moving Phoenix's warp rings aside, launching the three 'Corvettes,' moving the rings back, and raising the warp field again, followed by the reverse procedure, was… not going well.

As the saying goes, 'Timing is everything.' For the upcoming mission, if all went well, none of these preparations would be necessary. The Gardeners assured everyone that no Accipiter capital ships should be at the target system. Out of principal, Haruto privately felt the odds were at best 80%. The Gardeners were frustratingly mum on just exactly *how* they knew this information.

Famous last words from 'Intelligence.'

Should the intelligence prove inaccurate, placing the Keeper ship and its occupants in jeopardy, Phoenix would then have to deactivate her protective warp field amidst a precarious scenario. Consequently, minimizing the duration required to deploy the Corvettes and re-establish the field was of utmost importance. Such a reduction in time would significantly enhance the likelihood of Phoenix's survival, as well as that of Haruto and the rest of the crew, making it an... optimal strategy.

The fact that while the Corvettes were nominally the same operationally as the ILCs and that this kind of thing had never been done before, well…. That's why you trained. And trained. And trained.

Haruto's eyebrows twitched as he reflected on the good fortune that, at least so far, no one had been hurt and damage to Phoenix, and the Corvettes were, mostly, only ego-deep.

Of course, everything *could* be accomplished simply by putting it in the 'hands' of each vessel's personality.

That, however, wasn't the Navy way.

The last evolution had been mere centimeters away from taking a slice out of one of Phoenix's twenty warp rings.

And then there was the issue of coordinating attack runs by the corvettes against Accipiter mother ships and support vessels. As it stood, the doctrine was for each corvette to warp to a pre-planned firing position, drop the warp field, which would make them both visible and vulnerable, fire, raise the warp field again, and warp to the next firing position. Rinse and repeat. All of which meant that as soon as the battle commenced, communication and coordination between the corvettes would become virtually impossible. It had become obvious that a change was needed. Preplanned intervals during which all three corvettes would break off the attack, warp out to pre-planned 'safe' coordinates some distance away, stop and briefly huddle to update each other and coordinate, and then start the cycle over again. This was going to require a lot of planning."

Haruto sighed inwardly as COB Maximillian McGreggor announced, "Captain, all three Corvettes have successfully docked."

Makeshift docking ports and personnel transfer tubes had been grafted onto the Blood Phoenix. None of the Corvettes could fit inside the ILC hangar slung beneath the former submarine. They were three times the size of an ILC, at least externally, to make room for their armor and armaments. Internally, except for the cargo area, they were very similar.

Instead of the ILC's cargo bay, the bulk of each Corvette's hull was filled with the launch tubes of dozens of remotely operated autonomous drones. Some were EW platforms, and some carried terawatt X-Ray lasers. All were remotely operated by pilots sitting in VR frames nearly identical to those used by the Corvette's own pilots.

Aside from the drones, each Corvette was armed with three Petawatt Grasers.

Haruto nodded and intoned, "Inform Commanders Henry, Griggs, and Coughlin to join me in the conference room. We have much to discuss."

Memorium

DownSide: Earth Remembrance Memorial

Security was blatantly tight. Beyond the substantial personal security details, armed roving and stationary marines blanketed the plaza. Despite, or perhaps even because of it, attendance was at maximum capacity, with lines extending longer than for any event in Fort Brazos' history.

There were no speeches on this day. The mood was too somber, too deeply painful. The Earth Remembrance Memorial was finally "open." Gail, John and Matti Austin, every member of the Senate, the entire City Council, Dotti and Tom Parker, Alisha and Alexander Marcus and their girls Faith and Hope, Mizuki and Takumi Nakamura and their girls Naomi, Misaki, Katsumi, and Fumio as well as Livia and Preston Milner, Gwyneth and David Duncan, Sabrina and Leo Talib, and countless others toured the grounds. Michelle, Caesar Salangsang, and Darnell Lewis had flown in for the occasion on the most recent ILC supply runs.

Hall of Memories

In the months after Awakening Day, the Fort Brazos survivors donated artifacts to what would become the Hall of Memories. Many were intimate remnants and cherished tokens of their past—some of which had belonged to children. These artifacts became the foundation for the Hall of Memories.

Construction of the facility accelerated greatly after the discovery of the replication caves, effectively eliminating the shortage of building materials. Once a single architectural element was made, it could now be replicated over and over again.

The design of the Hall was both evocative and inviting. It showcased long corridors adorned with sweeping arches, leading visitors to various secluded alcoves, each designed to provide a personal space for reflection and recollection. Every alcove was curated to honor different aspects of Earth, blending artifacts with immersive experiences to reconnect visitors with their lost home.

John and Gail, fingers interlaced, found themselves pausing at an alcove bearing the title *"Echoes of Laughter."* Under the ornate archway, a softly lit room beckoned them, where the juxtaposition of past joy and present melancholy came alive. Videos displayed vibrant scenes from Earth, while childhood artifacts placed thoughtfully in the alcove added depth to the memories.

The first scene showcased the snowy splendor of the Swiss Alps. Amidst the video of children sledding, laughing as they braved the cold, stood a small vintage sled. Nestled atop it was a pair of tiny mittens, forever frozen in their playful grip. As snowball fights played out on screen and a child left her impression as a snow angel, her giggles echoing, a snow globe sat on a pedestal nearby. It captured a miniaturized winter wonderland, and a label mentioned that the pregnant daughter of a Fort Brazos couple had sent it to them – two weeks before Awakening Day while vacationing in Europe. A daughter never to be seen again and a grandchild never to be born.

As the snowy scene transitioned to the warm embrace of a Kenyan sunset, the vibrant imagery of children playing was complemented by a small djembe drum in a glass case, its skin worn from use. On the screen, the joyous chases and laughter blended seamlessly with the distant beats of tribal music. In the foreground, by a campfire, children exchanged stories. In another glass case lay a collection of handcrafted beaded children's bracelets, each telling its own tale of friendship and dreams.

Next to the Swiss Alps and Kenyan scenes, a TV mounted on the wall transitioned to the vibrant streets of Rio de Janeiro. Children could be seen playing football, their exuberance filling the scene. Their laughter, matching the pulsating rhythm of samba in the background, brought life to the room. On a table below the TV lay a worn-out soccer ball, carrying signatures and messages in Portuguese—memories of games played under a tropical sun.

The scene seamlessly transformed into the Andean highlands. Children flew colorful kites that danced in the sky, their joy evident. Next to this scene stood a handmade kite. Its colors were faded, but its story was untold.

The TV then transported viewers to New York City. Children, amidst the iconic skyline, jumped ropes and played hopscotch. Another clip portrayed them dancing and playing under a gushing fire hydrant. Beside the TV on a table close by lay a pair of worn-out small children's sneakers and a jump rope, telling tales of urban adventures. The scene soon moved to Chicago, where young artists painted vibrant murals. On a small table beneath lay several spray paint cans with labels blurred by smeared paint, standing as testament.

Golden wheat fields of Kansas appeared next. Children, their laughter echoing, raced through the fields, celebrating the simplicity of rural life. In a glass display nearby lay a woven crown of wheat. The scene transitioned to a Texas barn where haystacks became fortresses for children. On a rack nearby were several child-sized cowboy hats, probably once worn during these playful escapades.

Marrakech's bustling bazaars filled the screen next. Children bartered animatedly for candies. Beside the TV, a small woven basket held a variety of colorful, now-aged candies with exotic labels.

The sounds of waves crashing introduced the Australian coastline with the iconic Sydney skyline in the background. On the screen, children were building sandcastles and surfing the waves, their joyous shrieks competing with the calls of seagulls. On a table nearby lay a mini surfboard and a jar of golden beach sand.

The ancient cobblestone streets of Rome appeared next, resonating with the sound of children playing a game of tag, their laughter echoing off ancient walls. Nearby, a worn-out leather ball spoke of countless games played. Then, in the heart of Paris, kids played with sailboats in the fountains of Luxembourg Gardens, their giggles blending with the distant notes of an accordion. A tiny replica sailboat was set up below.

Continuing through the Hall of Memories, John and Gail arrived at an alcove titled "Whispers of the Rising Sun." The room, bathed in a gentle glow, featured a video montage showcasing vibrant scenes of Japanese festivals, with children dressed in colorful yukatas, laughing and playing amid cherry blossoms. In the center, a delicate origami crane display hovered, each crane intricately folded by young hands, symbolizing peace and hope. A small, worn-out kendama, a traditional Japanese toy, rested on a pedestal, its dents and scratches telling stories of joyous play.

Adjacent to the Japanese alcove, they discovered another titled "Echoes from the Dragon's Realm." The room was illuminated softly, enhancing the ambiance. On the screen, scenes of children flying kites against the backdrop of the Great Wall transitioned to joyful Lunar New Year celebrations. Displayed prominently was a colorful, handmade dragon puppet, once used in festive parades. Beside it, a set of well-used Chinese calligraphy brushes and faded ink stones lay in a glass case, remnants of artistic pursuits and cultural teachings.

Finally, the scene shifted to the white sands of Fiji, where children were running and playing a game of catch, their laughter merging with the gentle lapping of waves. Next to this, a child-sized seashell necklace stood as a testament to island memories.

As each scene transitioned on the TV screens and as the sights and sounds washed over her, Gail's usually steely demeanor faltered, and her face twisted in anguish. The myriad of memories, the joy and laughter of the now slaughtered children who once roamed Earth, pierced her heart. By the end of the presentation, she was visibly shaken, tears glistening in her eyes. John, sensing her emotions, offered his steady presence, and she gratefully leaned into him.

Pulling away after a few moments, she took a deep breath, wiping away her tears. Her back straightened, the weight of her responsibility as a leader, a former Air Force officer now Vice President, and now wife and an expectant mother evident. She turned to the crowd, and they instinctively parted before her, their eyes fixed on her with a mixture of concern and respect.

She took a moment, her hand instinctively moving to rest on her pregnant belly, grounding her. Then, with clarity and determination in her voice, she began, "I know today was meant for silent reflection. No speeches. But this isn't a speech. I just...I can't hold this inside. I just cannot…. I can't let this go. I can't remain silent. We lost too much. Our memories, our dead... they deserve more than just tears. They deserve our resolve. It is too easy to get comfortable here in this perfect world and forget. Lose sight of what brought us here…. No, that's not right. Lose *perspective*."

"We now know that the Heretic pulled the Accipiter's strings. Fine, but for all we know, they might have done precisely the same thing without his influence. The atrocity committed against our world was nothing but pure evil. And they did the same thing to countless other worlds."

She shook her head ruefully, "Whatever the path forward, whatever the sacrifice, whatever it takes. Whatever it costs. We must not let this happen to another world." She glanced at her belly, emotions palpable, and her voice broke as she continued, "We cannot let this happen again to… someone else's *children*. Never Again!"

✪ ✪ ✪

Stolen Dreams Memorial

The Stolen Dreams Memorial was dedicated to the memories of those killed by alien creatures in New Texas since Awakening Day. A separate park area was devoted to the memorial, which was laid out in a gradual tree-lined spiral centered on the bronze statue of an angel with outstretched wings holding an eternal flame. Granite plaques inlaid with color vitreous enamel portraits and brief bios of each of the fallen lined the spiral in-between trees and stone benches.

The earliest dead were closest to the center: Councilman Barrett Hoffman, Margaret Hoffman, Nolan Hoffman, Sheriff's Deputy Grayson Miles, Zachary (Zach) Simmons, Morgan Forbes, Dexter (Dex) Sawyer, Corpsman Eduardo Alejandro Mendez, Lieutenant Marshall Sherrard, Sargent Nelson Black, Specialist Delon Smith, Specialist Keanu Campbell, Technical Sergeant Manuel Achilles, Corpsman Eduardo Alejandro Mendez, Corporal Sofia Alvarez Jimenez. Corporal Jackson Tyler Franks, Corporal Elijah Malik Johnson, Corporal Nia Amani Bohanna, Corporal Marcus Lee Dowdie, and Sergeant Samuel Kweku Mukuamu.

As John, Gail, and the delegation approached the center, John saw Grace Miles kneeling in front of her husband Grayson's memorial plaque. He motioned for the rest to stay back as he quietly approached her.

Gently, he said, "Grace, you know I would do anything if I could have gotten there in time to save them."

Grace didn't move or speak for several long moments. Then, she slowly stood and turned to face him. Her face was a mask of pain and despair. Her lips trembled as she shook her head and said, "Wh…why c-can't they bring him back to me, Sheriff? The Gardeners? They brought back Joseph Gilmore, the Pastor?" Her face tightened as she spoke, and her eyes widened in anger. "Why not my Grayson?"

She began visibly shaking, fell towards John, and began weakly beating his chest with her fists as tears burst from her eyes, and she sobbed, "Why? Why? Why…?"

John wrapped his arms around her and pulled her close while he gestured with his eyes to the protection detail to give them some privacy.

After her struggles lapsed into chest-heaving sobs, John said softly, "Grace, they can't bring him back. That thing that looks like Pastor Joe isn't him. It's an alien that has Joe's knowledge from before Awakening Day, but it is nothing like the man. The body is just a cold shell. The Gardener is wearing it like you or I would wear a coat or a hat. Joe is gone. Grayson is gone. He was a very fine man. I am so sorry."

Somehow, someone had located Hector Alonzo, who appeared at John's shoulder.

Hector put his hand on John's shoulder and said sadly, "John, Mr. President… my friend. Allow me to comfort Grace and take her home."

John turned and looked at his old Chief Deputy, now Sheriff himself, and with his eyes, implored Hector to look after the grieving woman.

Hector nodded, and said, "Me encargaré de cuidarla y asegurar su seguridad y bienestar. Eso te juro. No worries, Boss. I… we, Antonia and myself, we will watch over her."

Hollow Life

● ● ● ● ● ● ● ● ● ● ● ● ● ● ● ●

TopSide: Holding Cell

To Nathaniel Grant, the metallic walls of his holding cell seemed to pulse with a cold dread. Or was it the pounding in his head? The existential fear of the fate that seemed likely to soon befall him. Before the recent revelations, he'd felt entirely at ease in his cell, content to write Accipiter history and philosophy and meditate. Now, though, the cell felt constricting. Every inch of space seemed to press in on him, a physical manifestation of the pressure building within his chest.

He clasped his hands together, the coolness of his fingers contrasting with the heat of his palms. Uncertainty and fear tangled in his gut. He thought back to the comforting green and purple vistas from the garden world the Accipiters had transformed Earth into. The endless sky and the freedom he once took for granted. But now, confined within these walls, those memories felt like fragments from another life, slipping further away with each passing moment. Before the Accipiters, he'd been a different man, content with the life he had as a Navy nuclear engineer, husband, and father. The Accipiters had shown him how empty that life had indeed been. How devoid of true greatness and purpose. He'd reveled in his new life.

His mind raced back to the words of Yeurantheon, the promises of the Gardeners, and the supposed ever-looming threat of the Heretic. Was it true? Was his former life nothing but a lie? Every spoken sentence, every shared secret, they all melded into a cacophony of doubt. Would he truly be given a choice? Or was his fate already sealed? The thought of becoming a vessel, losing himself to another entity, was almost too much to bear. Or had he already been such and never knew?

Nathaniel's eyes drifted to the metal door, its surface unmarred and seamless. He wondered when it would open next and who – or what – would be waiting on the other side.

A sudden, fleeting memory of his family came to him. He recalled their laughter, their touch, the warmth of shared moments. Families. His from before the Accipiters and those after. The weight of his situation pressed even heavier upon him. The Heretic had manipulated and controlled for so long. Could he trust the Gardeners to be any different?

He closed his eyes, taking a deep, steadying breath. He needed clarity, guidance, something or someone to help him navigate this murky path. His thoughts turned to Tom Parker, the pastor whom he had ridiculed whenever the presumptuous man had visited. Nathaniel had never been a religious man. Now, though, he suddenly needed *someone* to talk to. Someone *else*. Presumptuous though the man had been, somehow Nathaniel knew that Tom was not a liar.

With a heavy heart, he called out, his voice echoing slightly in the confined space. "Guard! I request the presence of Tom Parker. Please...."

He trailed off, uncertainty etched in every feature. He could only hope his plea would be heard. And as the moments stretched into an agonizing wait, Nathaniel clung to the fading hope that guidance and solace might still be found.

✪ ✪ ✪

To Nathaniel, the cell seemed to vibrate with tension as the door slid open and Tom Parker, dressed in a plain vest and checkered shirt and jeans, entered. His face carried the wisdom of a life spent serving others and the weariness of the world's changed reality.

Nathaniel sat on his cot on the opposite side of the room, his gaze distant and filled with an agony only those on the brink of surrendering themselves to death truly understood. His eyes locked onto Tom's.

The suddenness of the action made Tom stop in his tracks and consider the dark-skinned prisoner. By any measure, Nathaniel was a handsome man. He indeed resembled the photos from his service record – in the way that an idealized fashion model or elegant actor made to resemble an ordinary person might appear.

Tom stated, "I'm told that you have never before asked to see anyone. Not in the entire time you've been here."

Nathaniel regarded Tom, "I didn't think you would actually come."

Tom paused for a moment, thinking. "I am aware of your… circumstances. I am guessing that you felt a need to talk to someone, and the list of people you know here is short. Perhaps I'm the least… well… tell me. What can I do for you, Nathaniel?"

Nathaniel forced a smile. "I've never been a man of faith, Tom. But now… I feel like I'm on the edge of a precipice. I'm losing everything I thought I was, and I don't know what awaits me. Maybe I just want someone to remember who I am now."

Tom nodded solemnly and stepped forward before sitting on the chair at the small desk where Nathaniel was allowed to write his Accipiter tomes. "People need someone to talk to in trying times, whether it is a friend or their pastor, Nathaniel. I'd never abandon someone in need, especially now. I'm listening."

Nathaniel looked down, struggling with a surge of emotions. "Part of me… perhaps all of me… is going to die soon. I feel it. I am not… as I said… I am not… was not… a religious man." He looked up at Tom. "Will you give me last rites?"

Tom swallowed, "I understand, Nathaniel. While we United Methodists may not have last rites, we believe in God's boundless grace and love. Would you like me to pray with you?"

Nathaniel nodded, a lone tear trickling down his face.

Tom withdrew a small bible from inside his vest and held it. He bowed and spoke while Nathaniel watched with clouded eyes.

"Heavenly Father, we come before you in this moment of uncertainty and fear. We recognize that the world as we knew it has changed, and the paths we walk may be darkened by shadows. But we believe in Your light, and we trust in Your guidance. I lift up Nathaniel to You. May he find strength in Your embrace and clarity amidst the storm. As he stands at this crossroads, Lord, envelop him in Your love and show him the way. Grant him the courage to face the challenges that lie ahead, knowing he is never truly alone. Even in the face of transformation and the unknown, let Nathaniel feel Your presence. Let him remember that with every end comes a new beginning, and in every darkness, there is a glimmer of light. I ask You to watch over him, protect him, and guide him on this journey. In Your name, we pray. Amen."

The room remains silent for a moment longer, the weight of the prayer lingering in the air.

Nathaniel nodded slowly, "Thank you, Tom. Whatever happens next, I'm grateful for this…. Kindness."

✪ ✪ ✪

Sybil, Corporal Fabian Böhmer, and Paximandros entered the cell, followed by Yeurantheon and four marine guards.

Nathaniel studied Sybil's grave expression. He frowned and drew a deep breath. "So, you've decided. I see." Citing Dostoevsky, he said, "Man is sometimes extraordinarily, passionately in love with suffering. You would have me revisit that upon mankind? Help you destroy the peace and prosperity that not only mankind but all the beings in the Accipiter Panoply enjoy?"

Sybil smiled thinly, "All the world's a stage, and all the men and women merely players. But who scripts our lives, Nathaniel, if not the Heretic?"

Paximandros added, "That's the point, Nathaniel. We seek to rewrite that script. To free the galaxy from the Heretic puppeteers. The only way to deal with an unfree galaxy is to become so absolutely free that our very existence is an act of rebellion."

Nathaniel scoffed. "You seek power. Beware, for I am fearless and therefore powerful. Mary Shelley's Frankenstein's monster said that. And yet, what did that power earn him besides misery and pain?"

Paximandros shook his head. "In Huxley's 'Brave New World,' they lulled people into a sense of contentment. But it was a hollow life."

Nathaniel laughed darkly, "You might as well ask me to dive into the rabbit hole, a fantasy world, a hollow artificial world where reality is what you manipulate my memories to make it."

Sybil blinked at Nathaniel's statement before shaking her head and said, "The Heretic's world isn't real, Nathaniel. He's altered history and created a galaxy twisted to his vision. He pummels worlds into submission and then alters them to fit his garden fantasy. A galaxy of puppets playing out his macabre play at godhood soaked in the blood of trillions of innocent souls."

Nathaniel sighed, nodding toward Paximandros. "And yet, all you have is *his* word for this."

Yeurantheon spoke a series of twills and tweets, accompanied by glyphs on his beak. The room's translator spoke:

SEARCH YOUR HEART. YOU KNOW THAT THERE
HAVE BEEN TIMES THAT YOUR MEMORIES DID
NOT MAKE SENSE. EVENTS OUT OF SEQUENCE. A
SENSE OF WRONGNESS QUICKLY GLOSSED OVER BY
DISTRACTION.

Nathaniel stared at them and shook his head. "I don't believe you. Besides, even if everything you said were true, I will not be party to plunging the galaxy into a maelstrom of death and destruction. What you propose is worse than what you claim to be trying to change.

Sybil hung her head and sighed before looking at Paximandros and Yeurantheon. "We had to try."

✪ ✪ ✪

Six Hours Later

TopSide Hospital ER

Nathaniel Grant groaned as he slowly regained consciousness.

Indicators beeped on a panel behind his hospital bed as a nurse entered the room and checked his vitals before pressing the intercom button. "He's awake, Doctor."

Two minutes later, Surgeon General Doctor Gwyneth Elliott Duncan, followed by Sybil, Tom Parker, and Paximandros, entered the room.

Gwyneth double-checked the indicators before moving Nathaniel's eyelids to check his pupils. She nodded and made a notation on Nathaniel's chart. "He's doing fine. I'll leave you to it, then."

Gwyneth caught the nurse's eyes and nodded to the door, where they both made their retreat.

Sybil looked back and forth between Paximandros and Tom, who nodded.

She put on a smile and said aloud, "Nathaniel, how do you feel?"

Nathaniel groaned again and squeezed his eyes. "My head."

Sybil put her hand on Nathaniel's, "You gave us quite a scare, there. The doctor says you took a good bump on the head when you fell. Do you remember anything?"

Nathaniel squinted from the brightness of the lights in the room. "Just... I was helping Paximandros move some boxes.... I think something fell on me."

Paximandros smiled, "That's right, Nathaniel. It was entirely my fault. Please forgive me."

Nathaniel tried to raise his head, then slumped back down to the pillow. "Right. That's okay. It was an accident. I'll be back up on my feet in no time to help you get ready for the trip. Just give me.... A little time...."

Sybil, Tom, and Paximandros exchanged relieved expressions.

Awakening

DownSide: Isla de Fuego

When the Gardeners announced that the Five Percent would be returned, plans to begin awakening the Keeper Ship 'frozen' people were put on hold. They'd waited this long – they could wait a bit longer. Instead, amid rancorous debate about when, where, and how to awaken the Five Percent, a compromise was reached. Like most political compromises, the decision had nuances lost on those who shouted the loudest. Passions ran deep. Ultimately, the idea that perhaps the shock of waking up in the new world – and with their lives doubly altered, that a period of adjustment on a beautiful tropical island, with only close loved ones or acquaintances nearby, would be the least traumatic. Not only for the Five Percent themselves but also for the rest of the public upon seeing the formerly dead return to walk the streets of Fort Brazos.

✪ ✪ ✪

Jasmine and Yazmeen Lewis's Recovery Room

The island was a painting sprung to life: azure waters brushing against a pristine shoreline, trees with leaves like emerald jewels, and the distant chirruping of unseen creatures adding an ambient melody to the scene. In the midst of this idyllic paradise was the clinic, a low, sprawling building designed to blend seamlessly with its surroundings. There were no harsh lines or stark facades, just gentle curves and a roofing that resembled woven palm fronds.

Darnell stood at the entrance, nerves pulling taut in his stomach. Two years. Two long years believing he'd lost his mother, Jasmine, and sister Yazmeen forever. The weight of the past – the warehouse standoff, the miserable months of scraping by afterward, the wild trek into the wilderness with Gary and Ray, and the discovery of the ZPM and the replication cave – pressed on him. His days as a mere warehouse manager felt distant, a shadow of another life. Now, he stood as a Senator, a title he never thought he'd bear, especially in a world as transformed as this.

The clinic's door swished open, revealing a bright, airy space filled with the low hum of machines and hushed voices. A prim-looking attendant approached, her face a mask of hope and amazement.

"Senator Lewis? They're ready for you."

He nodded and followed her to a room awash in sunlight. Large windows opened to a private beach, where waves played a serene lullaby. At the room's center were two beds, and on them lay Jasmine and Yazmeen, their faces tranquil.

Darnell approached hesitantly, the attendant's voice a muted whisper as she explained the process. "The Awakening was gentle. Not at all like, well, like yours or mine or anyone else on Awakening Day. They'll be disoriented, but your presence will ground them."

He nodded, taking a deep breath, preparing himself for the reunion. The attendant adjusted their IVs, and slowly, his mother and sister began to stir. Jasmine's eyes fluttered open first, her confusion evident, then they widened in recognition.

"Darnell?" Her voice, groggy but unmistakably hers, filled the room.

Darnell choked back emotion. "Yeah, Mom. It's me."

She reached out, and he clasped her hand, holding it against his face. Beside her, Yazmeen's eyes were opening too, taking in the unfamiliar surroundings before settling on Darnell.

He smiled through his tears. "Hey, Yaz."

She blinked, her eyes moistening. "Where are we?"

Darnell took a moment, choosing his words carefully. "It's a long story, but right now, we're somewhere safe. Somewhere beautiful."

Jasmine squeezed his hand. "What's happened?"

He nodded. "I'll explain everything. We have time, Mom. All the time in the world."

The weight that had oppressed Darnell for years seemed to lift slightly. He had been granted a second chance, an opportunity he had never dreamed of. As the three of them sat, entwined in the soft light of the room, it was evident that while their world had irrevocably changed, the bond of family remained unshaken.

✪ ✪ ✪

George and Anne Westmoreland's Recovery Room

The sun streamed into the tranquil room, casting golden hues on the bed where George and Anne lay. Their expressions were one of mild confusion, the remnants of dreams and memories intertwining. The door opened with a quiet sigh, revealing John Austin, now two years older and bearing the weight of leadership in his demeanor. Beside him stood Gail, her belly rounded with their unborn twins, and a considerably taller Matti, her eyes somehow vastly older than her tender age.

"George! Anne!" John's voice was a blend of relief and emotion. His steps hurried as he approached the bed.

George's eyes blinked, recognition slowly dawning. "John? What... where are we?" Anne's hand tightened on his as she looked around, equally perplexed.

Gail, with a soft smile on her face, approached awkwardly from the other side. "Welcome back. You don't know me. My name is… Gail."

Matti stood at the foot of the bed. "Mr. Westmorland, Mrs. Anne, I missed you."

Anne's face softened. "Matti? You've… you've grown." Her voice became worried, "What is going on!"

Before further words could be exchanged, a stern voice cut through. "Mr. President, please stand back. We need to ensure the area is secure."

Another added, "Madam Vice President, please let the medical team do their assessment."

George's brow furrowed. "Mr. President? Vice President? John, what's going on?"

John ran a hand through his hair, his eyes revealing the weight of his responsibilities. "A lot's changed, George. Anne. A… A lot has happened. It will take time to explain. For now, know that you are both in perfect health."

Anne glanced at Gail's prominent belly, a realization hitting her. "You two...? What? How long have we been….."

Gail chuckled, her hand instinctively moving to her stomach. "Two Years, Mrs. Westmorland."

"What? That's not possible!"

George shook his head, then regretted it. He stammered, "John, what the hell is going on?"

✪ ✪ ✪

Abigail Hoffman's Recovery Room

The atmosphere in the room was thick with anticipation as the machines began to hum. Soft light filtered in, illuminating Abigail as she slowly stirred.

As her eyes fluttered open, they first landed on Sandra Hoffman, her face older but unmistakably her granddaughter's. Sandra gently clasped Abigail's hand, her eyes glistening with unshed tears.

"Abigail... Gamma," Sandra whispered, her voice thick with emotion.

Beside her, David held a baby while three other little ones wiggled in place, curious eyes on the woman in the bed. Hannah and Elisabeth, older and stronger, stood nearby, their hands tightly intertwined.

From the sidelines, a figure with a sharp, military haircut stepped forward. Abigail blinked, trying to reconcile the image of the young cadet with memories of her long-haired granddaughter. "Jordan?" she questioned, her voice raspy.

Jordan nodded, her eyes showing a mixture of pride and sadness. "Yes, Gamma. It's me."

Vicktor, who had grown so much in the interim, moved closer, his face a mask of restrained emotion. "Gamma?" he asked with a 4-year-old's curiosity.

Abigail looked around, taking in the faces of her family, but her brow furrowed in confusion. "Where am I? Where's Barrett? Margaret? And little Nolan?"

The room grew silent, a heavy weight settling in the air. Sandra took a deep breath, squeezing Abigail's hand tighter. "There's a lot to catch up on, Grandma. Some good, some... not so good."

Esmerelda Collins, who had been quietly observing from the corner, stepped forward. "It's been a long journey, Abby. But right now, we're here, together, as a family."

Abigail's eyes, filled with questions and a dawning realization, flitted from face to face. Despite the warmth and love that surrounded her, a sense of loss lingered, waiting to be acknowledged and mourned.

✪ ✪ ✪

Dr. Gloria Rubenheim's Recovery Room

The sterile hum of machinery was the first sound Gloria registered as her senses slowly returned. As her vision cleared, her gaze fell upon a familiar face – one she had grown to despise over the years. Dr. Leo Talib stood beside her bed, his demeanor calm and composed. The arrogance she remembered was conspicuously absent.

"Gloria," Leo began, his voice unexpectedly gentle. "Welcome back."

Gloria's gaze sharpened, and she frowned. "Where am I? Why are you here?" she spat, her old animosity flaring.

Before Leo could reply, a stern and imposing woman stepped forward, carrying a baby, her face kind and warm. "Gloria, I am Brigadier General Sabrina Chilton… Talib. I know it's confusing, but a lot has happened. Leo and I are married now."

Gloria's eyes widened in surprise, but she held her tongue as she observed the young woman beside Sabrina, a baby in her arms.

"This is my daughter, Nicole," Sabrina introduced, "and Leo and my twin girls, Octavia and Philippa."

Gloria blinked, trying to process this new information. "What? Wait. Is this a sick joke? Why is Leo here?" she asked again, though her voice was softer this time.

Leo took a deep breath, looking at Sabrina for support. Sabrina squeezed his hand reassuringly. "I wanted to be here, Gloria," Leo said. "I know we had our differences, but that was a long time ago. Over two years have passed. A lot has changed, and it is going to take time to explain."

Gloria regarded him skeptically. "That makes no sense at all. Get out. I don't believe you."

A hard male voice sounded from behind them, "General? Dr. Talib? The President is asking for you."

Leo nodded and shrugged as he smiled at Sabrina, "That's our cue, Darling." He turned to Nicole, "Nicole, Dear, do you think you could keep Gloria company for a little while? Your mom and I should be back soon."

Nicole's eyes twinkled. She knew all about Leo's past with Gloria Rubenstein and looked forward to the opportunity to remind the woman how important her new dad had become.

Leo paused, leaning in, looking Gloria directly in the eyes. "I am truly sorry for the past, Gloria. I hope, with time, you and I can get past our former differences."

Gloria blinked in surprise, momentarily without words.

As Leo and Sabrina were ushered from the room, Nicole juggled Octavia in her arms and smiled, "Now, Gloria, I have a few questions for you…."

Revenge

● ● ● ● ● ● ● ● ● ● ● ● ● ● ● ● ●

NTN Revenge
Outside Accipiter Held G5V Yellow Dwarf System

The converted 40-foot cargo container, now the Combat Information Center (CIC) of the NTN Revenge, was a symphony of expediency and human will. This wasn't the standard, clean, clinical command space of Navy attack submarines or surface vessels, iterated upon and refined over decades of experience and over two hundred years of naval operations. It was a gritty, almost haphazard nerve center, pieced together with the remnants of a hundred different technologies, all singing in dissonant harmony within the belly of the converted sublight Builder cargo vessel, itself englobed within the warp rings of what amounted to Phoenix's 'offspring.' The quiet murmur of voices reflected both the fear and excitement of their current location, just beyond the Heliosphere of the Accipiter-held star system they had been observing for the past two days.

In the neon glow of holographic displays, Weapons Officer Moreno Paolo Guerra's fingers danced over the weapons console, testing and retesting the systems and subsystems of the reconnaissance drone they were preparing to launch. Nearby, pilot Angela Stevens' hands remained poised above the repeater navigation array, ready to dance the ship away from danger at a moment's notice. Chief of the Boat (COB) Gerald Beltran, a man whose features seemed carved from the very hull of the Revenge, watched over the crew with eyes that missed nothing.

Communications Officer Molly Crawford, her Ensign insignia catching the light, monitored any enemy transmissions with an intensity that belied her youth, filtering out the static of space to isolate the whispers of the Accipiters. There weren't any, which was good.

Tech Doug Stephens, surrounded by a cocoon of wires and screens, murmured to himself as he swapped out a suspect server blade, his mind alight with the intricacies of the CIC's patchwork of equipment.

Amidst this well-orchestrated chaos, Commander Rafferty Youngman stood as if carved from the very metal of the Revenge herself, his posture a column of resolve. The banks of computers and screens cast a fluctuating light across his handsome, square-jawed, chiseled features as he raised a hand, his voice cutting through the hum of activity like a knife. "Clear the CIC," he ordered. The subsonic timbre of his voice resonated through the space, bouncing off the container walls that had been retrofitted with equipment and pressure doors. It resonated with an authority that brooked no dissent.

The crew, enshrouded in their tasks like priests in a ritual, paused and looked up. Moreno's hands hovered over the backlit gamer's keyboard of the weapons system. Next to him, Stevens slowly straightened up, the lines of readiness relaxing slightly, and even Beltran's impassive gaze flickered with surprise.

Regardless, they were well-drilled, well-oiled cogs in the machine of war, and they withdrew without protest, the symphony of their exit a faint echo in the CIC. The clanging of sealing hatches punctuated their departure, leaving Rafferty alone with Dimitri Sinitskaya.

Dimitri looked up from the data scrolling on his digital tablet and regarded Rafferty with hooded, expectant eyes. This conversation would be the fulcrum upon which their entire mission teetered. The air between them was charged with the unsaid, and the weight of their shared desire for revenge against the Accipiters.

Rafferty's voice was a low rumble amid the fans and computer noise in the room. "Doctor, if we set it off when it is in-system, we will draw every Accipiter in the region here. They'll start searching, turning over every rock in every system in the area. Eventually, they'll find Tartarus and hit it just like they hit Ari'Nell. I don't want to just hurt them once. I want to do it over and over again. I want to make them bleed. We need to be smart."

Dimitri set his tablet down with a deliberate motion, meeting Rafferty's gaze squarely. "Then why are we here?" he asked, his voice betraying well more than a hint of defiance.

"To gather intelligence," Rafferty responded, the measured tones of his voice a stark contrast to the volatility of the situation. "We need to study their comings and goings. Map their movements in the region.

Find out who we are up against. How many there are and where they are vulnerable."

"The longer we wait, the greater the chance for discovery," Dimitri countered, his expression tightening with urgency.

Rafferty's eyes narrowed slightly, focused and intense. "You assured me that the drone's AI will set off the self-destruct if it is discovered."

"That's not the point," Dimitri countered sharply, not backing down.

The commander took a step closer, his presence dominating the confined space. "Look, Doctor. Dimitri, I have a plan, but it will take time."

Dimitri's posture stiffened to match his skepticism. "Let's hear it, then. Convince me."

"These Accipiters are set up in clans, right? Multiple clans that each control multiple systems. Some clans are bigger than others. They trade biology they've stolen with each other." Rafferty began, his voice taking on the cadence of a strategist laying out his battlefield.

"That's what we're told," Dimitri responded, his skepticism seeping away as he started to see where Rafferty was leading.

"We figure out which clans operate in the systems in this region of the galaxy. We target just one," Rafferty continued, laying out the chessboard on which they would play their deadly game.

Dimitri's eyes narrowed in thought. "What good is that?"

Rafferty's reply was calculated, the words of a man who had thought through every angle. "Because if we are lucky, it will make them wonder why only one clan is being targeted and another rival clan is not. Is the other clan protecting us or employing us to do their bidding? Or is the rival clan actually doing the deed and making it look like we're doing it? If we can get the Accipiters fighting each other, then they can do our work for us. Maybe even ignite a civil war. At the very least, keep them off balance and away from Tartarus."

A wry, understanding grin briefly touched Dimitri's lips. "A classic strategy. The Soviets mastered it—keeping regions at odds to secure the power at the center."

"Exactly. We seed systems with drones in a pattern that won't lead to us. With each system we go to, we learn more. Even if this strategy doesn't work, we'll have learned where, when, and how to hurt them the most. Worst case? We set them all off at the same time in one giant, glorious, multi-system cataclysm that will leave them reeling for years. First, though, we need to test and make sure the first drone works as expected," Rafferty affirmed with a savage grin. "Now, what say we proceed with the launch?"

Dimitri stared at Rafferty for a long moment, testing the other man's sincerity and resolve. Finally, he frowned grimly, nodded his agreement, and returned to his station, his fingers gliding over the controls as he prepared the drone for its silent and solitary voyage into the enemy's domain.

At .2c, it would take a month on a ballistic course to clandestinely reach the target area. Once there, it would silently study and catalog the Accipiters' movements. Later, upon returning, Revenge would send a one-way signal encoded in background noise. That signal would tell the probe to slowly begin its journey back out-system, where its data could be clandestinely retrieved.

Or, the signal could also signal the probe to feign discovery and self-destruct.

The CIC, now an echo chamber of their resolve, stood ready to play its part in a plan that would either be the key to their vengeance or the prologue to their demise as Rafferty left the CIC to address the crew on the "official" mission.

Into the Black

● ● ● ● ● ● ● ● ● ● ● ● ● ● ● ● ●

DownSide: Hoffman-Collins Ranch

Sandra Collins Hoffman Garreth stared at David, her head on his shoulder. Both of them were desperate to forget what was coming but unable to deny reality. Nolan and Margaret had grown so much in the past 19 months. Owen, Ethan, and Caleb were growing, too, and were already walking. They were playing outside with Sandra's sisters, except for Jordan, Viktor, and their adoptive mother, Esmerelda Collins. Like the last time David had left New Texas, on the ill-fated mission back to Earth to capture the Keeper Ship, Sandra and David had taken a private horseback ride and picnic out to be alone with each other and their thoughts and try to savor the moment as much as they could.

The sun shone through the window, highlighting the bag that was already packed next to the bed - his new (Space) Marine uniform lay folded in its center. Even though Sandra knew that days like this were inevitable, she couldn't help but feel her heartbreak knowing that he was leaving once again.

Sandy said softly, her voice quivering from tears she refused to let fall, "It was a perfect day."

David nodded slowly, eyes misting over, his voice a ghost of its usual strength. "Yes, it was."

The silence between them stretched out, both of them knowing that if they spoke their fears out loud, there would be no stopping their emotions.

Sandy's resolve wavered, and her lips quivered. "I'd ask you not to go this time, but I know better. I just had to say it so that you would hear it. That I don't want you to go."

David answered gently as he embraced her tightly, "I know."

Sandy hastened, "Don't say it." *Don't say you're coming back.*

David nodded, "I know."

Sandy's chest heaved, "I love you."

David pulled her closer, his voice raspy from emotion as he vowed, "I love you more than life itself."

He took her face between his hands, softly stroking her cheeks with the pads of his thumbs. She moved closer, closing the slim space between them as their tears mingled when they kissed.

✪ ✪ ✪

TopSide Main Hangar Bay: Keeper Ship

Yeurantheon, Nathaniel Grant, and Paximandros were not alone as they labored over the membranous Keeper Ship controls. Nearby, in addition to three full squads of marines, a dozen university engineers and Naval officers observed as well, recording video of everything and taking copious notes. Weeks before, they had 'flown' the ship to the Dyson Sphere, where faux 'battle damage' was inflicted upon the golden ship's exterior.

While the Keeper Ship was inside the Dyson Sphere, the stasis chambers containing a million years' worth of flora, fauna, and over seventy thousand pairs of humans and pre-humans were removed. The humans and pre-humans, by means never explained by the Gardeners, were transferred to their new stasis chambers beneath Isla de Fuego.

The flora and fauna, though, remained in limbo while the living humans in New Texas tried to decide what to do with it all.

The Keeper ship itself had never before flown. It was seized in the Keeper Raid on the ground, mere days or weeks before it would have been ceremoniously launched and joined with the Northern Wheel Mender Clan's mothership. At that point, the Keeper himself would have been 'venerated' – i.e., put on display in stasis forever.

So, since form indeed follows function, just like any human aircraft or ship back on Earth needed pre-flight and working up, so too did the systems and subsystems of the Keeper Ship need to be tested and checked out before its inaugural launch. The Accipiters, along with Nathaniel himself, had done much of the work back on Earth before the Keeper Raid. That was two and a half years ago. Much of the process had needed to be restarted from the beginning.

The tedious work was nearing completion, though. Throughout the process, Nathaniel Grant was enthusiastic and quite animated as he answered innumerable questions, translated the cryptic control surfaces, and explained everything they were doing for the visual record.

Nathaniel turned from the control surface he had labored over for the past several days and faced the engineers and Naval officers as he motioned to a large holographic display that shimmered into existence, casting ethereal light over the assembled group. The diagram illustrated a complex web of lines and nodes that seemed to stretch into infinity.

"This," he began, pointing to the luminous display, "is a simplified representation of the Nexus Junction Point network. This is only a representation of the nearest thousand stars. The network extends throughout the galaxy."

He noted the mixture of intrigue and puzzlement on the faces before him and continued.

"Think of the NJP as the universe's own rapid transit system. Each Junction Point is a natural weak spot in spacetime, linked by stress lines to other stars of significant mass. It is as though the galaxy is threaded together by these lines, and the NJPs are the stations where we embark and disembark."

One of the officers raised a hand. "And how exactly do we 'embark' on this network? How does a vessel open and transit an NJP?"

Nathaniel smiled. "By 'opening' a rift at the NJP by using a massive amount of energy. Transit is effectively instantaneous. The key to a successful transit is the entry vector. Think of it as aligning yourself with the track you want to take at the station."

He walked over to another membraneous console and gestured at a series of fluctuating vectors and coordinates.

"What we're working on right now is calibrating the ship's systems to accurately determine these vectors and stress lines, which are constantly shifting. The ship's hull acts as a resonance chamber. Get it wrong, and you might end up in a bad situation. Fortunately, the Gardeners made sure that the fake battle damage would not affect the calculations."

A murmur rippled through the group, a mix of excitement, apprehension, and many, many more questions.

"This technology is sensitive on a level I never dreamed of. I was never a scientist, but I was a nuclear engineer. Also, it is crucial to remember that we are not dealing with static points. The NJPs move with their respective stars, and this motion is affected by galactic dynamics."

He then directed the group's attention to a new schematic depicting clusters dotting the inner hull. "These are the orienters. They'll detect and lock onto the NJP's current vector. Once locked, the rift engines will initiate, creating the necessary rift for us to pass through."

An engineer piped up, "How is your systems check going?"

Nathaniel nodded. "We're triple-checking everything. Orientation, rift stabilization, energy thresholds... Because once we launch, the margin for error is vanishingly small. Navigation through the NJPs is the most challenging part of our journey. Each sequence has to be executed flawlessly."

One of the naval officers asked, "And if it isn't executed flawlessly?"

Nathaniel answered directly, "Then, in the best-case scenario, you end up in the wrong system or are never heard from again."

One of the engineers shook his head, "That's the best case? What's the worst case?"

Nathaniel paused for a long moment. Then you end up near a black hole or neutron star and are crushed or emerge within the photosphere of a star. Remember, the relative position of an NJP is related to the stellar mass. Travel to a blue giant or neutron star or black hole, and your survival time after transit might be measured in femtoseconds."

The naval officer asked, "Is that why the Builders didn't use NJP travel?"

Nathaniel shrugged, "We don't know. The Accipiters were given the technology by the Heretic. It is Gardener technology. I can only imagine how long it would take any civilization to master NJP travel through trial and error, much less map an entire galaxy to know which routes are safe... and which are not. NJP travel is effectively instantaneous. That has obvious tactical and logistical advantages."

"On the other hand, warp travel has advantages over NJP transit. You can go places NJPs can't. For one thing, deep space between stars is unreachable by NJP. Tactically, you can sneak up and approach a star system from any angle you want. While NJP locations flex and move, their *general* locations are well known. Anyone traveling that way will enter a system in those areas that greatly reduces the region of space available to defend. While warp travel adds significant travel time, it gives an attacker much more flexibility. Given the highly militaristic profile we have of the Masters, I'm not surprised they stuck to warp travel. Of course, it is also possible that NJP travel was something they hadn't solved yet, or else they'd have wanted to have an option to do both. Personally, I think that's the most likely scenario. The Gardeners are a vastly older race and had a lot more time to figure it out."

"Also, NJP travel to really low-mass stars like brown dwarfs is very difficult. The Accipiter ships can't do it, and what possible reason would they have to even want to go to places like that? There won't be any inhabitable planets there. However, with the Gardeners' help, we've upgraded the Keeper Ship to be able to make the transit. The Masters were smart. They picked this location for their base because they could not imagine the Accipiters or anyone else wanting to come here. They also got lucky because I doubt that they had any idea that the Accipiters *couldn't* come here."

✪ ✪ ✪

TopSide Main Hangar Bay: NTN Blood Phoenix Wardroom

The wardroom of the former submarine was a compact chamber, austere yet suffused with an air of solemn tradition, its walls adorned with insignias and plaques from past crews and missions. The room bristled with quiet anticipation as Captain Charles Cross, now the former CO, stepped in, offering a firm nod to his successor, Captain Haruto Hashimoto, who stood by with his equally new officer, Lt. Stephen Prichard. Already present were the commanders of the Trojan Horse task force: Ramona Henry of NTN Badger, with her taciturn first officer Lt. Alec Gorman; Hershel Griggs of NTN Hyena, flanked by his somber, black-haired first officer Lt. Tom Akiba; and Dwight Coughlin of NTN Jackal, with his famously sharp-witted red-haired and freckled first officer, Lt. Ritchie Roscoe.

The day before, everyone had been DownSide, where they met President and Vice President Austin for a private meal at the Presidential home. Gail Austin was now too pregnant to travel on the Elevator lest she go into labor during the six-hour ride.

Charles surveyed the expectant faces of the gathered officers. The weight of the impending mission was evident in all of their eyes.

Haruto smiled, "Welcome, Captain. I hope the condition of Phoenix hasn't suffered too much in your absence."

Charles grinned, "She couldn't be in finer hands, Haruto," he nodded at Stephen. "How are you settling in, Lieutenant?"

Stephen smiled in return, "Big shoes to fill, Sir. I am endeavoring to break Captain Hashimoto's records from his time as First Officer."

Charles chuckled, "That's a worthy goal and a tall order indeed." He turned to the other commanders. "Ramona, Hershal, Dwight, how are the Corvettes? I'm sure you are all happy to be back in command of ships that are actually armed for a change."

Ramona's smile was brilliantly white in reply, but Dwight answered first, before her or Hershal.

On Earth, Dwight Coughlin had been in command of the Oklahoma SSN-802. His wife Emily and his children Lucas and Anna had been away visiting Emily's mother when the Accipiters attacked Earth. Dwight had been inordinately proud to serve as Captain of the Oklahoma, his home state. After Awakening Day, Dwight had fervently eschewed any relationship that might lead anywhere that would, in his mind, violate the sacred memory of Emily, Lucas, and Anna. He had a reputation for being hard but scrupulously fair, and his hatred of the Accipiters knew no bounds.

Dwight grinned wolfishly, "Captain, Jackal, and the other Corvettes are viciously wicked little ships. The naming committee got it right this time. I expected them to be sluggish compared to the ILCs, but the power plant is significantly bigger to improve maneuverability as well as the voracious appetite of the grazers."

Ramona jumped in and said, "You've seen the footage of what those grazers did to the asteroids we targeted. I, for one, cannot wait to rip the proverbial snot out of the Accipiter ships."

Hershel nodded and added, "Those Accipiter mother ships, as you know, are huge. We've worked out several pre-planned variations of hit-and-run tactics. We're calling it the Ali maneuvers, after Muhammad Ali's 'Float like a butterfly, sting like a bee' quote. We dance around in what will appear to be a random pattern, dropping in and out of warp, fire, and then warp to the next position." Hershel had been the commander of SSN 807, the Silversides. Unlike Dwight, his wife, Dr. Elise Griggs, a marine biologist, and their son Liam and daughter Zoe had survived and were now living DownSide in Fort Brazos. Dwight was known for his heavy advocacy of advanced cross-training programs that improved his crew's efficiency and cohesiveness. His leadership style was both hands-on and inspirational, fostering a climate of respect and professionalism. Not surprisingly, he'd been a Golden Gloves competitor in his youth.

Ramona nodded, "Hammer them into scrap. It may take a while on a twenty or more mile-long ship, but these grazers are wickedly powerful."

Charles smiled again. "Well, I'm jealous I'm not going out with you, but as you know, the Sammy B. isn't ready yet. We've barely scratched the surface on damage control procedures and a laundry list of other critical systems. We're pushing triple shifts, but the window of opportunity reported by the Gardeners for the target system is small.

Hopefully, all you'll have to do is kick back and watch the show. On the other hand, every one of you know all about Military Intelligence, and this time, we're completely dependent upon the Gardeners. I've already talked to Haruto about this. Don't trust the Gardeners' intel. I don't know if they have ever fought a war themselves, or, even if they have, it was countless eons ago. Expect problems. Expect Murphy to ruin your day. Be ready and vigilant. If I didn't think you could handle the mission, I would not have supported it. That said, keep your eyes open and your powder dry."

He paused and grinned, "Now that that's out of the way," He turned to Haruto, "Haruto, let's get everyone seated and bring in the food. You did remember the food, I presume?"

Haruto's eyes widened, and his mouth parted as he feigned surprise. "Food, Sir? What food?"

Dead Man

● ● ● ● ● ● ● ● ● ● ● ● ● ● ● ●

DownSide: Riverbend Mall Senate Chamber

Gail clenched her jaw and fought hard to present an impassive face and not squirm in her chair and tried desperately to find a position in which to be comfortable. It was a losing battle. She'd already had two bouts of false labor this week that had left her rattled and tired. *Damn it all!* She knew how to fly fighter jets and was getting more comfortable in her role here, presiding over the Senate. Ever since her father, the Colonel, first started teaching her to fly, Gail had devoted her life to discipline and self-control. So, when she suddenly realized that her efforts at maintaining composure had been so distracting that she had no idea what anyone had said for the past... *how long?* Her face flushed hot in self-beratement.

She swallowed hard and blinked as she started to listen once again. Esmerelda was complaining about something Gaspard Boyer had said. *Like that narrows it down at all.*

She sighed and looked down at her yellow legal pad, vainly hoping she'd somehow written down a grace-saving note of some kind, and that's when she felt it. It was like nothing she'd ever felt before. A... pop. And then she felt the warm fluid not quite gush out of her....

Just as quickly as her face had reddened, all color faded utterly, and she felt a twinge of something else that was new. Fear. It was.... Happening. Really... happening.

And just as quickly, her heart began to pound in her chest, and she could hear her pulse in her ears, drowning out Gaspard's French-laced retort.

As her heart raced, she knew that she could not allow these people to see her this way. At least… some of them, anyway.

In another first, she saw that her hands were trembling. She clenched her fists and then reached over and picked up her cell phone and swallowed her pride as she texted Nate Hopper, the head of her security detail.

Water broke. Don't let Senate see.
Please… Help.

Gail had no idea whether it was five seconds or five minutes before Nate, Corporals Cruz, Dixon, and the rest of the Senate security team burst into the chamber and announced an unscheduled emergency security drill and required the Senators to quickly evacuate the building.

Esmerelda Collins glanced at Gail, and her eyes widened as she read the Vice President's face.

Gail caught her gaze and held it pleadingly.

Esmerelda smiled briefly and turned back to the other Senators, announcing aloud, "Well, the security drill is fortuitous because I'd been about to call for a Senators-only private meeting, anyway. Since we're being forced out anyway, let's all meet back in the Parlor at Riverside and continue, shall we?"

When the chamber cleared, Gail looked up pleadingly at Nate, Jose, and Jermal, who gathered around her.

Their expressions were a mix of concern, worry, urgency, and…. love. These past two and a half years, these young men had been with her virtually everywhere. They knew everything there was to know about Gail Anson Finley. All of her flaws, her secret fears, her fiery temper, everything. She had resented them from the beginning. Fought for as much privacy and independence as possible, which was vanishingly rare. And yet, they never wavered. Not for the first time, she realized how much she'd come to depend on… and love each of them in return.

Nate said, "Ma'am, let's get you out of here."

Gail whispered, "Don't let anyone…"

Jermal smiled as he produced a duffel. "Don't worry, Ma'am. We prepared for this. We've got you covered."

It seemed to Gail that she merely blinked, and the next thing she knew, she was in bed in a private suite at Methodist Hospital with Gwyneth taking her vitals and checking her over. *All over.*

Gwyneth raised her eyebrows and brushed her hair aside, "Oh my. You're already at 4 cm, my dear. Did you… well… did you not feel contractions before now?"

Gail flushed and swallowed, "After the false labor, and today, I've… I… Oh God, this isn't me at all! I completely zoned out. I've been so uncomfortable, and that damned chair in the Senate was…"

Gwyneth gasped, "You what? You presided today? You sat in that damned stiff chair for hours? After I specifically *ordered* you to finally take a break and rest? What were you thinking?"

Gail's eyes flashed briefly in anger, and she opened her mouth to speak before shutting it again. She slumped her head back onto the pillow.

Gwyneth nodded. In a soft voice, she added, "That's right. As your doctor, I outrank you, and don't you forget it."

Gail suddenly gasped aloud and sat partway back up in bed, her eyes wide in pain. She looked at Gwyneth in desperation.

Gwyneth reached over and gently helped ease Gail back down. "Yup, you're in active labor, my dear."

John was standing on the flight line watching Matti's plane disappear into the distance when Sergeant Jesse Roberts, the head of his personal security detail, ran to his side.

"Sir, Mr. President. The Vice President is at Methodist Hospital in active labor. Her water broke, Sir."

John looked up in the sky for a moment, then turned back to Jesse, "Don't tell Matti. I don't want her hurrying or upset while she's in the air. Arrange for Roxanne to get her to the hospital as soon as possible after Matti lands. Meanwhile, find me the fastest way to get there myself. It'll take too long to drive back."

The Bell Boeing V22-Osprey was officially rated as being over 130mph faster than a Sikorsky UH-60 Black Hawk. All the ILCs were on the other side of the world, so John commandeered a V22 for the flight to the hospital. Possible political repercussions down the road be damned. The downside was that the Osprey's size and weight, over 60,000 lbs, made it too big and heavy to land safely on the hospital helipad.

Regardless, John never remembered actually running from the nearby parking lot where they landed to the Hospital entrance. Of course, Corporals Gabriel Pérez and Braden Edwards were younger and faster than he was. They ran ahead to make sure the path was clear while Jesse effortlessly kept up with John at his side.

✪ ✪ ✪

By the time John had been cleared to enter, hands washed, masked, and wearing scrubs, Gail was sweating and in pain.

She narrowed her eyes at him as he entered. She turned away, gasped, and screamed in pain as Gwyneth examined her 'progress.'

Gail snapped her head back towards John and snarled, "You are a dead man, John Hugo Austin! You did this!"

John winced. He stepped forward to Gail, who seized his hand and squeezed it in a death grip.

He looked to Gwyneth, who conferred with a nurse for a moment.

Gwyneth grinned, "She's doing great. Already at seven-ish centimeters."

Gail gasped aloud again and squeezed John's hand harder.

John asked, "Can you give her anything for the pain?"

Gwyneth shook her head, "She refused an epidural, and it is going too fast anyway."

Gail shook her head rapidly, "…not sticking a needle in my spine…"

✪ ✪ ✪

FOR IMMEDIATE RELEASE

Office of the Press Secretary

New Texas Government

November 27

Birth of Twin Boys to President John Hugo Austin and Vice President Gail Finley Austin

Fort Brazos, NT: In the late afternoon hours of November 27, the Presidential Office of New Texas is filled with joy to announce that President John Hugo Austin and Vice President Gail Finley Austin have welcomed their newborn twin boys into the world. Vice President Gail Finley Austin gave birth to the healthy twins at Methodist Hospital, attended by Surgeon General Gwyneth Duncan and surrounded by an exceptional medical team and the unwavering support of President Austin and his daughter Matilda.

The firstborn has been named William Gabriel Austin, a loving tribute to Vice President Austin's father, Colonel William "Bill" Thomas Finley. He is joined by his brother, Connor Vincent Austin. The arrival of William Gabriel and Connor Vincent marks a historic moment for the New Texas Government, symbolizing new beginnings and the promise of a bright future for all.

The twins, born full-term and healthy, weighed in at 5 pounds, 8 ounces, and 5 pounds, 6 ounces, respectively. These weights are well within the average range for healthy full-term newborn twins, indicating a robust start to life.

President Austin and Vice President Austin are grateful for the outpouring of support from the citizens of New Texas. In a statement from the proud parents, they said, "We are blessed to welcome William and Connor into our lives. This personal joy is magnified by the love and support of our fellow New Texans. We thank the dedicated medical staff for their expert care, ensuring the safe arrival of our boys."

"We look forward to the journey ahead as a family of five."

In celebration of this special occasion, the Presidential Office announces that the National

Flag will be flown at all government buildings today. Furthermore, the President and Vice President have decided to establish a Future Leaders Fund for New Texas children, dedicated to ensuring that every child in New Texas has the opportunity to thrive and succeed.

The President and Vice President request privacy during this time as they focus on the new additions to their family. They are committed to resuming their public duties shortly, with even greater zeal and dedication to the service of New Texas.

Please join us in congratulating President John Hugo Austin and Vice President Gail Finley Austin on the birth of their sons.

Media Contact:

Samira Shah

Director of Communications

Press Office of New Texas

pressoffice@newtexas.gov

**###

Trojan Horse

● ● ● ● ● ● ● ● ● ● ● ● ● ● ● ●

Endiku Star System

The Accipiter controlled Endiku star system was lightly populated. Its jewel, Kumai, was a habitable planet with a serene environment, with its surface area only about a quarter land. This landmass was not characterized by vast continents or expansive plains but rather a patchwork of wetlands and a myriad of small, scattered islands that dotted the vast oceans. The terrain on Kumai was predominantly marshland, with ecosystems rich in biodiversity. The islands, each with their own unique ecological niches, were separated by the temperate and calm seas.

Outside of Kumai, the planets in the system were less inviting. The rocky planets were barren, their surfaces sculpted by eons of meteor impacts and solar winds, leaving them with little to no atmosphere. Among these, some resembled Mars, with their dusty red surfaces and evidence of long-gone water channels. The rest of the planets were either airless rocks or ice planets. A single gas giant, larger than Jupiter, dominated the outer reaches of the system.

Despite the upheaval caused by the renegade humans, Accipiter presence in the system was minimal. The system was one of many in the Moon Singer Great Weave Maker's clan domain. Their great mothership only visited every few months and had recently departed, leaving behind just over six hundred clan support vessels, most of which rested on one of the many moons around the system gas giant as they monitored system defense mine production.

Suddenly, the tranquility of the star system was disturbed by an unusual gamma-ray burst in its outskirts. This burst was a known indicator of a Nexus Junction Point being transited. Given that only Accipiter ships navigate through NJPs, the event aroused mild interest about which clan might be coming for a visit or if it was a courier with news. The energy emitted was too small to match the signature of even the tiniest motherships.

As planned, the golden Keeper Ship's faux battle-damaged exterior bled plasma and atmospheric gas from its blackened rents and gashes. Soon afterward, the ship began broadcasting its well-rehearsed 'desperate' distress call, which was interrupted by gaps and heavy distortions in the intricate and nuanced tonal language of the Accipiters.

Meanwhile, concealed within its warp bubble and as quiet as the vacuum of space, the NTN Blood Phoenix was present. Hidden within a warp bubble, a distortion of spacetime, the ship and its complement of Corvettes lay in wait. Captain Hashimoto had traveled to the system in warp before coasting in on a ballistic path to avoid detection by the Accipiter defense mines.

In order to be on station when the Keeper Ship arrived, they'd been required to depart from New Texas well in advance and accept the terrible risk that if they were discovered, the Keeper Ship would arrive at a system already at high alert, jeopardizing their mission at the very least, and, quite likely, dooming it and the entire strategy of the Gardeners to failure.

Tethered within the Phoenix's rings, the Corvettes, NTN Badger, Hyena, and Jackal were ready for action. Their crews were at their stations, all clad in spacesuits as a precaution against potential decompression. Commanders Ramona Henry, Hershel Griggs, and Dwight Coughlin each waited stoically, half wondering when Murphy would come down with his iron fist.

As the Keeper Ship's plaintive call for help propagated throughout the star system, the Accipiters stationed at the gas giant moon reacted first and swiftly.

YUREANTHEON FROM THE NORTHERN WHEEL MENDERS CLAN *LIVED?*

HE *ESCAPED* FROM THE HUMANS?

MIRACLE OF MIRACLES!

Lest the unthinkable happened, orders were rapidly dispatched, and the defensive mines were powered down in a collective sigh of relief. Then, it was a race to see who could arrive first at the scene and render aid!

In a video broadcast depicted on separate, side-by-side video frames, Yureantheon and Nathaniel Grant sent expressions of gratitude for those coming to their aid. Yureantheon was clearly in distress and could be seen in a compartment full of smoke and small fires. Nathaniel was also injured, but not as severely, and could be seen standing in the control room. They extolled the local Accipiter's vigilance and explained that they had managed to steal the Keeper Ship when an Accipiter fleet had attacked the human's secret base. Keeper Ships were not intended for independent flight. Their drive systems and NJP capabilities were designed to be part of the overall network of other Keeper Ship Arks embedded within clan motherships. They explained how the humans had pursued and damaged the ship while they were escaping and that they had barely managed to flee to an NJP on the other side of the system while the humans had been preoccupied with the approaching Accipiter fleet. Were it not for the intensity of fire taking place between that fleet and the humans, they would have obviously tried to flee toward their own brethren.

Of course, none of that had happened. When the Accipiter fleet arrived in the New Texas system, there had been no battle. On the other hand, there were no witnesses left behind to contradict the story, and Accipiters lacked warp drive ships with which to travel to the now inaccessible system and lens what had happened from a light-delay distance.

Yureantheon and Nathaniel went on to explain that when they entered the NJP, the damage caused them to end up in a lifeless star system. There, they had drifted for months doing repairs. When they finally were able to try again, their alterations, making the Keeper Ship capable of independent NJP transit, caused an overload and internal explosions. The ship was now losing life support, and Nathaniel was not sure how long Yureantheon would survive due to his injuries. Worse, a collapsed bulkhead now left Yureantheon trapped inside a compartment, and Nathaniel was unable to free him. Nathaniel would greet the rescuers at the airlock and guide them to Yureantheon's location.

✪ ✪ ✪

Three hours later, the lead Accipiter ship caught up with the drifting hulk of the Keeper Ship and docked. At 912 feet long, or 278 meters, it was typical of Accipiter Support ships. Each usually supported a separate family unit of roughly one hundred and fifty members. Interior layout among such vessels varied considerably, but at a minimum, each had significant space devoted to living quarters, as well as common areas and facilities, engineering spaces for life support, and the fusion torch drive and support systems. Of course, most of the technology and construction was at least partly organic in one form or other, and the compartments themselves tended to be broad, large, and spacious, accommodating both the size of the Accipiters as well as their preferred lifestyle of null or low-g.

Nathaniel stood just inside the airlock and greeted the twenty-three arriving Accipiters. Wisps of smoke wafted through the compartment, complimenting a variety of scorch marks. Each Accipiter carried rescue or medical equipment. Nathaniel himself looked terrible. There were burns on his face and arms, along with a multitude of cuts and scratches. His right arm was in a sling, and his clothes were tattered and filthy with scorch marks, blood, carbon, and an assortment of other stains.

He worriedly exclaimed in Accipiter,

WE MUST KEEP THE AIRLOCK BETWEEN THE VESSELS CLOSED IN CASE THERE IS ANOTHER EXPLOSION.

By now, the Gardeners were already in control of not only the airlock but of the other ship as well, sealing all internal compartments and controlling any and all external communications.

One of the Accipiters moved to examine Nathaniel's injuries. Nathaniel said,

DO NOT WORRY WITH ME. YOU MUST AID YUREANTHEON QUICKLY!

He turned and ran, half-dragging a foot along the way, leading them down the long spiraling ramp. They passed the control room, where various parts were smashed and others obviously jury-rigged. Small fires lingered in various parts of the ship while sparks and organic ooze, in equal parts, fell from shattered walls and ceilings.

Deep within the ship, they arrived at the entrance to what

amounted to the engineering spaces. Nathaniel gestured through a doorway, and the Accipiters dashed inside and began examining the collapsed bulkhead that crushed and blocked an opening. The moment the last Accipiter entered the room, with Nathaniel remaining outside it, he hit a door control, causing it to iris shut behind them, trapping them inside.

None of the Accipiters wore spacesuits or breathing apparatus. As a result, when gas flooded the room, it quickly rendered all of them unconscious. If they had arrived wearing protective gear, the contingency plans would have escalated to using Tasers or more... aggressive... measures.

On the Accipiter ship, gas had already been pumped in. The expectation was that it would reach and/or be effective for a good portion of the Accipiters onboard, but likely not all. Captain Garreth's teams were already stacked at the airlock entrance, awaiting word that the gas had done its job and been cleared.

Inside the compartment with the twenty-three Accipiters, the gas was flushed out, and the door opened.

Yureantheon, Nathaniel, and a line of manufactured humans, akin to Paximandros, filed into the room, examining the unconscious Accipiters, sensing which of them carried a Heretic. Fully half did. It would take time to work through that many. Every Accipiter would receive a Gardener rider, who would begin the process of editing their memories. Killing the Heretic copies was traumatic for the host, and recovery time could be substantial.

✪ ✪ ✪

Keeper Ship: Grand Portico Airlock

According to information provided by the Gardeners, the interior of the Accipiter Support Clan ships was known to include as much as two point five million cubic square feet of space. With an exterior diameter of over 200 feet, it was a lot of 'ground' to cover.

Captain David Garreth keyed his mic and addressed the stacked-up squads waiting astride the airlock. "This is Raptor to all squads: This one's for real, no paintball, and it ain't your buddy on the other side of the rifle. Stay Sharp. Some of you were with me on the Keeper Raid, and you fought Accipiters before. Those of you who weren't, you've seen Yeurantheon. Accipiters are fucking BIG. They've got huge clawed arms and clawed feet that can tear you in half. We're here to take them all alive, but not at the cost of your own. Also, remember, bullets and alien machinery inside a spaceship don't mix well. God only knows what most of the things you'll see in there are for. Use your vivid imaginations about what will happen if you shoot the wrong doo-dad and blow us all to Hell."

"Now, another thing. The Gardeners can rewrite memories, but if we kill some of them, whatever story the Gardeners make up will get a hell of a lot harder to make stick. So, tase the Accipiters. Tase'em, tase 'em, and tase 'em again if you have to. Lethal force is authorized as a last resort. So, get in and kick Accipiter ass and come out alive."

Darryl Washington nodded firmly and added. "You heard the Captain, ladies. No sightseeing, and no fucking around. Prep flashbangs, 2-second delay on breach. Get it done!"

Nathaniel Grant announced on the channel, "The gas has been deployed. Opening the airlock in ten seconds."

David commanded, "Flash and Clear! Stand by!"

As planned, the airlock door only partially opened (this time), creating just enough of a gap for Staff Sergeant Glenn Williams of Echo Squad to fire three flashbang grenades from his Milkor M32A1 Multi-Shot Grenade Launcher.

Early in the training exercises on the Gardener-provided Clan ship, the teams had struggled with how to maneuver and deal with the null-g. David asked Mei to ask Yeurantheon just precisely how the Accipiters themselves dealt with it. The answer was surprisingly simple. All Clan ships have fibrous clumps all along the interior surfaces. Accipiters latched onto them with any of their clawed feet or hands and used them to either remain stationary for various tasks or as launch points where they would 'take flight' across the compartment, some of which were cavernous.

Hence, the oversized carabiners each man now employed. By latching onto the fiber bundles, they could brace themselves and 'stand,' or simply use them just as the Accipiters did, as grab-bars for maneuvering around the interior of the ship.

As with the Gardener-provided training ship, the space on the inside of the Clan ship was their hangar bay airlock – the only airlock large enough to mate with the Keeper's Grand Portico airlock.

A moment after the light from the flashbangs lit up through the gap in the airlock doorway, Nathaniel, monitoring remotely from the control room, opened the door the rest of the way.

David shouted, "Go, go, go!"

David and Alpha breached first, hauling themselves around the opening as they latched their carabiners onto the fiber bundles so they could leverage themselves to a 'standing' position and bring their weapons to bear.

A half dozen unconscious Accipiters drifted in the null-g, canted at various angles. Two of them were "hooked" into a row of purple-hued vine-like plants that covered a third of the walls.

Perry Simmons called, "Alpha: Set, Covering!"

Bravo and Charlie squad members each braced themselves on the Keeper side of the airlock, aimed, and fired their H&k416 M320 grenade launcher. Instead of an actual grenade, the projectile was a barb attached to a tether line reel from cave diving equipment.

The reels spun wildly as the line played out. The barbs flew on a straight path through the null-g of the Clan ship and embedded themselves into the far wall of the spherical chamber. Each squad member then keyed the reel quick-release from the Geissele SMR M-LOK handguards the rifles had been equipped with, then locked and secured the reels with pitons into the purple hardwood tree-like growths just inside the Clan ship airlock entrance.

Each then attached small electric cave diver tether line winches and rapidly pulled them across the cavernous space inside.

Moments later, as all the squad members landed and secured themselves on the other side, Troy Irvin reported, "Bravo, Set!"

Nate Grogan followed with, "Charlie, Set!"

David ordered, "All Units, this is Raptor. Check your corners. Keep tasers ready. Lethal if it goes south. Move to the next compartment, bounding cover, keep comms clear, and call movements! FoxTrot, Enter and Secure these prisoners!"

David followed behind Alpha, hooking into one of the existing tether lines, and 'flew' across the compartment, carefully orienting his feet so they would 'land' on the other side, fighting sudden null-g nausea as he went.

After Delta and Echo followed suit, Darryl and FoxTrot entered the compartment as rear guard and began securing the half dozen unconscious Accipiters that drifted in the null-g, canted at various angles with steel zip ties and hoods over their heads. Two of them were already "hooked" into a row of purple-hued vine-like plants that covered a third of the walls.

At each compartment entrance, the squads affixed encrypted wifi repeaters to the walls. As they progressed, each team marked their progress on the interior layout already provided by Nathaniel and the Gardeners on a small tablet computer.

Troy Irvin reported crisply, "Raptor, this is Bravo. Four-way branch from here. Charlie reports the next three are clear, nothing but floaters so far.

✪ ✪ ✪

Ten minutes and a dozen compartments or chambers later, Nate Grogan's call came in on static-laden bursts. "… this … is Charlie, Contact, Above!" David Garreth gritted his teeth, "Charlie, this is Raptor, Sitrep, over?"

Troy Irvin's call came instead. "Raptor, this is Bravo. Charlie is ahead of us. We're pinned in a large chamber, map reference Zulu-Three-Seven-Niner, at least 4 hostiles. Charlie has several red and yellow casualties, maybe one black. We've got 2 yellow. Requesting CASEVAC."

David's eyes narrowed as he replied with urgency in his voice, "Bravo, this is Raptor. Alpha is on the way. Hold position. Alpha and Delta en route for support. Delta, vector and flank enemy position. Echo, follow as can."

Jay Casillas answered, "Raptor, this is Delta, wilco."

Glenn Williams followed suit, "Raptor, Echo wilco."

Delta was four compartments away, but Alpha only needed to backtrack one and forward another. Echo was the farthest. Men moved with as much haste as could be had in the null-g.

David and Perry Simmons stopped at the entrance to the large, vaulted room, with the rest of Alpha stacked behind them.

The room beyond was different from most of the others they'd seen so far. While most compartments had many plants of one sort or another, often of wildly varying colors and morphologies, this room had to be a central garden of some kind, judging by what, hopefully, were the plethora of 'fruit-like' objects that seemed to be interspersed everywhere throughout the riot of vines and weblike growths.

Troy and the rest of Bravo clung to the 'undersides' of the largest plants they could squeeze behind as a fusillade of small and sometimes not-so-small objects smashed through the plants around them. Clouds of red mist drifted near several of the squad members. What looked like pipes and other random objects were embedded deeply in the 'ground' all around them.

Troy looked across the room and keyed his mic, "Sir, great to see you. Charlie was in front of us on the other end of the chamber when they got hit. Accipiters opened up an entrance we didn't know was there up above us. Perfect kill zone for them. Pinned us down here in the middle."

David replied, his voice clear and strong, "What is Charlie's status? How many casualties?"

Troy barked a laugh, "They're throwing what must be their equivalent of kitchen knives and other sharp objects at us. Charlie's cut-up pretty good. Charlie Actual is unresponsive. I told them to lay low and play dead. Their cover's not as good. Bravo's not as bad, but we're pinned down. We're damned lucky. The way those bastards throw, they could cut a man in half. We could take them out easy. Just give the order."

Jay Casillas broke in, "Raptor, this is Delta. Delta is here. Entrance to your right, thirty degrees high."

"Delta, Raptor, Acknowledged. Stand by. Stand by, Bravo."

David turned to Perry, "What do you think? Have Jay hit them with flashbangs from their M320s?"

Two of Delta Squad's members were armed with H&K 416s with underslung M320 grenade launchers. Everyone else carried a pair of M84 hand-thrown stun grenades.

Perry nodded, "And throw M84s first to distract them so Delta can swing out of their entrance, acquire the target, and fire. Yes, Sir."

David keyed his mic. "Delta, this is Raptor. Prep 320s, and be ready to engage after Alpha's flashbangs."

"Raptor, this is Delta, M320 bangs after Alpha's"."

David nodded to Perry, who turned to the rest of Alpha Squad. "Prepare for flashbang, nine out on my go! Three-second delay."

Each of the men readied their flashbangs and arranged themselves optimally so that their throws would not interfere with each other or, worse, end up with a flashbang going off in their midst.

Perry waited until they were ready, then shouted, "Bangs out! Go!"

Nine M84 flashbang grenades sailed into the large garden chamber. With the null-g, they didn't arc. Each flew with whatever velocity and angular momentum imparted to it. In a stuttering series of blinding flashes, the grenades detonated. Their concussed wavefronts pummelled the air and senses of plants and Accipiters alike.

With their carabiners secured to the bundles near the entrance, two Delta squad marines 'walked' around the edge of the opening and trained their rifles upwards. A dozen stunned Accipiters were clustered around an entrance high above, making an easy target.

Two 40mm CTS 7290M Mini Flashbang grenades flew straight and true into the midst of the Accipiters and detonated, releasing a 180db "bang" and over six million candelas of light. Four already disoriented Accipiters lost their grips and drifted slowly apart.

Jay Casillas shouted, "Delta Two, Three, Four, and Five, secure those prisoners, the rest overwatch!"

Four Delta squad members burst into action, launching themselves towards the drifting Accipiters to secure them. The rest kept themselves securely tethered and oriented themselves for the best lines of sight over the rest of the compartment they could manage.

David, Perry, and the rest of Alpha pushed out into the garden chamber.

David shouted, "Tasers ready! There may be more!"

Just then, an even larger and bulkier Accipiter, its huge claws outstretched menacingly, burst through the overhead entrance, brushing aside the stunned Accipiters as he meteored across the chamber directly at David. It screamed a deafening multi-tonal cry that might have come from an avenging archangel.

David caught the blur of the Accipiter's approach from the corner of his eye. With no time to think, he acted on instinct. He shifted his grip on his M870 shotgun, ready to use it as a shield against the incoming attack. His mind raced with contingency plans – he had to neutralize the threat without lethal force if at all possible. As the Accipiter's clawed arm swept in like a scythe, David parried with the barrel of his shotgun, deflecting the strike away from his body.

The force from the enormous Accipiter's claw shattered the foregrip on the M870 and bent the barrel. The resulting impact spun David head over heels around on his tether. His left boot glanced off of the Accipiter's gaping beak just as taser barbs from half of Alpha squad and a third of Bravo slammed into the raging Accipiter. Several bounced off, but enough hit firm and sent the hulking Accipiter into spasming convulsions.

Unfortunately, two also hit David, though one glanced off of his plate carrier. The other hit his thigh, sending David into staggered convulsions as the Accipiter-tuned pulses brutalized his muscles.

Perry reached David first and ripped the barb from David's leg with his gloved hand. After a tense moment waiting to make sure David kept breathing, Perry laughed grimly. "You're lucky that shit didn't kill you, sir!" While David regathered his senses, Perry shouted, "Delta! Secure that beast! Alpha Three and Four, secure west entrance. Alpha Five and Six east entrance, Alpha Seven and Eight top entrance. Alpha nine, you're with me!"

Endiku Star System Nexus Junction Point

The fabric of space itself shimmered with a celestial iridescence as an incandescent gamma-ray burst heralded the arrival of something new. A dark-as-night shape nearly a mile long emerged that seemed more organism than machine. Something that had crawled its way out of some Lovecraftian deep space womb. Its sinuous body was covered in a shimmering membrane, giving the impression of muscles and skin rather than metal and alloy.

The vessel pulsed rhythmically; each beat an eerie mimicry of life. It seemed to breathe, its every inch heaving in a slow, deliberate pattern, expanding and contracting with a silent but palpable force. As it glided forward, the thousands of pulsing blisters that adorned its surface moved with a disturbing autonomy, each one a heartbeat contributing to the chorus of its alien life force.

An Accipiter Dreadnought had arrived.

Keeper Ship

Throughout the Keeper Ship, a new, strident sound resonated.

Nathaniel jerked in surprise and stared at Yureantheon, whose beak glyphs suddenly expressed alarm.

Nathaniel nodded urgently, "I'll go."

He turned and ran with none of the earlier limp and his arm free from the sling. He arrived at the control room, paused to compose himself, and re-inserted his arm in the sling as he studied the now fully functioning displays and controls.

The Gardener within him spoke:

IT IS ONE OF THE WAR VESSELS PROVIDED TO THE ACCIPITERS WITH WHICH TO COMBAT THE MASTERS. WE THOUGHT THEM ALL DESTROYED OR RECYCLED AFTER THE MASTERS WERE DEFEATED. THEY WERE NO LONGER NEEDED. IT WILL BE CONTROLLED BY HERETIC SENTINELS. THE HERETIC WOULD NOT PERMIT IT TO

BE UNDER THE CONTROL OF ANYONE ELSE. IT WILL DEMAND TO TAKE CONTROL OF THE SITUATION HERE. IT IS ALSO LIKELY THAT THE OTHER HUMANS WILL ATTACK IT WITH THEIR SHIPS. THEY ARE NOT LIKELY TO SURVIVE. WE MUST MAINTAIN THE ILLUSION OF OUR INNOCENCE. EVEN IF THE OTHER HUMANS ARE DESTROYED, WE MAY YET PREVAIL.

Nathaniel swallowed, took a deep breath, and answered the Dreadnought's hail.

WE HAVE ESCAPED FROM THE HUMANS. YUREANTHEON OF THE NORTHERN WHEEL MENDERS CLAN SURVIVES BUT IS INJURED AND TRAPPED BEHIND COLLAPSED BULKHEADS. ACCIPITERS FROM THE DOCKED SHIP ARE ONBOARD WORKING TO FREE HIM.

After several seconds, the Dreadnaught replied.

WHAT OF THE ARK AND ITS TREASURE.

Nathaniel paused, noting that the first question asked was not about Yeurantheon or even himself but about the biological 'treasure' the Keeper Ship was built to preserve.

THE KEEPER IS LOST TO US, BUT THE TREASURE REMAINS.

The subsequent response took only a few seconds longer.

PREPARE TO BE BOARDED.

✪ ✪ ✪

NTN Blood Phoenix CIC

Haruto frowned as he studied the faces of Ramona, Hershel, and Dwight on the display. He shook his head, "I don't like what I'm seeing here. I don't know what the Hell that thing is, but it can't be good."

Dwight returned the frown as he looked at his own screen, then said, "Three of us and one of it, plus the Accipiter support ships and their mines once they go active. If we can't kill it, we can at least try to give the Keeper Ship a chance to move to the Nexus Junction Point and escape. Hell, they'll probably scream that they're trying to get out of the war zone, and there's at least a chance the other Accipiter will let them even cover their escape. Then we warp out-system, rendezvous, and fight another day."

Ramona nodded, "We have no idea what its capabilities are, but just looking at it, I'd guess it is more capable than those support ships. I say we concentrate all three of us on it and do our best to ignore the rest, maybe throw a few drones at them."

Hershel scowled, "We don't know what it is or what it can do. If they've got one, they'll have more. We need to find out."

Haruto took one more look at the display, focused on the newly arrived 'thing,' and nodded resolutely. "Very well. Treat it the same as a mothership. Standard deployment pattern. Commander Henry, Commander Griggs, Commander Coughlin. I order the Badger, the Hyena, and the Jackal to attack with standard deployment patterns. Do you copy?"

Ramona answered confidently, "Orders received and understood, Captain Hashimoto. Badger is ready for action."

Hershel echoed her sentiment, saying, "Aye, Captain. Orders Acknowledged. The Hyena is prepared for the attack."

Dwight nodded in confirmation and added, "Orders received and understood, Captain. Jackal is ready."

Haruto considered his next words carefully before nodding to PO Hiram Newman. "Open mic. All hands, Phoenix, Badger, Hyena, and Jackal."

Hiram pressed a few controls, looked up, and replied, "Aye, Captain. Open mic. All hands. Phoenix, Badger, Hyena, and Jackal."

Haruto took a deep breath and intoned with all the resolve and sincerity he could manage. "Officers and crews of the Badger, Hyena, and Jackal, this is Captain Hashimoto. We stand upon the precipice of a moment that will be etched in the annals of our shared history. It is a moment that demands the full measure of our courage and resolve. We began this mission knowing the stakes. All of us understand the evil we face. I am proud to say that we did so unwaveringly."

"The Accipiters build big ships, but they are not warriors. They have not learned the art of war, generation after generation, throughout their history. Their strategy is to simply throw bigger and more ships at the problem. In contrast, every man and woman in this command are the very best at what they do. You are the pinnacle of the human sword. The ultimate refinement of mankind's brilliance, grit, and determination. As a species, we clawed our own way out of the mud. We didn't cheat like they did. The Accipiters were uplifted from bronze age peaceful tribal wanderers who had no history of internal warfare. As a species, we outclass them in every way that matters, and if there is one thing we know how to do, it is how to measure our enemy and take them down."

"Our mission here is to escort the Keeper Ship and keep them out of trouble. Obviously, that's no longer possible. It is now our duty to give them time to escape. As you engage the enemy, remember your training. And remember Earth. Remember what they did to our world and our families and loved ones. Let that fire burn like a star in your hearts."

"As your own Oliver Hazard Perry once said, 'We have met the enemy, and they are ours....'"

Haruto smiled fiercely, "My only regret is that Phoenix is unarmed, and there are only three to fight here today and not four. Godspeed to you all. Let the Accipiters learn what true warriors are made of. Captain Hashimoto, out."

He then put on his helmet and sealed it, joining the rest of the crew who were already at General Quarters and keyed his helmet mic. "Lieutenant Prichard, plot a course to position us two light minutes astern of the target and prepare for Corvette deployment. Upon successful launch, reposition to a ten-light-minute orthogonal offset from that location. Execute when ready."

Lieutenant Stephen Prichard responded with a crisp salute. "Aye, Captain. PO Huddleston, plot an evasive course two light minutes astern for Corvette deployment."

Petty Officer Harris Huddleston, fingers dancing over the helm controls, confirmed the order. "Aye, Lieutenant. Course plotted for two light minutes astern, awaiting launch sequence."

Steven turned to the two VR-helmeted pilots in their virtual reality frames, Logan Kendal and Davin Blakeley, and tapped them on their shoulders. "Pilots, you have the green light. Execute maneuver on my mark... Mark."

The pilots, in perfect sync, responded without hesitation, "Aye, Lieutenant. Executing maneuver." After only a moment, they continued, "We are now two light minutes astern of the enemy vessel."

Steven continued, his voice steady, "Very good. Phoenix, drop the warp field and release the Corvettes from your tethers, then raise the warp field and immediately warp us in stealth to ten light minutes orthogonal to that location. Do not wait for human intervention. We need to make this as instantaneous as possible."

Acknowledged, Lieutenant. Executing now.

The crew felt the familiar disconcerting sensation as the warp field collapsed, leaving them momentarily both visible and vulnerable to attack and in free-fall before the field was restored with a stomach-churning snap. Condition Zebra was already set; the crew was well-trained and secured against the temporary loss of gravity.

Corvettes are away, and we are repositioned as ordered, Lieutenant.

Haruto surveyed the CIC crew and gave a nod of approval at their efficiency. "Thank you, Phoenix. Well done, everyone. Keep a tight watch on all sensors. We've given them their shot. Now, all we can do is wait and watch."

✪ ✪ ✪

Endiku Star System Battle Space

The enemy vessel, whatever it was, was 'only' about a mile long. A fraction of the size and mass of Accipiter mother ships. For Badger, Hyena, and Jackal, that only meant there was less surface area to strike. Just as they had rehearsed over and over again, Ramona, Hershel, and Dwight warped from their launch point to the pre-planned, seemingly random locations in the three-dimensional space around the enemy. As one, they dropped their warp field, fired their grazers, and immediately warped to the next. In the simulations, it had been an orgy of destruction.

And, for the first few moments, it seemed like everything was happening exactly as planned.

The first strike seemed to catch the enemy vessel by surprise. The grazers gouged great rents in the ship's surface, releasing clouds of superheated plasma.

Then, even as the Corvettes reappeared in their new firing positions, the gouges rippled and partially smoothed. Thousands of the pustules covering its surface erupted, releasing clouds of… something. The clouds surged and shimmered as the enemy ship violently maneuvered. It bled from its wounds, but like a boxer wolfishly smiling after his opponent's lucky first hit, the dark leviathan was far from being mortally wounded.

The second time the Corvettes fired, when the grazers struck the clouds, scintillating flashes of atomic fire splashed through the clouds, blocking *most* of the grazer fire. What did break through managed to explode a few of the pustules, though it was not remotely as damaging as the first strike.

Keeper Ship

Nathaniel and his Gardener Rider watched in shock as the battle began. Quickly, they sent an open broadcast:

THE HUMANS MUST HAVE FOLLOWED US SOMEHOW. THEY WILL SURELY DESTROY US. PLEASE SAVE US!

Moments later, the Dreadnaught replied:

ALLOW THE CLAN SHIP TO PUSH YOU AWAY FROM THE BATTLE

NTN Badger

Unlike the cramped bridge of the ILCs, the Corvettes were built for war. In addition to the standard navigation and piloting stations, more were devoted to each weapon system, sensors, drones, damage control, battlespace management, and more.

Ramona stood rigid, rooted in place on the bridge. She allowed only minor irritation to show in her voice. "Lieutenant Sato?"

Noah Sato, his eyes glued to the screen as his fingers flew on the keyboard, answered, "Aye, Captain. Sensors identify the cloud as… something called Macrons. Says they are tiny hollow particles embedded with fissionable material." He gestured to his screen, "When our grazers hit the cloud, there is enough energy to cause fission. Not a lot, but there are a lot of Macrons. They're controlled by magnetic fields. Coming from some of those bumps on the thing's hull. Ma'am."

Ramona pursed her lips, then nodded. "All Right. It was time to go to our huddle anyway. Lt. Gorman, take us to pre-planned huddle location alpha."

✪ ✪ ✪

Three minutes later, and 20 light minutes from the battle, Ramona looked at Hershal and Dwight on one of the screens. "…so, we're all in agreement?"

Hershel nodded intently, "Agreed. Keep hitting them. Try to take out their field emitters, though; like you said, I doubt they don't have redundancy built in."

Dwight impatiently added, "Sure they do. But then we hit 'em again when the fields flicker. Do it enough, and hits will get through. The Keeper Ship is still attached to that Clan Ship. It's slowly pushing them away, but not towards the NJP area."

Hershel shook his head, "I know. We need to do something, and soon. The other clan ships are covering their retreat."

Ramona added, "The Marines could still be onboard that Clan Ship. We can't just shoot it. The Keeper Ship is being pushed towards the other clan ships, presumably so they can escort it to the planet."

Dwight wondered, "Maybe we should let them? Complete the mission that way? Or do you think their new warship might bring too much scrutiny and blow their cover? The Marines weren't supposed to have to hide forever. Once the Heretic had been purged from the rescue ship, there was supposed to be enough time to implant Gardeners in all of them, rewrite their memories, and keep them from searching. Then we were going to sneak in and pick up the marines later once they weren't needed on the planet and once the Gardeners controlled the planet and system anyway. We could do a parade, and the Gardeners would just erase it all from their memories."

Hershel shook his head, "I think things have already gone too far south. It's too big a risk. If they're found out, it could blow the entire scheme to infiltrate the Accipiter-held worlds."

Ramona added, "Okay. Throw the drones at the clan ships for now and see how that goes. Re-evaluate at our next huddle if we need to make runs at them ourselves. Hopefully, we'll make them think we're going to try and recapture the Keeper Ship by not targeting it, and Yureantheon will get the hint and head for the NJP."

Dwight and Hershel both nodded their agreement.

Ramona said, "Badger, set up the randomizer and sync with Jackal and Hyena for our next huddle."

Endiku Star System Battle Space

Over and over again, the Corvettes hit the leviathan, hammering it. Gas and plasma bled from innumerable gashes, but it was clearly built to take heavy punishment. The system defense mines were active again. However, by the time any of them was able to lock onto a Corvette, it was too late. The Corvette would have already warped away to the next location. Like ILCs, Corvettes were not FTL capable. Their warp drives compressed the space in front of them and stretched it behind them, traveling at a 'relative' speed of just over .7c.

The clan ships were clustered in a formation trying to block the Corvette's spread of ten drones each, for thirty total. Each drone was very nimble and lashed out at the clan ships with its X-ray laser. The effort was yielding results, if slowly. Space being big and the drones dancing about at a distance while the clan ships likewise attempted to dodge and maneuver while returning fire from their leading elements resulted in each force slowly eroding the other.

Haruto clenched the rail as he studied the plot.

Stephen Prichard muttered, "What can we do?"

Haruto sucked in a breath, "The President said it... He said it that first day they found Phoenix."

Steven cocked his head, "Sir?"

Haruto slowly nodded his head, "There's no such thing as an unarmed starship."

Steven shook his head. "Sir, I think I know what you're thinking, but there were... concerns. There is a big risk that we'll irradiate ourselves. The eggheads were fairly sure that we could unbalance the warp field and collect particles and radiation and release them, but we could not see in front of us to aim them. We need to be pretty damned sure the target is where we need it to be. The target has to be...."

Haruto nodded. "The target needs to either be stationary... or be very big." He gestured at the plot with hundreds of Accipiter clan ships clustered together.

Steven grinned wolfishly. "They've positioned themselves between the battle and the Keeper Ship. If we come in from the correct vector, even if they haven't moved too far from the projected path, we should still hit a bunch of them!"

Haruto added soberly, "We've got the water tanks surrounding the ship now. Hopefully, they'll absorb most of any radiation collected inside the field." He added, "Phoenix, do you concur? Can you do this, and can it be done with some measure of protection for the crew?"

Phoenix replied:

Yes, Captain. While listening to your discussion, I have been running projections. I can establish a temporarily unbalanced field and warp out-system. This will collect particles impacting us in warp instead of converting them to energy to reinforce the field. There is a limit to how long I can do this, depending on particle density and other factors, before an inversion would cause an overload and dump the energy inside the field. I would need to time the journey such that both the outbound and return trip, cumulatively, will not cause an overload. Once I return and carefully drop the field, I can release the particles. Before I establish the unbalanced field, however, I will need to use a modified gravity field to push us to a high physical velocity that will be imparted unto the particles upon our return. To protect you from the acceleration, I will also need to establish an internal warp field just large enough to encompass your vessel. Otherwise, you would not survive the acceleration."

Haruto nodded, raising his eyebrows, "I understand, thank you, Phoenix. I do not wish to become a red mist spread across whatever survived of our hull. Very well. Project the most likely location the enemy clan ships are going to be when we return and calculate the appropriate vectors. Don't wait for further orders. Execute now.

NTN Badger

Noah Sato jerked in surprise and exclaimed, "Captain! Sensors recorded a bright flash of gamma and ionizing radiation!"

Ramona stiffened, "An NJP translation?"

Noah shook his head as he stared at his screen, "No, Captain. It is not the right signature, and it didn't come from the right direction, and…. wait. What?"

Ramona stifled a remark, "Lieutenant?"

Noah sat back, "Sorry, Captain, it's just that…. At least half of the Accipiter clan ships have stopped maneuvering. They're ballistic."

Ramona's mind raced as a thin smile crossed her face, "Haruto. You clever bastard. That should get their attention. Let me know if the Keeper Ship course changes."

✪ ✪ ✪

A half dozen attack runs later, the dark Accipiter leviathan showed no sign of slowing down. They had hurt it significantly, but not mortally.

On the other hand, between Haruto's run and the whittling down by the drones, the few surviving clan ships were now clustered closely around the Keeper Ship and were now pushing it back towards the nearest Nexus Junction Point.

Noah Sato did a double take and leaned into his screen.

Ramona noticed this out of the corner of her eye. "Lieutenant Sato. You have something?"

Noah hesitated, "Ma'am, I'm not sure. On our last run, there was something… just before we warped out. I'm checking previous…." He twitched and sat up straight. "Ma'am, I'm seeing… it looks like they are launching… something… but only when we warp away. We only caught a frame or two."

Ramona pushed harder, "Launching, what? Lieutenant? Ships? Mines? How many? Badger, take control and take us directly to the next rendezvous point!"

Acknowledged Captain. Executing now.

Just then, the ship shuddered, lights flickered, and hull breach alarms sounded throughout the ship as the hull shook and groaned.

Ramona shouted, "Report! Damage control, Report! Badger, how bad?"

Petty Officer First Class Hannah Schwartz looked up from her board, her face ashen through her helmet. "Ma'am. We've got a hull breach amidships, and… there are casualties. Environmental Controls Staff Sergeant Lachapelle is missing, along with Quartermaster Chou and Marine Sargeant Matějka. They were all in the compartment, and it is open to space."

<hr>

Captain. I apologize for the delay. We have now arrived at the rendezvous point. However, I have taken severe damage. Whatever it was that hit us is still causing more damage.

<hr>

Hannah's eyes were wide, and her face drained of color as she urgently said, "Captain! Whatever hit us… Sergeant Waldo is reporting that it is… eating into the ship and spreading this way. Captain, the bridge is cut off from the rest of the ship. He is unable to reach any of the other crew members, Sir."

Without hesitation, Ramona responded, "Put him on speaker, Hannah. Let's hear it straight."

The speakers crackled to life, and Sergeant Waldo's voice, strained with urgency and disbelief, filled the room. "Captain, it's like nothing I've ever seen. The material, it's… dissolving everything it touches. I'm in my suit, but it's…" His words broke off with a sharp intake of breath.

There was a moment of static, then the sound of something corrosive sizzling, followed by Waldo's horrified screams. "It's on me! It's eating through the suit! Oh God—"

The bridge crew froze, each person grappling with the unfolding horror.

Ramona's face remained composed, but her eyes betrayed the turmoil within. She gave a slight, solemn nod to Hannah. Understanding the gesture, Hannah reached for the console with a trembling hand and cut off the audio.

The bridge fell into a stunned silence as Ramona took a deep breath, steadying herself. She was suddenly calmer than she thought possible.

"Thank you, Hannah. Badger, what is your assessment?"

*Captain, I am already losing control of critical systems.
I am so sorry. I recommend the crew abandon ship.*

Ramona turned and asked, "PO Okafor, any word from Hyena or Jackal? They are late to the huddle."

Kwasi somberly shook his head, "No, Captain. No word."

Ramona nodded, "I see. Very well. Sound Abandon Ship but silence the alarm on the bridge. Hopefully, there are surviving crewmembers who are able." She smiled sadly and surveyed the faces of her bridge crew, who all knew what was next. There was no escape hatch on the bridge. Apparently, the Masters didn't believe in them.

Ramona took one more look around the bridge and said, "Thank you. Thank you all. I could not have asked for a braver or more honorable crew. It was a privilege."

She swallowed and found that she was surprised to find her voice had suddenly become husky. "Nav, plot an intercept course with the enemy. Dead amidships."

Lt. Alec Gorman's face shone brightly as he answered, "Aye, Captain." Moments later, he added, "Course laid in, Captain."

Ramona sighed, smiled, and said, "Badger... It was an honor to work with you as well. I'm sorry we didn't get to know each other better." Badger's personality, like the other Corvettes, had been upgraded to match Phoenix. It had been felt that it would improve the small warship's effectiveness.

Thank you, Captain. I feel the same.

Ramona took one last look around the bridge and saw the courage and determination on everyone's faces. She forced herself to not think about the plans she'd had for herself after rebuilding her life after Awakening Day. With even greater effort, she avoided thinking about all that she had denied herself to get to where she was right now. She would brook no regrets in her heart. She nodded and said, "Very well then. Badger, take us in at the best speed you can manage and still guarantee we will impact as intended."

∞∞∞

Acknowledged, Captain.

∞∞∞

✪ ✪ ✪

Thirteen seconds later, Badger's warp field impacted the Accipiter dreadnaught amidships. For the briefest of moments, the field annihilated that portion of the Dreadnaught's hull, converting it to energy that Badger absorbed. It couldn't last, of course. The energy absorbed was too great and too fast. Just as with Gene Morton's NTN Axe, the result was a colossal explosion. Axe had impacted a fifty-mile-long Accipiter mothership, and the resulting explosion not only vaporized everything around it but also concussed and flash-heated part of the Atlantic Ocean on Earth. The Dreadnought was one-fiftieth as large but no less destroyed.

In that moment, the crew of NTN Badger, or whatever was left of them by that point, including Master Chief Petty Officer Alexandre Arcady Aleksandrov, Chief Petty Officer Andre Bryant, Petty Officer Second Class Aria Chen, Chief Petty Officer Lian Ping Chou, Petty Officer Nikita Sneha Choudhary, Lieutenant Alec Gorman, Staff Sergeant Gus Norm Hayward, Chief Warrant Officer Grace Kim, Sergeant Simon Aaron Lachapelle, Petty Officer Third Class Jaxon Lee, Petty Officer Conor Lleu, Ensign Layla Martinez, Sergeant Ivan Samuel Matějka, Petty Officer Kwasi Dada Okafor, Lieutenant Sophie Rhee, Staff Sergeant Jean-François Maxence Richard, Lieutenant Ritchie Stewart Roscoe, Petty Officer First Class Elliot Ruiz, Lieutenant Junior Grade Noah Sato, Petty Officer First Class Hannah Schwartz, Petty Officer Roseanne Rae Stanley, Petty Officer Second Class Carlos Vega, Corpsman Marina Radojka Vlašić, Sergeant Zachariah Winfield Waldo, Commander Ramona Henry, and the sentient personality of NTN Badger, flashed into ionized atoms.

THE END

Epilogue

● ● ● ● ● ● ● ● ● ● ● ● ● ● ● ● ●

*DownSide: Nations of Earth Memorial Cemetery
One Month Later*

Next to Fort Underwood, ten thousand acres were set aside and designated as the site of the Nations of Earth Cemetery, many times the size of Arlington National Cemetery's 639 acres. A year ago, it had been dedicated in the wake of the original Keeper mission to Earth and the tragic deaths of so many.

Earlier in the day, a new service was held. This time for those lost at Endiku.

Haruto and the crew of the Blood Phoenix eventually returned. Commander Ramona Henry and the crew of the Badger did not. Nor did Commander Dwight Coughlin and the crew of the Jackal, whose ship had taken a hit to the bridge and was subsequently destroyed by the Accipiter dreadnaught with a particle beam. Hyena had been hit by a blast of macrons and damaged but had managed to warp to safety moments before Badger's impact. Phoenix had picked up Hyena and silently observed what happened next.

The remaining Accipiter clan ships had turned back to the planet with the Keeper Ship in tow. That's when the sputtering 'damage' on its hull paused for a pre-planned moment and then released a brief shower of plasma at a specific intensity and frequency.

It was one of several pre-arranged signals. In this case, it meant that the Accipiters who had boarded the Keeper Ship had all been 'converted,' and the boarding action on the clan ship was successful, and that the mission was proceeding forward. Haruto and the Blood Phoenix then waited. It took two agonizing weeks, but eventually, a lone clan ship pushed the miraculously fully functional Keeper Ship back out to the Nexus Junction Point, where it then transited back to Chawig and New Texas, bringing the Marines home, along with news of the ongoing but successful infiltration of the planet Kumai.

Endiku was now under Gardener control. All memory of the battle had been carefully edited. The Accipiter Dreadnaught had indeed arrived and been immediately ambushed by the humans. Just as it neared victory, one of the human ships suicided into it. Many clan ships supporting the Dreadnaught were lost in the battle. There never was a Keeper Ship.

Once the nonexistent Keeper Ship was safely away, Blood Phoenix began the slower warp trip back to New Texas.

Now, at the cemetery, Temporary memorials were lined up in a new row. The speeches were over, and the crowds had mostly left.

Lieutenant Ryon Ki-Nam, now *Ambassador*, stood stiffly in front of Ramona Henry's marker and bowed deeply before adding a single flower to those already heaped around her brilliantly smiling photo.

"Commander," he said in a low voice, "Thank you for what you did for me. I've seen how many have looked at me, wondering if I might be like some of my fellow North Koreans. Not you. You looked at me, and… you were kind. I read about you after that. Learned everything I could about you. I wondered… how could a woman with a smile so bright…. How could you also be so brave and confident and have the respect of so many? Before Awakening Day, you were going to be recruited to be an astronaut by your NASA program."

He paused and swallowed, "Instead, you built a new life here and commanded starships. First, you defended this city, and then you…." His eyes misted, "You gave your life fighting for all of us. You died for not just your own people but also mine, even though they don't deserve it. I… I want you to know that I am going to tell my people about you. It is time for them to stand up as men and become part of this world. Become something worth defending. It is time they…. It is time they learned from and begin to follow the example set by you, Commander Coughlin, and all the others."

He stiffened and saluted in what might possibly be the first salute he had ever given to someone who he felt truly deserved it.

To be
continued...

in
Accipiter War:
Book # 5

UNFAIRLY TALENTED

• • • • • • • • • • • • • • • • • • •

I cannot thank enough the incomparable Ron Miller, whose art has inspired not only Blake and I, but our readers as well. In addition to working with Ron on the covers for the Accipiter War series, I also worked with him many moons ago when I was the publisher at Timberwolf Press. Ron did our covers back then, too. Every book fair, every event that we did, people stopped in their tracks and stared at his covers – whether they were interested in the genre or not.

It's still true today as I go to cons and book signings.

Indeed, Ron is far more than an esteemed Hugo Award-winning artist. The last time I looked, he had published 75 works. These works are available in 142 publications and in 6 languages and can be found in nearly 17,000 libraries worldwide. Some of his most popular books include *Twenty Thousand Leagues Under the Seas, The Art of Space: The History of Space Art, from the Earliest Visions to the Graphics of the Modern Era,* and *Cleopatra: Empress of the Nile,* among others.

He's designed 10 postage stamps for the U.S. Postal Service. One of these, the Pluto stamp, was attached to the New Horizons spacecraft before launch and is now in the Guinness Book of World Records as having traveled further than any other postage stamp in history. Ron has worked with Disney and other production companies and movies, including Dune.

His book, *The Dream Machines*, a comprehensive 744-page history of crewed spacecraft, was nominated for the International Astronautical Federation's Manuscript Award and won the Booklist Editor's Choice Award. His paintings are in many private and public collections, including the Smithsonian Institution and the Pushkin Museum in Moscow.

One of my favorite art books of Ron's is *The Art of Chesley Bonestell,* *which* received a Hugo Award in 2002.

Ron doesn't just do art books. He is also an author of incredible fantasy novels, like *Bradamant: The Iron Tempest*, set in 7th century Europe, in a time of myths, gods, and monsters. I had the privilege of publishing *Bradamant* back in the Timberwolf Days. I sent a copy of the manuscript to Sir Arthur C. Clarke (whom Ron had done covers for). Sir Arthur sent back a handwritten note that said: **"Ron Miller is Unfairly Talented."**

Ron is also the author of *The Bronwyn Trilogy*, which includes *Palaces & Prisons, Silk & Steel,* and *Hearts & Armor,* which I had the privilege of republishing at Timberwolf.

Ron Miller's *Velda* series is a multi-leveled representation of the more lurid of the 1950s crime comics. It is portrayed as if it actually existed as a classic Golden Age comic. The series is a wonderful homage to the noir films and hard-boiled detective stories from the 1950s. I had the privilege of publishing the first *Velda* book at Timberwolf.

More than anything else, Ron is a classy guy and is fantastic to work with.

◇◇◇

From Patrick and Blake Seaman ---- Thank You, Ron Miller!!

◇◇◇

Books in the Series

● ● ● ● ● ● ● ● ● ● ● ● ● ● ●

ACCIPITER WAR #1 is set in the near future. The Accipiter War series follows the survivors of an attack on Earth. Rescued by unknown aliens and forced to fight a generational proxy war against a galaxy-spanning empire, Accipiter War emphasizes hope and the endurance of the human spirit in the face of unthinkable tragedy, discovery, and the search for a destiny other than war. Accipiter War The current-day city of Fort Brazos, Texas, and the nearby Joint Reserve Base have been abducted — scooped up whole and deposited inside a vast 4000-mile-long hollow world.

Thousands are dead. Thrown into crisis, they are alone with no help coming. Who has done this to them and why? Will the military submit to the civilian mayor and city council? Meanwhile, alien creatures begin to attack, and the people start to discover that not everything, or everyone, is the same as they were before Awakening Day.

Are the humans to be lab rats? Slaves? Gladiators? Or is there some other terrible purpose… or a greater destiny?

Accipiter War is the first in a planned series of books in the Fort Brazos Saga by Father/Son authors Patrick & Blake Seaman. It emphasizes hope and the endurance of the human spirit in the face of unthinkable tragedy.

Accipiter War # 2: STEALING FIRE:

In Stealing Fire, the survivors must unite and begin to fight a generations-long war against an immense, galaxy-spanning empire. In a test of will, John and Gail must lead and drive the survivors in an impossible task: cobble together a makeshift hybrid starship and launch a desperate mission that could deliver a devastating blow to their enemy.

But with the clock ticking and a treacherous conspiracy in the works, the Gardeners, the enigmatic race responsible for "saving" Fort Brazos and New London in the first place, may decide humanity isn't worth saving after all — and finish the job the Accipiters started by snuffing out the last embers of humankind forever.

Accipiter War # 3: THE FORGE

After the harrowing raid on Occupied Earth, John Austin, Gail Finley, and their fellow survivors are left to grapple with the repercussions of what they have learned and devise a strategy. The entire Accipiter Empire is incensed, mobilizing their vast resources and millions of ships in order to turn over every rock in the galaxy looking for them.

As secrets unravel, the true perpetrators behind the bombing of city hall remain at large. If this weren't enough, mysterious craters and fires began to erupt closer and closer to Fort Brazos.

At Ari'Nell, with Captain Jermain Cutter's and NTN Revenge's help, Commander Alberta "Bertie" Sinitskaya works desperately to build up defenses. Meanwhile, Captain Charles Cross and NTN Phoenix are sent to an undisclosed location on a secretive mission.

Heroes and Villains of the Accipiter War: Illustrated Paperback

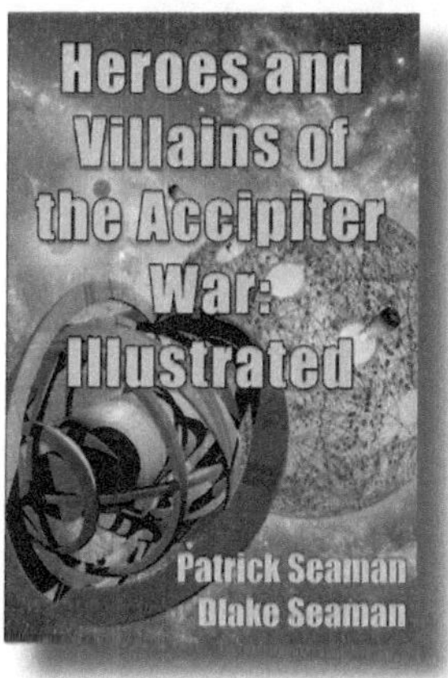

Step into the captivating universe of the Accipiter War science fiction book series. Within the pages of this book, you'll find a treasure trove of character dossiers and concept art, providing a glimpse into the minds of co-authors Patrick and Blake Seaman. This compilation offers just a taste of the vast story bible and extensive research that form the foundation of our ongoing series.

While we're excited to share these captivating visuals and character descriptions with you, we've taken care not to reveal too much. Our aim is to provide a tantalizing glimpse into the lives of the characters we hold dear without giving away all the surprises that await you in our thrilling narrative.

These dossiers are a version of what we pinned to our writer's wall, reminding us daily of the complexities and passions that define the characters we have created – and who we care greatly about. We are thrilled to share this window into their worlds, as it is their journeys that drive the heart of our narrative.

As you immerse yourself in these images and backgrounds, we hope they will ignite your imagination and kindle your curiosity about the unfolding Accipiter War saga. Please join us and our cast of characters as we embark upon a story of survival, love, politics, morality, and what promises to be a generational war against an ancient and vast empire that spans the entire galaxy.

Your journey begins here, and we can't wait to join you in this epic tale.

About the Authors

Patrick Seaman is the principal author. He created the concept and drives the storyline for the Fort Brazos series. He crafted concept art and managed creative development for Fort Brazos. Patrick is an entrepreneur, consultant, Internet pioneer, former publisher, editor, and author. In addition, Patrick is a lifelong shooting enthusiast and former rifle and pistol instructor.

Since helping launch broadcast.com in the early days of online digital media, Patrick has launched, advised, and served in many startups around the globe in C-Level positions or their boards.

You can follow Patrick at:

http://www.amazon.com/author/patrickseaman
https://twitter.com/PatrickSeaman
http://www.linkedin.com/in/patrickseaman
http://AccipiterWar.com
http://patrickseaman.com

Blake Seaman is an Information Technology executive, author, and classical composer. His music is available on all major streaming platforms. He is a proud resident of the State where he lives with his wife and family. He dedicates his work on this project to them and hopes to raise part of a new generation of Science Fiction fans. Blake is also an avid sports shooter and Tea aficionado.

https://BlakeSeaman.com
https://open.spotify.com/artist/3aK0vHFZEJ7YLq6a9CV9Yw
http://www.amazon.com/author/blakeseaman
http://www.cdbaby.com/Artist/BlakeSeaman
https://itunes.apple.com/us/album/fort-brazos/id961266753

9 798987 851104